SIMI [illegible]

The agent—A [illegible] figure from a shadowy organization whose purpose is clear enough: find the canisters before they explode.

The football star—His sister is murdered and they want him the same way. A horrible death awaits him in the jungles of Nicaragua.

The canisters—What horrifying new force, sealed within them, threatens the future of the entire planet?

THE VALHALLA TESTAMENT

An unforgettable novel of the world in peril by the bestselling author of THE EIGHTH TRUMPET, THE ALPHA DECEPTION, and THE GAMMA OPTION.

Also by Jon Land:

THE DOOMSDAY SPIRAL
THE LUCIFER DIRECTIVE
VORTEX
LABYRINTH*
THE OMEGA COMMAND*
THE COUNCIL OF TEN*
THE ALPHA DECEPTION*
THE EIGHTH TRUMPET*
THE GAMMA OPTION*

*Published by Fawcett Books

THE VALHALLA TESTAMENT

Jon Land

FAWCETT GOLD MEDAL • NEW YORK

For Sensei, who knew

A Fawcett Gold Medal Book
Published by Ballantine Books

Library of Congress Catalog Card Number: 90-93048

ISBN 0-449-14634-0

Manufactured in the United States of America

First Edition: August 1990

ACKNOWLEDGMENTS

THE creative process in my case is in many respects a collaborative effort. Without the help and guidance offered by those whose names follow, this book especially could never have reached its full potential. As always, my apologies to those I have inadvertently left off and special thanks to those whose names have become regular inhabitants of this page.

I start as always with Toni Mendez, as great a human being as she is an agent, and the backbone of my career. Listening to editors becomes more crucial with each book and I have been blessed with two: Ann Maurer, whose own standards keep mine high; and Daniel Zitin, who proves that the *complete* editor can still exist in today's often chaotic world of publishing. In fact, all of the Fawcett family under Leona Nevler is doing its utmost to refute the stereotypes burdening the book business today.

For techincal assistance, I am once again indebted to Emery Pineo, who keeps his title as the smartest man I know.

Dr. Mort Korn, meanwhile, having suffered through another first draft, makes his tenth consecutive appearance on this page. His input is more important now than ever, as is that of Tony Sheppard who feasts on early drafts that would make anyone else cringe.

Thanks ever so much for Andi Gruber (my number one fan in Europe) for his help with the geography of Vienna and its Opera House; to David Torgan for the same in Tegucigalpa, Honduras; and to Steve Fortunato for Nicaragua.

For techincal assistance above and beyond the call of duty, my heartfelt thanks to Commander Paul Dowd and especially Richard Dube, now of Newport Helicopters and formerly an attack pilot with the 101st Airborne. Without their help, together with that of Richard Levy of Corporate Air Newport, this book's climax could not have been written.

Lastly, thanks to former Headmaster George Andrews and the students of St. George's in Newport for letting me get to know your school.

PROLOGUE

"FOR *those passengers awaiting the arrival of Amtrak train number 216, the Metroliner, from Washington with service to Boston, that train is now approaching the station. . . .*"

The announcement brought Trask up from his bench in the seating area of New York's Penn Station. Once again, as he had been doing for the past twenty minutes, he carefully examined the entire area around him. The long Columbus Day weekend had turned an already busy Friday into chaos. All trains in and out of New York were delayed, the result being a cluster of fidgety travelers hovering around the huge track board. Trask had watched them with no small measure of amusement. What did the fools think, that by staring unceasingly at the board, they could speed up the posting of their track, or quicken the train's approach into the station? No more than gazing at your watch can make time pass faster. Trask almost could have laughed.

He slid among them in the central concourse, his limp more pronounced from the long period of sitting. Bodies rushed past him, many of them students, judging by their sacks and duffels. Trask had to twist to avoid their onslaught. Many seemed impervious to his presence. Time had already been stolen from them, plans threatened. To the young it was the stuff of nightmares, Trask reckoned, strangely undaunted by the jostling.

He was taller and far better dressed than virtually all those around him. His long overcoat hid a hard, taut body honed by practice as well as experience. Part of that experience had been to dive in front of an undersecretary of state an instant before a terrorist bullet would have killed him. Trask ended up losing a chunk of his thigh from the exploding shell and receiving a commendation in return.

Not exactly the fairest of trades.

He was a courier now as a result, and rather relieved to be out of the forefront. He had been pushing his luck for too long. It was unusual for a field man to have a family, and thoughts of them had begun to intrude toward the end. Today's job was typically bland. Just a routine pickup from the courier coming in on the Metroliner. Trask didn't question the precautions. The same route was never used twice, and this often led to a roundabout trek for the incoming material. The big boys had their reasons, and that suited Trask just fine.

A porter he had tipped earlier whispered the Metroliner's track number to him ahead of its posting. Descending the stairs toward it brought him against a horde of arriving passengers. The flow upward resisted his descent, but Trask patiently made his way down through the crowd. He had the bottom in sight when a girl not much older than his daughter lost her grip on a shoulder bag. It tumbled and spilled its contents everywhere, stalling the line's progress. Trask saw the girl smile as he stooped gingerly to help her retrieve her possessions.

He saw her hand, too, but simply assumed she was reaching for one of her fallen cassette tapes when it jerked suddenly upward. Trask caught the blade's glimmer at the last; two years ago, before the leg, he might have been able to escape its path. As it was, he managed only to arch his frame upward, the motion throwing the balance of his weight on the bad limb. The leg buckled and Trask was reaching desperately for the railing when the blade whipped across his throat. He was in the middle of a breath when the steel touched cold and fast, and that was where it ended, where everything ended.

Trask collapsed into the oncoming crowd, his bulk shoving them backward and catching those closest in the outpouring of his blood. His killer, meanwhile, left her possessions scattered over the steps and rushed upward in pace with the panic that spread through the mass of travelers.

Riverstone hadn't been close enough to the stairs to hear the commotion. Instead he had lingered by the specified section of the train, prepared to pass on the material to Trask and then climb back in for the continuation of the trip to Boston. Impatiently Riverstone checked his watch, decided he would give Trask another two minutes.

A nagging feeling in his gut told him to scrap the mission and reboard the Metroliner now. Riverstone had never been a field man per se, but his experience as a courier was second to none in this network. He'd experienced these feelings before, and there was almost always something to them. Yet this was strictly routine, a run-of-the-mill drop quite befitting a man nearing sixty with retirement in his sights.

The two minutes passed without any sign of Trask. Riverstone started to climb back on the Metroliner, then hesitated. He had to report the anomaly. Somebody somewhere had fucked up, and he didn't want the blame to fall on him. A quick call from one of the concourse phone banks and he'd still have a chance to reboard the train before it pulled out.

Riverstone swung left and started walking. He didn't want to emerge in the station near any of the Metroliner passengers in case someone other than Trask was watching. Attention to such details was standard procedure for him, even if it wasn't for others. Trask would probably show up to meet the next train in one hour, with a communication snafu undoubtedly to blame.

Riverstone realized he had walked beyond any of the exit flights upward, and swung around again. Behind him on the left-hand track, another train was coming in from the south. Perfect. He'd lose himself in the cluster of passengers emerging from it as they climbed for the station. Riverstone slowed his pace as the train squealed to a halt.

In front of him a cripple pushed himself along on walking sticks, listing alternately to the left and right. The doors of the incoming train had opened when Riverstone drew even with the cripple, prepared to join the flow of passengers upward. He saw the cripple turn toward him and seem to stumble. Riverstone reached out to stop the man from falling and felt something press against his side. Before he could respond, a trio of what felt like savage kicks split his ribs and stole his air.

Now it was Riverstone who staggered. He could feel the warm wetness oozing from him as he slumped against one of the concrete standards.

I'm dying. Oh Jesus, I'm dying. . . .

Riverstone registered that final thought as he crumpled into the path of what would have been his cover. The cripple had already disappeared into the surge ahead with the clacking of his walking sticks marking his path.

The director's face was pressed close enough to the fish tank to seem a part of the rocks and plants held within.

"Sit down, Richards," he instructed the man who had just entered his office.

The director shifted only slightly behind the glass as Richards obliged.

"I've already been briefed, Captain, so you can spare me the details. What else have you been able to learn?"

"We've lost contact with the remaining three agents along the Jubilee network, sir. The murders of Trask and Riverstone were not random."

"I was afraid of that. Has Sapphire been compromised?"

"By all indications, no. The penetration occurred somewhere up the line. None of the couriers knew of her existence, so we can assume she's safe."

"At least for the time being you mean, Captain," from the director.

As a former military officer himself, the director was most comfortable addressing his operatives by their military rank when it applied. When it didn't, they seldom rose in the CIA as far as Richards had. The director came up from behind the fish tank, his gaunt face losing the refracted pudginess the view through the glass had provided. Richards thought he might have looked better with it.

"I believe, Captain, we should pull Sapphire out."

"My feeling is that would be a mistake, sir."

"I don't want to lose any more agents."

"Sir, the strike against the United States the Jubilee network latched on to has to be coming soon. We're going to be hit and we're going to be hit hard. Recall Sapphire and we lose our last hope of finding out when and how."

The director sat down in the high-backed chair behind his desk and sighed. "What's the alternative to recall?"

Richards eased a file folder toward him across the desk. "Sir, our basic problem now is that we have been cut off from Sapphire just as she has been cut off from us. Any attempt to reinitiate contact along traditional lines will place her in far greater peril than she is presently in. With that in mind, I've developed a contingency."

The director opened the folder and skimmed the several pages forming its contents. His eyebrows flickered.

"Not something you've thrown together over the past twelve hours obviously, Captain."

"No, sir, I've been working on it for some time."

"Impressive logistics."

"Thank you, sir."

"Don't thank me yet. I said impressive, not viable. I don't like using civilians."

"The risk in this case is minimal."

"The risk is never minimal, Captain, *especially* in this case."

Richards's eyes tilted toward the manila folder. "The plan takes that into account."

"Obviously."

"We only have two choices open to us, sir. One is to recall Sapphire. The other is to proceed with this contingency."

The director scanned part of one of the pages again. "How accurate is your intelligence on this civilian?"

"Very. It came from Sapphire herself."

He looked up at that. "Then she's willing to accept the risks as well."

Richards nodded.

"The question, Captain, is: Are we?"

"Sapphire understands the stakes, sir, just as we must. It took us over a year to arrange this placement. She doesn't want to throw everything away with culmination so near."

The director closed the folder and shoved it back toward Richards. "You'll destroy this, of course, along with any other direct evidence of this operation's existence."

"Of course, sir."

"We can have no record, nothing whatsoever that can lead back to us, even if the operation is successful."

"I understand."

"Make sure that you do, Captain. Make sure that you do."

PART ONE

Casa Grande

New York: Wednesday, six A.M.

CHAPTER 1

"WE had us any balls, Ivy, we'd drive back downtown and chuck their asses out the window."

Jamie Skylar turned to the huge shape in the Jaguar's driver's seat. "Wouldn't change anything, Monroe."

"Nice payback, though, something you become quite the expert in," Monroe Smalls said with a smile.

Jamie smiled back at him and reached for the latch. "Thanks for the lift."

He had started to hoist the door open when Smalls's huge hand closed on his forearm. They were parked in one of Kennedy Airport's forbidden red zones, but none of the patrolling traffic police seemed eager to argue the point.

"You ready to tell me where you're going, Ivy?"

"Vacation," Jamie lied. "NFL board of standards and practices gave me six weeks off, so I figure I might as well enjoy it."

Monroe Smalls smirked at him. "Yeah, and the Pillsbury Doughboy's my first cousin on my mama's side."

"I can see the resemblance."

Smalls let go of Jamie's arm. "Just keep your ass in shape, Ivy. Six weeks done, the Giants'll be waiting. Shit, you don't miss the play-offs, you don't miss nothing."

"Take care of my locker, Monroe."

"Least I can do on accounta how you took care of my ass."

Jamie slammed the Jaguar's door, and his reflection looked back at him in the glass. He looked tired. Worse, he looked sad and weak. The long, wavy brown hair that sometimes slid out the bottom of his helmet seemed limp. His face was normally smooth and angular, but it wasn't just distortion from the glass that made it appear puffy and drooping. His crystal-blue eyes, usually so bright and vital, were shown in the window as lifeless spheres. Even his powerful shoulders seemed to be sagging.

What the hell is happening to me?

It had been only the day before that Jamie appeared before the National Football League Board of Standards and Practices. Their preliminary investigation had been completed with uncharacteristic swiftness, but Jamie wasn't surprised.

"Mr. Skylar," board chairman Walter Mount had opened as he took off his glasses, "the purpose of this hearing is to hear final testimony in the matter of your purposeful injury of one Roland Wingrette of the Philadelphia Eagles. For the record, this incident occurred on Sunday, October second. Also for the record, are we to conclude that you have decided not to retain legal counsel for this hearing?"

"You are."

The board members glanced at one another disdainfully. The room was laid out just as Jamie had pictured it: deep and rectangular, with Mount and the four others hidden behind a conference table set near the front wall. Before it, a number of chairs had been arranged in neat, precise fashion, the effect purposely that of a courtroom. A big-screen television dominated the right-hand wall. Against the left-hand one sat a stenographer whose black machine had already spit out a curled ream of paper. Jamie had taken a chair set forward from the rest directly in front of the chairman.

Walter Mount was nodding. "Then let us turn our attention now to the monitor. . . ."

With that, the big-screen television jumped to life. The sound blared briefly before Mount muted it. Giants Stadium.

Seventy-six thousand fans screaming their lungs out at an early season game with play-off intensity. Kickoff coverage team lining up on the field following a Giants touchdown, Jamie third blue shirt in from the right.

Six years back, Jamie had figured Scranton High stadium would hold the biggest crowd he'd ever play before. A senior on a decent team with a decent chance of making second-team all-state or honorable mention wouldn't ordinarily have much of a career ahead of him. But a Brown University recruiter saw him and took a chance. Brown had won a grand total of five games over the preceding three years, so the smart talent, as the recruiter put it, wasn't exactly breaking down the doors to play there. Jamie liked what the man had to say. Play football in exchange for a degree in engineering if the financial aid came through. Scholarships didn't exist in the Ivy League, the recruiter explained. It was the best they could do.

He had been the leading rusher on Brown's freshmen team but hadn't turned all that many heads. The big transition happened over the summer before his sophomore year. He took up lifting weights for the first time and saw his weight jump from 185 to 205. Another inch and a half of growth put his height at a nice round six foot two. When he came back for summer two-a-day practice sessions, he did the forty in 4.6 flat, beating his best previous time by three-tenths of a second. Coaches made him run it again the next day just to make sure their clock had been working right.

The real change, though, was on the field. All of a sudden people were having trouble catching him, and when they did, they couldn't bring him down. Not a single defender on the whole Brown team could manage the feat one on one. It was as if Jamie had tuned into a new kind of balance, could juke his upper body one way while his lower body went the other. Sometimes he could even feel the parts separate, felt he was two people. He saw the holes and hit them at the same time and had become the prime ingredient in the Brown offense by the opening game against Yale. Nine hundred yards as a sophomore and twelve hundred more as a junior. People started to take notice.

Senior year proved to be the best of all. Nineteen hundred yards—an average of almost two hundred per game. *Sports Illustrated* came to do a story. ABC carried one game and ESPN three. Brown went 10–0 and stormed to the Ivy League title for which each member of the team was rewarded with a golden ring set with a big blue jewel. The only time Jamie had taken it off since was when he was playing or practicing. He received enough votes in the tallies for the Heisman Trophy to come in fifth, the best showing ever from the school where John Heisman himself had gone. Before he knew it, a call came on draft day from the Giants and he signed a three-year contract for $250,000 a year, with the first two guaranteed. A half-million bucks to play pro football with a Superbowl contender.

The tape was rolling, but Jamie didn't watch it. The incident was too well etched on his mind, planned out far in advance. The Eagle return man had taken the kickoff on the two and been piled up just short of the twenty-yard line. Jamie saw this out of the corner of his eye while the rest of his vision was poised on Eagle offensive lineman Roland Wingrette, who'd been blocking on the left. The whistles had long blown when Jamie crashed into him from behind. The much larger Wingrette had gone flying, landed, and hadn't gotten up. A sea of white Eagle uniforms swallowed Jamie for a brief instant before the blue of the Giants joined the pileup. Jamie was hit several times, but he didn't feel it through the pads. All he felt was good.

Walter Mount had stopped the tape and removed his glasses. "Mr. Skylar, it is the contention of this committee that you willfully and maliciously sought to do harm to Roland Wingrette. And in so doing did cause a concussion and third-degree separation of the right shoulder. What do you have to say in this matter?"

"Nothing."

Mount hastily redonned his glasses, as if his eyes were deceiving him. "You are admitting a totally unprovoked, potentially career-threatening attack on a fellow football player?"

"Not at all."

"But you said—"

"The attack was provoked."

"Mr. Skylar, we could find nothing on the game film to indicate actions of Roland Wingrette toward you."

"Not me."

"What?"

"Rewind the tape, Mr. Chairman. To the ten-minute mark of the third quarter."

Mount cleared his throat. "We do not have the complete game film readily available."

"Fine. Then just answer a question. What position does Roland Wingrette play?"

"Offensive line, reserve."

"But he was in for that one series in the second half, wasn't he? He came in after our all-pro defensive lineman, Monroe Smalls, had flattened their quarterback for the third time in the afternoon. First play in, Wingrette chop-blocked Smalls behind the knees. Refs didn't see it, but the players did. On both sidelines."

"These are serious charges, Mr. Skylar."

"Bullshit. You've heard them before and you didn't do a damn thing about it."

"So you took it on yourself to extract punishment."

"Apparently." Jamie looked closer at Mount, who had lapsed into silence. "You don't plan to review the films, do you?"

"The relative honorability of your intentions does not change the facts here."

"He's done it before, you know. Hell, every time that fuck wad coach of theirs sends Wingrette into a game, it's to take someone out. And instead of doing something about it, you condemn me."

Mount pulled off his glasses again. They trembled in his hand. "You could have brought it to our attention, Mr. Skylar. There is a procedure for these grievances. There are proper channels."

"You ever play football, Mr. Mount?"

"Er, no."

"Too bad. You'd know a hell of a lot more about procedure

if you had. There's a code on the field, Mr. Chairman, that's got nothing to do with standards and practices. All of you should really come to a game sometime. You just might learn something."

Mount held his ground. "And yet with all these incidents you allege Roland Wingrette was behind, you were the first to act upon it."

"Nope. Just the first to get it right."

Mount stared ahead, expression trapped behind anger and stupefaction. "Mr. Skylar, this committee is prepared to decide on your punishment for willfully rendering a fellow player inactive for six weeks, and you seem to have no regrets whatsoever."

"Only that I didn't put him out for the season, Mr. Chairman."

It took the committee only twenty minutes to call Jamie back into the room. Against the left wall, the stenographer's fingers were keyed like a gunfighter's ready to draw.

"Mr. Skylar," Mount began with glasses in the on position, "it is the judgement of this committee that you be suspended from the National Football League for a period of six weeks, during which time you are prohibited from taking part in any practice or meeting. Giants Stadium is off limits to you, as are the stadiums of any team the Giants are playing on the road during that period. Additionally, you will be fined the sum total of your salary for that six-week period. If you wish to appeal this judgement, the NFL council will inform you of the proper procedure to follow. . . ."

Mount had more to say, but Jamie didn't listen. This committee would never understand why he had done what he had. Simply stated, Jamie owed Monroe Smalls, owed him more than he owed anyone.

Jamie ruefully recalled his initiation to training camp the previous summer. He was hog-tailed and slammed to the ground on his very first carry by Smalls, who wore the vast majority of his 300 pounds as sheet steel muscle. But when the all-pro had finally let him up, grinning, Jamie shoulder-tackled Smalls back to the turf and began flailing at him. The blows must not have had any great effect, because Smalls had the tables turned before anyone could even break the scuffle up. He was still grinning when he lifted Jamie from the turf.

"For an Ivy League man, you got shit for brains but rocks for guts," the big man told him then. "Keep hittin', Ivy, and you might just find yourself a job here."

And he did, in no small part because Smalls pushed and prodded him at every opportunity. Smalls had been a two-time all-American at Army and had been granted a special dispensation in order to play pro ball. In return, in the off season he did twelve weekends reserve duty and repeated the ten-week Special Forces course every spring at Fort Bragg after minicamp. The latter had been Smalls's idea, his way of getting keyed-up for the season. In preseason it got so Jamie was looking for the all-pro every time he got the ball even when Smalls wasn't in the scrimmage. Got so he could read the holes the instant faster that you had to in the pros. Smalls was all over him, dogging him and making life generally miserable, and in the end Smalls was ultimately responsible for his making the team as a third-string tailback. Jamie figured decking Roland Wingrette didn't even begin to even out the tally sheet.

The window slid down and Jamie was glad to see his reflection slide away with it.

"Remember, Ivy," Smalls said as Jamie looked back into the Jaguar from the curb, "I'm paying your fine."

"Whatever you say, Monroe."

"You're fuckin' A right whatever I say. And I also say six weeks done, all this gonna be just a baaaaaad memory. Plenty of shit worse than this been known to happen."

Jamie almost told him it already had.

The telegram had come the night before. Jamie hadn't mentioned it to anyone, including Monroe Smalls. Nor had he told the Giants front office or anyone else where he was going. He'd explain it all when he got back. There weren't many things in the world more important to him than football, but one of them was the reason why he was sitting in a first-class seat on a plane bound for Nicaragua forty minutes after Monroe Smalls had dropped him off.

A man who had been watching him from a distance in the departure lounge waited until the jet had begun its taxi before moving for the phone.

"It's a go," he reported. "Skylar's on his way."

CHAPTER 2

"ARE you checking in, miss?"

Chimera regarded the doorman politely and smiled. "No," she replied. "Just meeting a friend."

Chimera continued on through the 42nd Street entrance of New York City's Grand Hyatt. The escalator was directly to the left, rising toward lobby level to the sounds of water cascading in an endless cycle through the large fountain. She had been to the Grand Hyatt only once before but recalled the layout well enough. The lobby sprawled from a wall-length reception desk, across a lounge area complete with built-in velour seating, to the gleaming Sun Garden restaurant which overlooked 42nd Street. Chimera edged forward, noting only peripherally the endless line of conventioneers waiting to register; briefcases held, coffee sipped, a few already with peel-off labels affixed to their lapels.

It wasn't hard to fine Crane; he would be in the spot Chimera would have chosen had the circumstances of desperation been reversed. Keep the back covered and the sides as easy to watch as possible. The rectangular island of brown velour seating designed around an indoor planter was the perfect choice, and she spotted Crane an instant after spotting it. He was sitting on the segment that looked out toward the wide end of the lobby, dominated by the piano bar and Sun Garden restaurant. His back was to the front desk, but he couldn't be seen from there. A drink diluted with melted ice rested on the white square table before him, right next to the nearly finished house of straws he'd been constructing one piece at a time.

Chimera slowed her approach, disturbed by something wrong with the scene. If there was any such thing as a legend in the world of killers she was a part of, it was Crane. No job had ever been too difficult, no challenge too great. When all else failed, you called Crane. The right people knew that, and some of the wrong ones as well. His speciality was knives, but he could handle just about any other weapon as well.

He had done his best work for Israel in that country's early days, but he made his legend with The Outsiders, a group so named because they existed "outside" of all sanctioned authorities. For a price, anything could and would be done by operatives who were outsiders themselves, outcasts who had made mistakes that left them nowhere else to go.

Halfway across the room, Chimera stopped short. This man couldn't be Crane. The shoulders were too stooped, the frame much too thin. The Crane she knew was a big man, but this one looked to be the product of some crash diet. And yet it was indeed Crane, and Chimera's thoughts lingered briefly on whether his appearance was somehow to blame for the desperate message that had brought her here. One Outsider arranging to meet with another was totally unheard of, but Chimera would not have dismissed Crane's plea no matter what the cost.

Chimera could tell by Crane's progress on the house of straws that he had been here awhile already, which was bothersome since she was not late. Men like Crane never lingered too long in a single spot unless they had a pressing reason.

She was approaching him from the side across the brown and white checkerboard carpet when the legend spoke.

"Hello, Matty."

Chimera sat down on the seat next to Crane's. "To be trite, it's been a long time."

"Right. Years. How many? Two?"

"Two and a half."

He gazed at the auburn hair which tumbled past her deep-set brown eyes to her shoulders. "God, you look great, hell of a lot better than the first time I saw you in that bar. Cairo, wasn't it?"

Chimera nodded and tried to look relaxed.

"I hope I didn't take you away from anything."

"I'm due somewhere tomorrow. It can wait."

"Damn," said Crane, and she watched his hand tremble as he moved another straw into position. In the incandescent light of the lower lobby, something looked wrong about that hand. A straw slipped from its grasp, and Crane held it up for Chimera to see. The fingers had grown knobby and twisted, fat at the joints.

"Arthritis, Matty." Another laugh, humorless this time. "I spend over thirty years out here, the best of them with The Outsiders, outlast them all, take on all comers, only to be done in in the end by bad genes. Fifty-five isn't so old, is it?"

"It shouldn't be."

"Doctors say if I'm lucky, it won't get worse. Don't worry, they tell me, I can still lead a normal life, do all the tasks required of me. Should I have bothered to tell them that my life hasn't been normal since before I can remember? That the prime task required of me is to wield a knife, both killing and throwing variety? They'd probably laugh. Those days are over. Told me to squeeze rubber balls for therapy ten minutes a day. Can you picture it, Matty, me squeezing rubber balls?"

Crane used both hands on the straw this time and managed to get it settled into place. The roof was the hardest part of the structure, and his arthritic hands were fighting him all the way. This kind of thing wasn't supposed to happen to legends. It was too mundane. Legends often died, but they never, never deteriorated.

"I need you, Matty," said the legend. "I know when I brought you into The Outsiders I warned you never to need anyone. But this is different."

Chimera listened patiently.

"I've latched on to something I wasn't supposed to. It was

quite inadvertent and I don't have any proof. That doesn't make me any less sure, though.''

''Sure about what?''

Crane didn't speak right away. ''There's a group working behind the scenes, its purpose being to affect everything that occurs in front of them.''

Chimera waited for him to go on.

''They don't make policy, they create it, manufacture and manipulate it. I know this because we, The Outsiders, are their soldiers. They created us, too.''

''We're independent, Crane. That's the point.''

''It's another illusion. Listen to me, Matty. I was there close to the beginning, and the scenario's not hard to figure. Korea had ended disastrously, we were losing the Cold War as well, and no one was heeding the warnings about Cuba. Some of the best minds in the country figured it was time to take matters into their own hands, and created a kind of shadow government.''

Crane hesitated very briefly.

''Think of all the people The Outsiders have killed, all the elections we've disrupted and governments we've helped destabilize. We always thought, those of us who bothered to think, that we had been retained by individual parties to do a job no one else could. But what if it was always the *same* party, Matty? What if The Outsiders were no more than the private soldiers of this shadow government?''

Chimera saw the legend's fingers were trembling now, the arthritis making it impossible for him to hide his fear. ''You wouldn't have contacted me if you hadn't decided on the answers already.''

''I contacted you because my pension's come up. The shadow government knows I'm on to them, and no one's allowed that. A few years ago I still would have been able to hold my own.'' He paused to gaze down at his hands. ''But not anymore. They can't be allowed to get away with it. Somebody has to stop the group that's pulling all the strings.''

''Stop them from what?''

Crane seemed not to hear. ''Escalation. On every level. The checks and balances have eroded. The subtleties are gone. They're making their move.'' His eyes sought Chimera's. ''What do you know about Pine Gap, Matty?''

''It's some sort of research station in the middle of the Australian Outback.''

''*Weapons* research. The Outsiders sent me there to smuggle out some explosives.''

''What kind of explosives?''

''Something called Quick Strike. It's new and volatile. Beyond that, I don't know a thing. I took out twelve canisters about the size and weight of one-liter soda bottles—two crates, packed six in each. I never planned on delivering the crates to the next step up the line. They were going to provide the proof I needed to expose the truth about The Outsiders, about what *we* have become. I arranged with my contact, Kirby Nestler, to retrieve the crates from a drop point, but when he arrived they were gone. The Outsiders knew where to look because they were watching me. I was supposed to die after I finished my part. Maybe they knew I was on to the force that really controls us, maybe it was just coincidence. Managed to stay one step ahead of them, though. And I've also managed to keep the state of my hands a secret, so they're not about to act rashly. I'm even still carrying, loaded up with throwing knives from chest to calf, even though I doubt I could make them work anymore.''

''You're saying this . . . group has the crates?''

''With the full intention of using the Quick Strike charges they contain. I don't know where or when, and I can't surface to find out.'' His eyes narrowed. ''I need you, Matty. Not just me either. Get the Quick Strike back. Whatever it takes, you've got to get those charges back.''

''Who was your conduit?''

''Stein the bookseller. If he's still alive. The doors on this are all being closed. Locked up tight.''

''If this group is as good as you claim, they wouldn't sacrifice controls like Stein merely because of his connection with you. Too difficult to replace. Too much attention drawn in the process. Let me make a call.'' Chimera started to stand up, then thought better of it. ''When I get back, we'll turn our attention to you. I've got resettlement routes, plenty stashed away for when the time comes.''

Crane's face brightened. ''It was me that taught you about resettlement routes. But they're not for me. I don't want to waste away; I've been doing that enough lately. This is my retirement villa here,'' he said, pointing at his nearly completed house of straws. ''It's all I need. The memories fit neatly inside.'' Crane looked up from the house and back at Chimera. ''I saved you once, didn't I, Matty?''

''And I owe you everything for it.''

Crane smiled and in that instant looked like the Crane of old, as if a sudden burst of strength pulsed through the gnarled and weakened fingers. ''Then go make your phone call, Matty.''

Chimera moved to the phone bank in an alcove beyond the sprawling registration counter. A pair of calls confirmed that the bookseller Stein was alive and well, but she stopped short of arranging a meet. Better to take the bookseller by surprise, especially if, with Crane on the lam, he had reason to take precautions. Time to get back to the legend, convince him to accept some help, maybe rehash more of his better times.

But Crane was gone. His house of straws, its roof complete, remained on the table. Chimera approached the well-stocked lobby bar across the way, heart thudding, fearing it was already too late.

''Excuse me.''

The barmaid looked up.

''I'm looking for a friend of mine. Older gentleman. He was sitting over there.''

Before she could point the way, the barmaid nodded. ''He left with a few friends.''

''When?''

''Just a minute ago.''

''Where? Did you see where?''

''Off toward the shopping alcove.''

''How many . . . friends were there?''

''Four, maybe five.''

Chimera moved swiftly through the lobby for the Hyatt's

shopping alcove, which housed an antique shop, a jewelry store, and a pair of sundry stands. The only way out of the building, once in the alcove, was through a heavy exit door with an L stenciled over it. She breathed deep and plunged through.

Five men . . . Five was a tough number to take under the best of conditions, and these were hardly optimal. Chimera could never hope to do it alone, but, then, there was no reason to.

Because there was Crane to consider as well. Crane would be expecting what was about to happen. The legend would be ready for it.

Chimera burst through the steel door into the dim of the stairwell, Sig Sauer nine-millimeter pistol in hand. A few of the pensioning team had reached the top of the stairs, the others still had a few steps left to go. Crane was amidst them.

Chimera's first shots were simple. Even in the half-light, the lowermost men made inviting targets. Their efforts to whip out their weapons were futile. Almost before two of them were tumbling down the steps, Chimera dove and rolled hard against the wall to steady the Sig's next shots. These would be tough ones, because two of the remaining three gunmen had fanned out and were firing away. Only one man was left with Crane.

Crane . . . the legend, capable as only a legend could be.

With bullets everywhere, all Chimera could do was spin away from the wall to the floor, and find meager cover beneath the first step. But Crane could do far more. He moved just enough to free himself of the grasp on his right arm, and ducked a hand immediately into his jacket. It emerged with a knife, which he promptly buried into the stomach of the man who'd been holding him. The gunman on the left flank swung toward Crane while the one on the right continued to aim automatic fire at Chimera. Wall fragments showered down, keeping her pinned. Crane had a second knife in hand by then, and both gunmen were potential targets.

He went for the one with the machine gun firing down on Chimera. She caught a glimpse of the throwing knife in his hand. Then it was in motion forward, as straight and sure as ever, time turned back in the flash of an instant it took for the action to unfold. The gunman was advancing down the stairs, and his bullets had almost found her when the knife found him. Flesh and bone were shredded en route to the heart, killing him between beats and pitching him downward.

The final gunman fired into Crane repeatedly.

"No!"

Chimera rose and fired four bullets into the last gunman. The man reeled backward and slammed into the wall with his arms flying, a trail of blood marking his slide down the beige wall. Chimera bounded up the stairs toward Crane, who had slumped over, partially propped up by the top stair.

The legend was well past words. His breath heaved and rasped, only bits of it ever reaching his lungs. But his eyes were full and alive. In the final instant of his life he had thrown a knife with no thought of his ruined fingers, and maybe that was enough for him.

But it wasn't enough for Chimera.

"I'll stop them," she promised, before Crane's eyes glazed over. "Whoever they are, I'll stop them."

CHAPTER 3

"It's for my son," the man repeated, thrusting the open memo pad toward Jamie.

"No problem."

"I thought it was you. I mean I was almost sure. But I figured it couldn't be because what would Jamie Skylar be doing on a plane to Nicaragua with the Packer game only five days away? Then I read today's *Times*. You got a raw deal. For what it's worth, I'm sorry."

"Thanks."

The man took his autograph and backed away with a smile. "I really appreciate this. Sorry to bother you. Best of luck."

And Jamie was alone again, glad that the man hadn't asked why he was going to Nicaragua. He closed his eyes and thought once more about the telegram from his sister that had greeted him on his return to his apartment the night before:

JAMIE:
IN TROUBLE. NEED YOUR HELP. COME IMMEDIATELY.
PLEASE.

BETH

His persistent attempts to call her failed, so he cabled her with his flight arrangements as soon as they were made. If there was no one waiting at the airport for him, he had the address where she could be found. They hadn't seen each other in two years, but she had been the most important person in his life for too long for that to matter.

Their separation had been brought about by nothing more dramatic than her career as a globe-trotting journalist of some high regard. Beth Skylar was a champion of left-wing causes the world over and had a prizewinning article or book to show for virtually every one of her stops. The latest stop, in Nicaragua, had been the longest. She had found paradise in the form of one Colonel José Ramon Riaz, a former Sandinista executioner better known as *el Diablo de la Jungla*, the Demon of the Jungle. The Contras had christened him that for Riaz's penchant for tracking down the most murderous of their number on their own turf ever since a Contra bullet had cost him an eye over a decade before. Riaz had an eye patch and a family, and now he had Beth, too. If her few letters were to be believed, she had fallen in love with him. As a result, she had shut Jamie out of her life, and he had pretty much resigned himself to that fact.

Until the telegram.

And now he was flying down to see her at Colonel Riaz's farm on the reinstituted direct flight out of Kennedy to Sandino Airport in Managua. After the 1990 election had toppled the Sandinistas and inserted the Chamorro government in their place, a new spirit of cooperation blossomed between the U.S. and Nicaragua. Nicaragua badly needed help rebuilding its ruined economy, and both American government and industry were more than willing to lend a hand. The signing of the Nicaraguan Accords resulted and now the country had been opened up to capitalist expansion. Accordingly, this flight was packed with businessmen, as were all flights to Managua.

What the hell happened, Beth? he thought, as the jet settled into its descent. *What the hell's going on?*

* * *

"Hey, superstar, can I have your autograph?"

His sister's voice caught him by surprise after Jamie had given up searching the crowded airline terminal for her. It was obviously not built to accommodate this kind of traffic, and work to expand the runways was constant. Bulldozers had replaced tanks around the tarmac. He found himself facing a huge patch of discolored khaki wall where a massive painting of General Augusto Cesar Sandino had been removed, though not replaced, since it would take the new government time to find heroes of its own. Jamie swung sideways at the sound of his sister's voice to find Beth leaping into his arms and to feel her long hair caressing his cheeks. He was instantly relieved to see her smiling.

"How about finding me a Nicaraguan skycap?" he asked after they had exchanged greetings.

She giggled. "You're looking at her."

Beth lifted his suitcase and left Jamie the carry-on. If the anomaly struck him, he didn't show it; she'd been carrying his weight since they were children and it was easy to slide backward. She had been seventeen, nine years older than he was, when their parents were killed in a car crash. The burden was one she shouldered willingly, raising him as both parent and sister rolled into one. She had never missed a football game until he reached college and her career in journalism started jetting her all over the world.

Her prizewinning articles over the past six years detailed her exploits from the Golden Triangle, to South Africa, to Central America where her strong belief in the Sandinistas led to her meeting Colonel José Ramon Riaz. Their affair made for better headlines and attention than her first-hand stories of his country's progress under its new leadership. The globe-trotting, prize-winning American writer taking up with the infamous *el Diablo de la Jungla* was enough to make even the gossip columnists look twice. And as a result, ironically, she had outlasted the Sandinistas who had drawn her down here in the first place.

"I told you in my cable you didn't have to come all the way out here to pick me up," Jamie said when they reached his sister's jeep, parked illegally against a curb along the airport's front. He had stepped out of the building's cluttered concourse expecting the same sights he was familiar with from other city airports. But Sandino Airport seemed to have been constructed in the middle of a wasteland. The rubble of buildings lost in the earthquake of 1972 pockmarked the scene. What structures he could see appeared to grow out of the rubble, looking out of place and unwelcome. The hum of heavy construction equipment in the surrounding hills sifted through the dusty air, evidence of American industry struggling to build Managua up again. He had seen the plans in magazines and newspapers and they were quite ambitious. Hell of a job the builders had ahead of them.

"Sure," came Beth's sarcastic reply, "and what were you going to do? Take a cab? What do you think this is, superstar, New York City?"

He stowed his bag in the back of the jeep and shoved his own shaggy hair off his forehead. "No, I thought your colonel friend could send a tank for me."

"He would have. But the driver was afraid you'd blindside him."

They hadn't seen each other in the more than two years she had been in Nicaragua but it might have been five times that, he thought as he scrutinized her face. Gone was the youthful vitality she had worn as easily as an old pair of jeans. There were bags under her eyes. Something was wrong with her smile. It made him think of the way his reflection had looked that morning in the window of Monroe Smalls's Jag.

Jamie hesitated before speaking again. "You look like hell, sis."

"You've looked better yourself, bro."

"But you were the one who sent the telegram."

She turned away and spoke without looking at him. "Yeah, well, we all make mistakes."

"Did I miss something here? Didn't I get a telegram from you last night that said you were in trouble, and you wanted to see me immediately?"

"Yes and no."

"Which?"

"I wanted to see you."

"Are you in trouble or not?"

"We're all in trouble, superstar."

"Save the literary bullshit for your readers. I'm here because you said you needed me," Jamie said from across the jeep.

"I do. I've felt like crap for the past few months. I kept trying to figure out what was wrong and I realized the only time I've felt okay is when I'm thinking of you."

"Why'd you call me down here, sis?"

"Because I had to know you would come. I had to know you were still there. I know you didn't approve of my relationship with Riaz. . . ."

"You never gave me a chance to."

"You didn't want one. You didn't approve and that made me feel like I had to make a choice."

Jamie eased himself into the passenger seat. "You asked me down here because you want my blessing?"

"I thought I could live without you as a part of my life, bro, but what I've realized this past month is that I can't. I had to get you down here to see how it really is."

"You said it was an emergency."

"Because I knew you wouldn't have come otherwise. I understand that people grow apart. You had your life and I had mine and it hasn't been easy for either of us. How many articles did I have to write before anyone noticed? How many yards did you have to burn up before the Heisman committee took heed?"

"And we're both doing our best to throw it all away. You end up settling down on a farm in Casa Grande and I get myself suspended for outdirtying a dirty football player."

She let the engine idle and looked at him the closest she had yet. "When that Eagle went flying, I knew it was you who hit him. I don't know how I knew, but I did."

"You watched the game down here?"

"The colonel had a videotape made off a government satellite. He picked it up himself when the game was over. You should have seen how excited he was."

"Please."

Her hands tightened around the steering wheel. "You think

I'm making this up so you'll like him. I don't have to. You'll like him anyway if you give him a chance; everyone does. He brought the tape home and gathered all his children around with us so they could watch."

"He has *children*?"

"Forget to tell you that, did I?"

"Yeah."

"Well, he's got four. Three boys and a girl."

"From previous affairs, I hope."

"All from a single wife who died four years ago. I wrote you about this in my letters."

"Must have missed it," Jamie lied.

Beth started to turn the jeep into traffic, then stopped. "I think it was watching the tape of that game last week that made me send that wire. I watched the hit, the fight, and it all came back to me. The high school games, then the college ones before I started with my work. Everytime you got hit, it was like I got hit too, the way it is for twins."

"We're not twins."

"No, we're orphans who raised each other, who did for ourselves because there was no one else. We only survived because we were together. I've been thinking about that a lot lately and I realized here I was—no, here *we* were—letting ourselves slip out of each other's lives."

She pulled into traffic at last and Jamie was grateful for the air rushing past his face. He had felt heat before but nothing like this. It was a choking heat that took his breath away. The air was thick like paste and hit his throat much the same way, leaving a dry residue on its way to his lungs. His shirt was already soaked through with sweat, and he could never remember a time he'd been more uncomfortable.

There was more to blame here than the heat, of course. All these years he had not stopped to think that his sister had depended on him as much as he had depended on her. The thought that it cut both ways was foreign and new and not altogether refreshing. He had *let* her cut him off from her life, wallowing in pity and self-righteousness. But never had he considered that it had hurt her as much as him. She hadn't visited him, yet he hadn't been adamant about visiting her either.

They drove on in silence much of the time, exchanging too much smalltalk. Beth pointed out many of the features of the countryside she felt Jamie should be aware of but a number caught his eye in advance of her words. The road was one of the major arteries in all of Nicaragua. Yet it was formed of simple black top, marred by potholes either untreated or poorly patched. The road was dotted on both sides by sporadic rows of small, shanty style homes with corrugated tin for roofs and curtains for front doors. Women in simple smocks went about their chores outside amidst chickens waddling about the camel colored dirt. American construction projects appeared in vast clearings from time to time, the powerful sounds of their green and yellow Caterpillar equipment seeming terribly out of place amidst the silent poverty of the countryside. The drive was hilly, but not altogether unpleasant, especially as they drew further toward Casa Grande in the fertile lands of the northwest. At times beautiful rich forests covered the road on either side. The jeep took the rolling hills easily and Jamie drank in a cool refreshing breeze to help relieve the parched dryness that coated his throat.

"I wired as soon as I heard about the suspension. Thought it would be a good time," Beth said two hours into a drive that still had one remaining.

"You must have pretty good sources."

"I've never been as far away as you think."

"Close suits me just fine."

"The operation is called Thunder Clap," Esteban finished after explaining the particulars to Colonel José Ramon Riaz.

"I can see why," said Riaz, leaning impatiently over the veranda railing.

The fat man rose to join him there. His gait was more of a waddle, sweat-soaked baggy suit swimming over his girth.

"Then you must also see why you have been selected as the perfect man to command it."

"Not really," said Riaz, tugging at his black eye patch. "Not at all."

"We need a man whose skills as a military leader are

equalled by his reputation as a Nicaraguan hero," reiterated the fat man. "A man who can keep a cool head and his wits about him. I would not be here if the Nicaraguan National Solidarity Committee did not feel confident about its decision."

"Your committee is an anachronism, Esteban."

"Like you, Colonel?"

"Apparently, the difference is I'm ready to accept that."

"And are you willing to accept the growing American influence in your country thanks to the weakness of the Chamorro government? Look around you, Colonel, look at this country you helped forge and nearly died to keep. The Americans speak of a new cooperation between our nations. But to demonstrate this they come here with their monstrous corporations and industries. Don't you see? When their bullets failed to topple us, they tried instead with dollars and we let them. They have bought us out, mortgaged our souls, and if something isn't done we will become nothing but their slaves."

"So it is left to the NNSC to stop them."

"We were once your allies, Colonel, your most loyal supporters."

"When you ran the government instead of being outcast from it."

Esteban's jaw hardened. "That will change, with or without your help. I am disappointed, Colonel. I came here expecting a different man."

"An NNSC puppet, for example."

"Operation Thunder Clap is the one hope we have to avoid becoming an American satellite before this decade is out."

"And would that be so bad? Is prosperity so bitter a pill to swallow? Do our people not deserve the chance American investment here is providing?"

"At what price, Colonel Riaz? Our own national pride, the fervor that led us to overthrow the pig Somoza? After all our sacrifices, can we return to his ways of concession and living as parasites?"

"You would prefer martyrdom?"

"The NNSC would prefer a Nicaragua free to chart its

own course without the same kind of American interventionism that has destroyed so many other countries. We want them out of here. Every man, every brick, every mainframe computer and assembly line. And what is best for us, Colonel, is also best for you."

"Best for our country also, of course."

"In our vision, yes."

Riaz almost laughed. "You think me a fool, Esteban? You come here with your words steeped in idealism when all you really seek is the means to return the Sandinistas to power. Make our country see the Americans as our dire enemy to give your old warriors a windmill to tilt at."

Esteban looked at Riaz as hard as he dared. "They are not the only enemy we face, Colonel," he continued, as he dabbed at his forehead with a damp handkerchief. "You are aware, of course, that the Chamorro government continues to welcome your great enemies the Contras back to the country in droves."

"They are not my enemies anymore."

"There remains a price on your head and the ones most likely to claim it are no longer pinned in Honduras. They fear our eventual return to power and are sure to take steps to insure it does not come to pass. Men like you and I will not be able to remain in this country safely unless the forces of the NNSC regain the government. And when we are gone there will be no one to fight off capitalist advances that will destroy the roots of everything we fought to create here. This is about duty, duty and nothing more."

"I do not need you to tell me my duty."

Esteban took a deep breath and gazed off the veranda at the fertile lands before him. "Yes, I do envy you, Colonel Riaz. I envy you your life, your land, and your family. They are all so precious, yet potentially fleeting so long as the Contras are running free without fear of prosecution."

Riaz took a large step closer to the fat man, one eye blazing forward.

"Don't mention my family. Don't *ever* mention my family."

But the fat man didn't back off. "The Contras have long

memories, Colonel, and after all your 'engagements' with them, it is only a matter of time before—"

"Get out."

"Colonel, I—"

"I was a soldier. What I did I did because we were at war. . . ."

"We *are* at war, Colonel."

"You are. I'm not. And even if I was, Operation Thunder Clap is not my idea of an engagement."

"We must vanquish the Americans and regain control of our nation's destiny, through whatever means are available."

The fat man felt Riaz's powerful arm grasp him at the elbow and tug ever so gently toward the steps.

"I wish you luck in that pursuit," he said simply.

"If you wish to reconsider, you know where to find me," the fat man told him.

"I'll do my best to forget," returned the colonel.

"I wish you luck in that pursuit."

"If you wish to reconsider, you know where to find me."

"I'll do my best to forget."

The recording of the conversation over, Sapphire pulled the headphones off. She felt cold and clammy. A thin layer of sweat coated her flesh. At last, the Jubilee network's surveillance of the Nicaraguan National Solidarity Committee had paid off. At last she knew exactly what the bastards were up to.

Operation Thunder Clap . . .

An instant later the microchip containing the digitized recording, smaller than a fingernail, was back in her hand. The equipment she had used was the most sophisticated anywhere. Dozens of miniature microphones planted around the house were rigged into a central voice-activated recording station. She had checked the LED readout and played back the chip at the first opportunity after returning to the farm with Jamie from the airport. Gazing at it centered in her palm made her tremble with fear.

It's worse than Richards thought, Sapphire reflected.

Her brother's telegram had been the signal that the network

had been compromised. If recall was mandated, Richards would have arranged her pull-out. Instead he had opted for the contingency. Otherwise the break they had been waiting months for would have remained closeted with no way to get the chip off the farm into the proper hands.

But there was a way now, thanks to Jamie, who was about to become her courier.

CHAPTER 4

ERNEST Stein's rare bookshop was located on 57th Street between Fifth Avenue and Madison, tucked neatly into a building that catered to private galleries and boutiques, one to a floor. His occupied the third, and Stein was there bright and early every working morning. As the first to ride the building's elevator, he always appreciated the absence of the stale smoke and expensive cologne which would dominate by the midmorning hours.

Stein had a nose for such things, had a nose for *everything*. Give him a rare book and he could date it not only by visual inspection but also by smell. In fact, scent was the first sense he used to enjoy a newly obtained volume. His three full rooms of elegantly bound volumes were full of the smell of book leather. He could sniff through a volume for the hundredth time as if it were the first. Customers were, or course, welcome, but Stein really didn't care if they bought or not. Each book meant something to him, and each sale detracted that much more from the olfactory beauty he had surrounded himself with.

He had just gotten over a cold and blamed this for the curious scent his nose detected in the elevator. Something unctuous, refined, yet unsettling in its vague familiarity. Stein couldn't place it and passed it off to both his cold and the first-edition Arthur Conan Doyle he had reread late into the previous evening. For most, Ernest Stein's life would have been intolerably lonely. But for Stein himself it was filled with bedfellows who made both loyal companions and entertaining mates. He wouldn't trade his books for anything.

Stein entered the glass-doored foyer of his shop, disconnected the alarm, and let himself in. The dead quiet of the shop embraced him, and Stein breathed it in, sniffed briefly, and then cocked his nose in puzzled fashion.

The same enigmatic scent from the elevator seemed to be present in the shop. He continued to attribute it to his cold and switched on all the lights before stripping off his overcoat. He lay it on the back of the nearest chair and set off for his ritualistic walk through the stacks. Books needed to be touched. Oil from the fingers kept them supple and alive. Stein was more than happy to give of himself.

He had gone barely a shelf when he noticed the first-edition *Lamb's Shakespeare* was missing.

"I needed something to read. Hope you don't mind."

Certainly words and smells do not travel as one, but Stein could have sworn the suddenly familiar smell from the elevator reached him with the voice. He pressed on his thick bottle-bottom glasses and scanned the room, coming quickly upon the figure seated in one of his luxurious leather reading chairs.

"Chimera?"

"Good morning, Stein."

There was never any doubt of the action she would take after leaving the Hyatt. She owed that much to Crane, owed everything to him for rescuing her from the life of Matira Silvaro. Her last days with the CIA had seen her stationed at the Company's African Affairs bureau. Too much was going down on the continent, and a number of Division Six personnel had been sent there to help safeguard American interests. She was involved in gathering intelligence on a trio of South African blacks, one of whom was making very suspicious friends. Matira passed her reports down the line and never questioned her orders until a backup team arrived with the leader's death warrant in their pocket. She was simply there to provide further intelligence. No sense risking her cover on a simple execution.

Matira couldn't stomach it. The black leader had done nothing other than rally the people against a government the United States rigidly supported. Yes, she had been involved in similar operations before, had even performed several killings herself, and quite successfully at that. But only against those who had been responsible for the deaths of innocents themselves, like drug overlords in the Central American backlands where she had learned her trade. That she could live with.

This she couldn't.

Based on the intelligence she provided, the hit team elected to wire the black leader's car with a bomb while he attended an afternoon luncheon. Once the car was restarted, the delay switch would be activated, and fifteen seconds later the car would be blown apart. Fine, for it made the response she had decided on all the easier. Once he was inside the building, she would simply call in the threat to the restaurant, and stress it was CIA-inspired. Her career was finished anyway as of that moment, so she might as well go out leaving herself with something.

As always, the intelligence she received was precise. The black leader was driven into the city, and Matira watched the hit team plant the explosive. They were disguised as workmen, which made no one question the street inspection that brought them under the car's chassis. Some putty to wedge the explosive home and a pair of wires to be spliced in. A minute's work, no more.

Matira was standing in a pay phone dialing the restaurant's number when her heart skipped a beat. The leader's wife and three children emerged from the building and climbed into the backseat. Frozen with shock, she watched as the car pulled out and exploded just a few yards from the curb.

She had never felt so worthless. She was ready to go to congressional authorities with the truth when the story broke. Matira got the news from a contact who was hiding her out.

She had been blamed for the killings! She had been marked

as a rogue agent, a renegade who had operated on her own. An all-out search was on for her. Matira had no illusions as to what that meant. Division Six operatives were not simply slapped on the wrist and reassigned to desk jobs. When you fucked up at Wet Affairs, you disappeared. No one ever saw you again. Forget being made a scapegoat; they made you an example.

So Matira Silvaro ran. The story reached the press somehow while she was holed up at a Cairo hotel, things progressing from bad to worse. She was at the bar trying to drown the memory of four innocent people in cognac when Crane appeared.

"Is this seat taken?"

"No, and it's not going to be either."

Crane's smile almost disarmed her. "Yes, it is."

"I think you better leave."

"Matira Silvaro, age twenty-seven," he said instead. "Born in the Canary Islands. Immigrated to the United States with parents at age of three. Joined Central Intelligence Agency 1982 after becoming first female Navy SEAL in that elite group's history. Assigned to Division Six—Wet Affairs—in 1984. Trained by Ross Dogan, better known as Grendel. Fluent in six languages. All assignments handled clean until South Africa six days ago." The older man smiled again. "Put it away."

"Excuse me?"

"The gun you're holding on me under the table. Put it away. They didn't send me."

"Who did?"

"You did when you ran and came here. Thinking of going back, turning yourself in?"

"The thought had crossed my mind," Matira answered, not bothering to add that whatever chance there had been for that was lost when the story reached the press.

"It always does about now, usually over brandy. Don't do it."

"Do what?"

"Go back to them. You'll regret it. Most of them do. But, alas, not for very long."

"Who *are* you?"

The older man tilted his head her way. "Someone who sat in that very chair, figuratively anyway, a long time ago. I'm here to rescue you, just as someone else rescued me."

The man lit up a Turkish cigarette and maneuvered it lightly between the long, supple fingers that made him a legend with knives. Recalling that moment now, Chimera couldn't help but contrast it with the sight of Crane's gnarled joints in New York. *You saved me, but then I wasn't able to save you. . . .*

"Can I call you Matty?"

"No one ever has."

"All the more reason. You can call me Crane. Not my real name. We don't use real names."

"We," Matira echoed.

"The Outsiders," said Crane. "Capital T, capital O, though you'll never see it written anywhere. Named for the fact that we work outside all intelligence communities. Also named for the fact that our numbers are composed of just that—outsiders, outcasts, people with nowhere else to turn. People who have made mistakes, or had mistakes forced upon them; who don't fit into the system anymore."

"You're offering me a job?"

"I'm offering you a lifeline. I'm your recruitment officer. I won't bother you with a discussion of the pay scale and retirement benefits. I'm sure you understand such terms, Matty."

"And what was your crime?" Matira asked him.

"Not a crime, a blunder made a lifetime ago. Cold war time. I was supposed to kill a man. I didn't because his family was right there. That wasn't part of the deal. My superiors didn't like me exercising moral judgement."

Matira smiled sadly. "If I had exercised more judgement, maybe I wouldn't be sitting here now."

"Not now, but eventually. For some it's inevitable."

"Nothing's inevitable."

Crane nodded his satisfaction. "An idealist as well. I can see why they picked me as your recruiter. We're both made up of incongruous parts, segments which shouldn't fit together but do, like that dragon in mythology. What was its name?''

''Chimera. Part lion and part goat. Breathed fire and made life generally miserable in Lycia.''

Crane smiled. ''A perfect anonym for you, Matty. I chose mine after the national bird of Israel since I did my first work in that nation. Better times. Simpler ones.''

''Anything but the present usually is.''

''We'll make you disappear,'' Crane assured her. ''They'll never find you. You won't exist anymore.''

''I like the prospects of that.''

Crane had been true to his word about The Outsiders. The work was challenging, though seldom fulfilling. Since she was a woman, countless avenues were opened to her. What she didn't know, Crane taught her, and on the rare occasions at first when she made mistakes, he was there to bail her out.

''The great thing about The Outsiders is that we're self-perpetuating,'' he had counseled her. ''Someday you'll recruit someone, just as I recruited you. You'll train them, help them, perhaps even name them, and that person will become your insurance. No one from within will ever move on your back, because it's always being watched over by someone who owes you, someone you saved. The ultimate deterrent and the only rule we live by.''

Chimera was living by it now.

''What are you doing here?'' Stein managed from across the room. ''You're breaking procedure. I have nothing for you.''

''But you heard about Crane?''

''Crane . . . yes, tragic . . .''

''There were five in all. I got three. Crane got two before he died. I rearranged the scene so they wouldn't know it was me. They'll think it was just one of Crane's old enemies come to even the score. Coincidence.''

''I had nothing to do with it! I *swear*!''

''What if I were picking something up? What if you had something for me?''

''I don't. I'm sure I don't.''

''You do. You just don't realize it yet.''

"Chimera, I—"

"You had something for Crane, though."

"Nothing!"

"Not today. But two weeks ago? Three perhaps?"

Stein pulled his bottle-bottom glasses off, as if preferring not to see Chimera at all.

"I can't talk about that."

"You had something for him then, didn't you?"

"Chimera, you know I can't!"

"Who's stopping you?"

"They'll kill me like they killed him!"

"They'll never know unless you tell them, and you won't because then you'd have to tell them you spoke to me. Now, back to business. Crane was working on something that took him to Australia and Pine Gap. He took out two crates of canisters that contained something called Quick Strike. Somebody's planning on doing a lot of killing, Stein, and I plan to stop them. So I need to know where the contact originated down the line."

"Even if I knew, I couldn't tell you."

"Sniff the air."

Stein looked puzzled but did as she suggested. He noted another faint scent that didn't belong, bittersweet and faintly medicinal.

Chimera showed a lighter. "I soaked selected areas with fast-drying sulfur oil. Evaporates fast, so no one will ever be the wiser providing you answer my question."

Stein returned his bottle-bottom glasses to his nose and waved his hands pleadingly. "Chimera, please!"

She flicked the lighter and a tongue of flame burned to life. "They'll burn fast, Stein. A total loss before the fire department could ever arrive. Think about it."

"Nicaragua!" the bookseller blared suddenly. "The retainer for Crane's Australian assignment was based in Nicaragua."

Chimera felt herself go cold. "Who was the contact?"

"A woman. A woman named Maria—"

"Cordoba," Chimera completed.

Stein's face twisted in puzzlement. "How do you know? How *could* you know?"

Chimera said nothing.

The bookseller adjusted his glasses. "What's going on here? Why are you doing this? You know the costs. You know what they'll do."

"I know what they did."

"No, this isn't about Crane. It's about you. You're doing this because you're afraid of ending up like he did," Stein pronounced boldly. "That's it, isn't it?"

Chimera almost told him, maybe it had been up until now, but it wasn't anymore. Her mind drifted back to an early exchange with Crane the day before.

"I hope I didn't take you away from anything."

"I'm due somewhere tomorrow. It can wait."

Tomorrow had become today. And she was due in Nicaragua, where she was supposed to meet a contact in a Managua bar.

A contact named Maria Cordoba.

CHAPTER 5

"No," Jamie said, adjusting the football in the boy's hand. "This way. Across the laces. Makes it spiral."

"Spiral?" the boy asked. At fifteen Marco was José Ramon Riaz's oldest son.

Jamie jogged forward. "Here, just give it a try."

Marco took an imaginary snap from center, backed up in the best tradition of American quarterbacks, and hurled the ball forward. It wobbled a bit but landed in Jamie's outstretched hands after he broke stride only slightly.

"Touchdown!" he proclaimed.

"Yes!" The boy beamed. He jumped once in the air, while his two brothers and sister clapped on the makeshift sideline.

Jamie met Marco halfway and tossed an easy arm over his shoulder. The boy's long hair danced in the breeze, and his smile was flashbulb bright.

"Now you can teach me how to kick."

"No!" protested his twin ten-year-old brothers in unison. "It's our turn. Please, Jamie, please."

They were on him by then, tugging and pulling. Strange, Jamie reckoned, how it always seemed the more you look to something with apprehension, the less you should have. The Riaz children were beautiful and polite. They showered him with praise and affection in perfect English. They had been waiting for him decked out in Nike warmup suits when his sister steered the jeep down the private road leading onto the property, past the armed guards standing vigilantly by the gate.

That was the only reminder of where he was and who the farm belonged to, because for his part José Ramon Riaz was nothing short of charming. Riaz had a warm smile that was a twin of Marco's and a face which claimed its false menace from the black eye patch dominating its left side. Beth explained that he had made up his mind to wear the patch as a constant reminder of the pain he had endured in the war with the Contras.

But about that Riaz had spoken not a word. Instead he had listened attentively to all conversations. Not that there were many. The children's fascination with an American football hero kept them about Jamie constantly with questions and pleas. Jamie had ended up tossing the lineless authentic NFL football around with Marco and the twins under the night floodlights. He forgot to take his Ivy League championship ring off and ended up scraping his fingers raw as a result.

Jamie was surprised by the simple beauty of the property that formed a stark contrast with much of the land he had passed in his sister's jeep outside Managua. The change seemed to have come with a cool breeze. He had looked up as they hit the crest of a hill and all of a sudden there was nothing but rich, lush forest enclosing the road on either side. Jamie knew they had reached the fertile volcanic lands of Nicaragua's central plain. They swung off the main artery onto a thinly paved route that would take them the remaining forty miles northeast to Casa Grande.

They passed many farms along the way and Jamie found Riaz's to be typical. Fields of rice that extended for acres were being tended by perhaps three dozen workers. Their quarters were located at the rim of the forest that bordered the farm's western edge. Beth was careful to point out that the colonel's workers lived better than any in the region, for he had built their quarters himself instead of merely supplying them with cheap materials as was the custom.

The Riaz house, meanwhile, looked rustic inside and out, yet featured up-to-date American influences such as a modern kitchen and a big screen television. The boys' rooms were notably American as well, walls crammed with posters of rock bands and a selection of pro football team pennants, the Giants' being the largest. Outside a hardpacked dirt flat surrounded the house and provided access to the nearby stables, corral, and barn that housed the animals.

The colonel's fourteen-year-old daughter Miranda was the only one in the household who did not warm up to Jamie immediately. Beth had warned him she could be cold; old enough to remember her mother and resent the younger woman who was taking her place.

Inevitably, though, Jamie's thoughts turned back to Riaz. He sat at the dinner table holding a twin on either knee, evidently happy just to puff away on his sweet-smelling pipe. Once Jamie's eyes were drawn to the scars that laced the back of his left hand, and Riaz quickly buried it behind one of the twins' backs. He was a man at peace with his life, who had left his past behind and was content to plan for a peaceful future.

The boys had taken the colonel's lead, treating Beth with warmth and affection. Again only Miranda held back but Jamie knew Beth would continue to take this as a challenge and confront it as she did any other. Beth had always loved challenges, thrived on them, the harder the better. Jamie supposed that was why she had accepted the responsibility of raising him so willingly and why later she had opted for a life that kept her in dangerous hotbeds of activity. In a twisted sense, he supposed, this business with Riaz could be looked upon as settling down. Certainly she was a hell of a lot more grown-up than he, a twenty-four-year-old who, without football, had nothing. He'd gotten his engineering degree, all right, but that kind of life had become unthinkable for him.

He slept comfortably that night and rose early with the rest of the Riaz household. He wasn't sure he was up to giving another day of intensive football lessons, but Colonel Riaz spared him further worry on that regard five minutes into a pancake breakfast.

"I have to go into town for a few hours. Plenty of sights to see you haven't seen yet, Jamie. I thought you might like to join me."

Jamie didn't hesitate. "Love to."

"Hey, can I come?" wondered Marco.

"Us?" chimed in the twins. "What about us?"

"You have school," their father said sternly. "Besides, I'd like Jamie to myself for a while."

They left thirty minutes later in Riaz's four-wheel-drive enclosed jeep, just the two of them. No guards or escorts. The only concession the colonel made was a nine-millimeter pistol packed into a back-hip holster that had him shifting about for comfort in the driver's seat.

Two miles down the single, unpaved road that led to the farm's private drive, they passed a pair of men squabbling over the best means of changing the flat tire that had stranded their ancient Chevy on the side of the road. The colonel's jeep was well past when one lunged into the Chevy's front seat and grasped the hidden microphone.

"Riaz is gone," he reported. "Tell the team to roll."

"This really is a beautiful country," Colonel Riaz said, observing Jamie taking in the scenery out of the open windows. The jeep was equipped with air conditioning, but both preferred to drive with the windows down.

"That's what the travel agencies have been saying lately. 'Paradise Unlocked' I think is the phrase that's going around."

Riaz shrugged. "Since the signing of the Accords, of course. We've still got plenty of problems—political, military, economic—more than our share, actually. But basically we're a farming country, just like we've always been."

"Even during the war with the Contras?"

The colonel's hands changed their grip on the steering wheel. "You know the worst thing about war, Jamie? It takes men away from their families and often never lets them back. Oh, they come back, all right, but they are not the same people who left. The jungle changes them. Putting on a uniform changes them. Being asked to kill changes them. We are a farming country, and the chain was broken during the war. There was not enough food to eat or sell, so we suffered. And we continue to suffer. Don't let the Accords or the travel agents fool you. The diehard Contras have not conceded at all. In fact, they detest our agreement with the Americans even more then the most militant Sandinistas, who have remained a powerful force,'' Riaz explained, thinking of Esteban and the NNSC. ''The Contras feel abandoned, and abandonment makes men hard. They are confined to the northeast jungles of the country, as dangerous as ever. Some things don't change.''

The colonel's one eye returned to the road, as the jeep cracked and crunched over the rocky gravel. Jamie's side of the road was lined by farmland for as far as the eye could see. The other side was thick, untouched forest, a reminder of what all this land had been like until cleared. A few farms dotted that side, but even they had chiseled their places in agreement with the land.

''You did,'' Jamie said suddenly.

''Only in part. I can escape who I was, but not the legend people made me into. They still stare when I enter the market. A checkout line is kept open, not because I'm a celebrity, but because the store wants me out as fast as possible. The other locals won't let their children associate with mine. I hired a tutor so they wouldn't have to go to school.''

''No one has a right to deny them school.''

''No one did. But if my children had attended, the other parents would have pulled theirs out. I came here to live in peace, not disrupt the peace of others. The people are simple here. Their memories control them, and all they remember is fear. I am a symbol of a different age.''

''But they don't understand what kind of symbol that is. You only went into the jungle after Contras, who had struck out at civilians. You talked the Ortega government out of conducting saturation strafing runs that could have totally wiped them out.''

''We are not butchers. A country that must kill its own to assert its own potency is the most impotent of all.''

Jamie smiled slightly. "The articles about you were filled with quotes like that."

"This is because your sister wrote most of them."

"Not all. 'The Poet Colonel,' one called you."

"It was 'Poet Devil,' I believe. Maybe he's right. I cannot explain myself any better than those who have sought to. I want to be a farmer, a father, a man of family instead of guns. I want to see my children grow up in a nation at peace with itself and the world, and I will do anything in my power to see that come to pass."

"As Señor Riaz instead of colonel?"

"The difference is one of approach, not beliefs. The weapons are different, the ideals the same. You of all people should understand that. What you did, why you did it—it was for an ideal."

"And now I'm out of football."

"We cannot control who we are or what makes us. Second-guessing makes men weak. In spite of everything, you have not once second-guessed what you did to that man from the other team."

"How do you know?"

"Because I wouldn't have," said Riaz.

CHAPTER 6

THE truck wobbled down the gravel road in first gear, brakes whining as it thumped and bucked. The guards in front of the Riaz farm recognized it as the vehicle that regularly delivered the propane gas that provided the farm with its hot water. The large tank would be filled and the smaller ones replaced with fresh canisters pulled from the back of the truck. The colonel had spent much money modifying the workers' cabins to take propane; he wanted them to live and bathe like human beings.

The truck turned halfway off the road and halted directly before the gate. The senior guard approached the open driver's-side window, while a second guard hung back in the shade by the guardhouse. Both had fingers on the triggers of their automatic rifles.

"*Buenos días,*" the senior one said to the driver, whose tanned elbow was propped on the windowsill. He was a young-looking man with a red bandanna across his forehead to hold his long hair in place and keep the sweat from his eyes.

"*Buenos días,*" the driver answered.

"You're early this week. I didn't think you were due until—"

The pistol barrel was propped under the man's forearm against the rubber window guard, camouflaged partially by the contrast between the bright sunshine outside and the shadows within the truck. The senior guard saw only the flash from its muzzle before the bullet tore into his chest and pitched him backward. The roar from the explosion drove the second guard into action. He was going for his gun's trigger and the alarm button at the same time, found the trigger but came up short of the button, when the driver's bullet pasted his skull against the guardhouse.

"Open it!" Maruda screamed to the man sitting next to him in the cab. The man moved fast to the guardhouse to activate the gate as Maruda pounded hard on the steel behind him to signal his men. "Get ready!" he barked. "We're going in."

The propane truck was a common sight on the property, nothing to cause concern as it wound its way down the narrow, tree-lined drive that led to the farm. A quarter mile from the gate, the farm came clearly into view. Five hundred yards later the road widened into the hard-packed area that surrounded the house, barn, stables, and corral. Maruda squealed the truck to a halt across from the house, almost directly in front of the barn.

The grazing horses stirred restlessly, looked up, and sniffed the air.

Maruda felt the sweat soaking into his bandanna and stepped down from the cab. His steps looked mechanical, almost robotic. Pistol held by his hip, he strode straight forward as the truck's back doors opened and his assault team began to spill out, led by Rodrigo.

Maruda's eyes fell on the giant fondly. Rodrigo stood as close to seven feet as six, his rectangular head shaven to show only a few days growth of black stubble. His massiveness made him appear slow, but nothing could have been further from the truth. No one here, including Maruda, had ever heard him speak, and with good reason. Once Rodrigo had been held prisoner and tortured.

They had torn out his tongue.

The damage done had left his face bent in a perpetual half smile, chilling in its contrast to his utter lack of emotion.

Maruda watched the colonel's son Marco emerge from the barn with a bucket of milk in either hand. The boy had actually smiled at him before noticing the armed figures emerging from the rear of the truck. The boy dropped the milk buckets from his hands and backpedaled, trying to turn.

Maruda's bullet caught him where he stood. It thumped into his chest and blew him backward. The spilled milk was splattered with rivulets of red. The clamor of the full buckets falling to the hard drive was actually louder than the gunshot, and Marco found himself staring up at the sky. Something hot and coppery filled his mouth, and a dark shadow crossed over the light, obliterating it.

Maruda had never broken stride. He fired his gun a second time from the hip. The boy's chest rocked from another impact. His body spasmed, twitched, eyes locked as they were. The first kill was always the best, but Maruda pressed on.

An old farmhand rushed from the barn with pitchfork in hand. Maruda shot him between the eyes and headed for the open door while six of his men moved off to surround the house. Seven others would be making their way to the fields by now. The workers would have heard the shots, would know something was wrong. The ones closest would run, all to no avail. Maruda's men would fell them all and then move on to their peasant homes to handle their families.

Maruda steadied his pistol and continued into the barn.

Beth Skylar wasn't sure what the sound was that had drawn her to the window. The kitchen looked out over the stables and western fields, and nothing in sight looked wrong.

But there had been the sound, and something about it had set her stomach fluttering. She moved quickly to the other side of the house. Visible from the side bay window were the barn and entry drive. The first thing she saw were the fallen milk buckets rolling back and forth on the ground, drawn to each other by the slope of the land. She had started to relax when a dark shape on the ground behind them caught her eye. All she could see clearly was a pair of legs clad in navy-blue sweatpants that were tucked into the tops of high-topped sneakers.

Beth's bowels turned to ice. She knew it was Marco even though the angle from the window kept his upper body from her. He must have slipped, she tried to reassure herself, tripped and fell.

The assurance didn't work. Fear gripped her, even before the man emerged from the barn, pistol in hand. She saw that he was young, not much older than Jamie, wearing a red-patterned bandanna to hold back his long hair. Her fleeting glimpse of him made Beth shiver, her throat clogging in the last instant before the professional in her took over.

She had moved away from the window an instant before it exploded inward. Beth dove to the floor, glass shards covering her and digging into her hands as she pulled herself across the rug.

There was another explosion of glass from the second floor, and that seemed to start the onslaught. Instantly automatic fire punctured her ears, coming from the fields. Though still lying prone with needles of glass prickling her exposed flesh, Beth could picture it all. A troop of gunmen was spreading out through the fields, cutting off all escape routes. Some of the workers and their families would try to run. Some might even succeed. But most would be cut down by the automatic fire that came regularly to her ears.

Beth pushed herself on toward the phone on the table nearby, thoughts never far from the young man wearing the bandanna.

"Señorita!" shouted the twins' tutor from partway down the stairs. "What is happen—"

"Get back upstairs!" Beth shouted back. "Protect the twins! Hide them! Do you hear me?"

Maria's response was to rush back to the second floor. Beth had pulled the phone off the table by then and pressed the receiver to her ear. Nothing.

Damn!

The line was dead.

She heard feet hurtling up the steps to the porch, then shuffling sideways. She could waste no more time. The many windows made it easy for anyone to follow her movements, but she had no choice. Marco lay dead outside, and all she could do was fight to keep the other children alive. No help would be coming from any other quarter. It was up to her.

Beth lunged to her feet and charged to the corner of the room dominated by José Ramon Riaz's gun collection, held in a custom glass and wood cabinet. For safety reasons, he always kept it locked, and she had no idea where he kept the key. Adrenaline surging through her, Beth grasped an ashtray from a nearby cocktail table and slammed it through the glass. She shoved her hand through the shards and unhooked the latch from the inside. With the glass doors opened, she went for the twelve-gauge pump-action shotgun and a box of shells.

Just then a shadow crossed before the window on her right. Beth hit the floor an instant before the glass blew inward, showering her yet again. She was already pushing the shotgun cartridges into their slot. It accepted six at a time, and she stowed the rest of the box's contents in her pockets. She picked another window, watched and timed her action to perfection with a shot of her own the next time the shadow passed. There was a scream and a thud on the porch beyond.

"Take that, you bastard!"

She had no idea how many were involved and hoped she could hit a few more to even the odds and perhaps discourage them. Terrorists, Contras, or whatever they were, they would never linger long once a battle was presented. Every second she could hold out added dramatically to her odds of keeping the children alive. Outside, though, screams alternated with gunshots, signaling harmless workers in the fields were being slaughtered as well. Why? It made no sense.

Beth slid back on the floor until her shoulders came to rest against an abutment in the wall that blocked any view of her through the windows.

"Madre?"

Startled, Beth turned toward the stairs to see the colonel's fourteen-year-old daughter, Miranda, already halfway down them with both hands clutching the railing. Something was dreadfully wrong.

"Oh God . . ."

"Madre . . ."

Miranda's white blouse was drenched in blood, and her face was bleeding from numerous glass pricks. Beth recalled the second explosion of glass that had come from the second floor. Miranda must have been drawn to the window by the sound of the first explosion, thus allowing one of the gunmen to seize upon her as a target.

"Miranda!"

Beth rose from her position of concealment and charged toward the stairs with shotgun held tight. Miranda's legs gave way and she moaned, hands sliding down the banister in a feeble effort to hold onto it. By the time Beth had reached the foot of the steps, the girl had let go and was tumbling toward her down the stairs. She nearly upended Beth in the roll that left her faceup with dead eyes staring at the ceiling. Beth was reaching down to Miranda when the front door crashed open. It hadn't been locked, and someone simply turned the knob to gain entry.

"You fucking bastards!"

Beth fired. The figure, already bloodied at the shoulder, was tossed backward through the open doorway. Beth fired again, doing more damage to the porch than what remained of the man's midsection. The shot was needed, though, to clear a path for her toward the door so she could close and lock it.

"Maria!" she screamed up the stairs, shoulders pinned against the now-bolted door. "Maria!"

The girl's terrified shape appeared at the top of the landing.

"Señorita?"

"The twins?"

"Safe. Hidden." Then, bravely, "I knew what to do."

"Get down here then. Hurry!"

Maria hesitated, but only slightly. At the bottom of the stairs, Beth eased the younger woman behind her and focused on the gun case in the den. Farther off, the automatic fire had become sporadic. The enemy could be retreating now, or remassing to launch an all-out assault on the house.

"Do you know how to use a gun?" Beth asked her.

"Here everyone knows how to use guns."

Beth moved away from Maria en route to the den and the gun case. The motion saved her life. The bullet that would have torn into her found Maria's throat instead and blew her backward. Beth twisted toward the window it had come from and fired her twelve-gauge as a bullet fired through the window opposite grazed her side and spun her around. She was going down when a second bullet slammed into her thigh, and she heard herself screech as she crumpled.

Beth tasted bile, the scent of her own blood, and fear welling up around her. Breathing hard, she pushed herself backward across the floor and up to the halfway point of the staircase. She wondered if a better strategy might not be to mount her defense from all the way on the second floor, but rejected that idea as quickly as it occurred to her. She couldn't risk drawing attention to the twins, hidden or not. So she would make her stand from here.

Here . . .

"The woman is good," Maruda mumbled to the commando closest to him behind the stone wall enclosing the house. "We have no time to be subtle. Bring me Rodrigo."

CHAPTER 7

"WHAT'S wrong?" Jamie asked, feeling Colonel Riaz applying the jeep's brakes well before they reached the gates to his property.

"The guards," Riaz replied. "I don't see them."

Jamie followed the colonel's eye and felt something shift in his stomach. It was true; the guards were nowhere in sight. The jeep snailed closer. He could see the guardhouse now as well as the gate.

The gate was open.

"Stay here," Riaz ordered mechanically, nine-millimeter pistol already in hand. He pulled the jeep to the side of the road and vaulted out.

Jamie lunged out after him and caught the colonel five yards from the guardhouse, where the first of the blood was obvious.

"Oh no," Jamie muttered.

Riaz stood there rigidly for a few seconds, as if to brace himself for what might be inside. Then he moved forward toward the blood and the guardhouse door. He turned away suddenly, then back again.

"What is it? What do you see?" Jamie asked, and started forward.

"Stay back! Listen to me this time!"

Riaz eased the door open enough for a clear view of what lay inside, and Jamie saw the booted foot.

"Jesus, no."

The colonel leaned over and came away from the doorway with an automatic rifle in his hand. He wedged the pistol back into his pants and moved to the road leading toward the farm. Warily he crouched and shifted the dirt about with his free hand. Then he stood up and headed back for the jeep.

"What's going on? What are you doing?" Jamie called after him.

Riaz swung into the jeep and gunned the engine. Jamie just managed to lunge in before it screeched forward. Only then did Riaz turn his way long enough to shove the automatic rifle toward him.

"Lean the barrel out your window and keep your finger on the trigger. If I tell you to, fire and keep firing at anything that moves."

"Okay, but—"

"Understand?"

"Yes."

Riaz gripped the wheel tight with his right hand while his left held tight to the pistol in his lap. Jamie's heart was pounding against his rib cage. His stomach seemed to turn over as the reality of what was facing them began to dawn.

"I think they'll be gone," the colonel was saying. "There were two sets of tracks inside the gate, one going in, the other out. A truck. They came in a truck."

Jamie looked at him, breathing in a panic. The road was as it always was, and he grasped at that for reassurance that everything was okay at the house.

That reassurance left as he gazed into the nearby fields and saw the fallen bodies of the farm workers scattered amongst the crops. Riaz, instead of driving toward the fields, was heading straight for the barn. The body of the farmhand was lying on its side with fingers still within reach of the pitchfork. Riaz pulled the jeep to a halt, half looked at Jamie with his one working eye.

"Give me the rifle," he ordered.

Jamie obliged, acutely aware he didn't know how to use it or any other gun. He climbed out after the colonel. Outside the jeep, Riaz had gone rigid again. Jamie drew even with him and followed the line of his vision.

Marco lay there, purple gore spilling from his chest and drying where it had spread all the way to the ground. Suddenly Jamie's whole head felt as numb as his mouth did after the dentist was finished shooting him with novocaine. He was aware of the crunching noise the colonel's feet made as he shuffled them forward over the hard gravel. Riaz knelt next to his son and smoothed the boy's hair. His face was untouched and looked strangely placid, as if death had somehow claimed his life but not his innocence.

The breeze picked up and Jamie twisted suddenly. He thought he had heard something, someone.

They could still be here! The killers could still be here!

The fear that prospect held for him was lost quickly when Jamie's eyes fell on the main house. The numbness he had felt turned into a sense of dread and he pushed himself into a charge.

"No!" Riaz yelled after him, starting to rise. "Wait!"

Jamie heard nothing. He was running with the same thoughtless abandon and daredevil stride that served him on the football field. He rushed around to the front porch and vaulted up on it, nearly slipping in a splotch of blood that had spread as far as the stairs. He approached the half-open door, shattered at the latch and punctured by irregular holes, aware dimly that not a single window remained whole. He saw Miranda first, her body twisted to one side of the stairs. The twins' tutor, Maria, lay to the right of the stairs, mouth gaping open and face twisted in agony above the throat shot that had killed her. He had the presence to think, at least it hadn't been like that for Marco, in the last moment before his gaze turned up the stairs.

The light had spared him this sight until last, and even then he held to hope, because surely this warrior shape with shotgun still near at hand could not be Beth, could not be his sister. . . .

Jamie eased his way up to the halfway point of the steps

without feeling himself do it. He was holding on to the banister and realized it was still sticky in places with what must have been drying blood. Behind him, Riaz was approaching after stooping briefly over Miranda. The colonel's hand reached for his shoulder just as he neared the body and looked down.

"Don't, Jamie."

It was too late. Jamie knew what he expected to see, but this, this— He felt faint. His legs went rubbery and he had to grasp the banister to keep from falling.

That's not my sister, he wanted to tell Riaz quite impassionately. *My sister had a face. . . .*

A hand grasped his shoulder from behind. Jamie looked back at the colonel, but neither spoke. None of it seemed real, the feeling of detachment oddly like the aftermath of being hit hard on the football field. He stood there over the faceless shape without seeing or feeling a thing.

Riaz had slid by him up the rest of the stairs. *The twins,* Jamie realized, snapping alert, *what about the twins?* Jamie followed Riaz to the top of the stairs, where the colonel stood rigid in the doorway to their room. Jamie had never seen a man stand so motionless, not even seeming to breathe. He moved closer to Riaz and peered past him into the room.

"Oh God . . ."

The twins were lying faceup on their matching beds, eyes obscenely open and bleeding from the identical slices in their throats. Jamie leaned over and gagged. Vomit sped up his throat.

When he looked up, he saw Riaz had entered the room. He approached each twin with the same silent care he might have exercised to cover them up late at night. But he stopped at each only long enough to close their dead eyes. Jamie followed his gaze to a section of the wall that was actually a door which led into a small secret room. The door was torn apart, ripped from its concealed hinges.

"They'll die for this," Jamie thought he heard the colonel mutter. "They'll all die for this."

"Who? W-W-Who did it?"

"Contras . . ."

Jamie could barely hear the colonel's words. Riaz brushed by him and moved from the room. He approached a linen closet down the corridor and pulled a floral sheet from within it. Then he descended the stairs to where Beth's body lay and gazed sadly downward before draping the sheet over her.

"What are we going to do?" Jamie asked, following him to the foot of the stairs. Riaz's only response was to strip down some bullet-ridden drapes to cover the body of his daughter. He seemed like an actor mechanically following his cues until a shuffling sound came from the front room. Riaz had his pistol out and readied before Jamie could finish his next breath.

There was nothing. Just the wind pushing the blinds about through the shattered window glass.

"Colonel?"

Riaz was shoving the pistol back in his belt now.

"Colonel . . ."

Riaz kept walking toward the front door, speaking without turning around. "Leave me alone, Jamie."

"Where are you going?"

"I have work to do."

"What about me? What about *Beth*?"

The colonel stiffened as he reached the door. "I can do no more for her here."

"Where then? I'm coming with you."

Jamie closed to just behind Riaz and grabbed his shoulder.

"No, you're not," the colonel said as he spun with all his pent-up fury and frustration. Jamie pulled his hand back but not before one of Riaz's hands shot out and grabbed him by the throat.

Jamie felt the blackness coming and lapsed into it as into sleep. Whatever the day had brought was lost in the darkness.

"*Señor* Skylar . . . *Señor* Skylar, can you hear me?"

As he came to, Jamie felt the eerie sensation of falling. He grasped on to the couch for dear life. A uniformed figure was leaning over to steady his shoulders. He realized he was lying on a couch in the spacious den to the left of the house's front entrance. The shadows outside told him it was late afternoon, and a cooling breeze blew into the room through places where windows used to be. A number of other Nicaraguan figures in uniform were milling about, some with notepads and at least one with a camera. They spoke quietly among themselves and kept their distance from the den now that Jamie was awake.

A picture of his sister's corpse locked in his mind and he shivered.

"Señor, can I get you anything?" the officer hovering over him asked. His English was excellent, marred only slightly by his native accent.

Jamie pushed himself to a sitting position. The pain in his head seemed to echo. He managed to look up.

"My sister . . ."

"We have taken her away. The others, too."

"Colonel Riaz?"

"I was hoping you could tell me, Señor Skylar."

"Wait a minute; how do you know who I am?"

The figure above him, still coming into focus, shrugged. "This is a small country, and Colonel Riaz is a most important man. We are well aware of all that affects him. You have been in Nicaragua for three days, no?"

"Whatever you say."

"Please, let us be friends. It will be easier that way." He paused. "What do you think happened to you?"

"I . . ."

"What was the last thing you remember?"

"Standing by the door with Colonel Riaz."

"Anything else?"

"Plenty."

"I mean of that moment."

"No."

The officer reached out and touched his throat. Jamie flinched.

"You have a nasty bruise there, señor, directly over your carotid artery. That's what knocked you out. Colonel Riaz knocked you out."

The memory of Riaz's hand grasping his throat came back in the flood of others.

"Who did all this?" Jamie's arm swept around him in an arc.

The officer seemed reluctant to answer. "Between fourteen and sixteen men, five of which were either killed or gravely wounded, from what we've been able to ascertain."

"That doesn't answer my question."

"It is the best I can do. Colonel Riaz is a hero to us, señor."

"And that makes him a sworn enemy of someone else, doesn't it? It was the Contras, wasn't it? It was what's left of the Contras that did this."

"Initial evidence points in that direction, yes. The guns the killers used were American M-16s. Their boots were U.S. army issue as well. They killed the colonel's servants as well: seventy men, women, and *children*."

"Bastards . . . animals!"

The officer nodded slowly. "I am sure you know of the colonel's past. There is no man the Contras had higher on their hit list."

"But instead of killing Riaz, they . . ."

"Yes, because a soldier is trained to accept his own death. This," the officer said, indicating the remnants of the carnage, "he cannot accept. This no one can accept. He must live with it, and there is no fate worse."

"They could have struck before."

"I suppose."

"But they waited until he had something to lose that mattered to him. The farm, peace, his children, my . . . sister."

The officer seemed pained by it all. "That is the way their minds work, señor. But we will catch them; you may rest assured of that." He knelt down so that the red bandanna holding his long hair in place was even with Jamie's eyes. "You have the word of Captain Octavio Maruda on that."

Night had fallen when Captain Octavio Maruda, still wearing his uniform, climbed into the back of the dark sedan.

"You are to be congratulated, Captain." It was the bulbous Esteban who spoke through the cigar-smoke-filled air of the rear compartment.

''Not yet,'' returned Maruda, stifling a cough.

''Complications?''

''Your intelligence was inadequate.''

''*My* intelligence?''

''The colonel's American girlfriend's brother was visiting.''

''And you were forced to kill him as well?''

''I wish it were so. He was off the grounds with Riaz when we arrived. They returned together.''

''And now?''

''We have the young man in custody,'' Maruda answered, evidently forgetting that he was a young man himself.

Esteban leaned back in obvious relief. ''Merely a loose end.''

''Should I tie it up?''

''No, Captain, you have other work ahead of you. Leave this to me.''

The bar was located in the Palama district of Managua, one of the city's seediest. Chimera's meeting with Maria Cordoba had been arranged for ten o'clock, but she arrived two hours early to watch the patrons coming and going from the outside. According to Stein the bookseller, Cordoba was the contact who had initiated the operation that cost Crane his life. And more than that, Chimera had actually been en route to see her when Crane's call came in. That meant she was supposed to have been a part of the operation, too. But she had been due the day before and was surprised to find Maria Cordoba still wanted to see her tonight. Precautions were, of course, in order. More than forty-eight hours had passed now since she had eliminated the team sent after Crane, plenty of time for The Outsiders to realize she had been responsible.

Chimera entered the bar at ten o'clock sharp. Its rank smell assaulted her even before she stepped inside. Perspiration seemed the predominant odor, hovering with stale beer in the clouds of cheap smoke thickening in the air. What little light there was came from a series of light bulbs dangling from ceiling chains. The room was small and square, the bar itself occupying a small portion of the rear wall. The men spread out among the dozen or so tables ogled her as she edged forward. A few whistled. Several whispered.

"You looking for a job, señorita?" asked a man in a polyester suit who seemed to be the manager.

"I'm looking for Maria Cordoba."

The man sized her up. "A job would be better."

"Just tell me where I can find Maria."

"She's upstairs, señorita." And he motioned toward a door at one side of the room.

Chimera nodded.

"Twenty American dollars, señorita," the manager said before she started for the door. "Payable in advance."

Chimera handed it over. The manager accepted it with a disappointed frown.

"This is truly a waste, señorita. Such a terrible waste. Second door on the right."

Chimera held her breath against the bar's thickening stench and moved for the stairs. On the second floor, she opened the proper door without knocking. Maria Cordoba lay on the bed naked in the thin light, fondling her own breasts. It took her until the door was closed again to realize who had entered.

"Not like you to miss an assignment, Chimera," she said, making no effort to cover herself, massaging her breasts harder now.

"You got my message. I was unavoidably detained."

"I got your message. You're needed for something else now. An execution, quite simple."

"They're never simple."

"This one should be. Your target's in jail." Maria was stroking her nipples now. "An American, Chimera. His name is Jamie Skylar. . . ."

Five hours later, Maria Cordoba walked the two-block distance back to her apartment. She was quite drunk, and the thickly sweet scent of marijuana accompanied her. It was hard making the keys work, and just as hard managing the door.

It was not hard to see two of the lights in the small apartment were on, one for each of the corpses propped up obscenely on the couch.

"They were waiting for you, Maria," said Chimera.

Maria Cordoba swung toward the origin of the voice. Chimera wasn't there.

"You've completed your usefulness," Chimera said, emerging from the shadows on the room's other side. "You're part of the same chain Crane was. They killed him and they would have killed you. I knew these two, Maria. They would have made it hurt."

Maria stood there speechless.

"I killed them because you're still useful to me. But if you choose not to talk, I'll finish the work these two were sent for." Chimera waited for the other woman to gaze at the corpses again. "And I'll make it hurt, too."

"Please," Maria begged. "*Anything!*"

"Sit down, Maria. Our talk may take some time."

CHAPTER 8

THE SR-71X Blackbird reconnaissance jet slid through the sky, burning time in its wake.

"Clark, this is Blackbird," the pilot said into the microphone that was part of his helmet.

"We read you, Blackbird," returned the com-link at Clark Air Force Base.

"Approaching recon coordinates now. Prepare for translink. Will transmit on my mark."

"Roger, Blackbird. Be advised we have Washington on line."

"Roger, that. Get you the best pictures we can."

Captain Bob McCord struggled futilely for comfort within the cramped confines of the pilot's seat. Nearly ninety minutes of flying at 1,500 miles per hour could take its toll, especially through unfamiliar skies. Critics might disagree, but McCord swore he could tell a difference as clearly as the one between distinct highways. His normal beat out of Clark Air Force Base in the Philippines was Asia, twelve-hour shifts in the air every other day to keep that part of the world honest. The SR-71X's incredibly sophisticated cameras could make 70,000 feet look like the view from across the street. He'd been scrambled out of rotation and sent off his beat before, but never ridden to his Blackbird with the base commander by his side in the jeep.

"This mission doesn't exist, Captain," he said gravely. "I want that clear from the beginning."

McCord kept looking at him.

"What do you know about Pine Gap?"

"Only that it doesn't exist either, sir."

"Answer the question."

"Rumors, innuendo, all sorts of things. From what most of us have gathered, it's some kind of research and development installation in the middle of nowhere."

"The middle of Australia, Captain, which is pretty much the same thing. The rumors you've heard are fairly close to the mark, except Pine Gap goes far beyond ordinary R and D. Ultrasensitive and top secret work only. Technology beyond either of our lifetimes tested smack-dab in the Australian Outback. That's where you're taking your bird."

"Sir?"

"Captain, seventeen minutes ago MILICOM lost contact with Pine Gap. Installation went black, clear off the grid. You hearing me?"

McCord nodded, weighing the prospects. MILICOM stood for "Military Communications," a watchdog facility which maintained regular and frequent contact with every major U.S. installation throughout the world. Plenty of explanations for a blackout came to mind, from a malfunctioning satellite to a radio operator who kept bringing up the wrong daily (or hourly) access code. But in the case of Pine Gap, no chances could be taken.

"We're the closest recon to the area," the base commander explained. "Your crew's already been dispatched. You can brief them."

The jeep had reached the holding area before the sleek silver jet that sat with its engines already warming. McCord had started to step out when the commander grasped him at the elbow, raising his voice to be heard over the Blackbird.

"MILICOM hasn't been able to raise anyone within the 100-mile sealing radius of Pine Gap. Start sending when you cross that point, all switches on auto. You understand what I'm saying?"

"Yes, sir."

Out of the jeep now, McCord turned back. "Why us, sir? We've got bases down there that could perform recon plenty faster and—"

"Because we've lost contact with them, Captain. It's not just Pine Gap that's off the grid, it's the whole fucking country."

Those had been the commander's parting words nearly ninety minutes before, and the hollow feeling that had settled in McCord's gut hadn't diminished since. If anything, with the send coordinates coming up fast, McCord felt a bowling-ball-sized hole where his stomach should have been. He cut the SR-71X's airspeed back to two-thirds and gave the controls to his copilot, so he could don the clumsy headpiece that gave him the same view the Blackbird's cameras had.

"Base," he said, and flipped a single switch on the console before him, "you have my mark. Transmission commencing."

"Roger, Blackbird."

The cameras mounted on the Blackbird's underside snapped off six shots per second, and with virtually no delay at all, these images were read by an on-board computer. The computer then transferred the images digitally back to Clark, where they were unloaded. The result was a sweeping array of whatever was lying 70,000 feet below on the barren lands surrounding Pine Gap.

McCord tightened the headpiece around his temples and took in the sights at ground level. "Base, I have clear down view. Nothing in sight but sand and brush. . . . Wait a minute. . . . What the hell . . . This can't be! Oh my sweet Jesus . . ."

"You're breaking up, Blackbird. Say again."

"Can't . . . lieve . . . ing . . . sible."

"Blackbird, you're still garbled. Blackbird, do you copy?"

Static.

"Blackbird, this is Clark. *Do you* copy?"

Only static again, though, returned the com-link's query, as the first of the Blackbird's transmitted recon photos slid from a slot in his computer frame.

CHAPTER 9

"You have our deepest condolences, Colonel Riaz. All those associated with the Nicaraguan National Solidarity Committee join me in—"

"Enough, Esteban," snapped José Ramon Riaz, pulling back from the fat man's cigar-ravaged breath.

They had met on Riaz's insistence halfway up Mount Acropia on a plateau that overlooked the Pacific central plain and Casa Grande. While waiting for the fat man, Riaz had let himself imagine he could see his own farm down there as it had been in the past, before the massacre. Yet the later memories intruded. He did not cry and, strangely, felt the start of hot tears not in his working eye but in his missing one.

Esteban cleared his throat. "After you called, I assembled all the reports the militia and our own people have accumulated on the attack."

"I've already heard them," stated Riaz plainly. "American-issue weapons and boots. A Contra informant who has come forward with some sketchy details."

"The others will be caught. You may rest assured of that."

But Riaz did not feel assured. "What is a man, Esteban?"

"Excuse me, Colonel?"

"A man is what he produces: what he makes of himself and what he makes of others. That being the case, what kind of man am I? I ran from what I made of myself and now what I made of others is lost." His eyes were frigid now. "Taken."

Esteban looked at him very closely.

"If I do nothing, if I let the killers be, then I am as bad as they are for I accept what they make me. And yet to be totally successful, I cannot only destroy them; I must also destroy what made them. For twenty-four hours now I have planned how I would hunt them down, but that accomplishes nothing. It is an atmosphere, a state of mind that must be altered, the state of mind that allows these animals to be." Now Riaz looked Esteban directly in the eye. "I can only be a man again if I destroy the source of their existence."

"Through Operation Thunder Clap . . ."

"I wish to lead it now."

Esteban's bulbous cheeks puckered. "Your motivations are admirable, Colonel, but Casa Grande has changed the circumstances considerably. As a result the rest of the NNSC may see you as too much of a liability."

Riaz grasped the fat man's forearm and squeezed until pain showed on his face. "Then it will be your job to convince them otherwise, won't it?"

"You will have to give me time."

"Thirty-six hours, Esteban. You will meet me back here then or I will dig a grave in your place."

"Thirty-six hours," the fat man repeated.

Jamie stared up at the ceiling, where the cracks in its plaster had become the dominant image of his world. The cell door was not locked; it had not been since Captain Maruda had escorted him here. But this was hardly a comfort. Fourteen hours had passed since he'd awakened on the couch in Colonel Riaz's living room. Maruda had brought him to this little-used jail building in Leon on the pretext of making immediate arrangements with the American Embassy in Managua. Up to now, though, as far as Jamie could tell there had been no contact. He had not seen Maruda since the preceding night and the on-duty militiamen had nothing to tell him.

Something was wrong.

He felt that with a cold certainty, as though he might be able to reach out through the stale air of the cell and touch it.

I'm never going to get out of here.

Maruda could have driven him direct to the embassy in Managua but didn't. So perhaps no official there had in any way been informed of his presence here and what had happened at Casa Grande. Or if they had perhaps, just perhaps, he had already been listed among those killed.

But why?

He shuddered and wrapped his arms about himself on the small cot to ward off the chill that was suddenly all-enveloping. The fact that the cell door was unlocked and he could get up and walk out at any time was of no comfort, for he had nowhere to go. Maybe that was what they wanted, what they hoped he would do. And perhaps this same mysterious "they" had been behind Casa Grande in the first place.

Jamie's thoughts veered in another direction. What of Riaz? Maruda had mentioned only that he had disappeared. Why had the colonel knocked him unconscious and abandoned him? The answer was all too obvious. It could only mean that he had become *el Diablo de la Jungla* again, determined to hunt down the killers of his family.

Jamie stirred on the cot and bolted upright. Some faint noise had disturbed his reflections. Then he heard a door creak closed at the other end of the corridor and the soft shuffling of footsteps approaching. Not the rackety clip-clop of the guards clumsily heading toward his cell, but the soft footfalls of a muffled approach.

He was standing rigid and ready when the door squealed inward, allowing a sliver of light to pass inside from the hallway. Then the door was opened all the way and he found himself staring at a dark-haired woman clad in a khaki militia uniform.

"Who the hell are you?"

"Whisper!"

"What?"

"Do what I tell you! Do everything I tell you!"

"What are you talking about? What are you doing here?"

"Saving your life," said Chimera.

"But who *are* you?"

"It doesn't matter," she snapped at him. Her features were obscured by the darkness of the cell and an army cap pulled low over her forehead. The hair that tumbled beneath it was dark, and the portion of her face that was visible appeared deeply tanned. "Just put these on," she continued, and tossed him a small bag.

Jamie opened it and found a uniform that was a twin of hers. He stripped off his clothes and yanked the pants over his sneakers.

"The sneakers!" she realized. "The damn sneakers! They might give you away. . . ."

"Give me away to *who*?"

"Just hurry!"

Jamie had barely finished buttoning the uniform's shirt when the woman grabbed his arm and half yanked him into the corridor. They sprinted down it away from the main exit, approaching a door at the very end. The woman grabbed the latch and turned it. It wouldn't give.

Before Jamie could react, she pulled a huge square pistol from a holster concealed on her calf and brought it up. He flinched as she fired, the noise of the explosions deafening in the enclosed space. She threw her shoulder into the door, and when it continued to resist, Jamie added his.

The door crashed outward and they emerged into the daylight at the rear of the jail building. A short, alleylike walkway separated it from another building.

"This way," the woman beckoned, and they rushed fast for the front of the neighboring building.

They reached the head of the walkway and swung right. The area in front of the building was adorned with the Nicaraguan flag and jammed with men and women in green or khaki uniforms.

"The parade will be passing this way any minute," the woman told Jamie.

"Parade?"

"Just follow me! Do as I do and be ready to move!"

Just then Jamie heard the instrumental sounds of a marching band, out of key and very brassy, coming their way. He saw that both sides of the street were lined with people, two rows deep in most places and stretching up to four or five in others. The band sounds drew closer. The people gazed into the sun toward its approach.

Jamie craned his neck to see the procession. At the head of it came a large flatbed truck adorned lavishly with flowers and fruit and packed with waving, smiling children. The marching band came next, and after it, a heavy complement of soldiers stretching from one side of the dusty street to the other. Their uniforms were of varying shades and descriptions, but they marched proudly in perfect unison. Behind them came an array of armed services vehicles, including jeeps, tanks, and half-tracks in a nationalistic display of strength to the people.

"We're going to join them," the woman said softly.

"The *soldiers*?"

"It's our only chance."

She grasped Jamie's elbow as the procession of soldiers was almost upon them. He felt her hand nudge his arm, knew a pull would be coming that would be his signal. They stood side by side at attention, already into the guise they were depending on to get them safely away.

Jamie felt the pull and stepped out into the formation. He squeezed between two rows of marching soldiers as deftly as he slid through holes in the line of scrimmage en route to the secondary. At first he thought he'd been separated from the woman, but a glance to his right showed him she was striding a single slot down. Neither spoke nor looked at the other. Those who might have noticed their entry into the parade must have assumed it was planned. Even their fellow marchers had given way and paid them no heed.

They stayed with the procession through town until the road narrowed and banked left. The marchers bunched closer together and the two of them strayed to the outside and then drifted off into the crowd just as they had left a similar one a half mile back. The woman took the lead again.

"This way! I've got a jeep waiting!"

Jamie followed her down another passageway between two buildings which led to a side street. Parked there was a rusty brown jeep, its paint peeling and bubbling. The woman jammed the key into the starter, but Jamie grabbed her hand and held firm before she could turn it.

"Uh-uh. First we talk. Who are you? How did you find me?"

"One question at a time."

"Take your pick."

"I was retained to kill you."

"You're not doing a very good job of it," Jamie responded without missing a beat.

"I've got my reasons."

"Let's hear them."

"Later."

"Now. Who are you?"

"Chimera."

"That's not a name."

"I don't have a name. I lost it a long time ago when the best friend I ever had pulled me out of the depths." She hesitated. "He was killed. It's why I'm here."

"Killed by who?"

"The same force behind Casa Grande, Jamie."

"Contras?"

"They had nothing to do with the massacre. That's what someone wanted Colonel Riaz—and the country—to think. It was all staged, a means to another end."

"That doesn't make sense!"

"It makes plenty. This force wanted Riaz to work for them, and Casa Grande was their means to convince him."

"And this same force hired you to kill me."

"Not hired—assigned."

"I don't see the difference."

"There's a big one," Chimera told him. "I work for a

group that's part of this. My friend who was killed was part of it, too, only they sent him to Australia."

"What does Australia have to do with Nicaragua?" asked Jamie.

"I traced the origin of my friend's mission to a woman here named Maria Cordoba, who had been waiting for me to show up anyway to fill an order."

"My death . . ."

"Not originally. I got that assignment in lieu of another one: the elimination of a camp in the jungle, Jamie, where the group that killed your sister is hiding."

Esteban rested his cigar on the ashtray and held the receiver tighter against his ear.

"Hello, Esteban," said the voice from Washington.

"I am happy to report that Colonel Riaz has now agreed to run Operation Thunder Clap," the fat man reported triumphantly. But the next words from Washington took the smile from his face.

"There are problems, Esteban. A thorough search was conducted of the Riaz farm. Some recording equipment was found, recording equipment of a most sophisticated nature."

Esteban swallowed hard. "But my men and the militia; we found *nothing*!"

"I am more concerned by what *we* didn't find: the microchip containing whatever was recorded. Your conversation with Riaz, for example, Esteban. The one in which you outlined the particulars of Operation Thunder Clap."

Esteban went quite cold, suddenly aware of the track the man's discourse was about to take.

"I will not burden you with the obvious," he continued. "The Skylar woman was quite obviously the agent-in-place whose network was interested in the exploits of your NNSC. She'd know quite a bit about those exploits if she had heard your conversation with Riaz, wouldn't she? But since the microchip was not found on her person, it stands to reason she placed it on someone else, the intent being to get it out of the country."

"Jamie Skylar," the fat man mumbled.

"If his execution has already been accomplished, I expect the chip to be salvaged from his corpse. Clear?" And, after an instant's pause brought no reply, "Clear, Esteban?"

"There's been a complication."

"I'm listening."

"Skylar escaped this afternoon. But he didn't act alone. By all accounts, he had help from a dark-haired woman wearing an army uniform."

"Why should such a fact concern me?"

"Because by all accounts, it was Chimera, the one we assigned to kill him."

Now it was the man in Washington's turn to lapse into momentary silence. When his voice returned, Esteban quivered at the cold intensity of his words, barely concealing the threat to himself they contained.

"Listen to me, Esteban. That chip contains a direct connection to your NNSC, and that could lead some enterprising sort to the truth, to Valhalla. Find it, Esteban. Whatever it takes, whatever you have to do, find that chip. . . ."

The director was feeding his fish when Richards stepped into the office. He sprinkled the saltlike powder methodically, as if to assure each of his pets an equal ration.

"Something new, Captain?" He did not look up as he spoke.

"We've confirmed that Colonel Riaz was not killed in the massacre, as reports indicated. We've also confirmed that Jamie Skylar survived the massacre as well, but his whereabouts at present are unknown."

"And the Nicaraguan authorities?"

"Behaving in a most cooperative manner, sir. They're convinced the last of the true Contras were responsible."

"With good reason, but we, of course, know otherwise."

"Only we lack the specifics. All we can assume is that Riaz's family was killed to coerce the colonel into joining the operation soon to be launched against us."

"Would Sapphire have known the details, Captain?"

"If she did, sir, then Jamie Skylar took them out with him."

The director looked up at Richards for the first time. "Did the Nicaraguan authorities mention anything about him?"

"They had no knowledge he had ever been there. All trace of his presence had been eliminated."

The director moved from the fish tank, and the light from the nearest lamp reflected the grimness etched over his features. "That does not bode well for the boy's chances, Captain, or ours."

"He survived the massacre, sir. If he's out there, we'll find him," Richards insisted staunchly.

"You're letting the personal enter in, Captain."

"You were right, sir. About civilians."

"In war, there are only soldiers."

"This isn't war."

The director gazed quickly at the photographs from Casa Grande spread across his desk. "It is to someone, Captain."

CHAPTER 10

CHIMERA drove the jeep northeast from León toward the remote and sparsely populated jungle regions of the country. The woods around them thickened as they drew closer to Siuna, and the road vanished altogether late in the afternoon after nearly seven hours of driving.

"We go on foot from here," she said after pulling the jeep into the cover supplied by the underbrush.

The drive had begun with more challenges and questions on Jamie's part. Chimera had done her best to ease his anxiety and confusion but succeeded mostly in compounding her own in the process.

"All right," she said, taking it by the numbers again, "my friend Crane went to Australia to pick up explosives he was convinced were part of the shadow government's attempts to take over the country."

"Through some kind of strike they needed Colonel Riaz to lead," Jamie completed.

"By all indications, yes."

"So they retained this hit team for Casa Grande and then retained you to eliminate the hit team. Alone. By yourself," Jamie finished, the meaning of that just starting to dawn on him.

"But I was detained in New York," Chimera said, ignoring his insinuations. "When I finally did arrive, they had a different assignment waiting for me."

"And then you rescued me instead. You still haven't told me why you took such a risk."

"Because the word being put out is that Colonel Riaz was killed in the massacre along with his family. You're the only proof that he wasn't, and thus is connected to something else."

"That base in Australia . . ."

"Pine Gap," Chimera acknowledged. "And the shadow government that sent Crane there. I've got to figure out how that ties in with Riaz. For now, you're all I've got."

"Until we reach this camp in the woods," Jamie picked up. "Until you find out who ordered the massacre."

"That's the hope."

After abandoning the jeep, they were able to cover seven miles through the woods before nightfall left them with no clear trail to follow. Their passage was further slowed by the thick foliage which scraped at their faces and gashed their ankles.

"We're almost there," Chimera said at last, and a few minutes later they approached the edge of a clearing, where Jamie could make out the shapes of tents, lean-tos, and prefabricated buildings thrown haphazardly together. It looked as if the camp could easily accommodate twenty people, and he went cold at the thought that he was this close to the killers of his sister.

"Wait!" she called back to him, rigid in her tracks.

Jamie drew even with her. "What's wrong?"

"I don't see any guards. There should be guards." She gazed back at him. "I'm going ahead. You stay here."

"I'll stick with you, if it's all the same."

"Suit yourself," she responded, and pulled her pistol from her belt.

Chimera slid catlike through the brush, her lithe figure disappearing almost instantly from view. Jamie did his best to keep up but couldn't match her skill in the dark as they entered the camp. Only when she stopped suddenly was he able to pull even. She moved at last to the closest tent and yanked back the flap.

Two sets of dead eyes gazed up at them, bodies twisted and bloodied. Flies buzzed about the corpses, and the stench from within forced Jamie's breath back down his throat.

Chimera rushed from the tent, and he followed. He reached her just as she was turning away from the doorway of one of the poorly constructed prefab buildings.

"They're dead, too," she reported, with disappointment in her voice. "We were too late."

"You don't sound surprised."

"The trail had to be covered. When I didn't show up as planned, they got someone else to cover it. I was just hoping that . . ."

Something made her stop in midsentence.

"Someone's out there," she said rapidly. "Get down!"

Before he could oblige, she had barreled into him in as hard a tackle as any he had ever felt on the field. A burst of shots rang out as he spit out a mouthful of leaves and fought to regain his wind.

"They know we're here, but all they can see are shadows."

"They," Jamie returned in a whisper. "How many?"

"I'm not sure. Not a lot or they would have rushed us already."

Another series of shots split the air around them. Jamie stayed low enough to smell the dirt. Chimera eased away, signaling him to be quiet.

"What are you doing?" he asked, disobeying.

She stopped her snakelike advance through the ground brush. "Circling around behind them. Take them before they take us."

He saw her check her calf to make sure an army-issue killing knife was still strapped there. Her face was taut with resolve.

What kind of woman was this, what kind of person?

"Stay where you are. Don't move. I'll come back for you."

A sense of cool precision permeated her assurances. Jamie

felt chilled by it. Killing the twelve men they had found dead in the camp would have been a simple task for her, because her skills placed her on a different level. He saw that now for the first time in all its clarity. He saw Chimera for what she was.

When he looked for her again, she had already vanished into the brush. Remaining prone on the ground, he strained his eyes to see into the dark distance beyond and searched for movement to fix shapes to. But there was nothing, not even any sign of Chimera.

The sound of brush crunching underfoot reached his ear. Jamie tried to pass it off to the wind but failed when it came again; louder, closer—a boot unmistakably responsible. Someone, barely raising his feet between steps, was coming up on the death-filled camp from the rear.

Jamie forced himself to remain motionless, controlled even his breathing. The boots shuffled sideways, then forward again. As soon as he was seen, he was dead, and being seen was inevitable. His only chance was to strike out himself, take this man on as he would a tackler in the open field.

The man was angling from the side, moments from seeing the bulge of Jamie's frame protruding from the small furrow in the ground. He would have to act before the man could, have to act before—

A soft gasp reached him in the night breeze, followed by the sound of something heavy dropping to the ground forty yards ahead in the woods. Chimera's work, it had to be! The man near him must have heard it as well, because the shuffling sound of his boots ceased. Jamie raised his head just a fraction and spotted the man off to the right six yards away. The man was big, bigger than him, dressed in civilian clothes. He rotated the barrel of an automatic rifle before him as if searching for the origin of the gasp in the forest beyond.

Jamie started to lower his hands beneath him to push off. This was his chance to take the man, when his back was turned and attention focused forward. He felt himself starting to shake, knew he could delay no longer. In the next instant he was up and charging forward, in his wake a swirl of dirt and leaves. The big man heard the sound and started to swing round when Jamie crashed into him with a football-style tackle. Impact was bone-jarring as Jamie's shoulder crunched into the big man's lower rib cage with the force of all his weight behind it. The rifle flew from his hands and he pitched backward with Jamie still latched on.

Jamie had felt the ribs recoil, but the instant of indecision that followed proved costly. The man was his to finish had he known how. As it was, though, he felt the man's huge, powerful arms surround him. He had planned to unleash a flurry of fists and elbows to batter the big man into unconsciousness. Now his arms were locked by his side, and the fallen figure beneath him was struggling to toss him off. The big man had almost succeeded when Jamie felt his knee pass over his dark-clad groin area. He launched a savage knee downward and felt it connect.

Hot, rancid breath poured from the big man's mouth. His teeth squeezed together in agony and his eyes bulged. But somewhere he found the strength to complete the motion of tossing Jamie off him. Jamie came down hard on the ground and rolled over to regain his feet. In the process he caught sight of the big man dragging himself toward the rifle. Jamie lunged and wrapped his arms around the man's throat from the rear, squeezing with all his might.

Jamie felt his biceps bulge and grow taught around the bulbous neck they were squeezing. The big man gave up his quest for the rifle and flailed desperately for Jamie's head. The blows were wild, and Jamie absorbed them easily until a finger jabbed his eye.

The pain exploded through Jamie's head, and a bright light flashed before him. His concentration wavered for an instant, long enough for the big man to pull him down and to the side. Jamie's head struck something hard and the light flashed again, the big man's throaty scream puncturing the return to darkness. Jamie saw the huge fingers coming at him straight as a ramrod and responded reflexively, rolling his head to the side. The big man's hand hit the ground, which pulled him off balance long enough for Jamie to ram a fist hard under his chin. Impact snapped the attacker's head back, and Jamie threw him to the side.

Jamie flung himself atop the man and pounded him with the fierce flurry of fists he'd tried for earlier. He smelled blood, scratched his knuckles on the man's teeth, was not even aware of his own breathing. He might have gone on forever if the sharp pain hadn't pierced his side. Everything stopped in that icelike moment: his breath, his heart, his thoughts. The man rolled dazedly away and Jamie sat there on his knees, feeling his hand wander to a slippery spot near his left pectoral.

He stabbed me! The bastard stabbed me!

The small semblance of reality he had held on to was gone. Everything turned surreal. He saw the big man, blood coating his face, staggering for him, massive blade glinting in the naked light of the night. The blade lashed forward and he deflected it, finding his feet again in the same motion.

His left side burned with agony, as he backpedaled. The big man stalked forward. Jamie heard the broken breath pouring from him, half-mixed with a snarl. The man's steps were uneven, every ridge in the ground threatening to trip him up. His knife hand, though, was firm and straight, and his knife hand was all that mattered.

Jamie backpedaled some more, nearly tripped on an exposed tree root. He tried to pull his arm from his side but couldn't, thought to protect it by turning his right in the bloodied man's direction.

How could he still be conscious, never mind alive?

Eyes half-closed, facial bones shattered, the man was still coming. Jamie felt a thin log beneath his feet and chanced the motion of stooping for it.

"AHHHHHHHHHHHHHHHHH!!!!!!"

The big man's scream echoed his rush, and Jamie came up swinging with his right hand. The log cracked his attacker squarely in the cheek, only dazing him. He lunged out again with the knife, and Jamie danced awkwardly from its path. He slammed the log down from straight overhead this time and could have sworn the big man's skull gave, but there he was whipping the blade in a side swipe again. Jamie felt the blade actually slice through his shirt, missing his flesh by that much.

He brought the log up under the big man's chin. The bloodied head snapped back, but he still kept coming, swiping at the air in relentless fashion as if it were Jamie.

Stop! Why won't you stop!

Still backing up, Jamie felt the ground level off and knew one of the prefab buildings would soon meet his shoulders. When he was pressed against it, his retreat would be cut off. He had to act now, chew back his pain and summon all the strength born of year-round conditioning.

Log still in his grasp, Jamie moved it left and joined his left hand to it. As he swung it, the pain exploded in fresh fire in his side. The impact stunned the bigger man, but still he stood there, knife held frozen before him.

"ARRRRRRRGGGGHHHH!!!"

Jamie screamed this time, as he brought the log around from right to left with all his force behind it. He felt it shatter on impact and watched the big man's body topple over like a felled tree, back and to the side. Jamie stood over him and gazed down.

The log was still whole in his hands. It was the big man's head he had felt break apart. Jamie could see only a misshapen mass atop a huge body twitching toward death. No feature above the neck was recognizable. Jamie sank to his knees. The warm blood slid down his side like shower water, and for some reason he still clutched the gore-covered log that had saved him.

"Jamie?"

Chimera was approaching softly from the front, dirt and leaves matted all over the front of her khaki uniform.

"What hap—"

She must not have seen the corpse until that moment. She froze in her tracks, the situation at once clear to her. She digested all the sights in the same manner a computer absorbs information.

"My God . . . you're hurt. Can you speak? Can you hear me?"

"Took you a long time," Jamie responded, and keeled over.

CHAPTER 11

JAMIE never entirely lost consciousness. He remained aware as Chimera eased him into the building he had collapsed in front of. Dimly he watched her searching about the room for something. Then came the sting of alcohol as she swabbed his knife wound, and the pressure of gauze wrapped tightly around his midsection to contain the wound and stanch the flow of blood.

"I killed a man," he heard himself mutter.

"He would have killed you."

"How should I feel?"

"How do you feel?"

"Tired. Weak."

"From the wound. Think of the man trying to kill you, end your life for no reason at all. Now think of stopping him. Think of the fact that you're still alive." She paused. "Now how do you feel?"

Jamie realized quite incredulously that his mind had cleared. He felt sharp and alert again. Focusing on the battle seemed to revive him, not repel him.

"Not as tired. Still weak," he offered.

"You've lost some blood. But as near as I can tell, it's just a flesh wound. No damage to ribs or organs. You'll be able to travel in an hour, maybe less."

"To where?"

"Anywhere but here, my young friend. Those men weren't the ones who wiped out the hit team that killed your sister. They came here looking for us."

"How?"

"They must have gotten to Maria Cordoba," Chimera said, as much to herself as to him. "They found out where I was headed, but their trap didn't work." Her eyes sharpened. "And when they don't check in, more will come in their place." Chimera's words came more rapidly now. "We're going into the woods as far as we can in the dark. At dawn we head east toward the Huaspuc River. So we don't forget that region used to be prime Contra territory, there will be plenty of mines and booby traps along the way to remind us. It's the most dangerous route, which makes it the best chance we've got to reach the Coco River and cross into Honduras. Get yourself ready to move."

Chimera pulled a pair of boots off the feet of one of the corpses. The boots, though not a great fit for Jamie, were infinitely preferable to his sneakers for travel through the jungle. The two moved off through the thick brush and had soon left the encampment far behind. The terrain was rugged and treacherous. The dark air carried the heavy scent of vegetation, yet Jamie scarcely noticed it, engulfed as he was by the scent of his own sweat and blood.

He stepped into a wide hole and nearly fell, relieved that it was a natural declivity and not a man-made trap. He endured the pain from his wound every step of the way, grateful for it since it kept him alert. The moon rose two hours into their trek, but the ground had become so uneven and the brush so dense that their progress came with agonizing slowness.

Suddenly a blast reached Jamie's ears as a loud *POOF*! Screams followed, one quick and the other bloodcurdlingly long. Contra booby traps had been tripped, evidence the reinforcements had found them already. But something wasn't right.

"That scream," he realized.

"It came from in front of us," Chimera completed.

"So we're surrounded. But how could they have come so fast?

"Because they've got nothing to do with the trap laid for us back at the camp."

"What?"

"They couldn't. They were dispatched separately in a much greater force. But I don't know why. I have no idea why." She swung toward him suddenly, the moon revealing the intensity of her expression. "There's a way we can make the fact that we're surrounded work in our favor."

"How?"

But she was already moving again, faster, taking less care of the ground before her.

"Come on!" she beckoned, turning back only long enough to utter the words.

Jamie followed and tried to match his steps perfectly to hers. The brush deepened, grew so thick that a mere yard even in the bright moonlight was enough to deny him view of Chimera as she made her way forward.

"This is perfect," she announced as she stopped suddenly.

"Perfect for what?"

"Listen, we can't outrun them. We're boxed in and they've brought good trackers with them."

"Trackers?"

"Natives of the jungle who could follow the trail of a mouse through the brush. But we can make their resolve work for us." With that, she stripped one of the Mac-10 machine guns she'd taken from the camp from her shoulder and thrust it his way. "I don't suppose you've ever fired one of these before."

He shook his head.

"It doesn't matter. The bursts can be wild. It's *better* if they're wild."

"Better for what?"

"Distraction, confusion, and ultimately our escape." She came closer to him. "You're going to follow the path we took back through the brush for fifty yards."

"*What?*"

"Let me finish! Find one of the depressions in the ground and conceal yourself with brush. Then wait, either for me to begin to fire or until you can see them approaching."

"I told you I don't know how to fire one of these things!"

"And I told you it doesn't matter. The sound of the bullets is all that matters. Your side will shoot, and so will mine."

"A cross fire!" Jamie realized. "You're going to catch them in a cross fire!"

"*We're* going to try. The trackers will be in the front. If we're lucky, the initial return bursts will take them. In the chaos we make our escape. Low to the ground, sticking to the underbrush when possible." Her ears perked up like a Doberman's catching a scent. "Now! You must go now!"

"How will we find each other?" he called when she started to move her own way.

"Keep moving. I will find you."

And then she was gone, out of sight. Jamie steadied himself and turned round. He covered the fifty yards in rapid fashion and searched about for a furrow suitable for concealing himself. No sooner had he settled himself under a thin cover of twigs and leaves than he heard the attackers approaching. Making himself be patient, he eased the Mac-10 into position.

Then wait, either for me to begin to fire or until you can see them approaching.

A shape in uniform appeared twenty yards to his right, clear and approaching steadily. Jamie started to bring the Mac-10 up. It felt light, almost like a toy.

He hadn't been intending to fire yet, was just testing the trigger when the first spray erupted. The soldier stopped as if he had crashed into a wall, and then the bullets threw him backward. Jamie heard Chimera's initial burst an instant before he locked on the trigger again, holding his finger there as he rotated the barrel from left to right. By the time it clicked on the end of the clip, chaos had taken over. Automatic and single fire filled the jungle and splintered the brush. Jamie draped the smoking, spent gun back over his shoulder and snaked back in the direction he had come from, arms and legs propelling himself over the brush at a far faster clip than he'd managed just a short time before.

rat-tat-tat . . .

The bursts continued to bang against his ears. Chimera's plan seemed to be working. The separate divisions that had been approaching from opposite angles after them were shooting at each other, bullet traded for bullet, death for death.

Jamie kept shoving himself along, never looking back. He heard screams and echoes of shouting intermixed with the constant fire now. Perhaps some of the soldiers realized what was happening. Even so, it would be some time before order was restored.

A hand grasped his ankle from the side. Jamie grunted, tried to kick free.

"Quiet!" Chimera ordered.

Jamie heaved a sigh of relief.

"We're going to make a run for it," she continued. "If we get away now, they'll never catch us."

"The mines, the traps, what about them?"

"We'll have to risk it. Just follow me and hope this area was one the Contras neglected."

They took off at an uneven pace, neither jog nor run, through the undergrowth and thick brush. Once, they tumbled together down a steep hill and collided at the bottom. Jamie's wounded side seared with pain, yet he was moving again as soon as he regained his feet. He could feel the sticky warmth of new blood flowing beneath the dressing Chimera had made for him earlier that night. It made him dizzy for a moment, but the feeling lasted only as long as it took to see Chimera moving on ahead of him.

He knew what it was like to play football with pain, how you could barely walk until you hit the field for pregame warmups, and then suddenly, miraculously, you began to feel better. He felt the same way now, the pain present, lurking, but his to control. The more he moved, the less he felt it. Jamie sprinted after Chimera, the sounds of gunfire behind them for now. When he caught up with her, she was squatting against the trunk of a tree.

"There's a funnel straight through that way," she said and pointed him in the right direction. "A clear path."

"What are we waiting for?"

Jamie could sense her next words before they came.

"I'm not going with you."

"I don't think I caught that."

"Listen to me, Jamie, together both of us can't make it. Alone we have a chance. I'm going to wait for them here. When they come I'll clear a path for myself back to the west. You'll take the path that's already open to the east. Do you have any bullets left in your rifle?"

"No."

"I'm out of clips, so just leave it. Take this," she said and stripped the massive killing knife from her calf, pressing it into his hands sheath and all. "It won't be easy. They'll be after you the whole way but you've got to cross the border to Honduras and get to the U.S. Embassy in Tegucigalpa. Stay with the original plan. Head northeast to the Huaspuc River and then due north to the border once you're past it. It's your only chance."

Jamie's mouth dropped and no words emerged as he stared at her in the darkness.

"Listen to me," Chimera told him. "Something's changed. They sent an army out here to find you. Not me, *you*!"

"You can't be sure of that."

"Yes, Jamie, I can. If they got to Maria Cordoba, they know everything I know. But you know something that can destroy them. Otherwise, they never would have risked such an all-out mobilization. Such strategies draw undue attention, and they should want to avoid that at all costs. Finding you has become more important to them."

"I told you everything I know. I'm not holding anything back."

"Nothing you're aware of. But it's there. Believe me, it's there." Chimera stopped, searching for the words to explain the next course of action she had already decided on. "The answers *I* need are in Australia. That's where this started for Crane, and where I have to go. But if they get to me along the way, our only hope will lie with you telling the American Embassy officials in Honduras everything I've told you."

"You haven't told me *anything*!"

"I'm not finished yet. When you get there, remember to tell them the force behind all this, the shadow government, has the explosives missing from Pine Gap, the Quick Strike. That's the key. It's got to be."

The sounds and shouts of approach rippled once again through the forest.

"There's no more time, Jamie. You're going to make it. I know you are."

In the time it took him to form a response, she was already gone, out of sight. With no other choice, he set off toward the east as instructed. Two hundred yards later, he heard a burst of gunfire punctuated by screams. A trio of explosions followed, and Jamie held to the hope they were Chimera's work. Either way, though, she was gone.

And he was alone.

CHAPTER 12

THE President sat on his exercise bike, towel draped around his neck and sweat turning his face shiny.

"I hope you're here to tell me what the Christ happened at Pine Gap," he said to National Security Adviser Roger Allen Doane, who had just arrived.

The President's legs started to churn easier as the Lifecycle's programmed routine passed into a straightaway, the RPM indicator hovering close to the prescribed eighty. Normally a meeting of this sort might have been held in the Situation Room or the President's study. But Bill Riseman found he thought best while exercising. The exertion kept his mind clear and active. The more stress he was exposed to, the harder he worked and the better able he was to deal with the issues at hand.

"On the other hand," Bill Riseman continued, "if you've brought the latest poll results, excuse me for not paying attention."

The election was barely a month away, and his challenger had grown nearly even in the polls. With momentum on the right-wing bastard's side, anything could happen, and God help the country if it did.

Roger Allen Doane came a bit closer. He was a thin,

academic-looking man who wore rumpled suits and too wide ties. The predominant expression on his face was a taciturn stare which intimidated many of his colleagues. It did not change now in spite of Bill Riseman's attempt at humor. His lack of emotions notwithstanding, Doane's performance as national security adviser had been nothing short of brilliant. He preferred working behind the scenes and had been an ally of Bill Riseman since the President's days in Congress.

"I'd like to take things by the numbers if I may," said Doane.

"These the same numbers that didn't add up yesterday?" snapped the President's chief of staff, Charlie Banks, from his perch on the bike's right.

Banks was as supercharged and direct as Roger Allen Doane was methodical and dry. He had been a friend of Bill Riseman's since boyhood and had directed the national campaign that had made him President. His hair was styled carefully to conceal as much as possible of his receding hairline.

"Whenever you're ready, Mr. Banks," droned Roger Allen Doane.

"Jesus," muttered Banks. "We lose the most important scientific installation in the grid and this guy looks like he just walked out of a boring Sunday service."

"Proceed, Roger," from the President, pedaling harder with the start of another hill sequence.

Doane lifted a remote control device from a nearby table. He touched a switch which plunged the front half of the exercise room into darkness. He hit another and a large screen descended from the ceiling to cover a good portion of the far wall. A third switch projected a postcard-perfect shot of a grouping of sand-colored buildings in the center of the Australian wilderness.

"Pine Gap was constructed this way to make detection from the air virtually impossible," Doane explained as if his audience were seeing it for the first time.

"The subject today, Rog," quipped Charlie Banks, "was supposed to be what destroyed it."

Doane's next press brought a second slide up, a bulky

mass of black with an irregular fringe of a lighter shade enclosing it.

"Pine Gap before and after, Mr. President," started the national security adviser. "This is one of the shots taken by the SR-71X Blackbird before seismic interference broke up her transmission. We've had people on scene in Australia for eighteen hours now, and their initial report just came through. The crater is the approximate size of Rhode Island and its average depth is twice that of the Grand Canyon. We have been unable to ascertain yet precisely how deep it extends in its center."

Bill Riseman's eyes were glued on the ugly splotch filling the screen. He mopped his brow with his towel. The red RPM readout on his exercise bike had climbed to eighty-five.

"On-scene analysis confirms the installation was not subjected to an outside attack," Doane continued. "Whatever destroyed Pine Gap did so from within."

"You're talking about human error."

"Or less possibly sabotage. Neither seems likely, because the complex was designed to rule out the mere conceivability of both."

"Looks like somebody ran out of room on his drawing board," smirked Charlie Banks.

"We can account for the crater alone any number of ways. The rest is inexplicable. The resulting seismic disruption was felt at varying levels through the entire continent of Australia. Sixty percent of the country has been blacked out since, turned into an electronic wasteland, which has vastly impeded our progress. Residents we've interrogated up to a thousand miles in all directions say there was a moment when the earth was pulled out from under them. Windows shattered. A number of buildings collapsed, and fissures ran like spiderwebs over the land. The Pacific tsunami net picked up the explosion on its instruments and has been issuing tsunami warnings since to anyone able to listen. In addition, people all over the western hemisphere noticed spectacular sunsets and a constant glow due to the dust and dirt that has collected in the atmosphere, residue from the blast. Transmissions coming out through normal channels are still garbled by electromagnetic disruptions in space. In essence, if seismological measuring instruments are to be believed, what you're looking at can be likened in effect to an earthquake approaching nine point five on the Richter scale."

As he spoke, Roger Allen Doane flicked through slides supporting his report. Charlie Banks for once was speechless. President Bill Riseman stopped pedaling his bike.

"What the Christ happened there? . . ."

A final flick returned the overview shot of the crater to the screen, the exercise room plunged into near darkness. "I can't tell you what happened yet," explained Doane, "only what didn't. Topical analyses of the crater confirm no evidence of searing, no blast residue, no rubble. Also, no evidence of radioactivity or radioactive fallout, so it wasn't a nuclear episode either."

Bill Riseman swung off his bike and stood up.

"Are you telling me this crater *wasn't* caused by an explosion?"

"An explosion, yes; but an explosion the likes of which have never been seen before."

The President's eyes were glued to the screen as he caught his breath. "Well, we're seeing them now, Roger, and I'd like to know what in the hell caused what we're looking at."

CHAPTER 13

THE white-haired man rose from his chair and lifted the crystal champagne goblet.

"My friends, I believe a toast is in order."

Around the conference table in the dimly lit room, the dozen figures joined him on their feet.

"A toast to our coming victory," the white-haired man proclaimed with his goblet thrust proudly upward. "I give you the future. I give you Operation Thunder Clap."

He touched the rim of the glass to his lips and sipped the drink that had been forbidden him for years. He neither smiled nor sought the eye of any person in the room; his stare was fixed on the middle distance. He spoke again.

"I give you loyalty. I give you total, unceasing devotion to a cause and a testament that has become this country's only hope for survival. The Valhalla Testament, my friends. Let no one question. Let no one doubt."

At that, a man standing near the table's center wavered. The crystal goblet slipped from his hand and smashed against the hard wood. The man reached out to right himself, but his knees buckled and he fell heavily, sprawled halfway across the table, mouth agape. He was already dead when his face hit the wood. His eyeglasses shattered on impact and mixed with the broken crystal. His eyes hung open. Despite their stares of shock, no one in the room dared utter a word.

"He doubted, my friends," said Simon Winters as he returned his goblet to the table. "He questioned. Worse than that, he told an associate of our existence. That associate has been eliminated as well."

A pair of guards entered through the double doors and roughly hauled the corpse from the room. The stares of the others remained fixed on Simon Winters through it all, wondering if they, too, might be about to drop. None bothered to question how the single poisoned glass had reached the proper hands; it had, after all, happened before.

The members had come to the mansion in Fairfax, Virginia, singly and at separate intervals to avoid drawing attention to their gathering. The mansion itself was surrounded by a ten-foot cast-iron fence so thickly lined on its inner side with plants and bushes as to make the view from outside virtually impossible. Such homes were hardly unusual in Fairfax and not apt to attract attention. All mail was delivered to a post office box, and the NO TRESPASSING GUARD DOGS ON DUTY signs did their part in keeping salesmen and maintenance people away.

"My friends," Simon Winters resumed with a strange calm, "you have just witnessed the fate of anyone who opposes us from within or without. I assume the rest of us are in agreement about our present course and strategy." He paused and looked about the room. "I say again, my friends. To the future!"

Simon Winters drained the rest of his champagne, but few of the others around the table ventured any more than a sip. The twelve individuals around the table formed the governing board of the Valhalla Group, the two nearest, along with him, forming the executive committee. None currently held government office, and only a few ever had. They viewed politics as merely a tool to help them accomplish their aims. It was power they understood: how to achieve and wield it, how to fashion it like a spear and aim it wherever they desired.

Simon Winters remembered the first day he had stepped

into a similar conference room, brought there by his grandfather, an Irish immigrant who had made his fortune in oil and gas. It was the day of his father's funeral. His father, killed on a Korean War battlefield for no good reason at all. Simon Winters was thirty-five, and that suddenly seemed very young. It was cold that day in Washington. Simon Winters remembered a light dusting of snow, remembered that the heat in the room had not been on.

"We're going to lose this war," the old man had said in his gravel-laced voice. "Your father—my son—will have died for nothing. Do you know why, Simon?"

Simon Winters had said that he didn't.

"Because of a poorly conceived plan, an act undertaken without consideration of all the elements. This bodes ill for the future of America, Simon. Look around you and tell me what you see, lad."

"Sir?"

"Tell me what you see in the room, damnit!"

"Only a table and some chairs."

"Close your eyes. Visualize those chairs occupied by men who have a proper vision of the future. By men who know which direction to steer this country." The old man looked away from his grandson. "Your father died because these chairs are empty today."

Simon Winters swallowed hard.

"What is Valhalla?" his grandfather asked him.

"The hall of Odin where Norse warriors who died in battle were received."

"Heaven?"

"For some."

"For who?"

"The bravest, the most noble, those who died with a sword in their hands."

"And thus died defending their land. Am I correct, lad?"

"Yes, sir."

The old man looked back at him. "We shall have our own Valhalla. The group will meet in this very room, and from it we shall defend our land against fools and enemies. That will be our testament." The old man came closer and touched

Simon's shoulder in a rare display of affection. "Your father would have been with me. Now that task has fallen upon you."

It was a task the young Simon Winters had readily embraced. The notion of the Valhalla Group was that of a secret, permanent government *behind* the government. Officials at all levels were placed, manipulated. Candidates were chosen and pushed with an inexhaustible supply of resources. Everywhere maneuvers, mechanizations, undertaken toward the consolidation of power.

There were no elections in Valhalla, only appointments. The men and women chosen for the Group at first desired more to be makers of a kingdom than kingmakers. What changed their minds was the rise to power of Castro in Cuba and their own failure to prevent a communist government takeover just ninety miles from U.S. borders. It became clearer that working behind the scenes was not enough. To accomplish their vision and preserve their testament, they needed to do more, to *be* more.

Simon Winters's grandfather chaired the Valhalla Group until his death in the early seventies. His later years, when he stubbornly held to his chair, were marred with errors and miscalculations. Many of the members blamed him for failing to use the Group's power to prevent such fiascoes as Vietnam and the Arab oil embargo. The Group became hopelessly mired in bickering and lost its sense of mission.

With his grandfather's death, Simon took his place as head of the Valhalla Group, determined to renew its order and purpose. A single member rose to oppose him and Simon did just what his grandfather would have. He called the man a traitor and shot him in the head. With the body lying there, Simon Winters gave the rest of the shocked members that one chance to leave. None had taken him up on the offer.

The grandson of its founder carried the Valhalla Group into a new age. Instead of merely reacting to world events, the Group now actively contrived them to suit the best interests of the U.S. Assassination was common. Blackmail and extortion became familiar tools. Hatred of communism and attempts to crush it figured largely in their plans. But the breakdown of communism in Eastern Europe they had helped bring on only served to increase their resolve. There was always an enemy to find if one looked hard enough and Valhalla realized their greatest enemy resided at home now.

The Nicaraguan Accords were what precipitated the Group's boldest round of action yet. The Accords symbolized to them the impotence of the U.S. government. Believing the Chamorro government could solidify its hold on power was an absurdist's notion. The Sandinistas, through their newfound puppet organization the NNSC, would find their way to power again and this time they wouldn't reliquish it. The vast billions of dollars now being invested in Nicaragua would then be nationalized. It was inevitable. The U.S. would be reduced to groveling in support of a government that went against every principle she stood for or risk losing everything she was now building. Nicaragua, meanwhile, would find itself with the dollars and machines that could enable it to destabilize and conquer the entire region.

The Accords came to symbolize a weakness, a complacency, in the very core of America. The United States was crumbling more from within than without. Drugs were running rampant through the streets. The blessed freedoms the country had built herself on were being battered and abused. People burning flags, *flags*! It made the Group's collective flesh crawl. But what to do?

Another crossroads, another crisis, and once more Simon Winters stepped forward. To meet the challenges presented, the Valhalla Group would have to rule from the closets of power instead of the shadows. To achieve this, though, men who spoke with Valhalla's voice would have to come to power. For years these individuals had been eased into place in the political forefront. Above all, the candidate opposing incumbent president Bill Riseman belonged to them. All the Group's plans were centered around his winning the presidency in four weeks' time. And so the disgrace of the administration had to be assured, leading to sweeping changes on election day. To accomplish this Valhalla planned to use the

Nicaraguan Accords to destroy Riseman. This tragic error would provide the means to help bring about his undoing.

And Operation Thunder Clap was born.

"Were you able to toast with us, Captain Marlowe?" the white-haired man spoke toward a brown speaker that rested in the center of the conference table. Some of the glass from the dead Group member's goblet glistened around it.

"Indeed, sir," returned the voice, slightly altered by a scrambling device. The voice belonged to the fourth member of the Group's executive committee and its military representative, the architect of Operation Thunder Clap. On Marlowe's own insistence, only Simon Winters knew his actual identity.

"Splendid," Winters said, speaking to all of those before him now. "My friends, do we not stand here on the verge of something great, something awe-inspiring? It has too often been the lot of this group to salvage what it could from the foolish mistakes of others. We have been repairmen rather than builders. That is about to change. Four weeks remain until the election that will bring us to power. Our role will be to speak for the people of this country and correct the errors and injustices that have been perpetrated upon them. One month and the Valhalla Testament will be the doctrine that holds sway.

"The changes will be subtle at first but more overt with the passing of months. Most will welcome the return of controls and discipline, welcome even the drastic steps we must take to insure this coming to pass. You know the long-term plans. You know how far we have to go to make sure we go far enough. Unmitigated freedom is a privilege, not a right, one this country has sadly lost. The homeless, the drugs, the fifty percent dropout rate at many of our schools in an education system on the verge of collapse—these are the harbingers of the future if we do not step forward and bring in the reins on a way of life going astray."

Simon Winters's eyes blazed as he spoke. The others looked at him mesmerized, their own resolve reinforced by the power and vigor of his words. Once more he raised his glass.

"I say again, my friends: to the future, to *our* future!"

His speech over, Winters moved away from his accustomed spot at the head of the table. The others took this accurately as the sign for their departures. They left as they had arrived: alone, in separate directions.

When only the three members of the executive committee remained, Simon Winters retook his seat at the head of the conference table.

"Let's get back to business, shall we? Mr. Pernese, your report please."

Benjamin Pernese sat on Winters's right, his appearance innocuous except for an untreated cataract glazing his left eye. Pernese hated hospitals and doctors to an equal degree. His wife had died years before during a routine operation, and he had sworn them off forever as a result.

"Ten days from now," he started, "our assets in the world of finance assure me that three of the nation's ten largest banks will close their doors and file for government protection. We've all read the projections. Economic panic will ensue and the entire economy will be frozen on the verge of collapse."

"Left for us to get moving again, of course, following the election. Now you, Margaret."

The woman on Winters's left was the first female member of Valhalla ever to serve on the executive committee. Margaret Brettonwood had dedicated her life to the service of her country. It was her husband, children, filling all those respective needs and filling them well. She had served as ambassador to three different countries and in the United Nations for two different presidents. Twice mentioned as a possible vice-presidential candidate, she did not aspire to that or any chair other than the one she sat in now.

"Three weeks from now police in five major cities will stage a collective walkout. Our assets indicate the army will be called up within twenty-four hours, forty-eight at the outside."

"Thus setting the precedent for the actions we will be taking after the inauguration," Winters completed. "The societal curbs this country is in such dire need of." He leaned closer to the brown speaker. A piece of crystal lay on its top. "Of course, the central part of our plan remains Operation Thunder Clap. Mr. Marlowe, you may now discuss the specifics."

Marlowe proceeded to provide the details of the training segment of the operation, along with the timetable for the strike team's subsequent entry into the United States. He spoke for ten concise minutes, finishing with a brief overview of the strategy involved in taking the island that was the operation's target.

"The logistics are extremely complicated," noted Margaret Brettonwood.

"Necessarily so, ma'am, as they are in all missions of this nature."

"Are the responses of our government and military so easy to predict?" asked Winters.

"Even if they are not, my final bit of insurance will assure us of success."

"But this final bit of insurance is the most complicated business of all," said Brettonwood. "Can you really get such an apparatus in place?"

"Work will begin Monday. The arrangements have already been completed. The mandated covers have been secured."

"I am more concerned with Colonel Riaz's role in all of this, Mr. Marlowe," interjected Benjamin Pernese.

"Then let me reiterate, sir, that the colonel was not chosen at random. His psychological profile made him the perfect candidate. So far we have accurately predicted each and every one of his responses to the stimuli we have provided."

"What will the members of the team be told?"

"To obey Riaz implicitly. With the exception of our plant and his man, they are men from the Nicaraguan National Solidarity Committee. Esteban has arranged everything for us. They believe they are doing what is best for their country."

"Which leads me to the irregularities we have recently encountered in Nicaragua," said Pernese, changing the subject. "Exactly who is this woman who has damaged us?"

"An Outsider known as Chimera. We've used her quite often in the past. We have now positively identified her as the operative who met with Maria Cordoba, as well as the one responsible for the deaths of those five agents in New York."

"They were dispatched to execute one of their own, were they not?" Pernese wondered.

"Yes. He had outlived his usefulness after he completed the Pine Gap segment of the operation. We had no way of anticipating Chimera's presence."

"She killed them all?" asked Margaret Brettonwood.

"At least three."

"She must be very good."

"We wouldn't have used her if she wasn't, ma'am."

"Don't be coy with me, Marlowe," Brettonwood snapped. "Since we know Chimera spoke with Crane, she must be aware of our pickup from Pine Gap. And reaching Maria Cordoba can only mean she has made the connection with Nicaragua. The link between those two factors, Mr. Marlowe, is us."

"None of her actions indicate she knows anything of us, ma'am."

"Yet," said the woman, "by your own admission, we are dealing with an extremely proficient operative here, perhaps the best The Outsiders have to offer. If anyone can make the proper conclusions and respond accordingly, it's Chimera."

"I'll grant you that, ma'am. But I remind you that less than a week remains before our operation begins. We'll find Chimera well before then. There are only so many places she can go that might lead her closer to us. We can and will cover them all."

"The status of this football player she helped to escape disturbs me as well," said Pernese. "You are certain he can do us no harm?"

"Absolutely," responded Marlowe, carefully concealing the existence of the microchip that was surely somewhere on Skylar's person. What the reaction of the board would be to this information was entirely unpredictable. "Chimera only helped him in the hope he might be able to do the same for her. When she realizes he can't, she will abandon him, and may well have done so already."

"Which brings us to the subject of the explosives, Marlowe," said Simon Winters, eager to be off this subject. "What has been your determination concerning them?"

"Sir, due to the potency of the Quick Strike charges, I've arranged to have them shipped directly to the target area. They will be waiting when Riaz's team arrives just where he is expecting them."

"Your reports indicate the explosives must be stored under certain conditions," reminded Brettonwood.

"Indeed," Marlowe acknowledged, and went on to elaborate on the specific arrangements.

"Brilliant," complimented Simon Winters with a light clap of his hands. "Positively brilliant."

"Thank you, sir."

"Not only are the logistics sensible, but additionally they serve to keep the explosives out of Riaz's hands for as long as possible."

"And," Marlowe picked up, "keep in mind that the colonel will be dead before our planned time of detonation."

"Too bad he didn't agree to work with us when Esteban approached him directly," said Benjamin Pernese.

"It wouldn't have mattered, sir," Marlowe told him. "His death would have been called for anyway."

"Sorry I'm late, Colonel Riaz," Esteban greeted, shuffling his bulbous frame toward the mountain ridge that looked out over much of the country.

Riaz did not turn to face him. "Just speak."

"I have good news, Colonel. Your request to lead Operation Thunder Clap has been approved by the NNSC."

Esteban had expected some reaction, a bit of thanks, at least a satisfied smile. Yet Riaz merely turned toward him, his expression chiseled in the same cold granite as it had been the last time they had met.

"You think I should be grateful or perhaps even reverent, don't you, Esteban?"

"If you have changed your mind . . ."

"Nothing has changed. I do what I do because I must, but I take no pleasure in it. I have chosen to follow this path to avenge my family because it is the only one open to me. The fact that my work will also serve the end of your NNSC's so-called patriots is meaningless to me."

"Even though it serves Nicaragua as well?"

"When does it end, Esteban? Must innocent lives always be placed in jeopardy to achieve our ends?"

"Like the lives of your family, Colonel?"

"Different."

"Yes, indeed. The lives of the hostages will be in the hands of the American government. They will have a chance. Your family had no chance," the fat man reminded at the risk of infuriating a man he already stood in dread fear of.

But Riaz showed no emotion. "The training ground?"

"Construction was completed yesterday. Everything has been built to scale. We have even the sea itself to use as a prop. Your suggestions as to the kind of personnel were taken to heart. I have twenty dossiers in the car for your inspection."

"I shall require only fourteen men."

"We had arrived at twenty as an optimum figure."

Riaz remained standing there. "Fourteen."

Esteban nodded rapidly. "As you wish, Colonel. Make the cuts as you desire. Five days' training is all we've been able to allot."

"Five days is more than enough. This island where the training will take place . . ."

"I will escort you there personally."

Riaz looked toward the fat man's car. "We should get going, then."

"There is one more thing. The choice of team members is, of course, up to you. Our only request is that we be allowed to place our own man as your second. Precautions, you understand."

"Depends who it is."

"A fine soldier with a record worthy of your esteem."

"I'll be the judge of that. Just tell me who he is."

"His name is Maruda. Captain Octavio Maruda . . ."

CHAPTER 14

IT was not until midmorning on Saturday that Jamie caught his first glimpse of the pursuers. Standing on the highest point of a tall hill, he could see them scurrying in the undergrowth far below, the metal from their guns flashing irregularly in the bright sunlight. He pressed himself against a rock for cover and peered out.

There were dozens, fifty troops at least! He calculated the distance and tried to figure how far behind him they were. Hard to say, but it was a few hours in any case.

After leaving Chimera the night before, he had walked northeast in the direction of the Huaspuc River until exhaustion overcame him. He slept fitfully, covered with brush, almost burrowed into the ground. He had never been an outdoorsman. A high school summer interlude spent in an Outward Bound program in the Midwest was as close as he had come.

He had come fully awake with the sun and kept moving with barely a pause. His sole source of refreshment came from small brooks with the sweetest water he had ever tasted. The terrain grew steeper and steeper until Jamie realized he was trudging almost entirely uphill. The higher he rose into the hills, the scarcer became the foliage he used as cover.

Never far from his mind was the very real possibility that he might come upon one of the traps laid by the Contras to safeguard the last of their territory. A few times he was quite certain he found their markings and narrowly avoided them.

Finally, at an indiscernible distance, he glimpsed a rush of blue that could only be the northern reaches of the Huaspuc River as it wound its way toward the Honduran border. He reached it by late afternoon, with all of his lead over the pursuing soldiers intact. Chimera's advice had been to simply keep it on his right as he moved up-country. Continuing to follow the river north on foot, though, would subject him constantly to the possibility of capture by the pursuing soldiers. On the other hand, if he could swim across, his lead would become insurmountable.

The Huaspuc was a half mile in width at its narrowest point. Even under the best of circumstances, hardly an easy swim, but easily the best option available to him. He sat down on the rocks and removed his boots, then carefully tied them by the laces to his belt, one on each side to keep his weight balanced for the swim. Then he left the shore of crusty brush in favor of the rocks rimming the river and lowered himself into the water.

It was colder than he expected, and Jamie felt the drying sweat over him had chilled to ice. He rotated strokes between crawl, side, and a semblance of the breast. He mostly swam the crawl, to make time. The others were used for rest in motion, their rotations growing longer as he drew farther into the cold center of the river. Exhaustion threatened to overcome him several times. His breath came with difficulty. His periods of slow-stroking became longer, and then the crawl all but disappeared when his legs rebelled against further kicking. His wounded side stiffened and began to lock. Time passed with agonizing slowness, the distance covered discouragingly small.

Yet the opposite shore drew methodically closer. When it at last sharpened in view, the sight charged Jamie with the energy displayed in his initial strokes. The rocky bottom came up without warning and his feet grazed it as he stopped to tread water. He pawed along a bit more until he could stand comfortably. The breaths that followed had never tasted so good. A feeling of exhilaration, of triumph, filled him. His wound had not stopped him, the soldiers had not stopped him, and now neither had the river.

I beat you, damnit, I beat all of you!

And then something brushed against him in the water. Jamie felt a slight jarring against his side, something pushing against him. Not a fish, he thought next, not a fish . . .

He saw the dark shape angling in from the right and hoped for a brief instant that it was a stray log or battle-ruined tire left to stray down the river. But the next instant showed him the same shape bent into a curl that was everywhere at once. His arms flailed wildly, thrashing to escape, the awful pressure closing on his chest with viselike strength.

"Ahhhhhhhhhhhhhhh—"

Jamie heard his own scream echo through the woods, choked off at the same time as his breath. The snake wrapped itself around him, one with the water, layers of it enclosing his midsection and climbing for his throat. His hands tried to grasp for it but couldn't get a hold, so huge was the snake's circumference.

The thing hissed and tightened its grasp. The hideous, bulbous head, a mere extension of its body, flapped up and down. Jamie didn't think it intended to bite him, had risen merely to help its own cause of dragging him beneath the surface. He felt his rib cage contract further as the snake tightened its coil. It must have been fifteen feet in length, and most of that was wrapped around him, squeezing ever harder.

Jamie's hands desperately sought the creature's head. His flailing knocked him off balance and he lost the secure footing he'd gained seconds before. He and the snake sank beneath the surface and were encased in the dark murkiness of the river. Jamie struggled valiantly for the surface that shone in the light above, but the snake's weight and thrust carried him farther downward. His lungs bursting for air and his vision growing dim, he fought the grip of mindless panic as well as the snake's.

The knife! Chimera's knife!

Jamie heard the words in his ear more than he thought them. There was a heavy puffiness in the fingers of the hand he lowered to his belt, the other one remaining fixed beneath the thrashing head of the beast. The fingers locked on the hilt and stripped the blade free. He brought it up into the darkness before him.

Jamie jabbed the knife forward toward the vague shape of the snake's head. The blow pierced the beast's thick reptilian skin. He twisted the blade and jammed it forward like a saber. The thing's head shook madly. Jamie felt warm wetness pouring onto the hand that continued to shove the blade through as it tore upward.

The pressure on his chest slackened. The surface was just above him and he bounded for it with the snake's body still wrapped tight around his midsection, thrashing and spasming. The welcome air that poured into his lungs gave Jamie the strength to tear the rubbery layered thing off him. Its head split down the center, it nonetheless continued to writhe and fight. Jamie watched it finally sink beneath the surface and pushed himself toward the shore.

Gasping for breath and coughing, he staggered out of the water onto the rocks and brush at the river's edge. Each breath and each cough was awful agony for his bruised rib cage. He collapsed and lay there trying to calm himself, keeping in focus the fact that he must push on if he hoped to elude his pursuers.

Push . . . on . . .

Jamie opened his eyes. The last rays of light were just visible. He must have blacked out after reaching the shore. He realized his breathing was coming easier. Much of the pain had retreated as the tensed muscles, damaged by the snake's embrace, had relaxed. How long, though, had he been out? Four hours at minimum, judging by the sky, as many as six perhaps.

He rose to a sitting position and gazed across the river. Jamie froze. There, on the opposite bank, he saw a large complement of the soldiers he had seen coming in pursuit earlier in the day. Shifting and moving about, working objects into the river.

Rafts! Rubber rafts!

Jamie knew in that instant all the ground he had gained on them was gone. But they hadn't seen him yet or their motions would have been more excited and frantic. That was reason for hope, and Jamie pulled himself along on his stomach, careful not to let any sudden motion give him away. Once within the cover of the brush, he stopped to pull his water-darkened boots over his soaked socks.

Jamie found his feet and hit the fastest pace his body would give him. In minutes he could hear the sounds of pursuit behind him. Branches snapped. Muted voices were exchanged. Jamie charged through the woods in reckless fashion to put distance between him and them.

The ground dropped off suddenly and he plunged downward, rolling and then sliding over the rock-infested brush dirt. He could feel his damaged ribs clawing at his flesh from within and came to a halt on the verge of passing out once more with the soldiers' boots thrashing closer.

Jamie fought to rise. Half-bent over from the searing pain in his ribs, he tore through the woods. He scraped his hands raw mounting a sharp rise. It leveled briefly and then shot downward, and Jamie used the slope to generate some pace. It seemed he had done just that when his legs were pulled out from under him. His first thought was of one of the Contra booby traps, and he tensed. But something was still wrapped around his lower legs, still pulling, and Jamie recognized the feeling as that of being caught from behind by a tackler who'd cut off his angle.

He felt the shape surge over him in the next instant and was about to struggle when the cold steel of a killing knife pressed against his throat.

"*Keep quiet! Don't move!*" a voice whispered in his ear.

Jamie spoke Spanish, but even if he hadn't, the commands would have been quite clear. Jamie obeyed them and let himself be dragged into a thicket which parted easily to accommodate both him and his captor.

"*We wait for them to go,*" the voice whispered next, and Jamie realized it sounded quite young. Even in the darkness he could see the arm holding him from the rear was thin and frail, the hand attached to it small and covered with dirt.

Jamie made a motion to turn, and his captor's response was to press the steel blade harder against his flesh.

"Okay," he relented. "Sorry."

The soldiers approached the thicket seconds later, muttering to one another. Flashlight beams sporadically split the night, thin slices finding their way through the well-covered thicket. Jamie could feel eyes searching.

The sounds of the soldiers gradually lessened. With the night at last silent again, his captor urged Jamie around, keeping the knife pressed against his throat. What little light the night gave up illuminated his face, and Jamie found himself looking at a boy no more than fourteen or fifteen. Considering the territory, he must have been a Contra.

"You will come with me," he ordered in Spanish.

"Whatever you say." Jamie answered.

The boy prodded Jamie out of the thicket and kept a hand on him as they walked, the knife always a scratch away from his flesh. The boy knew how to use it; that much was certain.

They walked for twenty minutes, their route so erratic that Jamie couldn't say for sure which direction they had taken. The terrain was very treacherous, and when Jamie slipped down, the boy impatiently yanked him back up, the knife a constant reminder of who was in charge.

Halfway up the steepest rise, Jamie felt the boy pull him sideways toward a dense tangle of undergrowth. His captor parted the branches to reveal the opening to a cave. The soft glow of lanterns emanated from within, and the boy eased him the final bit of the way inside, spewing out a chain of Spanish too fast for Jamie to decipher.

And in the thin light, he found himself being stared at by a dozen young faces with ice cubes for eyes.

CHAPTER 15

"Do any of you speak English?" Jamie managed to ask, hiding his astonishment while his escort pulled the branches together to conceal the cave's entrance once more.

"Yes, American fuck face," snapped the oldest-looking of the bunch, rising to his feet. His body was taut and lean, his hair grimy and gnarled like wire. "But you got to have reason for me to talk to you."

The boy grasped a squat-looking automatic rifle from the ground of the cave and trained it on Jamie.

"See, American fuck face, you wear the uniform of our enemy."

"Only as a disguise to help me get away from them."

The oldest boy came closer. "How we know you not lying, fuck face?"

Reflexively Jamie shot his hand out and knocked the gun barrel away. "The soldiers were chasing me, in case you didn't get the right story. They're more my enemies than yours."

"They been chasing you all your life, fuck face?"

"No."

"Then they not as much your enemies as ours."

The boy who had brought him here spoke too rapidly in Spanish for Jamie to follow.

"He say the men after you aren't regular soldiers," the leader translated. "He say they different."

"So am I."

"Why they want you?"

"They don't want me to get out of the country. I can hurt the men who sent them if I get out of the country."

"Then you will have to get out of the country, fuck face," the leader said with a smile.

The group had placed lanterns in a circle on the most level part of the cave floor and gathered around their light. Jamie counted ten boys in all, ranging in age from eleven to the leader at sixteen or seventeen. They were all dressed like soldiers. The older ones wore camouflage fatigues in small men's sizes while the younger ones wore older uniforms that had been pieced together to fit them. Though the leader was the only one fluent enough in English to carry the conversation, the others sat around in transfixed silence, occasionally trading a whispered translation.

"You hungry, American?" the leader asked.

Jamie hadn't realized till then just how ravenous he was. "Only if you have enough to spare."

"We can get more."

One of the younger boys scampered on his knees to the rear of the cave and returned with a can of food like K rations Jamie felt certain must have come courtesy of a long-ago American supply drop. He started pounding the can with a rock until one of the older ones pointed out it had a pull tab. The rest of the boys laughed. Since there was no fork, he dug some out gratefully with his fingers and shoved it into his mouth. It tasted like some kind of processed meat. Jamie wolfed the food down gratefully.

"Are you Contras?" he asked between mouthfuls.

"We nothing," replied the leader. "Contras that didn't go back after the election are still across border in Honduras. They don't want us. Say we're too young."

"So why don't you go back?"

"What you mean back, American? We never there. We born, we raised right here," the leader insisted, jabbing a finger into the dirt. "We got nothing to go back to. We get old enough, we cross border. Not easy, though. Border with Honduras closed tight and patrolled to keep Contras from making raids."

Jamie felt his heart sink. "So how am I going to get across?"

"You can't now. You must wait. Like us, but not as long."

"Wait for what?"

"Jungle storm, American. Lots of water fall, lots of light flash. Soldiers stay inside when weather bad."

"I can't wait that long."

"Must if you want to get to Honduras."

Jamie shoved the last of the can's contents into his mouth. "I'll leave tomorrow morning," he said finally.

"Bad idea," the young leader cautioned.

"Why?"

"Men dressed as soldiers want you bad, eh? Probably went another mile maybe after missed you in the woods. In the morning they double back, check everything again."

"In that case I should leave now," Jamie offered. "Keep them from finding you."

He stood up and winced from the pain in his ribs and the knife wound.

"You hurt, American."

"I'll be all right."

"Chest bad, ribs bad. You cough blood?"

Jamie looked at him. "How did you know about—"

The leader aimed his eyes at the boy who had saved him in the jungle. "Arturo see you kill snake. Say you're brave."

Jamie nodded at the boy who had brought him here. "I didn't know I had an audience."

"Why you come down here, American?"

"To visit my sister."

"Huh?"

"They killed her and now they want to kill me."

"You not spy? You not CIA?"

Jamie shook his head. "I play football."

"I mean for business."

"That's it. I play football."

The leader translated, and a few of the boys snickered and mocked throwing and catching balls. *Here's my Ivy League championship ring to prove it,* Jamie almost said.

"You fast then, eh, American?"

"I have my moments."

"You gonna need one tomorrow when we get you to border."

The leader, Alberto, spread dirt over his first map and fashioned another of only the northeast part of the country from the Huaspuc River on. He added a deep furrow at the top to denote the Honduran border and finished by wedging his stick into the ground to represent their present position.

"How far are we from the border?" Jamie asked.

"Fifteen miles to the Coco River. Cross river and you there. Five hours to cover it. Maybe six because we move at night."

"I thought you said morning."

"I did." He shook his head. "Bad idea. Too many patrols, not even counting the soldiers looking for you. We leave before midnight. We leave in one hour."

"What's the plan? We've got to have a plan."

"You have a plan for getting here, American?"

"No, I just got lucky."

"Then maybe you get lucky again."

In fact, Alberto did have a plan, and a good one at that.

"We travel at night to border river. On our way no problems from the soldiers. Problems start when we get there," he explained.

"How so?" Jamie wondered.

Alberto went back to his stick, still watched by all the boys. He drew a bold line along the deep furrow denoting the border.

"Government now controls this whole stretch. Where they don't control, all there is is water. No way to get across. Too wide to swim across like you did today, American." And then, with a smile, "Too many snakes."

"What does that leave us with?"

"Quickest route. Steal a boat from government camp on river."

"What?"

"Yes! It's easy to do and safest way." He made an X with his stick. "Here is closest camp. Sure to be lots of boats. We arrive just after dawn. Soldiers sleepy. Not notice us as much."

"Dressed this way?"

"We change. Have other clothes here. Dress like peasant workers. Soldiers have plenty loading and digging. Don't pay for shit." Alberto flashed a bright smile, and in that instant he reminded Jamie of Marco, Colonel Riaz's oldest son, full of excitement and enthusiasm.

Then he remembered Marco's body and shuddered.

"You just stick close to me," Alberto was saying. "We make it look like you take boat because you supposed to. By the time they notice anything different, you across river to Honduras."

Jamie gazed down for a time at the stick-drawn map. "You really think this is going to work?"

"Who knows? You rather stay here?"

"Stop!"

Alberto called out the command as they at last neared their destination. He ordered the boy named Arturo to drift back and check the woods. Arturo returned minutes later. His news turned Alberto's face grave.

"The soldiers after you know we're here," he reported.

"How do they know it's us?"

"Your boots."

"My boots?"

"If skilled Indian trackers are along, they will know your mark from them." An idea struck Alberto. "Pietro, come here!"

A younger boy bounded forward obediently and Alberto

issued him a series of commands in Spanish. Pietro sat down, pulled off his sandals, and gave them to the leader.

"Take your boots off and squeeze these on, American."

"I don't want them going after this boy," Jamie told him, aware what he was planning.

"They won't for long. Soon they see only one track there. But we find more time. Hurry!"

Jamie pulled off his boots and handed them over to Pietro. The boy put them on and packed soft dirt into the empty areas left by the difference in their sizes.

Of the ten boys only five had been outfitted to make the trip that had commenced just over five hours before. Besides Alberto, Arturo, and Pietro there were Tomás and Alejandro who wanted to be called Alex. Alex and Pietro were the youngest, both barely in their teens with voices that had just started to change. Tomás was nearest in age to Alberto. He rarely spoke but his hard black eyes missed nothing. He kept his hair cropped short, while the others left theirs long and unattended.

They had fitted Jamie with the largest set of civilian clothes available; they were rags, but the fit nonetheless was cramped and uncomfortable. The pants were much too short and pulled at the crotch, while he could barely keep the shirt tucked in.

"Is better," Alberto had assured. "Look more like native this way."

The small group set off as planned a half hour before midnight. The night had remained cloudy and although they had taken along a single flashlight, Alberto expressed his intentions not to use it except in the most dire emergency. Even talk among the group was prohibited, unless absolutely necessary. Tomás led the way, fifteen yards or so ahead of the rest. Jamie couldn't even see him but Alberto could and that was all that mattered. He walked immediately behind the leader with Pietro and Alex next and Arturo bringing up the rear. The procession remained in that order over the long journey through the night, exchanging as few words as possible and stopping only occasionally for water or rest.

Pietro finished lacing the boots Jamie had given him and spat out some Spanish too soft for Jamie to make sense of.

"He says it is his pleasure to do this, American," Alberto translated. "He says we fight the same enemy."

The boy spouted off some more.

"He says not to worry. He will be all right. This is not the first time he has done something like this. His father taught him how, and he is not afraid."

Pietro waited until the rest of them had continued on before breaking off on his own. The rest continued on and soon reached a low barbed wire fence enclosing the government's shoreline camp. Alberto sliced through it effortlessly with an American-issue knife and signaled Tomás to slither under it first. The rest of the group followed, heads down and stomachs pressed flat, and moved together to the last cover of foliage.

Jamie was amazed at the sight. The scope of the camp was impressive, much more sophisticated than he had anticipated. Machine-gun and small artillery bunkers were set up across the perimeter of the shoreline facing the woods as the first line against any attack. Behind them a series of tents and supply huts had been erected to house the large complement of soldiers assigned here. Jamie could see a number of men walking about routinely in regular patrol while others appeared groggily from the living areas, stretching in the early morning light.

"Is like I said," Alberto whispered. "We get here at perfect time."

Even more important, a fair number of locals dressed similarly to themselves were busy loading equipment onto trucks and starting breakfast over open fires. Since the locals were not armed, the boys would have to leave their rifles behind before approaching.

In the river, boats of all sizes and varieties were moored. Many of the faster craft were undoubtedly used to patrol the river, while the slower ones were supply vehicles used to ferry equipment here from larger installations. The gasoline dump was a simple shed overflowing with kegs. The tents and prefab buildings formed the southern perimeter. Most ominous of all was a raised machine-gun nest in the center, well fortified and manned even now.

A man's shout reached them all at once from the rear. Alberto tensed.

"The soldiers," he muttered. "Closing fast."

"But the diversion," Jamie grasped. "Pietro—"

"Didn't delay them long as I hoped, American. We move now. Just follow along. Pretend you belong. Pretend you zipping up fly so anyone who sees will think we went to take a piss. Then keep walking. See those dinghies near the water?"

"Yes."

"You will take one. Row out to nearest boat. Key will be in starter."

"Some security."

"No one wants to be responsible for losing it." He took a deep breath of his own. "Now. We go."

The next moments took on a surreal afterglow all their own. As Jamie walked into the camp, he felt as though a part of him were outside his body watching what was happening. Exhaustion played a part in it, fear an even larger one. He did as Alberto had instructed, and when the young leader boyishly pushed at him, Jamie pushed back. Arturo and Alex slapped shoulders. Only Tomás took no part in the playacting, holding himself rigid and unblinking as always. Their rifles had been abandoned back near the barbed wire. All but Jamie carried American .45-caliber pistols, relics from past wars and past times. The baggy clothes did well enough to conceal the bulges they made, but against the awesome firepower around them, the pistols didn't add up to much.

As they reached the center of the camp, Tomás broke off from the group and leaned over as if pretending to tie his shoe. Alberto scolded him for a time with his eyes but then seemed to grasp his intention while Jamie remained befuddled. Alberto shouted something in Spanish to a local hauling bags from the back of a supply bed. The man nodded and waved him forward.

"We are going to join this man to blend in," Alberto

whispered. "I am going to shout something to you in Spanish when we get there. It will be instructing you to get something off the white boat moored closest to the shore. Just nod your head and do it. Don't look back. Move fast but not too fast. Like football, American, eh?"

"Yeah," Jamie said, trying to smile.

"If there's trouble, we help you. But whatever happens, don't stop. Don't turn back."

They reached the peasant unloading the shipment in the next few steps and as explained Alberto spit out some loud orders in Spanish directed at him. Jamie did his best to look stupid, a lumbering oaf taking orders from a boy. Behind him he could hear Alberto picking up on the ruse, probably making fun of him, and then everyone laughing.

Jamie didn't turn back. The shore and the dinghy upon it now held his undivided attention. He kept his shoulders and back tense, expecting someone to rush or shout at him. But Alberto had been right. Not many in the camp were about at such an early hour and those that were paid him no heed at all.

He reached the dinghy and eyed the land across the way. A mere mile across to Honduras, to freedom. He pulled the dinghy into the water and walked out after it. He was too nervous to climb in casually and was afraid his clumsy attempts might have drawn attention from the shore. Then he remembered his guise as an oaf. If anyone were watching, his awkwardness would work in his favor. Reassured, he finally managed to swing himself into the small row boat.

He had already elected to disobey Alberto in one regard: the closest boat, the white one, was a cabin cruiser and wouldn't be able to give him much speed. But a few yards beyond it a luscious blue speedboat lay moored. This craft would suit Jamie's purposes far better, providing the speed he sorely required.

Jamie grabbed the oars and pulled rapidly away from the shore with his eyes still trained on it. He had almost let himself relax when he saw a group of soldiers burst from the forest and fan out through the camp. Undoubtedly they were the men who had been pursuing him and now, at last, they had caught up. Though they were not real soldiers, their uniforms did the job well enough; especially at such an early hour in a border camp occupied by simple grunts. The shouts and rifle shots fired into the air by the arriving forces rousted the billeted camp soldiers out of bed and sent them scurrying to their posts. Something big was obviously going on and poor response would cost them.

Jamie picked up the pace of his rowing and strained to reach the blue speedboat. He saw men rushing about in all directions, the men masquerading as soldiers mixing with the real troops. The peasant workers were herded harshly together. Finally a few of the stares fell on the water, on the boats. On him. They hesitated at first but not for long. Before Jamie could reach the speedboat, a host of uniformed figures was charging for the shoreline with rifles pointing at him. Orders were shouted, hands waved to alert the others that the object of their pursuit had been found.

Jamie could do nothing but keep going, flinching against the certainty of bullets soon to be speeding his way.

Instead of the expected rifle shots, though, a different sound reached his ears. Alberto and the two young boys had drawn their .45s and commenced firing straight into the line of soldiers drawing a bead on him. Taking them totally by surprise, the first barrage felled the uniformed figures like dominoes; the others rushed for cover in order to regroup. This was just the few extra moments grace Jamie needed to reach the speedboat. He vaulted over the side, but his eyes stayed on the burgeoning battle. One of the younger boys, Alex he thought, used the brief confusion to dash forward and grab a pair of automatic rifles that were leaning against one of the huts. He tossed them to Alberto and Arturo and then dove to the sand beneath the first barrage of return fire.

Alberto dove low, too, spinning with the automatic in his hands and firing in the direction where the soldiers had retreated. Arturo fired the second automatic as he backed off with Alex toward the cover promised by the gasoline kegs and supply huts.

Jamie unmoored the speedboat and moved for the starter

switch. The key was indeed there. It turned quickly, but he hesitated before speeding off across the Coco toward Honduras.

By then the onslaught directed the boys' way was constant, and Alberto had to draw back as well. Soldiers from both the pursuing troop and the camp advanced boldly in the face of their token return volleys. The boys tried to take refuge behind the gasoline cans, but bullets cut through the steel, spilling fuel upon the beach. It seemed hopeless, and would have been if not for Tomás.

He must have reached the machine-gun nest and overcome the guard at the start of the chaos. Now he turned the gun and opened fire into the heaviest concentration of soldiers, taking full advantage of the camp's most strategic position. The soldiers fell in their tracks to the high-caliber rounds, as Tomás's fire continued to spray them. Alberto and the younger boys seized the advantage by opening fire on those soldiers rushing to flee the assault.

They're winning!

Jamie shoved the boat into gear and gave it gas, turning the wheel at the same time. Its nose crested, then dropped when Jamie eased back on the throttle. The advantage the boys held was only temporary. Soon they would be cut down and slaughtered, bodies pounded with bullets. They had helped him, and now they would die for it. Unless, unless . . .

The emergency kit flashed before his eyes, affixed to the bulkhead above the steering wheel. He yanked it down and snapped it open. Inside was a flare pistol and three flares—the very things he had been hoping for. Holding the kit in one hand, he spun the speedboat around and headed back for shore.

The scream of the speedboat's revving engine covered the sounds of the shore, but he could see well enough what was happening. An all-out assault had been launched on Tomás's position. Bullets rained on it from all directions, and when the soldiers rushed toward it unhindered, Jamie knew Tomás was dead. The others would soon join him unless he did something.

"Alberto!"

Jamie's scream was lost in the wind rushing past his face, but he didn't care, and screamed the boy's name again. In that instant his own life meant nothing, and never had he felt so without fear. Alberto and the other two boys were pinned hopelessly down, ammo exhausted, one of them obviously wounded. Jamie screamed his name again.

This time he heard the shout and turned toward the speedboat rushing for the Nicaraguan side of the river. Surprise and gratitude showed in his face. Taking the two younger boys by the arm, he started for the shoreline.

They're not going to make it. . . .

Fear filled Jamie again as he grabbed for the pistol and loaded the first flare.

Alberto had reached the water but was going down, hit in the leg. Arturo leaned over him, and Jamie saw his head explode, simply break apart under the force of the shell.

"Bastards!"

Jamie fired the flare.

Whereas the bullets had merely punctured the storage tanks of gasoline, the flames ignited them. On impact, a huge burst of fire blew up and outward, spreading fast wherever the gasoline had flowed. A wall of blazing orange and coal-black smoke rose along the shoreline and separated the soldiers from the boys. The speedboat closed on the shore and Jamie spun the wheel, turning the craft just when he was on the verge of beaching it.

"Come on!" he screamed at Alberto, who was limping through the water dragging an unconscious Alex after him. The dead Arturo had been claimed by the river.

The soldiers continued to fire their rifles blindly at the wall of fire, the shots wild and desperate. Jamie grabbed for Alberto's extended hand and dragged him and Alex into the boat. In the same instant he spun the speedboat around and gassed it. The boys toppled to the bottom of the boat in a heap. Alberto raised his head.

"You a fool, American."

"Save it for the other side," Jamie responded as the nose of the speedboat crested over the currents, casting white foam behind it.

CHAPTER 16

COLONEL José Ramon Riaz gazed at Captain Maruda from across the table that had been set up outside the tent.

"They are good men, Colonel. All of them."

"And did you help Esteban in their selection, Captain?"

Maruda pulled off his red bandanna long enough to tuck his hair back beneath it. "He asked for my input, yes."

The island training ground lay twenty miles off the Nicaraguan coast. It was totally deserted and held no interest for locals or tourists at all. Still, patrol boats swept the waters twenty-four hours a day in case someone ventured too close, either by chance or otherwise. The island itself was considerably larger than the one they would seize in Operation Thunder Clap, but the exact boundaries of the target had been fenced off to provide precise scale for their maneuvers.

"Yes, Captain," Riaz conceded. "They are good men. Anachronisms like myself."

"Colonel?"

"They do what is asked of them. They do not question. They have ideals; but their devotion is to their duty. We will be asking much of them, more perhaps than we have a right to. More perhaps than any man can be expected to give."

"Their lives?"

"The cold-blooded taking of others. It is never easy, Captain. Believe me, it isn't."

Maruda nodded as if he agreed. It was good Riaz had been out of circulation by the time he began to make his mark. In fact, the captain's brutality had made him somewhat of a legend even before his twentieth birthday. In the war against the Contras, collaborators and sympathizers had to be punished, too. Twice Captain Maruda had hung men by their genitals. Once he hung a woman by her breasts until the hooks driven through her flesh forced her to bleed to death. He became more subtle in his midtwenties by killing the children of collaborators instead of the collaborators themselves. His greatest stroke of genius, though, was what ultimately led to his being reassigned to the militia, while attracting his present true employers to him. On three separate occasions he made parents suspected of being collaborators kill one of their own children on penalty of him killing all if they refused.

Maruda never made a secret out of the fact that he enjoyed his work. He liked to compare himself to Colonel Riaz in his days as *el Diablo de la Jungla*. But they really had nothing in common. Riaz functioned as a soldier and fought with dignity and honor. Clearly death was a necessary by-product to him, to be avoided wherever possible. For Maruda, killing was the only thing that mattered, both a means and an end. The best thing about his new employers was that they gave him a chance to exercise his finest skills again. Still he continued to gaze across the table at the colonel in apparent agreement.

"We go into this mission to confront an enemy who has done nothing to us," Riaz was saying. "Speak of symbols all you want, but triggers must be pulled at people, at faces who don't understand why they must die."

"They will only die if the Americans make it so," Maruda reminded him. "The triggers belong to them, not us."

"And yet the hostages we will take are not the people directly responsible for the ruin of our country."

"But it is through them that we will reach those responsible. Without this operation we will become another U.S. satellite, a helpless and dependent puppet."

"You sound like Esteban, a helpless and dependent NNSC puppet."

"You must agree with what the committee is trying to do. After all, you are a part of it."

"*Was* a part, Captain. What I do now, I do for myself. Yes, I've been trying to convince myself what you say is true ever since I told Esteban I wanted to lead this operation. I haven't quite succeeded."

"But, Colonel, it is the dollars pouring into Nicaragua that trained the men and bought the weapons that killed your family. Without Operation Thunder Clap, our whole nation will die just as your family died, if not in body, at least in spirit."

Riaz looked at Maruda differently. "Do you fancy yourself a poet, Captain?"

"I fancy myself a soldier, sir."

"Then as a soldier, you must be bothered by some of the logistics confronting us with this mission."

Riaz rose and walked in silence up the rising slope of the island until the hastily constructed shells of buildings were in sight: six of them built to the exact size and specifications of the target. Unlike the true island, this one lacked any fields or manicured grounds whatsoever, so additional shorter fencing had been set up within the greater perimeter to denote where trees, shrubs, and open areas would be at the actual target site.

"The drills are going quite well." Maruda spoke from just behind Riaz.

"On the mock-up," the colonel conceded. "The real thing might prove something else again." He turned to Maruda. "We will reach the actual target by bridge, correct?"

"Yes."

"It disturbs me that a facsimile is missing from our mock-up."

"The logistics proved too difficult. We have the pictures."

"Scale is difficult to gauge."

"Crossing it is just a formality. Exactly one mile, more of

a causeway actually, easily destroyed to eliminate the only route onto the island."

"And," said Riaz, "the only route off."

"I'm afraid our efforts to locate Skylar have failed," Esteban reported to the man in Washington. The words jackknifed in his throat. "He made it over the Honduran border this morning."

He held his breath through the silence that followed.

"Was the woman with him?" the man asked deliberately.

"By all accounts, no."

"Then they separated."

"My people feel she might have been killed in the skirmish in the jungle."

"They've separated," repeated the military representative of the Valhalla Group. "You realize, of course, that if the Americans latch on to Skylar's microchip before we do, the operation will have to be scrapped."

"But Colonel Riaz is progressing so well on the island. I thought perhaps the timetable could be, er, advanced."

"Everything has been planned out too precisely to move up now. Besides, that's not your problem. But two of your problems have now become mine. Chimera and Skylar. You've caused me considerable embarrassment on this end."

Esteban could barely get the air down through the clog in his throat. "I can explain."

"Spare me your explanations, Esteban, and just keep me informed of the colonel's progress."

"I'm listening, Roger."

News that National Security Adviser Doane was en route with the latest findings from Pine Gap had reached the President while he was starting his regular run on the treadmill in the White House exercise room. Sweat was glistening on his face by the time Doane arrived. He was into his fourth mile and geared the machine down to a modest trot. Nearby, Charlie Banks leaned against one of the Nautilus machines.

Doane seemed to be having trouble issuing his report to Bill Riseman's bouncing figure. "Sir, the information I have just obtained pertains to the cause of the blast. On-site inspection and analysis by our team at Pine Gap has confirmed that the explosion and its subsequent effects were brought on by an accidental release of a substance not properly contained."

"*What* substance?"

Roger Allen Doane paused. "Antimatter," he said finally.

The President turned the machine down to a walking pace and wiped his face with a towel. "What in hell were they doing with antimatter at Pine Gap?"

"Sir, the scientific Frontier Bill you signed gave—"

"Now, hold it right there," roared Bill Riseman, picking his pace up ahead of the machine's. "The bill I signed allocated the usual multiple-zero figure for research into the use of antimatter as a propulsion catalyst. You helped sell me on it. Where'd we send it? Somewhere in Switzerland, wasn't it, Charlie?"

The President's chief of staff moved away from the Nautilus machine. "The European Center for Nuclear Research."

"Did some of that money end up at Pine Gap, Roger?"

"Yes, sir, it did. To research possible employment of antimatter in weapons use."

"And were you aware of this research?"

"Yes, sir, I was."

The President turned the treadmill back up to a runner's pace. "Goddamnit, Roger, what's going on here? I brought you into this administration. You were a man I trusted. How could you hold something like this back?"

"The research was in the most elemental stages," Doane answered. "There was really nothing to hold back. And the experiments at Pine Gap were actually benefitting the work in Switzerland by manufacturing anti-protons for their use as well. The existence of antimatter has been known since 1935, the problem always being how to store it. That's what they were working on at Pine Gap, you see."

"No, I don't see."

"I'm no scientist," Doane sighed, "but I'll do my best to explain. Antimatter is just what its name indicates. For each type of subatomic particle in normal matter, there is a corresponding particle of antimatter that has the same mass but the opposite electrical charge. For example, protons are positively charged, while their antimatter counterparts are negatively charged."

"I suppose I'm even less of a scientist," the President said, sounding short of breath. "You're losing me."

"Think of antimatter as a mirror image of normal atoms: identical, but with all features reversed. The explosive potency derives from the fact that the two elements cannot exist for more than a millisecond together. Once they come into contact, both are destroyed and transformed into energy of incredible magnitude."

"An explosion . . ."

"Beyond nuclear. Beyond everything. As I said before, the problem for years has been one of storing antimatter, learning how to contain it. Since it can't exist for more than that millisecond in the presence of regular matter, an electromagnetic vacuum containment shell in which subatomic positive particles could not exist at all was the only hope." Doane paused. "Some time ago, thanks to coinciding experiments in the development of ceramic superconductors, Pine Gap created that vacuum shell."

"But their vacuum was breached, wasn't it? Their shell cracked," the President fumed. Doane started to reply, and Bill Riseman rolled right over his words, as the sweat poured off him. He mopped his brow with his sleeve. Until he spoke, the hum of the treadmill dominated the large room. "They fucked up big time, and Australia's got a crater the size of Rhode Island as a result. Answer me this, Mr. Doane. How much antimatter did it take? How much slid out of that cracked shell to leave us with a hole that size and send ripples for thousands of miles in every direction throughout Australia?"

"The mass, approximately, of a marble."

"Good Christ . . ."

"I'm afraid there's more, Mr. President. Another of the things our on-site team has been able to determine with certainty was that the blast originated on Pine Gap's sublevel seven."

"So?"

"All work whatsoever on antimatter was conducted on sublevel nine."

Upon hearing those words, the President turned off the machine and leered down at Doane. "I'm a little confused here, Roger. First you report Pine Gap was destroyed by an antimatter explosion, and now you tell me the blast originated on a floor where there wasn't any."

"That's the problem, sir."

"No, Mr. Doane, that *was* the problem. The problem now is finding out how."

PART TWO

Pine Gap

Australia: Monday, three P.M.

CHAPTER 17

CHIMERA would have felt out of place even if she hadn't been the only woman in the smoky, overheated Poria bar.

"Aye, miss, Kirby Nestler comes here often enough. Not since yesterday, though. What's it to ya?" the bartender asked her.

"I've got business with him, that's all."

"Do ya now? Well, how 'bout then I direct ya to his patch?"

"I'd be most appreciative."

She passed the money over, and the bartender snatched at it as if afraid she was going to change her mind.

"Two miles due west outta town," he directed. "Only mailbox you'll come to. Kirb's place is down the hill a ways."

Chimera started to back up, but the bartender spoke again.

"Next time you come through, miss—" he winked "—drinks're on the house."

Armed with the bartender's directions, Chimera set out to find Kirby Nestler, Crane's Australian contact who had helped with the logistics of his final operation. She had obtained the address of the bar from Stein, in New York, and at least she knew he had been alive as of yesterday. A long chain of flights had gotten her first to Melbourne and then aboard a commuter flight to Adelaide. From there a rented four-wheel drive vehicle brought her north past Port Augusta and into the Flinders Ranges. The landscape was surprisingly lush and fertile en route, especially considering that Poria, located just north of Leigh Creek, made its living off coal mining.

A township more than a town, with a population of barely 700, Poria boasted only a pair of general stores, a combination post office and bank, a small rooming house, and a camping park, in addition to the bar she had just left. The road toward Nestler's address quickly turned desolate.

She found herself growing tired and opened all the windows in the rental just to keep herself alert en route to Nestler's house. Times like these set her mind wandering, and her thoughts, not surprisingly, turned to Crane. She couldn't refuse him when he had contacted her in New York and couldn't decline the charge he had passed on to her, even if she had wanted to. She thought again of what he looked like sitting there at the Hyatt, a frightened old man whose fingers had betrayed him.

She was the best, as Crane had been the best. But following in his footsteps meant taking the bad with the good. He had not died alone, because she had been there, and in that final act he was helping her again, guiding her, showing her the way out even as it was forced upon him.

You're doing this because you're afraid of ending up like him, Stein the bookseller had said to her in New York.

No, she realized now, *I'm doing this because he couldn't let me end up like him.*

She turned her attention back to the road leading to the home of Kirby Nestler. It was not straight at all, as the bartender had indicated. It curved and dropped until what seemed like far more than two miles had been covered. Chimera was about to turn back when she spotted a single dilapidated mailbox hanging half-off an unsteady post. She pulled her jeep down the drive just after it. The sudden plunge jolted her as the jeep plummeted down a steep hill. She braked desperately and settled into a bumpy ride toward a small house. The drive banked into a rise the last stretch of the way, which helped her at last slow the jeep.

Jumping down, she stretched her limbs in the bright afternoon light and climbed the porch to the front door.

"Mr. Nestler?" she called after several knocks brought no reply. "Mr. Nestler?"

She turned the knob and found the door open. She entered slowly, clinging to the hope that Kirby Nestler was inside and for some reason hadn't heard her. A quick search of the modest, unkempt three rooms showed her the house was empty. It hadn't been for long, though; she could smell the lingering odors of a recent meal. Chimera considered the possibility that she and Nestler might well have passed going in opposite directions. If she went back to Poria's single unnamed bar, she'd probably find him there. She left the house with just that notion in mind.

She was halfway to her jeep when she saw a sight that froze her blood. Five huge crocodiles, at least ten feet long, were pawing toward her from under and around the jeep. Chimera backpedaled until a sound that was a cross between a hiss and a snarl stopped her dead. Turning on her heels, she saw another four of the creatures emerging from beneath the porch. A quick glance to each side revealed more crocs closing fast, surrounding her and effectively cutting off her escape.

Her pistol was in hand by then, but she held no illusions as to its effectiveness. It would take half a clip to kill a single of these creatures, never mind well over a dozen of them. She could try for the jeep, but unlatching the door and lunging in would cost time she did not have. She could bolt through a gap between the creatures, but to where? And a croc could cover her pace twice over. She would wait for them to circle in on her closer, get them as far away from the jeep as possible before making her move. A long shot, but what other choice did she have?

The crocs coming from the porch charged suddenly. Chimera twisted sideways, which brought her dangerously close to two of the creatures approaching from the jeep. Her only chance was to leap over them and take her chances. . . .

"Halt!" came the command of a husky voice.

The crocs instantly froze in their tracks.

A tall, bearded man approached, shotgun in hand, from the shadows on the side of the house. He was lean and lanky, taut bands of sinewy muscle covering his arms. His hairy shoulders and chest were exposed outside the fabric of a dark tank top soaked at the stomach with sweat. He wore a thick handlebar mustache, which looked strangely menacing beneath his thick crop of hair as dark as that matted over his upper body.

"Drop your gun, miss."

Chimera obliged.

"You got thirty seconds to speak your peace 'fore I feed ya to 'em, miss."

"You're Nestler!"

"I reckon twenty-five now. . . ."

"Crane sent me. I'm here because of Crane!"

"Sorry. Don't know no Crane. Fifteen seconds, miss."

"An American! You worked with him on a job two weeks ago, a little less maybe. Two crates smuggled out of Pine Gap."

Nestler's eyebrows flickered. "Back!" he screamed at his creatures.

A few of the crocs sauntered reluctantly away. The rest continued to eye her hungrily.

"Back, I say!"

The rest followed suit after hissing as if to challenge Nestler's orders.

"I raised these babies," the tall man said, folding his shotgun neatly over his forearm as he advanced closer. "Folks say no way they can be trained. I say bloody bull. Anyway, miss, you got my attention." He leaned over and picked up her gun, but he wasn't ready to hand it back to her yet.

"You remember Crane."

"Called himself Mr. Bird."

"It figures."

" 'Scuse me, miss?"

"Nothing. I'm here because I've got to find out where those crates went after they left Australia."

Nestler eyed her warily. "What makes it your problem?"

"My friend died because of those crates, Mr. Nestler," Chimera said, only half lying. "It was important to him that the contents get back to their rightful owner, and that makes it important to me. I owe him. He saved me a long time ago."

"Saved your life, did he?"

"You could say that."

Nestler didn't bother to press. "Yeah, he was a good bloke. Up front all the way. Paid me more than was fair. Say, just what do I call you?"

"Crane called me Matty. Short for Matira."

"What was his name, Crane or Bird?"

"Neither. People like us don't use our real names. We choose another that somehow fits the way we are, the way we work."

"What's yours?"

"Chimera."

"What's that?"

"A mythological dragon formed of various parts from other creatures."

"Any of them croc, miss?"

"Sorry."

"Too bad. But I won't hold it against you, Matty." Nestler knelt down and stroked one of the slower-retreating crocodiles. "Wrestled them when I was a boy. Got a hundred scars to show for it, but that's when I started to figure they could be trained. Wrestlin' with 'em, I could swear they had their chances to kill me. But they didn't 'cause they were havin' too much fun." Nestler stroked another. "Lots of the time they get older, they get too ornery to keep. This lot's the best of the bunch. I'm too old to train a new batch, so I'll die with these."

"But you were ready for someone to come. You were *expecting* someone to come."

"Damn right, miss. After what happened, I figured somebody might be payin' me a visit."

"What are you talking about?"

"You come here about Pine Gap, you should know."

"I came about Crane and what he brought out of Pine Gap."

"Then you got a problem, Matty mate, 'cause it ain't there anymore."

"What isn't?"

"Pine Gap."

Chimera looked at Kirby Nestler dumbstruck.

"It's gone. Big hole in the ground where it used to be, and for plenty of miles beyond. My figurin' was, somethin' your friend did made it happen. So I decided anybody catches on, they might come alookin'."

"But you stayed," Chimera said, still trying to collect her thoughts.

Nestler's eyes swept about his crocs. "Anywhere I can't take all these bastards, I don't go. You follow? You understand friendship, loyalty, so I guess you do."

"What happened at Pine Gap?"

"Blew itself to hell and took a good chunk of the world with it. All that's left is a hole that maybe goes all the way to the other side. Take ya a million days to spit across it. Course, they told the damn country it was an earthquake. Area's sealed up tight as a wanker's backside, but you can't keep nothin' secret from the Aborigines since they talk to the land. Land musta told 'em the truth, Matty mate."

"Think the land can tell them where those crates ended up?"

"Not quite, but somethin' else might interest ya some. The hole left where Pine Gap was ain't all the Aborigines been talkin' about. Seems like an army's invaded the area and set up camp. Monster supply planes landed one after the other for a while. Americans, by the way they tell it, packin' men, machines, and miles of wire into a settlement. Aborigines call it Circuit Town."

Chimera digested these new facts, a fresh plan already forming. "Can you get me there?"

"I'm a guide, Matty mate. It's what I do."

"Wait. I'll need some supplies, not exactly run of the mill . . ." Then, after she had detailed her needs to him, "Can you do it?"

Kirby Nestler winked and handed her back her gun. "Man who trains crocs, mate, can do just about anything."

They flew north to Alice Springs by private plane. The airport in "The Alice" had been closed since the explosion that had destroyed Pine Gap, but Nestler knew the man who ran it, and made the arrangements. He also arranged for a jeep to be waiting to take them deeper into the Northern Territory and the Outback toward Pine Gap.

They drove northwest out of The Alice on the Tatami Road, the heat growing more intense and the air drier as they plunged farther into the Outback of the Simpson Desert.

"Don't let this fool ya, Matty mate," Nestler advised. "Tonight when we hit Circuit Town, you'll need a jacket to keep from shiverin'."

Before setting off, Nestler had spread a map over a table at the airport and traced the line of their journey with a long, thin finger, finishing near an X marked in red.

"This is—used to be—Pine Gap. She's located spittin' distance from the border with Western Australia. Way the Aborigines tell it, the crater extends through the Tropic of Capricorn south to maybe a hundred miles from Ayers Rock. North they ain't bothered to measure yet. The land we're headin' for is Aboriginal Land, and you need a pass to drive through it. I'm on good terms with them, though, so we don't have to worry."

"I notice the equipment I asked for isn't in the jeep."

"Fear not, Matty mate, it'll be there when we need it."

"We'll still have to get awfully close to Circuit Town. The risk of being seen is gonna be big, Kirby."

"Don't sweat it. We'll take cover in the hills."

"The map says the land around Pine Gap is all flats and plains."

"That's what it used to be."

An Aborigine party was waiting for them at a prearranged point two miles from Circuit Town. Its members camouflaged the jeep while Chimera and Kirby Nestler continued on their way.

Dusk had fallen, and true to Kirby's prediction, Chimera needed a jacket to ward off the chill. It had taken them over four hours to get this far, and much of the ride had been bumpy and uncomfortable. Not to mention the uncontrollable thirst that plagued Chimera. No matter how much water she drank, she could not relieve the dryness in her mouth, and she welcomed the cool night now for the relief she hoped it would provide.

The land they walked upon to reach Circuit Town was bumpy and irregular. The ground swelled in some places, dropped in others. Hills and gullies appeared where none had been two weeks ago. A few times Chimera found unfinished fracture lines in the surface of the earth itself, running like stitches across a gaping wound on the planet.

The lights of Circuit Town were visible from nearly a mile away, a dull glow growing into a luminescent haze and finally a near daytime brilliance. The closest hill overlooked the outskirts of the makeshift settlement from a hundred yards away.

"Here we are then, Matty mate," pronounced Nestler as he handed her a pair of binoculars.

She gazed down through them to find a number of Quonset huts, along with trailers and moderate-sized prefabricated buildings and tents. Everything was strictly functional, no space or manpower wasted.

Beyond Circuit Town there was, simply, nothing. A dark splotch was all she could see of the massive crater left by the explosion of Pine Gap, and even this was mostly obscured by the endless cloud of dust over it.

What could have caused this? she dared to ask herself at last, shivering from the sight of it more than the cold. *What in God's name—*

"Yup," the big man said with eyes still glued to his binoculars. "Just like the Aborigines said."

"What about the supplies I asked for?" Chimera asked him.

Nestler responded with a wink. "One computer coming up, mate."

"How?"

"The Aborigines. They stole what you need."

"From where?"

"Where else? Circuit Town."

"Should be here any minute," Nestler continued.

Since trespassers were not expected, security in and around Circuit Town was fairly thin. And even if it hadn't been, Chimera didn't doubt the Aborigines could heist the materials she requested out of the installation easily without being seen.

"Don't bother looking for the Aborigines, Matty," Nestler advised, seeming to read her thoughts. "You won't be able to see them till they're good and ready."

True to that word, the first time she saw the natives was when they appeared next to Nestler holding a dust-covered Psion laptop portable computer. Forty megabyte storage capacity. Eight-and-a-half hours of use from its battery pack. The most advanced machine of its kind and perfect for the chore of collating and analyzing data in the middle of the Outback.

"They found it in one of them buildings down there," Nestler explained. "Figured it was pretty much what you were looking for."

It was indeed. Chimera popped up the small attached monitor screen and switched the Psion on. Her hope was that all data Washington had possessed on Pine Gap would be contained inside the machine's memory for simple access on site. And since they wouldn't have expected visits from interested parties there would have been no reason to employ overly complicated passwords or entry procedures.

"You figurin' on findin' out where those crates that friend of yours took out ended up, mate?" Nestler wondered.

"If not that, at least some clue as to how he pulled it off and who on the inside might have helped him. That's a start."

Chimera brought up the disc's menu and breathed easier. It was all here, everything. She accessed the heading AVAILABLE ANALYSES first. Two clicks later, she was scanning rapidly through the single-spaced reports filed by the on-site investigative teams. Most of the data held no interest for her but one word grabbed enough of her attention to freeze her finger in place over the scan key:

Antimatter.

She peered closer, squinting, eyes training themselves.

"This can't be," she muttered. "It doesn't exist."

"What's that you're saying?"

"Antimatter," Chimera replied. "This report details the process of how it destroyed Pine Gap after being released accidently."

"Never heard of this antimatter."

"My God," Chimera followed mostly to herself, "Pine Gap must have discovered a way to safely store it, at least they thought. . . ."

"I can't hear you, Matty."

"It doesn't matter. Circuit Town would have accumulated all the data we need. Let's see if we can tap into some. . . ."

She went back to the menu and pressed out a new set of keys.

"What you doing now?" Nestler asked.

"Checking the logs the day you and Crane picked up the crates of Quick Strike. Yup, here it is. The shipment is recorded right there. I won't bother checking the inventory codes, because I know they would have been falsified."

"By who?"

"That's what I need to find out next."

Chimera knew how Crane's mind worked and how he would have gone about securing a contact on the inside. She brought up the personnel logs for the day in question and every ensuing day up until the last. No anomalies showed. All personnel were present and logged on. She felt defeated.

Where to go? *Where?*

She went back four days *prior* to the day of the shipment and found the same result. Everyone was accounted for. Pine Gap personnel worked in three-month shifts without ever leaving the complex. Crane couldn't possibly have penetrated that security, nor would he have tried, so where would he have thought to look for someone who could? Very likely it would be someone who'd just completed his final rotation. His or her name would thus have been removed from the personnel logs. The person would be free to act, knowing that he or she would never be returning to Pine Gap again.

Chimera's fingers started across the keyboard beneath the light of Nestler's flashlight once more.

"What you got, Matty?"

"I'm not sure yet. Let's see. . . ."

She was bringing up a list of all those personnel whose last rotations ended within a week of the shipment Crane had brought out of Pine Gap. Five names flashed across the screen, along with their last known civilian addresses.

"One of 'em got a funny mark by his name," Nestler noted. "What's it mean?"

"That he's dead, apparently," Chimera answered, seeing it, too. "Let's see if we can prod out the details. . . . The man was killed, along with his son, in a car accident two days after the shipment went out and two days before Pine Gap blew."

"Guess that leaves us with only four."

"No, Kirby. I found what I came for."

"The dead man?"

"They killed him because he was a part of this, just like they killed Crane. But he may have left something behind. Time to go, Kirby," she said, checking the dead man's address. "We're heading to Melbourne."

CHAPTER 18

"ANSWER my question, Mr. Danzig."

The diplomatic attaché saw the cold resolve on Jamie's features and simply shrugged. "It's procedure."

"Two armed guards outside the door of someone who just wandered in?"

"You didn't just wander in," the attaché corrected. His name was Danzig and he looked to be about the same age as Jamie. "You were brought in by American military advisers after a high-speed boat chase across the Coco River."

"Semantics."

"Procedure," Danzig repeated. "In case you've forgotten, you landed on our doorstep with what, by your own admission, was a pretty wild story, remember?"

"All of which is true," Jamie said as he eased himself forward. "Just tell me when I can go home."

"We're making the arrangements. As soon as possible, I assure you."

" 'As soon as possible' ended after my first night here. I've told you what I came to tell you, and I don't want to sound ungrateful. I've just had enough with Central America. Excuse me for not wanting to see the rest of Honduras."

Danzig shrugged and took his leave.

The little of the country Jamie had seen was a dim flutter in his memory. The explosions and fire on the other side of the Coco River had drawn plenty of Honduran troops to the shore to greet his arrival. Jamie beached the speedboat and called desperately for the soldiers to come help him with Alex and Alberto. Both were wounded, though far from mortally, and a helicopter flew them all to a military base, where the boys would be cared for.

The same helicopter brought Jamie to an airfield where a dark sedan was waiting for him with Danzig in the backseat. Jamie had steadfastly refused to say anything to anyone until he reached the U.S. Embassy in Tegucigalpa, so the ride was made in silence. He was given a room at the embassy with a shower and left alone to feel human again. When he came out, a doctor was summoned to re-dress his knife wound and tape up his damaged ribs. Then Jamie dressed in a fresh set of clothes Danzig had obtained for him.

He lay down on the bed just to rest and didn't open his eyes again until darkness took over the room, except for a single low-watt bulb. Someone had drawn the blinds while he was asleep. He realized he had been stirred finally by someone knocking at the door, and rose to answer it.

"Everything all right, Mr. Skylar?" Danzig asked.

"Everything except you calling me mister," Jamie said sleepily. "Call me Jamie. What were you doing out there, standing guard?"

"You're our guest, Jamie. I wanted to be around when you came to. We have to talk. Remember?"

Jamie tried to stretch. "God, I still hurt everywhere. What time is it?" He gazed at the drawn blinds.

"Eight o'clock. You've been out for six hours. I thought you might like something to eat."

"You thought right. How about the biggest steak you can lay your hands on?"

"Done," Danzig said, and moved to the phone on Jamie's nightstand.

"We can talk while I eat."

Danzig asked permission to tape their conversation, and Jamie gobbled up his food, speaking between mouthfuls. For a time, Danzig stopped him for questions, then simply settled back and listened, transfixed by the tale. In all, it took two hours to relate both the chronology of his flight and the various claims made by Chimera as to what she perceived to be going on.

"When can I go home?" Jamie asked at the end.

"As soon as the ambassador okays it."

"Okays what?"

"Just a formality. He's only just returned to the embassy. I'll have your statement transcribed overnight and on his desk with his breakfast."

But now the morning was already half gone, and not a word had been mentioned about his going home. It reminded Jamie curiously, and fearfully, of the treatment Captain Maruda had afforded him back in Nicaragua. Put up a polite front while killers were waiting in the wings. This might have been the American Embassy, but he was a stranger who was way out of his league, and there were guards outside his door. Why? To keep him safe or to keep him where he was?

Stop it! Stop it!

But paranoia reached out and grabbed him, like a cold hand in the middle of the night. A knock broke off his thinking.

"I'm back, Jamie," the attaché, Danzig, announced, and opened the door. "We're going upstairs."

"It's about damn time."

Danzig led him down the hall, the two guards not far behind. There was a strange expression on his face, almost fearful. They climbed two flights, bypassing the arrows for "Ambassador's Office" on the third floor for a conference room on the fourth. It featured a long dark wood table and separate sitting area. Danzig led Jamie to a couch and had barely taken a chair for himself when the door opened again. Danzig bounded up as if launched by a spring. A man with thick salt-and-pepper hair and wearing a dark suit strode purposefully forward with a file folder under his arm. He had the stiff walk of a soldier used to standing at attention, and he strode by Danzig without acknowledging his presence.

"I'm Gordon Richards, Mr. Skylar. Director of operations,'' the man said, and took the hand Jamie had reluctantly extended.

''I was expecting the ambassador,'' said Jamie.

''Indisposed,'' Richards told him. ''I'll be handling you.''

''What do you mean 'handling' me?''

''Getting you safely home. That is what you want, isn't it?''

''And that's what a director of operations does?''

Richards forced a smile. ''Among other things.''

''You don't have a tan.''

The remark caught Richards off guard. ''What did you say?''

''I said you don't have a tan. Everyone else here could pose for a Coppertone ad, and you barely qualify as Casper the Friendly Ghost. Or, excuse me, spook.''

''You finished?''

''Close. Your suit's wrinkled, Mr. Director of Operations. Looks like it's been through a long plane ride. How's the weather in Washington?''

Richards's eyes flared in Danzig's direction. ''I think you can leave us now.''

''I think you can stay,'' Jamie followed instantly, and the attaché looked suspended in midair until Richards's grudging nod bid him to retake his seat.

''This is a delicate situation, Mr. Skylar,'' Richards said next. ''Your celebrity makes it even more delicate.''

''Really? How so?''

''That's what I'm here to explain.''

''I thought you were here to get me home.''

''One is directly linked to the other.''

''I'm being debriefed. That's the word for it, isn't it? Hasn't the CIA got anything better to do? Christ, I already told Danzig everything. Just read the transcript.''

Richards's eyes were frigid. ''I already have. Last night. It's why I came down personally.''

''Well, I'd like to see the ambassador personally,'' Jamie said, and pushed himself back to his feet.

''The ambassador does not wish to see you.''

"Maybe he wants to see the Redskins next time the Giants are in town. . . ."

"Sit down, Mr. Skylar."

"Tough tickets to come by, even for you diplomatic types. But then, you're not a diplomatic type, are you, Mr. Richards?"

"Please, sit down."

Jamie's eyes met those of Gordon Richards. What he saw in those eyes scared him enough to silence him. He may have handled 300-pound linemen who'd spent their lives with barbells, but Richards was a whole other species, maybe not as strong but plenty more dangerous. He remained expressionless. Finally he spoke very quietly.

"Sit down, please."

Jamie complied and heard Danzig let out the heavy breath he'd been holding.

"What do you know about your sister, Mr. Skylar?" Richards asked.

"I know that she's dead."

"What about before?"

"She was a journalist. Great reputation. Won a few prizes. Never made much money like her kid brother, who got himself suspended from the league."

"She worked for us," Richards said, and the blow to Jamie felt like a blindside tackle. "CIA, Mr. Skylar, for the last five years. Her code name was Sapphire. Look, I know this isn't easy for you, but the truth is, she was a top operative in Dry Affairs."

"Nonviolent infiltration assignments," Richards added after a pause.

"It got plenty violent." Jamie was dimly aware of his body sliding back into the couch.

"Not her specialty. Minimal training at best. Unfortunate. Someone more seasoned could have survived Casa Grande."

"Jesus Christ . . ."

"She was with Riaz because we made it possible. She was spying on him and forces he was connected to, namely a Sandinista backed organization called the Nicaraguan National Solidarity Committee, the whole time."

"She was . . . in love with him."

"A front, most of it anyway. We—I—needed her down there to keep her eye on the diehard members of the NNSC. We knew it was only a matter of time before they moved in a big way against the Chamorro government and I don't have to tell you that wouldn't be in the best interests of the United States."

"Yes, you do."

Richards just kept talking. "Then word reached us that they were planning something all right, except it was aimed directly at us. The goal of their operation was to destroy the Accords and the present government along with them. Get us out and Chamorro follows in turn went the thinking and your sister was already in place to uncover the means." Richards took a deep breath. "We knew you had survived the massacre. We did everything we could to find you, but no one knew anything. Everything became clear when I read your statement."

"Not to me," Jamie muttered.

"Excuse me?"

"I said not to me. Why were you looking for me, Mr. Richards? How did you even know I was in Nicaragua?"

"Because we arranged that, too," Richards continued as Jamie's features twisted in disbelief. "The couriers and conduits who relayed your sister's intelligence were uncovered and killed. We needed another means, a contingency, that would allow her to get whatever she was on to out to us." Richards hesitated. "You were that contingency."

"You son of a bitch!" Then, as quickly as the rage had fired in him, Jamie felt a numbing calm. "The suspension . . ."

"Our work as well, yes," Richards confirmed. "We simply took advantage of the situation presented. If it hadn't been that, it would have been something else."

"I'll bet. But the telegram . . . You knew I'd go down there. How could you know?"

"Your sister. She knew. Using you was her idea, Jamie."

Jamie got up and paced to the wall. "I can't believe this. . . ." Again confusion pasted itself over his features.

"But you didn't come down here out of a guilty conscience, Mr. Richards. You don't give a shit about me."

Richards's features grew reflective. "I gave a shit about your sister. I was her control. I placed her with Riaz. I set it all up."

"You killed her."

"No. I got her killed. Maybe it's the same thing. You can be the judge, but first you've got to help me. And her."

"I'd say she's beyond it."

"Her work was everything. It didn't die with her."

"What the fuck are you talking about?"

"Listen to me, Jamie. The massacre was only part of a much greater whole. You've already figured that much out for yourself, but you don't know it all any more than we do. Sapphire—Beth—was the only one on to the whole truth, and she would have made sure that truth made it out even if she didn't."

"How?"

"She had equipment: recording, processing—you name it. All capable of storing material on miniature microchips. The network of couriers had been bringing them out. That's how we were able to learn what little we do know." Richards took a deep breath. "We searched the farm, Jamie. There's a chip missing, a recording chip."

Jamie looked at the CIA man incredulously. "You think she gave it to me?"

"I know she gave *something* to you."

"If she did, I left it in Nicaragua." Jamie raised his arms to better make his point. "Hell, these aren't even my clothes."

"You were the contingency, *her* contingency, remember? She wouldn't have called you down there if she wasn't sure she had a foolproof way of getting the chip out with you. We would have been waiting when you came back . . . if all had gone as planned."

"It didn't. Jesus, listen to what you're saying. She could have put the chip anywhere. My luggage maybe, and in case you haven't noticed, I'm traveling light."

Richards shook his head. "She would have placed it where it would never leave your person."

Jamie came back to the couch, his memory stirring. "In the jungle, Chimera knew the soldiers had come for me, but she didn't know why. This explains it, doesn't it?"

"Part of it," the CIA man acknowledged as he opened the manila folder resting on the coffee table before them and removed a single eight-by-ten black-and-white headshot. "Is this the woman you knew in Nicaragua as Chimera?"

Jamie took the photo. It was a bit blurred, and although many of the features were different, he could tell it was indeed Chimera.

"Yes," he replied.

"Her real name is Matira Silvaro. She's a former operative of ours, too, except the affairs she handled were very wet, quite different from your sister. She turned rogue five years ago after killing four innocent people. She went underground for a while and then resurfaced under the anonym Chimera. We've been able to link her to at least a half-dozen politically motivated assassinations. Strictly top-drawer stuff. She always was one of the best Division Six had to offer."

"Division Six?"

"Wet Affairs," Richards elaborated.

"She saved my life. . . ."

"And gave you information linking what your sister had uncovered in Nicaragua to something much greater."

"A shadow government behind the government about to move out of the shadows. They had a plan to take over the country, Chief, and Chimera was convinced the massacre happened to make Riaz a part of it. You telling me you didn't know about this?"

"About the Nicaraguan National Solidarity Committee's part in it—yes. About another group manipulating the NNSC—no. If Matira—"

"Chimera," Jamie corrected.

"If *she* is right about this shadow government, then they must be using the NNSC to accomplish their ends for them. A plant on the inside speaking their words, maybe even proposing *their* plan."

"Wait," Jamie said suddenly. "I'm remembering something, the last thing Chimera said to me." His eyes sharpened and bore into Richards's. "She said to tell you they had the explosives from Pine Gap. The Quick Strike."

All of Richards's features seemed to freeze. "You're certain she said Quick Strike?"

"Absolutely."

"Did she say how much?"

"No. What is it? What does it mean?"

Richards looked at him, the stare more telling than any words he could have mustered. "It means we know what they're planning to hit us with, and we've got to find out where and when. You're our only hope to do that, Jamie."

Jamie got up again, nervous now, needing to move. "But I don't have the microchip. Goddamnit, I don't have it! I'd tell you if I did. You've got to believe that!"

"I do. But your sister was a pro. If you could find the chip, it stands to reason the enemy could as well. So she would have put it somewhere only we could find it. Taking that into account, we're not going to look until we get you to a safer place."

"As in the U.S. of A.?"

"You're going home, Jamie."

CHAPTER 19

"I'M here about your husband," Chimera said to the woman who opened the door to the sixth-floor apartment in a fashionable Melbourne high-rise.

With the help of Kirby Nestler and his trusty pilot friend, she had made the long, tiring trip here straight from Pine Gap. By late Tuesday afternoon she had found the address of the late Sam J. Minniefield, the Pine Gap worker she felt sure had been Crane's contact inside.

Minniefield's building was jammed between other concrete and glass monoliths in the city's downtown district. Finding the proper apartment and negotiating the lobby were both simple affairs. The only person who gave her so much as a second glance was a janitor dressed in blue overalls. Then he, too, dismissed her and went back to his chores.

"What about my husband?" the woman inside the apartment asked.

"It's rather complicated. If we could talk inside . . ."

"*What* about my husband?"

Chimera gazed into the eyes peering out at her above the chain. "Mrs. Minniefield, I believe your husband was murdered. Those same people have been trying to kill me, and plenty more are going to die unless I can find out who they are."

"Murdered? But my, my . . ."

"Yes, Mrs. Minniefield, your son, too."

"My God . . ."

"Let me in. Please."

The door closed again, and she heard the woman fidgeting with the chain lock. At length she swung it open for Chimera to enter. Chimera stepped into a moderately sized and furnished apartment. Everything was neatly arranged and tidily made up. No dust or dirt. The burnt orange pile carpeting was streaked with the marks of a vacuum. There were bookshelves and an entertainment center. The kitchen was open to the living area and featured a long U-shaped counter island. It, too, was immaculate. Chimera smelled air freshener, sufficient to have wiped out any trace of what Mrs. Minniefield had made herself for lunch.

"We can talk in the living room," she said, and guided Chimera toward it.

Nervously Fran Minniefield seated herself on the couch. The woman held her hands between her knees, rubbing her palms together constantly.

"I know how hard this must be for you," Chimera began, as she settled into a chair opposite Mrs. Minnefield.

"No, you don't. You couldn't."

"I don't mean the loss you've suffered. I mean listening to me."

"The police said it was an accident. I knew better, I did. Sam was too careful a driver, especially with Jory in the car. Who did it? Who are these people?"

"Your husband worked for them. He didn't realize it, but he did."

"My husband worked for Pine Gap!"

"As an inventory control officer. Yes, I know. That was why he was retained, that and the fact that his tour was about to end."

"Why *who* retained him? To do what?"

"Smuggle something out of the installation."

"That's impossible!"

"He found a way, and after he did, after he had outlived his usefulness, they killed him."

"No!"

"Your husband's tour at Pine Gap ended two weeks ago. But he stayed on unofficially for several days afterwards, didn't he?"

"Yes," came the woman's reluctant reply.

"Could your husband have left anything . . . some papers perhaps, something in a safety deposit box?"

"No, I tell you! *No!*" She rose, trembling. "I want you out of here now."

"Mrs. Minniefield—"

"Don't call me that. Don't call me anything. I don't know you. You come here with an incredible story and expect me to—I don't know what you expect, and I don't care. Just get out before I call the police."

Chimera was about to protest but thought better of it. She didn't wait for the widow to show her the door. She turned back once on her way to it as if to speak, then shrugged and let herself out.

Shaking visibly, Fran Minniefield moved into the kitchen and set the water to boil for tea. She was spooning her usual three sugars into a cup when the door opened and the janitor with the blue overalls entered.

"Well?" he asked.

"She knows. Everything almost."

"Who the bloody hell is she?"

"She didn't say exactly. Not one of those the old man told us to look out for, though. I'm pretty sure of that." She paused. "There'll be others now. It's only a matter of time."

"Then the sooner we get out of here, the better," responded the man, striding down the hallway.

Fran Minniefield stormed after him. "But you said we should listen to the old man. Do what he told us."

"It isn't safe anymore."

She reached out and hugged him. "I'm scared. Oh God, I'm scared. . . ."

The teakettle's whistle prevented them from hearing the

door open and close again, followed by the soft footsteps toward them as they embraced.

"You should be, Mr. and Mrs. Minniefield," said Chimera.

"How did you guess?" the man dressed as a janitor asked.

"I had a feeling from the start because I know how Crane, the old man as you call him, would have worked it out. Then there was something about the apartment that bothered me. Not what I saw, but what I didn't see: children's toys."

The Minniefields looked at each other, then at Chimera.

"There weren't any around," Chimera continued. "When a child dies, parents never clean up all his toys. They leave them about as if it might bring him back. But if he's not dead, if he's off visiting relatives somewhere, then he'd have to take his toys with him."

Sam Minniefield swallowed hard. "You got kids of your own, do you, miss?"

"No," said Chimera quietly.

Minniefield's arm slid firmly around his wife's shoulder. "We'd like to see our boy grow up. If that's not to be, we hope you'll at least leave him alone."

"I'm not here to kill you. Otherwise, you'd be dead already. I'm here to help, just like I told your wife."

"I don't follow you."

"This is all starting to make sense to me now. Crane taught you how to rig the car accident so everyone would believe you were dead."

Minniefield nodded. "How do I know you know this Crane fellow? How do I know you're working with him?"

"He was in his late fifties, early sixties maybe, but he might have looked even older. His hands were bad."

"Called himself Mr. Bird."

Chimera couldn't help but smile again at Crane's private sense of humor at work. "He meant a lot to me. He was my friend and a whole lot more. He died because of what you were a part of, Mr. Minniefield. He changed the scenario because he wanted to see that you and your family lived." Chimera paused. "You smuggled two crates of Quick Strike charges out of Pine Gap for him. When he realized what they were to be used for, he changed his mind and tried to get them back. But he failed and was killed. Now I'm taking over for him."

"But I have no idea where they are. How can I help you get them back?"

"You've got to try. Everything's changed: the stakes, the costs—everything. What have you heard of Pine Gap lately?"

"Nothing. I've been lying low."

"It's gone."

Sam Minniefield's features froze.

"I was there. All that's left is a crater, an abyss, in the center of this country."

"The earthquake," Sam Minniefield said, realizing now the story of it had been a hoax. He looked closer at her. "But only one thing we were working on could have that kind of effect."

"Antimatter," from Chimera. "An accidental release was what destroyed Pine Gap. But it was Quick Strike you smuggled out for Crane."

"Yes. A new type of explosive, it was. Incredible density. Each charge could manage the same destruction as maybe two hundred pounds of C-4 plastic explosives. It's light, undetectable, and easily carried. Short of an atomic bomb, the most powerful explosive ever developed."

"You're describing the ideal weapon for a terrorist."

"Or *anti*terrorist, which is what it was conceived for. 'Infiltration devices' was the phrasing, I think. One man could walk onto a base and level it with a single charge carried in a briefcase or a knapsack, without leaving any nuclear-type residue." Minniefield paused. "Your friend gave me some notions how to pull the heist off. I altered inventories on the computer and created a shipment that didn't exist so that the eight charges could be delivered to him."

"Eight?" Chimera raised, noting the number was different from the one Crane had provided in New York. "But twelve were smuggled out, six to a crate."

"That's . . . not possible," Minniefield returned unsurely.

"Crane wouldn't have been wrong about something like that."

"Twelve," he muttered, then his face went pale as something came together in his head. "Twelve . . . Oh Christ, no. It can't be! *It can't be!*"

"What can't be? What are you talking about?"

Minniefield's breathing had picked up, almost to the point of hyperventilation. He looked panicked.

"You're sure about Pine Gap? You're sure antimatter was to blame for its destruction?"

"Yes."

"An accidental release," the man said, repeating her words from before. "A containment shell opened because they thought it was something else, a containment shell that had been mislabeled and stored in the wrong place, on the *wrong level*!"

"You're saying that the additional four canisters actually contain *antimatter*?"

"Yes! My God, yes," Minniefield said rapidly. "Listen to me, Quick Strike's unstable properties made us use virtually the same ceramic construction for its canisters we used for the antimatter containment shells. Do you understand what that means? These containment shells were almost identical in appearance to the Quick Strike canisters." His voice became soft and reflective. "Somehow when I altered the inventories, I must have ordered them moved. The computers would have taken care of everything from there, even relabeled the shells accordingly."

"Then they opened a containment shell they thought was a Quick Strike charge at Pine Gap," Chimera surmised.

"And as soon as it was released into contact with regular matter, the explosion resulted and the installation was gone."

"Not all the installation, though," reminded Chimera. "Twelve canisters had already made an unscheduled trip out, and four of them contain antimatter. But whoever has them doesn't know that. They *couldn't* know that. What happens when they detonate, Mr. Minniefield? What happens then?"

Minniefield looked clearly terrified. "An explosion simultaneously releasing the contents of four containment shells would be beyond comprehension. . . ."

Minniefield stopped when a loud buzzing filled the room.

"Someone's downstairs," said his wife.

"Let them go on buzzing," Chimera instructed.

"Them," noted Sam Minniefield. "You were expecting this, damnit!"

"Do you want to see your son again?" Chimera challenged.

"What do you mean?"

"Answer me!"

"Of course," the husband answered for both of them.

"Then you've got to do exactly as I say. By the letter. No deviation. Clear?"

The couple nodded in unison. Chimera's thoughts were coming fast. The assailants downstairs had come here because they had traced her steps. But they wouldn't have rung the bell if they had known she was already here.

"We're going to get out of this," she assured the Minniefields.

"How?"

"You've got to do exactly as I say." A short burst of the buzzer sounded again. "You're going to the stairs. You'll wait for me in the stairwell and then we'll walk down together."

"Right up to them? No!"

"*Trust me!* You trusted Mr. Bird, and that's the only reason you're alive now. Now you've got to trust me!"

Sam Minniefield shrugged. "All right. Just tell me what to do."

"Take those overalls off. They might be looking for them if they've got things figured the same way I did." Chimera realized her use of Circuit Town's computer might have been discovered. It would be a simple matter from there to discern exactly what she had learned and piece together her trail that way. "Take nothing with you," she advised. "It'll be a while before you can come back; but it doesn't matter. You'll live to be with your son. That's what matters. Into the corridor. *Now!* They'll be coming."

Resisting no further, although clearly terrified, the Minniefields advanced into the corridor, with Chimera right behind them.

"Lock the door," she ordered Minniefield. "If they come this far, it'll slow them down."

The man did as he was told. Chimera pointed toward the stairwell.

"Quickly! Move!"

The door beneath the EXIT sign was still closing when she found the fire alarm. The shrill wail began instantly, a blaring, ear-wrenching screech that made her flinch. Perfect. It was the end of a working day, and the streets would be thronged with people returning home.

Chimera bolted toward the stairwell and joined the Minniefields.

"What now?" the husband asked.

"We wait."

"Wait? For what?"

As if in answer to his question, the descending crowd, alerted by the alarm, circled down upon them at a well-paced clip. Chimera drew the Minniefields into the crowd, and they were lost in the descent.

"They'll know what I look like," Sam J. Minniefield muttered fearfully. "They'll know what *you* look like."

"Of course."

"Give me a gun," Minniefield demanded. "I'm good with guns."

"No guns. We'd never get them all. You don't know how these people work."

"Then what do we do?"

"I've taken care of it."

Reaching the swell of bodies in the lobby, Chimera was able to see out into the street. The already cluttered traffic had snarled to a halt amid a chorus of raging horns and distantly approaching sirens. She saw the two green delivery trucks double-parked, one behind the other, on the other side of the street, with a van a few spaces in front of them. Coming around one of the trucks was the lanky shape of Kirby Nestler.

Chimera grabbed the arms of both Minniefields. ''Keep it slow until I tell you to move.''

Nestler was out of sight now, but the rear doors of his trucks had been raised open.

''When I tell you, move through the door and leave the area. Make sure you separate. Don't look back and don't look at each other. Don't move any faster than everyone else. Blend in. Is there a place you can meet up?''

''Yes,'' from Fran Minniefield. ''Barney's Pub.'' Her eyes strayed to her husband. ''Where we first met.''

''Tonight at eight o'clock. Not before. Do you hear me?''

Both nodded.

They had reached the center of the lobby when Chimera saw the first crocodile. It dropped from the truck to the pavement with a light splat, followed by dozens of other similar sounds as the occupants of both trucks spilled out. It took a while for the crowd of bystanders gathering on this side of the street to notice them, but they were alerted finally by the screams of passersby across the way. They began to disperse, slowly at first and then more quickly as the creatures maneuvered through stalled traffic. Those tenants exiting the building joined the flight as the creatures slithered toward the sidewalk, jaws clapping from side to side. Traffic skidded to a screeching halt. Some drivers rolled up their windows and locked their doors. Others abandoned their cars and tore away down the street with the crowd.

''Go!'' Chimera urged, shoving the Minniefields ahead of her out through the lobby doors.

The couple did just as she had instructed them and darted in opposite directions with the fleeing crowd. As quick as that, they had disappeared.

Nestler's crocs were pawing their way over the sidewalk now, further scattering the mass of bystanders. Since the crocs were merely rushing at the people in their way, it was clear to Chimera that Nestler had fed them just before boarding the trucks. But they weren't her major problem in any case.

She knew somewhere in the crowd was the backup for the Outsider team that was certain to have already entered the building. The chaos and panic were working in her favor, but those advantages would last only as long as it took for the Outsiders still out here to recognize her.

With that in mind, her first objective was to reach the safety promised by Nestler's trucks. She had started toward them when a pair of gunshots burned into her ears. A man who had rushed in front of her in that instant crumpled to the sidewalk. Chimera dodged his falling frame, while those immediately behind her tripped over it. Her eyes swept the area but found nothing. The Outsiders had mixed with the crowd as well, guns already hidden, impossible to pick out. They knew who she was, had been warned about her. Show themselves and they'd be dead in a heartbeat.

A surge from the side pushed Chimera forward into a man who had fallen, and she toppled to the ground. Her fall brought her within breathing distance of a hissing croc with jaws open. Strangely, that gave her an idea.

Chimera pushed herself up, preparing to break away from the mass enclosing her. She saw a slight crack in the crowd and bolted through it into the center of two dozen crocodiles pawing through the street, several having risen atop stopped cars. She zigzagged through the minefield of chopping teeth in the hope it would make the remaining Outsiders expose themselves.

A monstrous croc rose up before her, and Chimera leaped atop a car hood to avoid its jaws. Another was waiting for her when she leaped downward, and her lunge carried her just out of snapping range. Behind her a car window exploded under the force of a bullet. A series of shots fired in rapid succession forced her to dive for cover amidst the crawling crocs, where she steered clear of one snarling snout only to turn headlong into another.

Chimera pulled out her pistol. She was starting to rise when blood exploded in a jet from the back of the croc nearest her. The creature twisted and snapped at the air, hissing horribly.

"*Son of a bitch!*" a voice wailed from the other side of the street.

She caught only a quick glimpse of Kirby Nestler's elephant gun before its huge barrel erupted. The Outsider who had shot his crocodile was blown backward into a car windshield. The glass spider-webbed as the blood from his torn insides spread downward and followed the lines. The barrel erupted again and a second Outsider's head exploded, showering the remnants of the panicked crowd with blood and brains. Confusion ran with the chaos now; there were bullets to be avoided as well as crocs. The final Outsider lunged from within the mass. Out of Kirby's line of vision, but not hers.

Chimera pumped two bullets at him, hedging her aim with the rampaging crowd to consider. The one bullet on line merely grazed him, but the man tumbled toward the waiting jaws of an angry, frightened croc. The man tried to push himself back, but the beast lunged and closed its teeth around his head.

Nestler was by her side now, helping her up. A stiff whistle from him had all the crocs circling back for the ramps he had lowered from the trucks. The one who had clamped onto the last Outsider was dragging his writhing body across the street. Police and fire officials were closing fast, but the snarl of traffic had proved an impenetrable obstacle. Kirby urged his ungainly troops up the ramps of the trucks, hoisting the wounded one in himself. When he climbed into the van Chimera was already sitting in the passenger seat.

She motioned for him to wait before pulling off, and kept her attention on the doors to the apartment building. Among the last to emerge were a pair of men who looked utterly dumbstruck by the carnage, the last of the Outsiders returning empty-handed from the Minniefields' apartment. Despite the shock of seeing their dead cohorts, they didn't linger. They knew the procedure to be followed in such an event.

Chimera watched them climb into an illegally parked Alfa Romeo.

"Let's go," she said, and Nestler pulled out into traffic.

"We headed anywhere special?"

"Wherever they go will do just fine. It won't be long. That's a given. Hand me the binoculars."

Nestler changed lanes and came within four cars of the

white Alfa Romeo. Chimera knew that procedure for its occupants now required a report to be made to the proper parties. But those proper parties had no idea what she had learned and what The Outsiders had been ultimately responsible for:

Four of the canisters stolen from Pine Gap contained antimatter!

She considered that for the first time. Crane had been right all along, more right than he could have possibly imagined. As bad as he had deemed things, they were worse. People were going to die in untold numbers if the shadowy group in possession of the canisters intended to use them. And Chimera had no doubt it did, for it never would have gone through such an elaborate heist unless that was the full intention.

The Alfa passed the first of several outdoor pay phones, and Chimera had started to worry when the car's driver pulled round a corner and parked. The man in the passenger seat climbed out and headed for a phone attached to a brick building between a deli and a clothier.

''Pull over,'' she told Nestler.

By the time he had swung into a red tow-zone, Chimera had the binoculars pressed against her eyes. She had sunk low, head just high enough over the window ledge to see out of the van.

The pay phone was a dial variety, and the binoculars were powerful enough to flesh out the shape of the man dialing but not the numbers themselves. Chimera calculated it for herself by counting the holes the gunman was working his fingers through. She memorized the numbers one after the other. It was an in-country call, but to another region of Australia. She could see the man's lips moving now.

Forty seconds was all it took to give his report. The speaker hung up and returned to his car. An instant later the Alfa was back in traffic and Kirby Nestler was gunning the van's engine.

''No need, Kirb,'' Chimera told him.

''Got what you need, have ya?''

''Let's get to another phone, one a bit more private, and I'll find out.''

There was no rush. Time had to be allotted for the proper

wheels to be set in motion. Nestler brought her to the nearest hotel, where she found a bank of lobby phone booths. Chimera inserted a coin to gain an outside line and then dialed in an access code that patched her directly into the AT&T international system without any sign or record. The number she dialed was the computer resource center of INTERPOL, the international police organization she had learned how to access years before.

"*Enter desired entry area at the tone,*" a computerized monotone instructed.

beep . . .

"Seven, zero, Charlie."

"*Thank you.*"

"Phone bank," greeted an actual voice seconds later. "State designation."

"Victor, Abel, six, one, niner, Delta."

"You are cleared. Please continue."

Chimera provided the phone number she had watched dialed.

"Location found."

"Search numbers dialed from that exchange in last fifteen minutes."

"Hold, please." It took twenty-five seconds. "Ready. Single call two minutes, twenty-nine seconds in duration. Number dialed as follows . . ."

Chimera memorized that, too, but there was something more she wanted. "Location of subject matter."

"Hold, please."

Forty seconds this time as the computer searched for the proper data feed. Such a lag told Chimera the report issued by those who had received the Outsider's had gone beyond Australia to the next link in the chain. A link who knew everything perhaps.

"Ready," came the woman's voice, and she recited the address.

CHAPTER 20

"YOU'LL be home in twelve hours," Richards said to Jamie in the backseat of the sedan as it inched its way through the Tegucigalpa traffic.

"Washington isn't my home," Jamie answered, stretching his legs as best he could. The front seat on the passenger side was loose, and every time he kicked it, it wobbled.

"You won't be there long."

"So you say."

"Your sister was a top operative, Jamie. We'll find the chip, because she would have hid it somewhere that would make it easy for us."

"Then you could have searched me here, but we're two thousand miles from home and maybe the chip doesn't make it back to Washington, right?"

"I'm playing it safe," Richards conceded.

The embassy Volvo was being driven by one of the well-dressed guards who had stood watch outside his room. The other guard sat in the passenger seat. Getting to the airport meant negotiating the snarled, hilly streets of the Honduran capital. It reminded Jamie curiously of San Francisco, a city he knew thanks only to a Giants road game earlier in the season. Motion came in brief, maddening spurts, often followed by equally maddening jolts.

The road finally leveled off in the section of the city devoted to outdoor markets. The markets had been stocked with fresh produce, and the people had come in droves to gather a share, the overflow spilling out into the streets. Many of the shops had been set up out of makeshift carts, which were nothing more than boxes with wheels connected by rope to rear-mounted steering wheels. The carts were most practical for selling, but they reduced the traffic flow to a narrow single lane on each side, leaving motorists to battle for position. Tegucigalpa's many poor hovered about the market in search of handouts. Merchants swore at them and shooed them away with brooms and sticks. The air reeked of car exhaust, and the noxious vapors seemed to gather in the valley. The car's brakes kept squeaking as the driver inched along, which added even more to the anxiety wrought by the tense silence that dominated the interior.

Jamie stretched his legs again, and once more the seat in front of him wobbled on impact.

The driver hit the brakes, and this time Jamie could see the road ahead had been totally blocked by a produce truck that had wedged itself between two parked cars while trying to negotiate a difficult turn. People stood around arguing, no one doing much of anything to rectify the situation. The poor hovered about in the hope of securing spilled refuse. Richards's eyes gazed about him in search of potential detours. Finding none, he settled back uncomfortably next to Jamie.

"I'll call for them to hold the plane if it comes to that," he said, trying to sound reassuring.

Jamie wasn't paying attention. Waiting at the airport or waiting in traffic didn't seem much different to him.

Most of the locals continued to mill about, while the beggars seized the opportunity the traffic jam provided to approach any likely-looking car for American money. The driver waved several off, but one who had approached from the front was incessant, tapping now on the passenger-side window, smiling to reveal brownish yellow teeth. The hum of the air conditioner drowned out most of his pleas, and the result was a continuous chorus of moving lips blended with the constant tapping.

"Fuck it," Richards relented. "Get rid of him."

The guard in the passenger seat moved his hand to the power window switch. Instantly the window began to glide down, rancid, exhaust-laden air flooding the air-conditioned cool of the car. Jamie's first hint that something was amiss was noted quite casually. The beggar's hands, instead of being stretched out to receive his change, were hidden below the window level. He almost paid the anomaly no heed until he saw the man's eyes were too steady, his stare focused and sure.

Jamie was already in motion when the beggar's hands came up cradling a machine pistol. He collapsed himself to the floor an instant before automatic fire splintered the car's innards. His eyes recorded the muzzle flashes and he felt the warm blood splash upon him from the ruptured head of the guard in the seat ahead of him. The beggar shot the driver and Richards with the same burst and their screams exploded with the blood.

The beggar leaned farther through the window to inspect his handiwork, fully believing his bullets had found all the occupants. Jamie's shoulder was square against the loose passenger seat, and he knew instantly what he had to do.

He rocketed the force of all his weight and strength forward and up. Not much different than striking a tackling dummy during training camp. The seat jetted forward, torn from its sprockets. Impact struck the beggar square in the face and neck, and Jamie kept shoving upward to keep him pinned. The man still held on to his machine gun but was unable to use it.

Jamie, meanwhile, rose with the seat. Reaching over and around it, he found the beggar's squirming head and cracked it hard against the windshield. The glass shattered and Jamie smashed the head forward again, all his strength behind the blow this time. The beggar's head crashed bloodily through the glass and lodged there.

Jamie's first instinct at that point was to jump out and run. But a flash of cold reason made him pause and turn back. He reached for the blood-splattered chest of Richards. The CIA man's head was tilted back, dead eyes staring at a ceiling sprayed with scarlet. Jamie forced a trembling hand into his inside suit pocket and came out with a packet containing his temporary passport and airline ticket home.

Insurance.

Then he dropped out of the car, keeping low amidst the huge snarl of traffic about him. The street was chaos, people running everywhere, cars left abandoned, and screams replacing the whine and squeal of brakes. Many of the mobile pushcarts had already been toppled, and goods spilled over onto the streets. Jamie knew other gunmen might have accompanied the beggar. They could be approaching him now, knowing him while he did not know them.

But he had the crowd.

He caught up with a swelling throng and mixed with it, moving as the people moved, screaming with them as well. He had no idea where he was in relation to the embassy, several blocks away in any case, which was too much to cover under the circumstances. He had to find a phone and call Danzig.

The throngs had spilled over onto several adjacent side streets and Jamie continued on, half expecting gunmen to steer toward him from the rear. He kept his pace brisk, ears tuned for a possible rush in any direction, knowing it would come to him the same way the sense of an imminent tackle did. But if he turned back, they would pick him out amidst the crowd.

Jamie kept walking. He slowed his pace only when he was clear of the crowds and began to search in vain for a phone booth to call the embassy from. He headed toward a boulevard dominated by buildings rising above the others he had seen so far. He prayed a hotel would be among them, a big one with a host of touchtone phones in its lobby.

His walk brought him out from the market area, and while some of the buildings grew newer and sleeker, they still had to battle neighboring shanties for space. There were no zoning regulations in Tegucigalpa, and the result was unchecked squatting on the part of the many homeless.

At last the huge marquee of the Hotel Maya caught Jamie's eye just down yet another hill. He was drawing close to it when the sign diagonally across the street caught his eye: AMERICAN EXPRESS TRAVEL OFFICE.

The first thought through his mind as he veered toward it was of the many commercials he had laughed off highlighting all the terrible things that happened to travelers. Jamie passed through the entrance and into the air-conditioned coolness of an office with three separate counters, manned by women in identical clothing. Two were available, and Jamie chose the one farthest from the door.

"I need to use your phone," he said softy. "It's an emergency."

"Yes," the woman replied in accented English. "May I see your card?"

"I don't have one. I mean, I have one; I just don't have it with me."

"Your name, please."

"It really is an emergency."

"I understand. But I still need your name."

"Jamie Skylar."

"Would that be under James?"

"No—Jamie."

"Address?"

Jamie provided it, anxiety starting to pool like acid in his stomach. He stole a glance at the door, half expecting a pair of dark figures to be standing just outside.

"Here we are," the woman announced after feeding the information into her computer terminal. "Do you need a replacement card?"

"I just need to use the phone." Again a new thought occurred to him. "I could also use some cash."

"Your card entitles you to a $2,000 advance."

"I'll take it."

"I'll just need your signature. . . ."

"What about the phone?"

"Sign here and you can make your call while I fill out the form."

She thrust a slip at Jamie, who signed it mindlessly. Then

the woman brought a phone out from beneath her station and placed it atop the counter. "Can I get the number for you?"

"Is there somewhere more . . . private?"

"I'm afraid this is the best I can do. Just tell me the number and I'll dial it."

"I don't know the number. It's the American Embassy."

The woman regarded him strangely. "That's not even eight blocks from here. If you wish, I could get you a taxi and—"

"I need to speak to someone there. I need to speak to them now."

The woman brought the phone back toward her and dialed the proper number. After the first ring, she handed the receiver to Jamie.

"American Embassy," a cheerful voice said.

"William Danzig, please."

"Who should I say is calling?"

"Jamie Skylar."

A pause.

"I'm afraid Mr. Danzig is in a meeting and cannot be disturbed."

"This is an emergency. Disturb him."

"Yes, sir."

Jamie grasped the phone base and dragged the whole apparatus as far down the counter as the cord allowed. The woman was busy filling information in on his cash requisition slip. The seconds passed and Jamie thought he was starting to have trouble breathing.

"Danzig."

"Jamie Skylar here."

"I thought they had made a mistake. Why the hell aren't you at the airport?"

"We were ambushed en route. A beggar with a machine gun. Everyone in the car is dead."

"*What?*"

"Don't make me say it again."

"Richards?"

"Everyone! I said everyone!"

"Christ, I don't know what to do. This isn't my department. Let me find someone who can help. . . ."

"No! There isn't time! For all I know, they could be watching me right now."

"Where are you?"

"American Express Travel Bureau across from the Hotel Maya."

"All right, hold tight. Or better yet, wait in the hotel lobby. I can send an embassy car with a few marines for you. That will give me time to brief someone on the fourth floor."

Richards's floor, Jamie remembered.

"No," he said suddenly. "Just you. You're the only one I trust. Don't tell anyone until I'm there."

click . . .

"What was that?" Jamie demanded.

"What was what?"

"A noise, like someone picking up another extension."

"There *is* no other extension."

"I heard it, I tell you!"

"Jamie, calm down. . . ."

"No! They heard this whole conversation. They're probably already on their way."

"You're not making any sense."

"Watching three people get shot didn't make any sense either, but it happened maybe fifteen minutes ago."

"I'm sending a car, Jamie. As soon as I get off this phone I'm sending a car. Just hang on."

"Forget it, Danzig. It's too late. I'm pulling out."

"Where? *You can't!*"

"No choice, cowboy. If they plowed through Richards and his men, how much better do you think your marines will fare?"

"It's your only chance! Listen to me, Jamie, settle down and listen."

"I'm plenty settled and I'm also going to hang up."

"No, don't! Let me give you a secure number." And, after he had recited it, "Get somewhere safe and call it in two hours. I'll have help standing by."

Jamie's mind was already out the door, but still he spoke.

"You're right, Danzig; this isn't your department. Can't you figure out they've got people planted inside? Can't you figure out that's how they nailed Richards in the street?"

"They *who*?"

"That's it for this dime, pal. Talk to you in two hours."

With time to kill before calling Danzig back, Jamie took to the streets. He walked with apparent aimlessless but there were both purpose and direction in his steps. He traversed no street more than once, and avoided smaller side streets altogether. Three times he stopped in cafés and found himself a table with his back to a wall and a view of the traffic before him. Satisfied he was not being followed, Jamie let himself linger at the last of the three cafés and ordered a pair of large Cokes. There was no ice, but the drinks were fairly cold and fountain-sweet. They soothed his desert-dry throat and relieved the powerful thirst induced by the melting heat of the city.

The café had a pay phone with instructions for use printed in English as well as Spanish. It seemed as good a place as any to call Danzig from, and he could only hope the young attaché had by now been able to arrange safe pickup for him. The force that had pursued him through Nicaragua was still after the microchip Richards had alluded to, as determined as ever to get it.

Jamie inserted some of the change obtained at the American Express office into the proper slots and dialed the number Danzig had provided. It had barely finished its first ring when it was answered.

"Jamie!" came the attaché's voice.

"Got my taxi ready?"

"I can't talk now. We've got to meet."

Jamie felt the fresh fear grip him. "What's wrong?"

"Not here. You were right, Jamie, more right than you realize."

"What's going on?"

Silence filled the line before the attaché's voice returned reluctantly. "The murders this afternoon, Richards and the others—you've been blamed for them."

The receiver nearly slipped from Jamie's hand.

"Are you there? Jamie, are you there?"

Jamie felt wobbly.

"We've got to get you out of this country. Get you back home, where this can be sorted out."

"Just do it."

"I'm working on it. No one else knows. Haven't told a soul. Listen, Richards had a temporary passport made up for you."

"I've got it. I took it from him before I left the car."

"Good thinking. Should make my work a little easier. The thing is, I'm trying to handle this alone. The whole place has been crazy all day as it is, and I doubt anyone's even noticed me."

"I just want to go home."

"A few more hours. That's all I need to—"

Danzig's voice stopped abruptly, and Jamie heard a loud thud through the receiver.

"Bill, are you there? . . . Bill!"

The phone clicked dead. The dial tone returned. Danzig was wrong: someone *had* noticed him. Jamie slid the receiver back to its hook. The café suddenly seemed very crowded, the eyes of all upon him. He backtracked in his mind. How long had he spoken with Danzig?

Long enough for the call to be traced. That much was for sure. He had to get out of here, move and keep moving until he was free of yet another country where so many wanted him dead. And now his pursuers had complicated that task no end by branding him a killer.

The embassy was looking for him. The Honduran police was looking for him. The force behind the true killers was looking for him.

Jamie moved out of the café slowly into the street, another man joining the late afternoon crowds. The woman just ahead carrying the baby might whip around with gun in hand. A knife could be thrust into his ribs by the businessman a yard to the rear.

Just keep moving.

A bus teeming with people at the corner up ahead had

started to inch its way back into traffic. Jamie sprinted the short distance to it and squeezed himself on, eyes cheating back to check for possible pursuit. There was none.

Of course, they could have reached the bus ahead of him.

Or been on it waiting for him to jump on.

The circle of madness widened around him as the bus pulled away from the curb.

CHAPTER 21

CHIMERA stood on Vienna's Kartner Street, opposite the famed Opera House. Another tour of the building would be commencing in a few minutes, and she steadied herself before moving to gain the access she so sorely required.

Kirby Nestler had helped her get out of Australia and eventually here after a maddening trek across continents and time zones. INTERPOL had pinned down the Palais Schwarzenberg as the locale of the number dialed from Australia. Located in a fashionable hotel by the same name, it was one of Vienna's most exclusive restaurants, owned and operated by a man named Leopold Fuchs, a longtime control for The Outsiders.

Like Stein, Fuchs fit the profile of an Outsider conduit perfectly. They were men of exorbitant tastes, men who formed their covers around their own indulgences. Chimera had worked for Fuchs several times when the portly little man had gone by another name in Venice. Fuchs had a taste for incredibly expensive wines and young boys. The latter had created quite a mess in Venice, and The Outsiders had resettled him here. Now, two face-lifts and a tummy tuck later, Fuchs was still operating as a top man in the network.

His well-earned reputation as a dandy made him a character wherever he settled, and Chimera was surprised that The Outsiders permitted Leopold Fuchs his eccentricities. Then again, that was the point, she supposed. Operatives like Chimera were bound to them by the fact that they had no one and nothing else. Higher-ups like Fuchs were bound to the organization because it alone knew how to keep them happy and out of trouble at the same time. All this aside, he must also have been the conduit who had handled the routing of the crates Crane had obtained from Pine Gap. Right now he was Chimera's only hope of tracking down the dozen canisters which included four antimatter containment shells.

A new production of *Don Carlo* was premiering that very night, and Chimera knew Leopold wouldn't be able to resist attending. That was where she would get him. All the materials she required for her work were contained in a cheap-looking burlap shoulder bag. Chimera had dressed herself as a student, a disguise that still came easy for her and invariably seemed to dispel suspicion.

The explosives held in her bag were crude at best. The circumstances made it impossible for her to contact dealers on the chance they had been warned to expect her presence. So she had purchased several items at a drug store and small market upon arriving and spent the night fashioning what she needed. A mini travel clock would serve as timer, crude as well, but effective.

The work had been painstaking, and the lack of sleep these past few days was beginning to tell on her. Years before, she had learned how to cram eight hours of sleep into two, but had planned to deny herself even these until she began to nod out at the most crucial—and dangerous—stage of her construction. Two hours of slumber gave way to three, and after a shower, she was barely able to finish her work by ten A.M. No way to test it, of course, at least not until the moment it had to work.

After taking Vienna's U1 subway to Karlsplatz station, she grabbed a quick breakfast at, of all places, McDonald's. She then paced about the pedestrian district studying the outer layout of the Opera House until noon came. The building remained a focus of life in Vienna, one of the chief symbols of resurgence in the wake of the city's destruction in World War II. A night of bombing had nearly destroyed it, but determination had long ago restored all the beauty of its mid-nineteenth-century construction. The Opera House's byzantine structure was formed of aged yellow granite, with hand-chiseled doorframes and ornamentations. Its multi-layered construction was clear even from the facade, but Chimera's plan required a far more thorough scrutiny once she gained entry.

The coming of noon was her signal to make the five-minute walk to the State Theater Booking Office at 3 Hanuschgasse. The Booking Office was the only place she could obtain the location of Fuchs's private box. It was closed daily during the noon-to-one lunch hour, and its front door posed only a minor impediment for her. Inside, she quickly located a steel drawer full of file cards listing the season ticket holders. A few panicked moments ensued when she found nothing under the Fs, but a check of the Ls found her quarry's box listed under "Leopold."

That information in hand, she returned to the Opera House just in time for the one-o'clock tour. She waited only to catch her breath before crossing the street to join the line forming outside. She would drift away from the group at the first available opportunity and disappear into the maze of serpentine halls and catacombs. Within lay a labyrinth of passages and rooms, no longer used and thus forgotten.

Separating herself from the tour group proved no problem, just as she expected, and she began her own exploration of the cavernous, multilayered structure. Once or twice she lost her way and had to backtrack anxiously in order to recover her bearings. She found the power box in the cellar just before two o'clock but elected not to set her explosives charge until after all the daily work crews had departed. There was always the chance they might venture down here and uncover her handiwork. By two-thirty she had found the backup box sensor, which triggered the emergency lighting once the main power died. She continued on through the corridors, charting, memorizing, imagining contingencies that might require the knowledge to be employed that evening.

Chimera hid in the dark subterranean layers of the Opera House as the day dragged on. She waited until silence claimed the corridors at five P.M. before retracing the steps that had taken her to the damp, musty tunnel. Setting her homemade explosives charge took only three minutes, and she moved immediately to the backup station controlling the emergency lights. Chimera would need total darkness when the time came, and for this she needed to "fool" the sensor. She wired a slightly modified Walkman radio into the system, designed to push current through as soon as the rest of the juice died. Still sensing incoming power, the sensor would fail to activate the emergency lights, leaving the Opera House in the total darkness she had created.

Preparation and timing was everything. For her plan to succeed, Chimera had to be just outside Fuchs's private box when the charge went off at 9:00, an hour after the start of the performance.

With the first note pounding from the orchestra, Chimera began her quick trek back to one of the serpentine hiding places, where she had stowed her toolbox. Reversed, her jacket was the same shade as that worn by the electrical crews she had glimpsed in the corridors through the afternoon. That, along with the tool pouch and belt she had brought with her, would serve as her passport, to go anywhere she wanted to go.

At 8:56 she reached the hall adjoining the one on which Fuchs's box was located. She knelt, set her tools down beside her, and pretended to work on an electrical socket. Her attention seemed riveted on the task, but her eyes were focused on the door leading into Fuchs's private stall.

8:59 . . .

Four or five men would be inside the box with him. She had a knife and her hands, and that was all she needed.

9:00 . . .

She had held her breath for a fearful instant before all the lights in the Opera House died. Chimera reached the door to Fuchs's stall in the blackness and felt his guards poised within it, effectively enclosing him. She didn't care if they caught the sound of the door opening. Once inside, they were hers.

thud . . .

"*Was war das für ein Lärm?*" she heard Fuchs demand in response to the sound of the first of his men falling. "*Was geht heir vor?*"

A thump followed, and then a gasp.

"*Wer ist da?*" Fuchs's voice was desperate now, terrified. "*Haltet sie auf!* Don't you hear me? *Stop them!*"

A snap like a bubble bursting.

A swish and then a brief gurgle swiftly extinguished.

Fuchs was about to scream when a powerful hand closed over his mouth.

"Don't move, Fuchs," a voice whispered into the dandy's ear.

"Chimera," he realized.

"You should have been expecting me after Melbourne."

"I don't know what you're talking about. There's been a mistake. Can't you see that?"

"It's dark, Fuchs." Chimera tightened her grip on the dandy. "No, I think you were expecting me. But you were so sure of your bodyguards, you got careless. They weren't bad, Fuchs."

Chimera kept her palm over Fuchs's mouth as she yanked him quickly into the corridor. The darkness was hers now, but the success of her plan demanded speed as well. Shapes were milling about them. She could sense the panic, as much her ally as the explosive charges in the basement had been. She dragged Fuchs into one of the passageways she had found and descended onto a cryptlike plateau that smelled like the sewer that ran around it. Chimera flicked on a small penlight.

"I know what you did to Crane, Fuchs, and for that, I should kill you. But I'm going to give you a chance to live."

"What do you mean?"

"I mean you can tell me about the mystery group that has the explosives Crane lifted from Pine Gap. You've been running that part of the operation from the start. Crane had started to catch on to the truth of who you were running it for. Even before Pine Gap, he had started to catch on. A shadow government, he called it, on the verge of coming out of the shadows and taking over. A quiet upheaval. A revolution going on that no one could see. Talk!"

Fuchs swallowed as hard as he dared. "They'll kill me if I do!"

Fuchs gasped when Chimera showed her knife, a strangely thin blade just visible in the thin light. "This knife is more like a razor. Peels the skin away instead of slicing. A patch at a time. The scars, Leopold, think of the scars."

"How could you?" he screeched.

"Simple. The same way you could kill Crane."

The dandy pulled back reflexively, but Chimera pressed the tip of the curved blade against his cheek.

"A revolution, yes," Fuchs said at last, "but not one that anyone will be in a position to stop. It will seem at first like a subtle shift in power voted for by your country's people." His train of thought veered. "But it doesn't matter what I tell you, because you can't stop them. Give it up while there's still a chance."

"If I give it up, Fuchs, it's the world that won't have a chance."

"What are you talking about?"

"Crane came to Australia to pick up eight Quick Strike devices. He left with an additional four mislabeled canisters containing antimatter. Your shadow government has them now, and they don't even realize it. They're going to detonate them, and there might not be a world left for them to control."

"You're lying!"

"I'm not that creative. Who are they, Fuchs? Where can I find them?"

"You can't! *I* can't!"

Chimera moved her blade just a fraction, and a neat stream of blood poured down the dandy's cheek.

"Stop!"

"Talk and I'll be glad to."

"They call themselves the Valhalla Group."

Chimera felt her heart quickening.

"They've been operating behind the scenes for years, but

now they believe your country desperately needs what they have to offer."

"Which is?"

"Virtual totalitarian rule. The abolition of freedoms for the sake of security. Drugs, crime, rampant political and civil corruption. They will use any and all means to sweep these away. But the cornerstones of your country will be swept away with them."

"My country won't stand for it."

"Your country will *beg* for it. Valhalla are masters of manipulation. They manufacture events as they need them. They will have your country calling for what they want without realizing what it is."

"How?"

"Think, Chimera! Elections will be taking place in your country in three weeks. Valhalla has taken steps to make sure their people, including a President, are elected."

"Steps," Chimera echoed. "You're talking about Nicaragua."

"That and more, but Nicaragua is the key to disgracing the administration and swaying the election their way. Valhalla infiltrated the NNSC and commandeered its plan to strike at the United States for that very purpose."

"The Quick Strike charges . . ."

"It's why the Group needed them. They were the centerpiece of the plan from the beginning, innocent lives lost dramatically, with the Nicaraguan Accords—and thus the present administration—to blame."

"How? What is this plan?"

"That I don't know! You must believe me. Only Valhalla knows."

"Right, and you know where I can find them." Chimera pushed the scalpel-like instrument farther under the dandy's skin, a jerk away from scarring him irreparably. "You're going to tell me, Fuchs. You're going to tell me now."

The President reread the report while churning his legs up the Stairmaster. The automatic speed control on the constantly revolving steps was set at the halfway level, but he seemed to be laboring. He wore a monitor on his left-hand ring finger, and the readout on the machine's screen showed his pulse to be much too high and climbing as he flipped through the pages.

The wall before Bill Riseman was mirrored, which allowed him to look at Charlie Banks and Roger Allen Doane without turning around. He closed the report.

"The CIA control responsible for this was killed in Tegucigalpa earlier today," he said, assimilating the facts for himself as well as them. "He thought his network was on to a strike by Nicaraguan Solidarity forces against this country. This report indicates it is no longer that simple." The President's legs kept churning. "A shadow government, ready to make their move out of the shadows. What does that mean to you, gentlemen?"

The two men had completed their readings of Richards's report as well, but neither responded from their positions on opposite sides of the Stairmaster.

"Talk to me, damnit!"

"The election," said Charlie Banks.

"You're damn right, the election. Someone is about to do their level best to overthrow this government electorally."

"Sir," started Roger Allen Doane, "constitutionally, you do have the right to put the election off."

"Only in the event of a national emergency."

"I'd say this qualifies," said Charlie Banks.

Bill Riseman eased the Stairmaster's control lever downward to lessen the pace. "And what would I tell the public, Charlie? That a secret group that's been operating unnoticed for forty years plans, in the guise of Nicaraguan nationals, to use explosives they stole from Pine Gap to disgrace us? Jesus Christ, I'm still having trouble believing it myself. No, gentlemen, we've got to stop them ourselves, which means we've got to find out where they're going to strike."

"Information apparently contained on the microchip planted on this—" Doane paused to get the name right. "—Jamie Skylar."

"And all the CIA can tell us is that he withdrew two thousand dollars off his credit card at the American Express office in Tegucigalpa and then disappeared."

"He'll be coming home, Bill," said Charlie Banks. "What else can he do?"

"That doesn't mean we'll be able to find him. You read the report. He survived Nicaragua and he survived Honduras. We can't sell him short."

"We're on *his* side," said Charlie Banks.

"He won't know that," said Doane.

"But he knows the shadow government has the missing explosives from Pine Gap, doesn't he, Roger? *What* missing explosives?"

Roger Allen Doane opened his memo book almost reluctantly. "A shipment was sent out to Israel in the time frame he mentions. Only, Israel never ordered it and never received it."

"A shipment containing what?"

"Twelve Quick Strike charges."

"So you're telling me that's what our shadow government has in its possession to use against us in this strike."

"It's not that simple. Only eight of the Quick Strikes had been produced for operation prior to the shipment."

"Get to the point!" the President roared, and his pulse rate soared to the monitor's highest reading of 240, holding there.

"All work on Quick Strike was conducted on sublevel seven, the level the antimatter was accidentally released on." Doane let his voice trail off as if his point had already been made. "The antimatter never could have ended up on the wrong floor unless it was mislabeled."

"Mislabeled so it could be smuggled out?"

"I don't think so, sir. The computer logs for the two elements are nearly identical, and the antimatter's containment shell is nearly identical to the Quick Strike canisters. I believe someone at Pine Gap altered the logs to arrange for an unauthorized shipment and when he did so, the computer relabeled the antimatter and transferred it accordingly. That explains how the antimatter ended up on the wrong floor, and it explains how Pine Gap was destroyed."

"Then the additional four of these containment shells went out with the eight charges of Quick Strike," the President concluded.

"In which case, whoever ended up with the shipment doesn't realize what they've got," added Charlie Banks.

"But they plan to use it, don't they?" demanded the President, holding tight to the handrails now. "That much we *do* know. What happens then, Mr. Doane? What happens then?"

"Mr. President, to answer that question accurately, I would have to know the exact logistics of the blast site."

"I know," said Bill Riseman, staring at the national security adviser in the mirror. "I've been reading up on antimatter. Wherever the blast occurs, though, we'll be facing enormous destruction caused by the hurricanes and tidal waves that will result from a massive hole torn in the atmosphere. And there wouldn't be much left around the blast site, except for a crater up to *four times* the size of the one where Pine Gap used to be. Am I right, Mr. Doane?"

Doane simply nodded.

The President at last looked behind him at Doane and Banks. "Our shadow government plans to use these canisters to destroy us, and by doing so now, they also destroy everything, including themselves. Then again, they're not really our shadow, gentlemen, they're our reflection. Well, we can make that work for us, too. It's time we let them see things from our perspective. Charlie, I want the truth of that missing shipment leaked. I want our shadow friends to know what they've got and what will happen if they go through with their plans. I want to see if they can cut it in the light."

"Think of the risks, Bill."

"That's the idea. They're not going to risk blowing up their own country, because their shadow world would die in the process. If there's nothing left to reflect, the reflection dies."

"Bill . . ."

"Put out the word, Charlie. All we've got to lose is everything, but it doesn't seem like very much right now."

CHAPTER 22

THEY entered the United States in small groups beginning Thursday, flying into different major airports. The passports they were carrying upon entry into the United States listed their point of origin as Mexico. A stamp from Nicaragua or any other Central American country might raise a flag.

The commandos then sat back to wait for the predetermined flights that would take them to the rendezvous in Boston. The closer they got to their ultimate destination, the less security precautions became necessary. They had already cleared the largest hurdle by entering the country without incident.

As a whole, the men traveled light, just a carry-on bag with bare essentials in order again not to stand out. Everything the men required would be distributed upon reaching their final destination. Their equipment and weapons had been funneled into the country slowly over the previous week.

Colonel José Ramon Riaz reached New York by way of a charter flight from Mexico City. The plane was all coach, and the air conditioning was not functioning well. He sat squeezed between two others in the center row, the noise and congestion denying him both sleep and the chance to be alone with his thoughts.

Riaz reflected back on the rigorous training of the previous six days. In all his years as a soldier, he had never seen a more deadly, efficient band than the one Esteban had assembled. The colonel recalled his brief association with Soviet *Spetsnatz* commandos and even the American Special Forces. The men who would accompany him and Maruda to the island were more than equal to these. They liked the taste of blood, the smell of it. And that was good, because plenty would be spilled before this was over.

The only problem Riaz faced was what to do with the giant, Rodrigo. His chillingly brutal effectiveness was undeniable, but so was the deficiency caused by his torture at the hands of the Contras. Since he couldn't speak, how was he going to communicate? Maruda came steadfastly to the giant's defense and insisted he could take care of it. They had worked together before, the captain explained.

The seizure of the island and roundup of the hostages would come easily. Almost all their time on the mock-up had been spent drilling on responses to the various assault and rescue tactics the Americans would employ. Such maneuvers relied almost exclusively on the element of surprise for their success. But that element did not apply in this case. The American commandos would come from air, sea, and land, and the American commandos would die.

A truckload of equipment was waiting for him in a warehouse a half hour's drive from the island. He would rent a car and drive there to keep attention from himself.

The plane full of Mexican tourists had started its descent. Riaz adjusted his eye patch and settled back as best he could.

The Valhalla Group met where it had met for a generation. Outside, a fall rainstorm pelted the windows. Thunder rumbled and the old house creaked under the strain of the wind.

"This is not meant as an attack on you, Marlowe," explained Simon Winters into the brown speaker. "But we must face facts. Because of Jamie Skylar and the information he obtained from Chimera, the government has been made aware of our existence, to say nothing of our operation.''

On the other end, Marlowe swallowed hard. The only thing he had going in his favor was that the microchip must still be in Skylar's possession. Otherwise, the logistics of Thunder Clap would have been forfeit as well.

''I beg to differ, sir. They know nothing of our operation.''

''Don't they? They know about Pine Gap. They know we have the explosives.''

''That does—''

''Mr. Marlowe,'' Winters interrupted, ''we have always provided you with freedom to act. How you accomplish our ends and what you choose to tell us has been and will continue to be up to you. However, this time we must face the facts that serious errors were made at Pine Gap. Not yours, not anyone's within our control.''

''Which changes nothing,'' insisted Benjamin Pernese, his cataract-covered eye twitching. ''The fact is we must retrieve both the Quick Strike charges and these . . . antimatter containment shells immediately. We cannot risk detonation under these circumstances.''

''You understand that means the cancellation of Operation Thunder Clap,'' said the voice from the box.

''We still have the two additional segments of our overall plan in place,'' stated Margaret Brettonwood. ''They may be enough yet to make election day ours.''

''And they may not, ma'am. What if I could reach the explosives,'' Marlowe suggested, ''and remove the four in question, even arrange for their return.''

''According to our sources, the canisters containing the Quick Strike charges are indistinguishable from the containment shells, impossible to tell apart by mere visual inspection.''

''And did you consider that these 'sources' may have created this story to frighten us off?''

Simon Winters shook his head. ''Would you also have us believe that the administration destroyed Pine Gap to add validity to its story? No, Marlowe, what they're saying is the truth, and we must face that."

"Never mind Pine Gap," blared Benjamin Pernese. "Thanks to Jamie Skylar and Chimera, they know about our existence as well. The responsibility for that lies with you, Marlowe. You are the one who allowed both of them to slip from our grasp, and as a result, far more than just Operation Thunder Clap lies in jeopardy."

"We have handled such problems before," Simon Winters broke in abruptly, "and we will handle them again. We must understand Mr. Marlowe's disappointment and his reluctance to see his operation abandoned. By the same token, Mr. Marlowe, you must understand that we have no option here other than the one we have chosen. We will rely on you to retrieve the canisters from the island and effect their return."

"Yes, sir."

"This will also mean recalling Riaz and his commandos. Is that a problem?"

"No, sir."

"Of course," Winters resumed, "there are the added problems of Chimera and Jamie Skylar. We have lost track of them, and both seem to be in positions to do us further damage, perhaps even continue on trails that lead ultimately to us. To me that represents as vast a threat as the antimatter, Marlowe."

"Leave them to me," the military representative of the Valhalla Group said with assurance.

"We left them to you before," countered Benjamin Pernese.

"But this time we know where they'll be going."

Outside, the torrents of rain continued to fall.

Jamie Skylar tried futilely for sleep on the flight from Chicago to New York, the last leg of a seemingly endless journey. He shifted and turned, trying to get his mind to rest, but it refused to shut down.

The abrupt termination of his phone call to Danzig at the embassy had crystallized his isolation. Escape by route of the Honduran airport had to be ruled out since it would be the first place the enemy would look. What then?

The answer had lain literally right before him. One bus ride became another and finally a third from Tegucigalpa to Guatemala City. The journey took a stifling eight hours, which ended with a cab ride to a jammed La Aurora Airport. It was another eight hours before a seat opened up for him on a Pan Am flight to Los Angeles, where he spent Wednesday night at an airport hotel. He forgot to arrange a wake-up call and awoke an hour past noon, stiff and no less tired. The first available flight out of Los Angeles brought him to Chicago, and he waited anxiously for the fog to lift before boarding this plane to New York.

And home.

But what good was home? What did he have to go back to? His sister was dead, and the truth of that was agonizing in its finality. Jamie had known physical pain often enough to consider it a close acquaintance. The pain of emptiness and loss, though, was worse. Every time he closed his eyes, Beth's face greeted him. Something had happened to his memory, though. He could see her only as he had last seen her: crumpled there on the stairs with her face obliterated. He searched in his mind for who she had been, but the picture would not come, because he had not known her.

She was a spy, an agent, an operative. He had rushed to Nicaragua because she needed him, though not for the reasons he thought. He had become her courier, her means to smuggle out the information that had cost her her life. The rage simmered in him through the sadness and grief. There was only one way to vent it, and that was to stay alive and destroy the force that had destroyed his sister. If he died, then she would have died for nothing. Somewhere, somehow, he still possessed the microchip and the proper parties, once he reached them, would find it. He could beat them because he had beaten them already. In Nicaragua and then again in Honduras.

They're scared of me, goddamnit. Maybe as scared of me as I am of them.

The fear meant that he could hurt them. And Jamie wanted

to hurt them. More than anything he had ever wanted before in his life, he wanted to hurt them.

He arrived at New York's La Guardia Airport exhausted, ravenous, and desperate for a shower. The stewardess had provided the exact time over the PA on the plane, but it took more than a quick thought for him to pin down the day.

Thursday. Yes, Thursday night just before nine o'clock.

Once in the terminal, nothing seemed as bad as it had been through the long course of the journey that had begun in Honduras. At last he could turn his attention fully to figuring out his next move. The FBI seemed as good a choice as any. He wondered if they maintained a New York office. He wondered if they kept office hours this late on a Thursday.

Perhaps they would for him.

He passed a newsstand and on a whim stopped to purchase a newspaper, the late edition of the *New York Times*. He handed a dollar bill to the girl behind the counter and glanced at the front page. The headline jumped off at him.

AMERICAN FOOTBALL PLAYER SOUGHT IN DRUG-RELATED DEATHS OF THREE FROM AMERICAN EMBASSY IN HONDURAS

He went cold standing there. He had been stupid not to have expected this.

"The murders this afternoon, Richards and the others—you've been blamed for them."

Danzig's words, a warning to him. Somehow Jamie had let the substance of that warning slip away.

"Sir?"

The girl behind the counter had his change ready. Suddenly he heard the sound of rapid footsteps clacking over linoleum in his direction. Jamie didn't even turn to look back.

He just ran with all the speed he could muster for the first sign he saw marked EXIT.

CHAPTER 23

CHIMERA knew something was wrong from the start. Her interrogation of Fuchs had taken her to Fairfax, Virginia, and the huge, fenced-in estate she had been hovering near for several minutes. Before reaching the house, she had contemplated a number of contingencies for gaining entry, all centered on overcoming or eluding the guards.

Except there were no guards.

The house itself was dark, but around it an eerie haze of floodlight spilled across the huge yard and garden. Some of the light splashed up against the house, where the shifting shadows of trees gave the only hint of life.

The diminished light provided the first indication of what had happened. A quick gaze up at the nearest streetlight showed that the glass was shattered; shards lay on the sidewalk on the other side of her car.

Shot out.

Chimera started warily toward the front gate. Under her black leather jacket, she had tucked the same Sig Sauer model she had used on Crane's killers. She withdrew the pistol just before reaching the gate. It was latched but not locked, and opened with a slight creak as she pushed it inward.

As she slid in the direction of a thick nest of shrubs to the right of the gate, her heavy breaths emerged as mist into the cool night. Her grip on the gun was very tight now and she was two feet away from the nest when she saw the first body. It had been tucked into the greenery so that only the lower half of a leg emerged. Chimera saw the shoe initially and crouched low to inspect the corpse. She shifted it to make use of the floodlights, and her hand came away cold and sticky. She didn't have to check her fingers to know it was blood; the sharp, coppery scent had already reached her nostrils.

Nestled farther amidst the shrubs she found a second body and then a third. The flesh was still warm, the blood wet. Whoever had done this hadn't been gone long, if indeed they were gone.

She continued on toward the main entrance, set back behind a trio of majestic pillars on a stately porch. She avoided the sprays of light en route on the chance that the killers were lying in wait within for more victims to arrive. The total darkness within the mansion made for the best camouflage at all.

The mahogany double doors were closed but not locked. Again she was not surprised. She opened the right-hand door and slid soundlessly inside, pistol palmed, her ears alert for the slightest of sounds. The marble of the foyer gave way to hard wood flooring draped with magnificent Oriental runners. Beneath one, the padding protruded just a bit. Someone, probably more than one, had come this way fast and disturbed the arrangement ever so slightly.

Her eyes had adjusted to the darkness now, enough stray rays from the outdoor floods to provide what light she needed. Her senses guided her on to a half-open door down the hallway. When she was nearly at the doorway, the feeling and scent of death assaulted her. Almost reluctantly she stepped over the threshold.

Branches played at the windows of thick glass uncovered to the night. There was no reason to cover them since this room was hidden from view at the side of the great house. The light from the floods was shallow, barely enough to illuminate a pair of figures drooped in their chairs tucked under a conference table. Chimera felt about the wall for a light switch, touched three, and flipped the center one.

A chandelier set over the conference table snapped on and illuminated the frozen-in-death expression of a man with multiple bullet wounds through his chest and face. Automatic fire had obviously been to blame, but somehow it had spared the corpse's cataract-covered eye, which stared obscenely outward.

Adjacent to that corpse, Chimera found the body of a similarly ravaged woman. The bullets had pinned the man upright, but the woman had flopped over so her face was not visible, and blood from her wounds had been sprayed over the wood surface of the table, reaching out toward a brown transistorized speaker device.

These members of the Valhalla Group had been butchered. But what of the remaining two? Fuchs had specified four leaders. Still clutching the gun, Chimera completed her visual search of the room. The other chairs around the conference table were all empty, but the one at the head had been shoved outward. Approaching closer, she saw its brown tufted leather was splattered with blood that had reached the carpet as well. The splotches formed a clear trail leading out of the room. Chimera followed it through the door and left into the corridor.

The trail led toward the back of the mansion, where she could see a second open door. A dull orange light flickered from inside it. She passed in, gun first, and observed a small fire directly ahead. The flames crackled, lighting the paneled library room. Sitting there beside the fire, eyes cast out through the huge bay windows that overlooked the estate's gardens, was another member of the Valhalla Group.

"This was always my favorite room," he said.

"Simon Winters," Chimera responded.

The old man turned his mussed white head toward her. He coughed a wet cough, and she could tell his death was near.

"The gunmen didn't check to see if I was wearing a vest," he said, forcing out the words. "Old habits die hard. But it didn't matter much. So many bullets. A few gaps. Enough." He coughed spasmodically again.

"Who did this?" Chimera asked him, drawing closer.

"You know who we are, don't you?"

She didn't answer.

Winters's eyes seemed to grasp her at last and showed what little surprise they could manage. "Chimera . . . Only you would have dared to enter this house alone. I knew you would find us. I knew from the beginning. . . ."

The old man's voice trailed into a cough, and his head rocked forward. Chimera feared death had overtaken him, but he clung stubbornly to life.

"Who did this?" she repeated.

"Marlowe," said Winters. "It had to be Marlowe. He called the meeting. I thought I heard him laughing over the speaker when his gunmen showed up."

"Speaker?"

"Security concerns prevented our military representative from ever meeting the others. I called him Marlowe after the Conrad character." Winters drew in a sigh that sounded like death itself. "I should have known, should have guessed it. He was too agreeable, didn't put up enough of an argument."

"To what?"

"Our decision to cancel Thunder Clap."

"The canisters," Chimera realized.

"Thanks to you and Jamie Skylar, the government figured out what we had. They realized it even before we did."

"You're saying Skylar's alive?"

"Of course he's alive. You saved him, after all."

"You decided to cancel your operation after learning of the antimatter," she concluded.

"Because of the risks. We sought to rebuild this country, not destroy it. But Marlowe had other plans."

"He can still be stopped." Chimera paused. "Where are the canisters now, Mr. Winters? What is Thunder Clap?"

The old man's mind drifted. "This was always my favorite room. I could sit for hours gazing out over the gardens, thinking how much the world is like them. Grounds to be turned and hoed, fertilized, and nurtured to achieve the precise arrangement one is looking for.'' His eyes sharpened briefly. ''You're a legend, you know that?''

Chimera thought of Crane and how it had ended for him. ''I'd rather not be.''

''But you can't run from what you are, and neither can I. We are much alike, the two of us, driven, determined, unstoppable when a goal lies before us.''

''Save it.''

''I'm just getting started, Chimera. Do you think that is a coincidence? Think again. Coincidences don't exist for us. Kill me and part of you dies, too.''

''Philosophy of the dead.''

''Indeed. I've been dead for a long time now, at least Simon Winters has. Just as you've been dead since the nasty business in Africa, at least Matira Silvaro has.''

Chimera stiffened at the use of her real name.

''We arranged for you to be part of that hit team,'' he continued. ''And we knew the children were going to get in the car and what it would do to you. And then we made sure the story was leaked so you could never go back.''

''No,'' Chimera muttered, even though she knew it was the truth.

''It made you an outcast, yes, an outsider. You were already one of us before Crane recruited you in Cairo.''

''You're mad.''

''And you're naive. To think a group as crucial as The Outsiders would accept their initiates at random. We chose our people,'' Winters pronounced proudly. ''You were the best, so we had to have you. *I* had to have you. So you see, when I said I always knew you'd find us, I was speaking from experience. I created you, Chimera, but first I had to destroy Matira Silvaro.''

Chimera came farther forward. ''She never died, Winters. She's still inside me, still right here.'' She tapped her heart.

The dying man shrugged. ''Truly unfortunate. For both of us.''

"You used me, Crane, all of us. There were no gardens for me. Just fields to be bulldozed, graves to be dug. Goddamn you, Winters. Goddamn you."

"He already has, Chimera. But he isn't quite ready for me yet," the old man rasped, and then a wicked, pained smile crossed his lips. "Or maybe hell is temporarily full."

Chimera came close enough for the fire's uneven light to catch her as it did him. She could feel the specter of death flickering with the flames.

"Not unfortunate," she said calmly. "Not unfortunate that Matira Silvaro is still in me at all. You're right, we are intertwined, you and me. If you die without helping me, then you die a failure. We all fail. Tell me where the canisters are. Tell me about Operation Thunder Clap."

"So much at stake, so much to lose," Winters rambled. "Control was ours to seize. We would have been content to remain in the shadows, but the country cried out for us and our testament. Mindless leadership had led her astray. It became our duty to set her back on course."

"Yes, by destroying the foundation on which our country was built."

"Not destroy, Chimera, *redefine*."

"Semantics. Don't you get it, Winters? You've become a despot, a tyrant, the head of a junta who alone knows what's best for his people. If you were so sure of your convictions, you'd create a platform and put forth a legitimate candidate who speaks for you."

"That's precisely what we intended to do, and our candidate would have won." A defiant smirk crossed Winters's whitening face. "Perhaps he still will."

"Not legitimately," argued Chimera. "And he might not be winning very much at all. Let's talk about survival, Mr. Winters, the world's as well as this country's. Tell me where I can find the canisters."

His smile this time was teasing. "I think I will, Chimera. I think I will so your quest might end in failure as mine has, and we will be linked together for eternity. In hell perhaps." He hesitated. "Castle Island."

"Castle *what*?"

"The Quick Strike devices formed the final element of our plan. With them the entire island could be destroyed. Terms will be issued, but destruction is the only acceptable result. From this, and the other elements of our plan, elections will sway in our favor, including the presidency! Think of it, Chimera. We will have taken over!"

"Your tense is wrong, Mr. Winters." And, after the old man's face had saddened with that reality, "You really think a man like Riaz will carry that scenario out?"

"He will not be in a position to. Another we have planted in his group has been given that task. Riaz has his own agenda. He knows nothing of Valhalla. He will believe to the end he is doing this for the good of his own country."

"Because you murdered his family."

"Sacrifices, Chimera. Casualties of war."

"Whose war? The children who were slaughtered? The American woman who died trying to protect them? I don't give a shit about your agenda, or the garden you're trying to grow, because you use blood for fertilizer. I've known people like you. I've *killed* people like you, and they're all basically the same. They think they're the only ones who've got things straight and their testaments hold the only possible salvation. Then watch the bodies fall as they try and prove their point. The only thing that makes you and your Valhalla Group different is that you lasted longer and did more damage."

The old man lost himself in another fit of wet coughing. Saliva slid from the corners of his mouth mixed with frothy blood. He gasped for breath and managed to hold on to life with an ever-fleeting grasp.

"It must hurt," he managed softly, "to come to me as an ally."

"Not really."

"If I don't help you, you'll fail."

"But you will help, because if I fail, so do you. Everything you've worked for, everything you've sown, lost in a moment of detonation. Might even cause tremors in hell."

"Damn you, Chimera. Damn you . . ."

"Tell me about Castle Island, Mr. Winters. Tell me about Marlowe."

CHAPTER 24

"WHERE'D you say you wanted to go?" the cab driver asked again.

"Just drive."

"East, west? North, south? Hey, it'd help if I—"

"Just drive!" Jamie ordered.

"Sure, buddy, sure. Take it easy." But after a few moments, and a few rapid glances into the rearview mirror, he spoke again. "Hey, bud, 'scuse me for asking, but you got the dough for this ride?"

Wordlessly Jamie flung a hundred-dollar bill into the front seat. The driver snatched at it eagerly as he kept driving.

"Take me to the Meadowlands," Jamie told him, his own eyes cheating out the back window.

"Where in the Meadowlands?"

"Sports complex."

"What?"

"Giants Stadium."

The stadium was a possible refuge and a place allies might be found. It was Thursday night. Jamie ran the timetable through his head and hoped he had it right. With a home game Sunday, team prep meetings at the stadium often went long into the night on Thursdays. Films were viewed, strategy discussed, final adjustments put into place. He had nowhere else to go, could think of no one else who would help him.

Help him *what*?

He wondered what credibility he would have with the FBI or any other agency. He was a suspected drug dealer accused of murdering three government employees; no, more than suspected. He had already been tried and sentenced. The shadow government had fixed everything.

Jamie reminded himself that their fear mirrored his. They were taking risks, exposing themselves in order to find him and the microchip. That microchip was still his salvation. Outside the back window, he could find no signs of pursuit. He let himself hope he had lost them in his dash from the airport. He would gain safe harbor in Giants Stadium before they were any the wiser.

The cab stopped at a red light.

"Look," Jamie said, "the hundred's all yours if you take some chances."

The driver screeched away when the light turned green. He ignored yellows and newly turned reds the rest of the way across the George Washington Bridge and onto the New Jersey Turnpike. The driver took the stadium exit off Route 3 and turned in toward the security gate manned nightly by a knobby-framed guard nicknamed Pop, who admitted to seventy and was probably closer to eighty. Pop's eyes had gone bad before the Giants' first modern play-off appearance in '81, and he hadn't missed a game for several decades before that.

Jamie rolled down his window as the cab snailed to a halt before the gate. Still no sign of pursuit from the rear. He watched the old man stir uneasily from his chair.

"Who's that?" came the gravelly voice.

"Jamie Skylar, Pop."

"Huh?" The old man leaned out the window for a closer look. "What the hell time is it?"

"I'm late."

"Late? I thought you were suspended."

"Just let me in."

The old man shrugged and pushed a button which opened the security gate and allowed the cab to pass on through.

The driver pulled up in front of a door around the side where Jamie had directed him. The driver muttered something and quickly drove off after Jamie had jumped out. He approached the door and tried the knob.

Locked. Locked, damnit!

He kicked at the steel and cursed his luck. It was never locked, never. Just then, Jamie thought he heard car doors slamming. The mere chance that the enemy had arrived was enough to make him raise his fist and punch hard at the glass. With the help of his Ivy League championship ring, the blow shattered it. Jamie reached in and unlocked the door, oblivious to the stinging pain and blood dripping from his hand.

He slid inside and was struck immediately by the uncommon quiet along the corridor. It could be the result of unusually intense meetings, meaning that very likely the Giants had been upset the week before at Green Bay. He continued on past the locker rooms.

Somewhere along the corridor a door slammed. Inside the complex. Someone coming out of a meeting perhaps. One or two of them might even be breaking up now.

But the silence persisted. There should have been some sound: the shifting of chairs, soft muttering, at least the voice of a coach providing narration for the game films. Jamie reached the first meeting room and opened the door.

Chairs all arranged in neat rows. Empty, the room deserted.

Jamie tried the next one and two more, all with the same results. No one was here.

Oh Jesus . . .

Had he miscalculated the team's schedule? Maybe they were on the road, after all this. Maybe the meetings had been changed around altogether. Either way, either way . . .

Now he heard footsteps in the corridor coming toward him. Jamie dared not wait to find out who they belonged to. Home had turned as unfriendly as the jungle, yet there was one crucial distinction: This was territory he knew. They were on his turf now, and even without the rest of the Giants to shield him, he could make do.

Jamie took off down the corridor, muffling his footsteps. This was Giants Stadium. He knew every nook and cranny of the complex, every potential hiding place. The best available would be within the structure of the stadium itself.

Jamie veered past the Giants' locker room down the ramp that led toward the east end of the playing field. He charged out to a field lit only by the moon and the few intermittent bulbs in the upper section and along the roof. His intention was to put as much distance as possible between himself and the footsteps he had heard back in the corridor. Dash across the field, and mount the stairs into the stands on the west end, where he could melt into the tunnels, ramps, and stairways. Let the bastards try to find him then, just let them.

The turf was covered by a tarpaulin, which flopped soggily beneath his feet as he ran. He had run the field a million times maybe, but never with the tarp still on, and never in shoes. This unfamiliarity subtracted a slight bit of confidence. In his mind he was trying to visualize this as a sprint for the goal line, but the tarp kept bagging up beneath his feet.

And then, as he neared the forty, the lights in Giants Stadium snapped on. The huge bulbs were of the gaseous variety that took several minutes to warm to their full capacity. But the soft glow that caught him seemed as bright as a spotlight. He continued to run until he saw the pair of figures emerging up the west-end ramp directly ahead of him.

Jamie froze in his tracks. Two well-dressed men eased forward, hands sliding into their jackets. Jamie turned to bolt back toward the east ramp only to find a trio of brightening shadows approaching from that end. These already had their guns drawn, and he felt the hopelessness surge through him. Since there were only two at the west ramp, he swung back to charge at them, not about to give up.

His eyes had just found the two men again when he saw the massive shape of Monroe Smalls closing in on them from behind. Smalls grasped a head in either hand and brought them together with a *whap!* that echoed through the stadium.

Then thudding sounds of impact could be heard from the other end of the stadium, and Jamie turned to find that the remaining three killers had fallen to the onslaught of at least twenty Giants in street clothes. They had been tackled hard to the stadium's red track and separated from their guns.

Jamie realized Monroe Smalls was rushing up to him, holding a pistol in either hand. Back behind the all-pro lineman, the downed shapes of the two gunmen looked like abandoned duffels of tape and ice packs.

"We best get you inside and patched up, Ivy," said Smalls.

"Think you should leave those two alone?" returned Jamie.

"They ain't gonna be wakin' up anytime soon."

"A water main busted beginning of the week in our locker room area," Frank, the trainer, explained as he finished swabbing the blood from the back of Jamie's hand, "so we've been using the Jets area since they stayed out west."

"Ouch," Jamie muttered when more alcohol drenched his bloodied, swollen flesh, and Frank went to work trying to pry his Ivy League championship ring off.

"Did a good job on yourself tonight, son."

"Just get me patched up so I can play the second half."

"You gonna tell us who the dudes with the guns were?" came the booming voice of Monroe Smalls, as he stepped through the doorway.

"Seems more important to thank all of you for saving my ass," said Jamie. "What'd you do with them?"

"Tied the sons of bitches up and locked 'em in the steam room, 'long with another one we found headin' toward the field from the light box. LT keeps hittin' the steam button, loosen 'em up a little. Course, you don't tell me who they are, I might throw you in there with 'em myself."

"You wouldn't believe me if I did tell you."

"Like I believe you were a drug-smugglin' murderer? Fuckin' A, Ivy, here I was thinkin' you got yourself suspended 'cause of me when it turns out you needed a few weeks off to whack some embassy dudes."

"I didn't think you read anything but the sports page."

"Article was continued in section B. Couldn't help it." Smalls's face broke out into a wide grin.

"You're enjoying this, aren't you?"

"I enjoy kickin' tail, 'specially when they about to unload on a bro and a teammate. But I would like to know what it's all about. Like what the fuck were you doin' in Nica-fucking-ragua? And why do these dudes want to make you eligible for the Hall of Fame early?"

"Sounds as if you read page one after all."

"Needed something for the shitter. Now talk."

"I got something that belongs to them, Monroe. Problem is, I don't know where to find it."

"Say what?"

"I told you, it's a long story. Starts back—" Jamie winced in pain when, with a final yank, Frank, the trainer, finally succeeded in prying his ring off. It rattled around on the training table and then dropped to the floor, bluish jewel separating from its casing.

"Fuckin' Ivy League must get their rings outta Cracker Jack boxes," Smalls smirked. He looked down. "Shit, though, they comes complete with a dime, case you gotta make yourself a call."

Jamie followed the big man's eyes to the small disc that had emerged from the ring. Not a dime, a . . .

"The microchip!" Jamie realized.

"Say what?"

"She hid it in my ring! She hid it in my ring! The jewel must have loosened up again when I smashed the window."

"Boy, you not makin' any sense 't'all."

"Get Coach Byte, Monroe."

"Say what?"

"Just get him."

Of course, "Byte" wasn't the coach's real name. He was a rotund slab of a man with Coke-bottle glasses who'd learned football as equipment manager of his high school and college teams. Computers gave him his in with the pros, and Coach Byte spent virtually all his time analyzing and programming the team's data.

Jamie watched him pull off his Coke bottle glasses and inspect the chip.

"It's not really a microchip," Byte said.

Jamie joined Monroe Smalls in shaking his head. "What?"

"It's a recording chip. You know, like a cassette tape."

"Except we can't just pop it into a deck and push PLAY."

"No," agreed Coach Byte, "but I've got another idea."

"See," Coach Byte was explaining ninety minutes later in his office inside the stadium, "this chip isn't much different than the kind they use in answering machines to record outgoing messages on. So what I did, I played around with my answering machine a little and managed to adapt the circuits for your chip's size."

With that, the coach slid his slimline Panasonic closer to Jamie. Thinking it was a cue, he reached out to push PLAY.

"Uh-uh," Byte said, grabbing Jamie's hand en route there. "It's the *outgoing* you want to listen to. Here . . ."

And the coach pressed a smaller button on the machine's side. After a few seconds, a metallic-sounding conversation in Spanish-accented English filled the room. Jamie recognized Colonel Riaz's voice instantly, speaking to a man named Esteban. He felt chilled from the start and got still colder as the part of the chip that had almost cost him his life was reached.

The site of the operation, Colonel, is Castle Island off the coast of Newport, Rhode Island.

You needed these explosives to take over an island?

Not quite. Castle Island is home to one of America's most prestigious prep schools, St. Michael's. We would like you to lead a group of commandos in the seizure of that school on the island. We want you to hold the students and faculty hostage under threat of setting off the explosives if the Americans do not meet our demands. You'd like to hear the timetable?

I'm sure you're going to tell me anyway.

It will begin one week from next Friday.

Very ambitious, Esteban.

The operation is called Thunder Clap.

I can see why. . . .

Jamie continued to listen, trembling outwardly now. It was all here, everything that Chimera had expected. Riaz had rejected the advances of the group represented by Esteban, and that group had killed his family and pinned it on the Contras so Riaz would change his mind. But it was the agenda of a much larger group that was behind everything. Chimera had said that much, and the revelation had plainly scared Richards back in Honduras.

Operation Thunder Clap.

St. Michael's School on Castle Island.

It was all happening tomorrow, and Jamie knew he had to be there.

PART THREE

Castle Island

Newport, Rhode Island: Friday, six A.M.

CHAPTER 25

THEY met at dawn in a small abandoned warehouse in Portsmouth, Rhode Island, fifteen miles from Castle Island and St. Michael's School. Maruda was there ahead of Colonel Riaz, and the two of them were joined by the individual groups of commandos right on schedule.

Maruda hoisted up the warehouse's garage-style doors to reveal two vans and a Ryder truck. Inside, Rodrigo had just finished single-handedly loading the last of the heavy crates.

"The bulk of our equipment," Riaz explained, "is contained in the truck. The eleven of you I've already designated will make the trip over the bridge in vans and disperse as indicated. You will not make any move until all of us are in position and you receive your signal from me. We don't want to risk any confusion. We want this operation to take place clean and sure, without complications."

Riaz didn't bother to ask if that was clear, because he knew it was. He was merely reiterating what they had practiced dozens of times on the scale mock-up. He adjusted his eye patch.

"When the island is secured," he continued, "the rest of you will bring the truck across and begin laying the explosives. Questions?"

"Why must we wait until twelve o'clock?" asked a commando named Javier. "The original plan called for nine."

"Because our information indicates only three-quarters of the students attend breakfast, while all are required to attend lunch. We want them confined when we make our landing. Better that way."

"The explosives to blow the bridge will be on the truck then?" asked Sanchez, the demolitions specialist of the group.

"Absolutely," replied Riaz. "That becomes priority one for your group once we've secured the area." He turned toward a small, squirrelly-looking commando. "Fernando, you will remain on the mainland with a roadblock to keep all comers off the bridge while the explosives are being laid. Once they are in place, you will ride the motorbike over to the other side before we blow it."

"You want to lose the whole thing, correct?" Sanchez asked.

"I want Castle Island isolated. I want no one to reach the school except birds and fish."

"They'll try, Colonel," noted Ishmael, which drew a smile from Rodrigo. "You know that."

"Yes," Riaz acknowledged. "They will."

Chimera had driven straight through the night after leaving Fairfax, driven until her eyes rebelled and she pulled off Route 95 and gave herself briefly up to sleep. It was the dawn that awoke her, with her mouth paste-dry and another two hours to Newport. Winters had indicated that the taking of St. Michael's School would not occur until tomorrow—Saturday at noon following the half-class day—so she had some time to spare. Not much, though, since she intended to spend today on the island preparing her defense. Gaining thorough familiarity with the grounds was the first order of business, followed by attaining the materials required to destroy Riaz's operation before it had a chance to get started. With time and surprise on her side, the advantage belonged to her.

Contacting the authorities was a possibility she considered but quickly dismissed. After all, based on what she knew of the Valhalla Group, how could she know she wouldn't be talking to one of their people? No, she had to finish this alone. She was most comfortable that way. The most pressing challenge before her was finding a legitimate way to gain access to the school. Sneaking about was out of the question. She needed to be accepted to prepare her work properly.

That thought foremost on her mind, she checked into a room in the Castle Hill Inn within sight of the island and the school. The room would become her base. With today's reconnaissance of the school complete, she would obtain the materials she needed and prepare them here. Saturday she would return to Castle Island before dawn and ready her assault.

It was while she was eating breakfast in the motel coffee shop that she found her means of access. A local paper rested on the counter before her, and on a whim she opened it to the back section. Her scan of the entries stopped halfway down the third column.

There it was, an entirely legitimate way of getting into St. Michael's School!

Chimera left the rest of her breakfast uneaten before her. It was all she could do not to break into a run for her car.

Forty minutes after Jamie Skylar finished up in Coach Byte's office, a plan hatched mostly by Monroe Smalls went into effect. A member of the coaching staff called the local police to report that death threats against the entire Giants team had been followed by the capture of six armed men inside the stadium. Police cars from four surrounding New Jersey communities, accompanied by a half-dozen state police cruisers enclosing a SWAT truck, arrived in a constant stream, sirens wailing. The players' parking lot filled with helmeted men in flak jackets bearing M-16s or shotguns across their chests. The six captured gunmen were ushered out first, their faces flushed and clothes soaked through, courtesy of their stay in the steam room. Immediately after, the Giants players began to file out under the watching eyes of the police. They hustled immediately to their cars, which had already been sniffed for explosives by specially trained dogs.

The players were escorted by local police in both directions on Route 3. Other units had been placed along the highway at strategic points to watch for possible snipers and pursuit. If the enemy came back in greater force, the intimidation factor surely would come into play. And if they didn't, the main purpose of the police presence, to deny the enemy Jamie Skylar, was sure to be successful.

After all the fuss was over and the last of the squad cars had left, a small group remained inside the Giants' locker room.

"What's the plan now?" Jamie asked Monroe Smalls.

"Me and the boys drive you wherever you want to go."

Jamie shook his head. "I can't let you do that, Monroe. You've done enough."

"This hero shit's running thin, Ivy."

"It's got nothing to do with being a hero. Too many people have got hurt trying to help me. I can't live with any more of that."

"You like dyin' better?"

"I'm not gonna die, Monroe," Jamie told him quite calmly. "If I was going to, it would have happened already in Casa Grande, or the jungles, or Honduras, or here tonight. Every time they miss me I get stronger, and right now I feel stronger than ever."

"You don't look it." Smalls looked down at him. "No way I can convince you to let me come along?"

Jamie shook his head. "Just me, Monroe. That's the way it's gotta be."

"You flauntin' your luck, Ivy. Fastest time in the forty anywhere look slow against a bullet."

"Not if it misses."

"I'm sorry," said Chimera, leaning back in the chair. "I didn't know."

The receptionist sighed. "Headmaster George likes to interview all the candidates himself."

"I can wait."

"He's tied up all morning. Did you bring a resumé?"

"I left it in the car," Chimera lied. "I can go out and get it."

"Later," the receptionist said, loosening a bit. "Just tell me your basic credentials."

"Emergency room, intensive care, and floor supervisor," Chimera said, items she knew would impress. The want ad section of the local paper had said St. Michael's was seeking a nurse, so she had come here as an applicant.

"And you say you can start right away."

"I'm from the area, like I told you."

Just then, a tall, lean man with close-cropped hair stepped out of the inner office and shook hands with a shorter man holding a briefcase.

"Until commencement weekend then, Tom," he said.

"Mr. George," the receptionist called to the taller one still in the doorway, "this is Miss Burke, *Nurse* Burke. She saw our ad in the paper and drove out straightaway."

Chimera rose to her feet and extended her hand. Headmaster George took it cursorily.

"I've got that meeting with the seniors at ten-thirty," he frowned. "If you could wait for just a few minutes."

"Could I take a walk around the school?"

"I don't see why not. Should we say eleven-thirty then?"

"Fine."

The headmaster of St. Michael's School shook her hand again and slid out into the hall.

The receptionist looked up at Chimera. "If you want me to call for a student to show you around . . ."

"Please don't bother. I don't want to be a nuisance."

"It's no bother at all."

"I just want to get a feel for the place."

"Let me give you the standard tour map. It's nothing elaborate, but it will help you on your way."

Chimera accepted it and stepped out the door. She now had a cover story if approached, and more important, she had free reign of the grounds to plan her defense against tomorrow's taking of the school.

In this regard the logistics of the locale itself dominated

her initial strategic concerns. Together with the towns of Portsmouth and Middletown, Newport was actually part of Aquidneck Island. Castle Island was located in the bay off Newport's southwestern tip. It was irregular in shape, as if some vast colony of sea monsters had torn frenzied bites from its shores. Those shores sloped up to the large plateau on which St. Michael's School had been built over a century before.

The island was accessible from the mainland by a two-lane causeway bridge extending out from Newport at Castle Hill. There was a trio of mooring docks as well, for those who came to St. Michael's by way of water. But it was the causeway Chimera focused on. It was easily the most defensible position, one where Riaz's forces would be the most contained and thus the easiest to take en masse. She needed fallbacks, though, and for this a detailed understanding of the school's logistics was required.

The cluster of school buildings stretched north to south across the island. They were layered in ivy-wrapped red brick or gray whetstone granite, their congruous appearance belying the fact that construction had been ongoing through the school's history. The original complex of buildings had been a simple square enclosing a courtyard. The central administration building had been constructed facing east to Castle Hill, while the steepled chapel directly behind it on the other side of the courtyard faced west toward the town of Jamestown across the bay. Over the years buildings had been added to both sides, though mostly to the one facing east, to the point where now the extension of structures, both interconnected and not, teased the sloping hills leading up to them from the shores. The separate buildings included a field house set slightly to the rear of the entire complex, and a number of dormitories constructed to meet the rising demand for space.

Nothing of the school's traditional beauty, however, had been sacrificed. St. Michael's maintained a kind of old English rusticity, unspoiled by time and modernization. The eastern front beyond the administration building was graced by a large, rolling green enclosed by a circular drive and bracketed on either side by combination soccer-football-lacrosse fields. The western front outside the chapel featured red and green asphalt tennis courts, a baseball diamond, and another pair of practice fields. There was no feeling of congestion, though the fields took all the space the plateau would give them. They were rimmed with thick green bushes and a scattering of trees whose leaves rustled softly in the breeze. Parking lots dotted the scenery here and there, with the largest hidden between buildings.

Chimera's walk about the school began on the steps outside the administration building, where she gazed at the part of the mainland visible across the causeway bridge. She wondered briefly if the best strategy available to her might be to force an evacuation of the island. The trouble with that scenario was the problem of securing the canisters of antimatter. Evacuation risked warning the colonel against showing up at all, which meant the containment shells would remain at large. It was clear that she had to leave everything just as it was supposed to be and then neutralize Riaz's forces in a way that ensured her controlling the containment shells.

Chimera ventured back inside the original complex of interconnected buildings, which now held the administrative offices and most of the classrooms. At the far end of the hall, one of the upper forms was holding a class meeting in a lounge that overlooked the small beach on the island's northwestern side. She skirted close to the doorway and, after consulting her map, climbed a set of stairs toward a series of classrooms down a hall; then she went down a narrow connecting corridor which led to the chapel. It was the school's most famous structure and also the one that would feature the largest selection of hiding places should she require one. Beyond that, its steeple strategically formed by far the island's highest point. It would be impossible to approach from land, water, or air without being seen from the vantage point it provided. Next she made her way into the science wing, drawn there by the smells and the promise of chemical weapons she could formulate from the array of bottles on the shelves. With class meetings still going on, she was free to patiently inventory the chemicals that might be of some use tonight from the lab areas and storage closets.

Chimera returned to the central administration building just as the form meetings were breaking up. She was a few minutes late to her interview with Headmaster George, and it took all her resolve to keep her mind focused on the questions he was asking. She smiled as she responded politely and forgot her responses as soon as they had been uttered.

"I think that does it," George said finally, bringing the interview to an abrupt halt. "When can you start?"

"Immediately would suit me fine."

He returned her smile. "After lunch, then." He flashed another smile. "Give you an opportunity to find out what sends most of our kids to the infirmary."

Headmaster George led Chimera to the dining hall along busy corridors she'd had to herself just minutes before. Because the dining hall faced out to the north, neither Chimera nor the headmaster saw the pair of dark vans slide onto the causeway bridge from Castle Hill.

CHAPTER 26

"I THINK we better start again," said the Newport police captain. "You say St. Michael's School is about to be taken by *terrorists*?"

"It may already have *been* taken."

The captain pointed to the phone. "They haven't called."

"Why don't you call them? Why don't you find out if anything is going on?"

The captain showed his impatience with a frown. "Look, Mr. Skylar, what is it exactly you want me to do?"

"I want you to evacuate the island. I want you to get all the kids off before he comes."

"Before *who* comes?"

"I told you—Colonel Riaz. And I also told you he was tricked into leading the operation called Thunder Clap."

"Which you learned from the microchip, too."

"Yes."

"Hidden in your ring by your sister, who was planted with Riaz by the CIA."

"And died when Riaz's family was killed."

"Okay. Now tell me again. Who killed all these people?"

"Killers hired by this Esteban, fronting for the group he *really* represents."

"A group that is doing all this as a way of taking over the United States government."

"In a nutshell."

"Oh Christ . . ."

Jamie felt himself grow calmer. "Listen to me, Captain. I know how all this must sound, but it's really happening. Never mind what happened in Nicaragua. Castle Island is about to be taken over by terrorists. I don't know exactly when, but I know it's soon, and you're the only one who can do a damn thing in time for it to matter."

The captain leaned forward. "Wanna hear what I know? I know you're wanted for murder and if I was smart, I'd throw you in jail and call the feds."

"Throw me anywhere you want. Call anyone you want. Just send help to Castle Island."

He pulled the phone toward him and eased the receiver to his ear. "Carol, get me St. Michael's School on the line." He lowered it to his shoulder and looked back at Jamie. "I think I'll let you talk to the headmaster yourself. Maybe you can convince him to ask for police protection."

"Captain?" The secretary's voice was barely audible coming from the receiver snug against the cop's shoulder.

"Yes, Carol."

"Sorry. Can't raise the school on any of their lines. Sounds like they're dead."

"Try again," the captain said less surely.

"Already have. Anything else?"

"Yeah," he followed with eyes on Jamie. "Have the nearest patrol car swing by here and pick up a passenger on its way to Castle Island."

"Will do."

The captain kept clutching the phone. "We got ourselves a heap of trouble if you're wrong about this, son."

"We've got a heap of trouble if I'm right."

"Disperse!" Riaz ordered into his walkie-talkie.

The men from the trailing van, all dressed in matching gray uniforms, climbed down without haste and fell in behind the colonel. At the same time, those from the lead van, including Rodrigo, spread out to their initial exterior watch positions.

"Captain, do you read me?" he asked Maruda, who was preparing to drive the Ryder truck across the causeway bridge.

"I read you, Colonel."

"We're about to go in. Give us five minutes. Repeat, five minutes, and then come on along."

"Roger, Colonel."

Riaz stuffed the walkie-talkie into his gray coveralls work uniform and signaled his men to head straight for the initial seizure point, the dining hall.

"This is Manuel, Colonel."

Riaz quickly retrieved the device, as the advance team slid by them in position. "Go on."

"All perimeter positions clear, sir. Looks like you've got the whole school eating lunch."

The colonel fingered his eye patch. "Just as planned," he said.

Chimera realized what was happening as soon as she saw them ease their way into the dining hall, realized that all her plans had gone horribly wrong.

How?

Marlowe! It had to be Marlowe! Valhalla's military representative had withheld the true starting time of Operation Thunder Clap from the Group, personal insurance on his part. Winters had told her the operation was going to begin tomorrow because that was what Winters thought.

She counted six figures entering the dining hall. They carried toolboxes instead of guns, and their dispersal was strictly by the book. All areas covered strategically.

Chimera gazed at the commandos and recognized them for the professionals that they were. She could tell by their eyes and the way they moved exactly how formidable they were. Even if she managed to overcome them all and secure the dining hall, an untold number of others lay waiting beyond.

Riaz was the last to appear, his black eye patch serving to identify him for her. At his entrance the students began to be aware something strange was happening in the room, and most of their conversation ceased. Members of the school administration approached the apparent workers to find out what had caused the gas company to arrive in such force. Riaz, meanwhile, made his way to the raised platform dominated by tables reserved for faculty and staff at the dining hall's front.

"You will stay calm, Mr. George."

"Excuse me?" the headmaster said, rising to meet him.

"I said you will stay calm. In exactly ten seconds my men will produce their weapons and you and I will address your students."

"What the hell are—"

"Five seconds."

George had just begun to complete his accusation when the dining hall filled with screams caused by the appearance of Uzis in the hands of the invaders. The guns had been concealed beneath their coveralls. Quite on their own, the students herded themselves in as tight a bunch as the center of the dining room would allow, putting the maximum distance between them and the potential bullets.

"Don't make me draw my gun, Mr. George," Riaz advised. "This will go better for both of us if we cooperate with each other."

"What's going on? Who are you people?"

"Who we are doesn't matter. What's going on is that we are taking your school hostage." Riaz beckoned him forward. "The mike, Mr. George. I believe we should calm your students down."

The headmaster gazed out the huge glass windows, as if hoping to see the police miraculously appear on the grounds.

"I have men posted outside, Mr. George. No one will get through them, believe me. The mike now. Please."

His voice was so calm in contrast to the frenzy in the room that it made the headmaster shudder. It was more like a tape recording, processed and rehearsed, with no hint of emotion or feeling.

"May I have your attention, please," George said into the

mike. "Settle down. Please." And, with his eyes on the one-eyed man, "You are in no danger. Please quiet down." He covered the mike and looked back at Riaz. "What else?"

"Get them quiet, get their attention, and then turn the mike over to me."

Chimera had let herself be herded into the bulging swell of terrified bodies along with the cooks and other kitchen personnel. She felt stupid, amateurish. She had come to Castle Island to prevent its capture and now found herself a victim of that capture instead. So much had rested upon her, and she had failed in every respect.

I should have known, at least suspected. . . .

Around her, children were whimpering. She could smell the fear, taste it. It strengthened her resolve. The one advantage she still held was that her identity was unknown to the gunmen. She would have to make that advantage work for her. She would have to find a strategy.

"Students of St. Michael's School," Riaz addressed them as if this were a commencement exercise, "your school has been taken hostage by members of the Nicaraguan National Solidarity Committee for crimes perpetrated by your nation upon ours. I know none of you are responsible for the vast injustices I speak of, but we all must live with and be accountable for the actions of our respective nations. If you cooperate, you will not be harmed. If you do everything we say exactly as you are told, we will inconvenience you as little as possible. For the time being you will return to your seats and stay calm. You may speak if you wish, but no one under any circumstances can leave this building. Your headmaster and I are going to have a talk concerning our agenda. None of you will be hurt if you cooperate fully. We have not come here to hurt anyone. That is the truth."

Riaz tossed an unspoken signal to his men, and Chimera watched as yet another part of the plan unfolded. His gunmen stripped off their overalls to reveal sport jackets, slacks, and ties beneath them. With overalls shed, if it were not for the guns, it would have been difficult to pick them out from the bulk of the faculty.

It'll keep the marksmen and spotters confused once they arrive, Chimera thought. *But not me. Not me . . .*

Maruda had driven the truck across the causeway just as planned, and deposited Ramon, Javier, and the demolitions specialist, Sanchez, right at the point where it joined Castle Island. Sanchez had held all the plastic explosives necessary to blow the bridge in a pack on his lap. Throughout the drive he cradled it affectionately. Unnerved at first, Maruda had quickly gotten used to it. After dropping the demolitions team off, he continued on for several hundred yards to the unloading point for the heavy armaments. So far the only weapon of note on the island was Rodrigo's .50-caliber machine gun, this because he carried it as if it were a normal rifle. The giant had already found a perch that allowed him a strategic view of the bridge. Maruda could see him eyeing it the way an animal does its prey, just waiting for a potential enemy to attempt to cross.

He had left Fernando back on the other side of the causeway dressed in the same Department of Public Works uniform Ramon, Javier, and Sanchez wore. Fernando was now erecting a typical roadblock of cones to turn away any traffic that might approach the bridge before the explosives were set. Drivers would be told a stress test was being performed.

And what a stress test it would be, Maruda joked to himself.

Twelve minutes to lay the explosives and fuses. Then Sanchez would call Riaz, and the order would go out to blow the bridge as soon as Fernando had reached the island side.

In the rearview mirror, Maruda caught a last glimpse of Sanchez supervising the work of packing the squares of *plastique* at key structural points on the bridge, starting three hundred yards from the island. Already he had Javier running the traditional fusing along the explosive line, a bit ahead of schedule even.

"We're almost there, kid," the older cop said back to Jamie. "Relax."

"You really play pro football?" the younger one in the passenger seat asked.

"For the Giants," came Jamie's mindless reply.

"Yeah, that explains it. I follow the Patriots. Can't tell you a name and number if they're not on the Pats."

Jamie shrugged and kept waiting for the clear view of Castle Island from where they were driving along Ocean Drive.

"There it is," said the older cop, who was driving. "To your left."

"Looks pretty normal to me," the younger one commented.

Jamie wondered if he expected a banner proclaiming ISLAND HELD HOSTAGE. DON'T BOTHER COMING OVER. How the fuck was it supposed to look?

"What?" the old cop asked him.

"Just talking to myself."

The squad car continued down Ocean Drive until the road forked left toward Castle Hill and the causeway.

"Looks like the DPW boys got here ahead of us," the young cop realized first.

"I don't have any report they were planning to work on the bridge today."

"Guess they didn't see fit to tell you, Sarge."

"Yeah, well, traffic gets closed down somewhere, the department gets a call. Regulations, pal. I think we'll have him move his orange cones so we can get a better look at what these boys are doing that they didn't bother telling anyone about."

"Come in, Colonel," Fernando said into his walkie-talkie as the squad car slid closer.

"I read you, Fernando."

"There's a police car approaching the causeway."

Riaz gazed at Maruda, who had joined him in the front section of the dining hall.

"Sanchez," the colonel said back into his walkie-talkie, "did you copy that?"

"Yes, sir."

"How long until the explosives are ready?"

"Another five to seven minutes."

"Damn . . ."

"Police car still approaching," came the voice of Fernando. "What do I do?"

"Leave it to me." And then Riaz spoke again into his walkie-talkie. "Rodrigo, go to the bridge. Repeat, Rodrigo, to the bridge. Hit your clear button twice if you copy."

click . . . click . . .

"Morning," Fernando said through the open window on the driver's side of the squad car. He was using his best American accent.

"You boys ever think to let us know you were gonna be closing the bridge down?" pestered the older cop in the driver's seat.

"This came up rather suddenly," Fernando answered, "but I thought you had been told."

"What's wrong?" asked the younger one.

"Possible structural damage. We're running some stress tests to check it out."

"We got business on the island. Okay to cross?" from the older one.

"Should be. Just go slow."

Fernando proceeded to move the line of cones aside and waited until the police car was well on its way before raising the walkie-talkie to his lips again.

"Something wasn't right about that guy," the older cop said to the younger one, fidgeting in the driver's seat.

Jamie leaned forward closer to them. "Maybe you should call for backup."

"Backup for what?"

"Those two guys standing off to the side up there waving to us don't have any tools."

"So?"

"How can you check for structural damage without any tools?"

The young cop looked across the seat nervously, already

reaching for the mike. "Hey, maybe the kid's got a point. Can't hurt to call in and check that guy back there's story."

"Jesus Christ," the sergeant muttered.

"Base, this is car seven."

"Read you, seven."

"Base, like you to check on a work order from . . ."

The young cop had just gotten those words out when a massive figure lunged out at the end of the causeway. The squad car was fifty yards from him when he squeezed the trigger of a huge machine gun that didn't even vibrate in his powerful hands. The windshield shattered, and the explosion of glass and bullets slammed the sergeant backward behind the wheel as the young cop ducked low as he could manage.

"Holy fuckin' Jesus Christ!"

"Seven, what's going on? Thought I heard—"

"We're under fire, that's what's going on! Repeat, we are under fire!"

The squad car swayed wildly from side to side, its occupants showered with glass. The sergeant struggled bravely with the wheel while his partner continued squawking into the mike.

"Oh shit . . ."

Directly in front of them the pair of workers on the bridge who'd been waving their arms were leveling smaller machine guns. Jamie saw the burst of orange from the rifle bores an instant before the rest of the windshield disintegrated. Blood showered the compartment from the sergeant's punctured body and the car went reeling out of control.

"Jesus Christ, get us help here!" he heard the young cop screaming. *"Help us!"*

Jamie ducked below the backseat as the next burst burned into the young cop's head and chest when he rose to grab the steering wheel. Fresh blood sprayed everywhere, and there was a *plop* as his head ruptured under yet another barrage. The sergeant's already dead frame was hit several times as well, and a spasm forced his foot down on the accelerator. The heavy car shot forward in the direction of the gunmen, who jumped out of the way, emptying the last of their clips.

Jamie felt the bone-wrenching collision with the steel safety rail and thought it would end there. But the approach angle carried the car up and over. It turned sideways in the air en route to the bay waters below.

The harsh impact was followed by a flood of cold, wet darkness, the light gone, swallowed by the sea that was about to swallow Jamie as well.

CHAPTER 27

"How long until we can blow it?" Colonel Riaz asked into his walkie-talkie.

"One minute," replied Sanchez, with the last explosive block in his hand.

"Make it thirty seconds."

"Sirens approaching," Fernando reported from the mainland side. "Four cars, I think, five maybe. Well spread."

"Come across *now*! Sanchez!"

"Sir?"

"Blow it as soon as he's with you."

"Will do, Colonel."

Sanchez got the last of the *plastique* in place, spread in a way that would force the last third to a half of the causeway bridge to crumble into the sea. Javier and Ramon strung the fusing out toward him and wedged it tight, returning in a rush to the island, with Fernando trailing just behind on his motorbike. Sanchez lingered for a time to inspect the beauty of his handiwork. Absolutely perfect, he reflected, backpedaling slowly. The wailing sirens grew louder, as the first of the police cars came screaming into view, but Sanchez seemed unfazed by them.

"Sanchez!" Riaz called.

"Sir?"

"Are you ready?"

"Fifteen seconds," Sanchez replied as Javier fastened the strung fusing to the detonator.

"Blow it!"

All the police cars reached Castle Hill at virtually the same time. The two from Newport and one from Portsmouth came by way of Ocean Drive, while the pair of state police cars pulled behind them off Ridge Road. The three lead cars moved toward the causeway in single file, close enough to make it seem their bumpers were intertwined. The last report from the squad car that was now off the air had made no sense, something about being fired upon. On a causeway bridge leading to a prep school? What in hell was going on?

Whatever it was, the response time had been incredibly quick. The lead cars swung onto the bridge to find nothing seemingly out of place. Across the way the structures of St. Michael's School winked at them between trees shifting in the breeze.

The state police cars were about to turn onto the causeway after them when the charge exploded. The world seemed simply to come apart in a horrific blast of orange that sent twenty tons of bridge rubble showering upward. The percussion alone sent the two lead police cars into the air as if the bridge surface had suddenly turned into a trampoline. The third car spun wildly and was stopped only by a hail of causeway remnants, which crushed and entombed it.

The state police cars had managed to stop just short of the bridge. Falling rubble shattered their windows and ravaged much of the steel composing their shells. Tires exploded under the pressure, and the officer in the second car back who'd maintained the presence of mind to duck under his dashboard now grasped for his mike.

"Base, this is seventeen. Somebody blew the bridge, goddamnit! Repeat, *somebody blew the damn bridge!*"

* * *

Chimera had not taken her eyes from Riaz once since he had completed his speech from the platform at the front of the dining hall. None of the hall's windows faced the mainland and the causeway, so she could only guess what was occurring and had no warning before the explosion came.

It shook the very walls of the old building. The earthquakelike rumble shattered windows and sent thick shards spraying inward. Blazer-clad students screamed their fear and dived headlong to the floor for safety. Some of the screams intensified as a few shards found their mark. In grotesque counterpoint, light fixtures toppled and the roof continued to tremble, plaster cracking into falling dust, well after the explosion had subsided.

Chimera knew Riaz had blown up the causeway; that would have been necessary for the success of his plan. The island had to be isolated. Now that it was, the options of the authorities had been significantly limited. When her eyes found the colonel again, he was speaking to Headmaster George; calmly, as if oblivious to the chaos beyond him. The toppled chairs and tables provided cover for the desperate students and faculty sprawled amid the broken glass on the dining hall floor. With Headmaster George by his side, Riaz spoke into the microphone. The blast had damaged the speakers, and his voice emerged muffled and slightly broken.

"Please bring the wounded to the back of the hall," he instructed. "If they are unconscious or too badly hurt to be moved, leave them as they are." He looked to George. "The headmaster will be in charge of taking care of the wounded. I have entrusted him the freedom to do whatever is necessary to keep them comfortable."

With that, Riaz yielded the microphone to a trembling Andrew George, one lens of his glasses shattered, who grasped the podium to steady himself.

"M-M-Miss Burke, where are you?" he called. "If you are in here, please come forward."

Chimera swallowed her shock at the turn of events before her. With no choice but to oblige, she shammed fear over her features and tottered to the front of the terror-filled dining hall.

Colonel Riaz looked on without interest as the woman he took to be the school nurse reached the podium. There were more pressing matters to consider. The operation's timetable had been advanced considerably now. The authorities would know what had happened here on the island and would be arriving in force considerably sooner than he had expected. That he would make adjustments for, but something else plagued him as well:

What had brought the initial police car to the island?

He felt in his bones it wasn't simply on routine patrol. Something had happened, something unexpected. He would in all likelihood never know what it was, and he fervently hoped it wouldn't matter. What did matter was that Maruda would now be in the process of distributing the heavy armaments for his men to take to their assigned positions throughout the island. The arsenal included Stinger missiles, .60-caliber machine guns, LAW rockets, and lots more—in short, plenty to make it possible for his team to defend the island from fortified positions within it. Not that he wanted to hide this reality from the Americans either. On the contrary, he *wanted* them to know exactly what they were facing so they would realize how hopeless any response other than capitulation would be.

Of course, they would never admit that to themselves; they couldn't. They would be coming in force, and not long from now, either. Good. Let them.

Riaz loved the challenge and was eager to display one at a time the cards he was holding. The hand was his and so was the island.

The squawking call from the walkie-talkie clipped to his belt broke his concentration. He snatched at it almost angrily.

"This is Riaz."

"Maruda, sir. I'm informed by one of our patrols that a survivor has washed up onshore."

"One of their policemen?"

"Judging by the clothes, no."

"Is he hurt?"

"Yes, sir. Seriously, from what I'm told."

Riaz found this quite strange. If there had been someone else on the bridge when Sanchez had blown it, he could hardly have survived. Perhaps, then, this man had been in the first police car that had plunged off the causeway after Rodrigo had machine-gunned it. But if the survivor wasn't a policeman, then who was he?

"Have him brought to the infirmary and treated with the others," Riaz ordered. "I'll want to see him for myself."

This time Jamie had believed he was dead for sure. Escaping from the steel tomb of the rapidly sinking police car seemed all but impossible. His desperate struggles with the door handle proved futile and his salvation actually occurred only after he had given up on them. Then simple buoyancy thrust him upward through the hole where the rear window had been.

All at once the cold of the water knifed through him. He clawed for the surface, with his chest pleading for breath, and broke through it, coughing and gasping for air at the same time. Wiping the water from his eyes, he treaded water and tried to find his bearings. The plunge had carried him far out into the water, closer to the island than the mainland. He had started swimming toward the island's shore when the explosion came.

The sound of it shook his ears, and there was an awful *crack*! on the top of his head that numbed him from skull to toes. Once again the water swallowed him, rising anew as if it had found an escaping prey it was determined to own. Jamie retained enough sense to hold to the surface as well.

His eyes burned and he realized with a start that more than the salt was blurring his vision. Everything was gone but light and dark, distant shapes that held the barest of contours. He was disoriented and looked to the causeway for direction.

It was gone, a huge portion of it anyway. The water still vibrated from the force of what Jamie now identified as a massive explosion.

Riaz had blown the bridge! The island belonged to him now, from shore to shore.

Jamie still had no choice but to swim toward it. He was too tired to thrash his arms or legs, could barely manage the slight paddle that carried him toward shore with the currents. Thoughts came and went sporadically. He kept drifting off only to latch on to consciousness again in desperation. He felt his feet touch bottom, and seconds later he collapsed into the surf licking at the shoreline. He dragged himself over rocks the last bit of the way into the sea grass and sand.

Well up on the sloping hill that formed the shore now, Jamie crumpled. The salty flavor of seawater mingled with the coppery taste of blood dripping down his face and into his mouth. He was too tired to probe with a hand toward the wound and was barely conscious enough to hear the sound of footsteps pounding toward him.

"Stay where you are!" a voice screamed at him in English, and then spat a report in Spanish into a walkie-talkie. Jamie turned his head in its general direction. There was seaweed in his hair and sand matted to his face. He could discern a pair of vague outlines, one of them huge, and nothing more.

"We are to take him to the infirmary," the one with the walkie-talkie was saying to the huge one. "The colonel's orders."

Riaz! Jamie realized. He could talk to him, reason with him. Something good might yet come of his presence here. He would tell Riaz everything he knew, everything he had learned from Chimera. The colonel would see he had been used, would see he had been tricked into working with a force whose interests extended far beyond Nicaragua. Jamie's mere presence here would be proof. Riaz would listen. Yes, Riaz would listen!

"Lift him up, Rodrigo," the one with the walkie-talkie

ordered, and Jamie felt a huge pair of hands close upon him.

Miraculously, most of the injuries suffered in the dining hall had turned out not to be serious at all. No broken bones or fractures. Since the glass had showered down more than exploded inward, there were just gashes, cuts, and lacerations, easily closed by someone with even the barest of training. Removing bits of glass from flesh, simple suturing, swabbing and dressing the wounds, were skills Chimera had used most frequently over the years, almost always on herself.

She dealt with the injured in order of severity. Through it all she reflected on just how much of a blessing the nurse's guise would be to her for the freedom of movement it would allow, the centerpiece of her revised strategy. She would become accepted by Riaz's troops and thus ignored by them. It was the last thing she could have reasonably hoped for, and yet it would provide her the means either to cut down the invaders one at a time or disable the explosives from Pine Gap once they were in place.

A quick scan of the infirmary's medicine cabinets also revealed she was anything but weaponless. Their contents included a number of potential poisons that could be injected into the opposition's forces, perhaps placed in their food. Some of the suturing instruments could help too, sharp and finely pointed as they were, instruments of potential death as well as life.

The infirmary was located not far beyond the dining hall, overlooking the northern shore of the island, so she still had not viewed the results of the bridge explosion. Nor, more importantly, had she been able to assess the full deployment of Riaz's forces. This was information she would have to come by before the time came for her to make her move.

Chimera had finished stitching a boy's arm and was affixing white adhesive tape around a gauze bandage when a huge commando still in uniform dragged a semiconscious form into the room.

"This one's been badly hurt," another commando behind the giant reported.

And as he continued speaking, Chimera found herself looking at Jamie Skylar.

The state trooper who had called in the report of the bridge explosion had managed to extract himself from his squad car and take cover behind a nest of trees to the right of the causeway's start on Castle Hill. A number of coastguardsmen approached from the station to his rear, but he waved them away. He was a lieutenant with fifteen years' police experience and a pair of tours with the Special Forces in Vietnam before that.

The constant whirl of sirens began five minutes later. The first policemen to arrive emerged with shotguns in hand, taking cover behind their squad cars and aiming quite ridiculously over a mile across the ruined bridge at nothing. The explosion had left barely half the causeway intact, jagged edges protruding outward like asphalt teeth into the vast open space where the rest had been. The squad cars came and kept coming from three separate communities and the state police. SWAT forces from nearby Providence were already en route as well, the lieutenant was told, and the coast guard had dispatched a cutter, two helicopters, and three crash boats to the scene.

The lieutenant accepted all this with a comical grin. None of these people seemed to realize they were up against absolute pros here. He knew the type, just as he knew that every police officer in the state of Rhode Island combined was no match for them. It wasn't a question of numbers; it was a question of style, and his own experience told the lieutenant the type of force that was needed in response.

Exactly twenty-one minutes after the explosion, the governor of the state of Rhode Island was stepping up to a podium to address a lunchtime meeting of the state's Librarians' Association. He had begun to ruffle through his notes when his chief aide stormed in from the rear of the room and carefully covered the mike before speaking.

The little color on the governor's cheeks vanished, and his lips replaced his aide's hand near the steel foil top of the microphone.

"I'm afraid something's come up, ladies and gentlemen, that requires my presence elsewhere. Miss Naismith," he said to the chairperson, "I'll return the microphone to you."

Without further word or explanation, the governor was gone down the center of the room, his pace approaching a jog under the befuddled, wondering eyes of the members of the Librarians' Association. He stopped on the steps outside and faced his aide.

"I hope I didn't hear you right back there, Dennis."

"You did. Details are still sketchy. I've been filling them in as best I can. We've got thirty police on the scene now, with another eighty en route."

"Christ . . ."

"I've alerted the FBI and I've got a helicopter standing by to take you to the scene."

"What about Washington? I mean, it seems like I should speak to someone in Washington."

"Bart Jacoby, head of the Bureau's Counterterrorism Division, is waiting for your call. He'll provide all necessary links for us."

"Links with who, Dennis?"

Cabral shrugged. "I'm new at all this, and there's no textbook to follow. My guess is the White House, the army, and everyone else who wants to stick their fingers in the pot."

"Gonna get them burned," the governor sighed. "And I, for one, can already smell the smoke."

"Mr. Jacoby, this is Governor—"

"Governor, I have the President's chief of staff, Charles Banks, on this same line. Can you hear me clearly?"

"Yes."

"Good. Your aide has informed me state and local law enforcement officials have been dispatched to the scene of the seizure."

"That's correct."

"Under no circumstances are those officials to approach the island. Is that clear?"

The governor almost asked how the fuck they were supposed to do that with no bridge to cross but simply said, "Yes."

"Under no circumstances are those officials to initiate or attempt to initiate any contact with the terrorists. Is that clear?"

Again, "Yes."

"If contacted by the terrorists, they will respond only that government authorities are en route and they are not authorized to speak. Is that clear?"

Hey, are you forgetting this is my state? the governor thought.

"Is that clear, Governor?"

"I'm sorry. Yes."

"You will remain by this line."

The governor swallowed hard. "I feel I should be on the scene."

"As you wish. So long as you are never out of contact. I can't overemphasize that, sir."

"I understand."

"And I appreciate it. We're going by the book here, but there are plenty of pages that haven't been touched upon before."

"Is there anything else?"

"Is there any way you can obtain a list of those enrolled and working at the school?"

"It's a private institution," the governor told Jacoby. "We don't have access."

"As I expected. What about general numbers?"

"Let's see. I spoke at their graduation last year. . . . Say, five hundred students and seventy-five administrative, faculty, and other personnel. The local authorities may be able to be more specific."

"I'd prefer to keep them out of it for now."

"Of course."

"Besides, what I really need is an overview shot of the

island. A photograph, perhaps the original blueprints of the school.''

''I wouldn't know where to look. No one would.''

''Something, there must be something. A postcard, a picture, anything.''

And then the governor remembered. ''What about a painting?''

''A painting?''

''Presented to the State House four years back and currently hanging in the rotunda. Provides an overview drawn damn near to scale.''

''It'll have to do.''

''I'll send it down to you.''

''Don't bother. Just have it ready for our people when they get there.''

''All right,'' the President said, trying to calm himself. He had been caught with the news halfway to the gym and had returned immediately to his study. ''What else do we know, Charlie?''

''That's it,'' the chief of staff reported, with Roger Allen Doane looking on. ''The school's been seized and the bridge leading to it blown up.''

''Then apparently our shadow government didn't get the message we sent. I submit to you that they're going through with this strike, Pine Gap explosives and all. What happens next?''

''Nothing until we get a man on the scene,'' replied Roger Allen Doane. ''There's an FBI specialist en route.''

''Who else do we have on the pipe?''

''Delta Force commandos are on security alert. They'll be ready for the flight north out of Fort Bragg in a matter of minutes.''

The President looked to his water glass and then back to Doane. ''And who's our top man in such matters?''

''Colonel Alan Eastman, currently serving in the Tactics Department at the Pentagon. He helped build Delta Force.''

''Then here's how I want to play this. I want Delta airborne and their CO on the horn to me from the plane. I want Eastman on another plane and I want him on the phone at the same time I talk to the Delta CO. Clear?''

''Yes, sir.''

''Okay.'' Bill Riseman stood up. ''We've found our missing antimatter, gentlemen. Now the trick becomes getting it back.''

CHAPTER 28

CHIMERA had stood there frozen for a long instant, the shock plain on her features.

"This isn't one of the students," she managed, hoping neither of the commandos had noticed, "or faculty either."

"We don't know who he is," the much smaller one said while the giant continued to hold Jamie effortlessly in his arms. A huge machine gun was draped over his shoulder. "He washed up onshore. Probably came out of that first police car."

"First police car?" Chimera asked, playing dumb.

"The colonel wishes to interrogate him personally," the commando ordered.

"Lay him on that table over there," she instructed the giant.

Jamie looked semiconscious at best. His legs dragged and his arms flapped helplessly by his sides as the giant lowered his frame onto the table.

"Can I finish with the rest of the students first?"

"You can do whatever you want. Just make sure he doesn't die before the colonel has a chance to speak with him."

She was able to deal with the few minor injuries remaining in a matter of minutes. The smaller commando had stayed behind and now looked extremely bored. Chimera insisted he could go on his way. Given the condition of the prisoner, she explained, he wasn't going to be waking up soon, if at all. The commando shrugged and took his leave. Chimera closed the door to the infirmary's inner room and rushed to the examination table.

"Jamie, can you hear me?"

His eyes fluttered. She lowered her hands to his shoulders and shook him gingerly.

"Jamie, you've got to wake up. Do you hear me? You've got to wake up."

His eyelids opened halfway, and he spoke in a raspy, hurt voice. "Can't . . . see."

She reached to the counter behind her for a penlight and held it before his right eye, prying it open. "You've suffered a mild concussion. Blurred vision is a fairly common response. It will pass soon."

His senses seemed to sharpen. "Your voice. I know your voice."

"You must speak quieter, Jamie."

Recognition flashed over his features. "*Chi—*"

The rest of her name was smothered by a hand pressed over his mouth. "Shhhh! Speak quietly!"

Jamie tried to raise himself, but his head made him pay for it. He squinted to improve his vision.

"What are you doing here?" she asked him.

"I was going to ask you the same question, but I guess I already know the answer. You went to Australia, and what you found there brought you here. And now you're playing doctor."

She almost smiled. "Nurse anyway. And what I found was worse than I expected. The shadow government I told you about before we parted in Nicaragua is called the Valhalla Group, and this school is the centerpiece of their plan to seize control of the country. Only, the plan began a day earlier than I was expecting."

"Operation Thunder Clap," Jamie muttered, senses gradually clearing.

"Yes! Yes!" she followed, recalling Simon Winters's words. "But how could *you* know?"

"It's what they were discussing on the microchip. But there wasn't anything about taking over the whole country."

"What are you talking about?"

"Wanna hear a funny one? My sister was CIA. Her whole writing career was a front. She was a spy and she was down in Nicaragua spying on Riaz. Dry Affairs, not Wet ones. But then, you know about that, don't you? At least you did when you were Matira Silvaro of Division Six."

Chimera felt a chill. "Never mind that."

"Why? The two of you have quite a bit in common: you both used me to get your messages out."

"Your *sister*?"

"She more than you. It's why she called me down to Nicaragua in the first place. When things got hot she planted a microchip inside my ring that contained a conversation between Riaz and some man named Esteban detailing something called Operation Thunder Clap." Jamie paused. "This."

"Esteban must have been Valhalla's man in the Nicaraguan National Solidarity Committee," Chimera elaborated. "And you made it out of the country, you made it out with this chip. But you reached someone, didn't you? That's how you learned about your sister . . . and me."

"I did what you told me. I ended up at the American Embassy in Honduras. Another CIA man filled in the holes. Then he had a few drilled into himself while we were on our way to the airport."

"Of course," Chimera said, realizing. "Your microchip was the only concrete link to Valhalla. They had to recover it at all costs."

"But there was nothing on the chip about Valhalla or what Operation Thunder Clap is really about."

"There was still enough to make Valhalla try to abort it," she explained, holding back mention of the antimatter. "Only, their military representative wasn't keen on the idea and killed the other members as a result. He's running things now."

"There's more."

"What?"

"What is it you're not telling me?"

"Nothing you need to know for the time being. I'm going to bandage your eyes and face. When the colonel arrives, I'll exaggerate your wounds to him. You must not speak to him. You will pretend to be unconscious."

"But I could talk to him. Let me talk to him!"

"And say what? Do you think he'll believe you? This isn't the same Colonel Riaz whose sons you played football with. Besides . . ."

"Besides what?"

"Never mind. A fragment of the bridge must have struck you in the head. Nasty wound. Lots of blood, but just a few other small cuts besides. A blessing."

"Why?"

"Gives me an excuse to bandage you, to hide your identity. I need you, Jamie."

Chimera stopped and swabbed the wound on the top of his skull with alcohol. He flinched in pain. It would take six stitches to close the cut, maybe seven.

"Need *me*?" he moaned between labored breaths.

Chimera shot some novocaine home and went to work with the sutures. Amazing how good she was getting at it.

"I can't stop them alone. With you, I'll have a chance."

Jamie winced as she pulled a stitch through. "How many are there?"

"Fourteen or fifteen," she said.

"Tough odds."

"Only for now. Soon there'll be hundreds of soldiers on the mainland."

"Might as well be in another country."

"Until we let them know they've got help over here."

"How?"

"I don't know. But I will. I have to."

"What is it you're not telling me?" he repeated, the stitching completed.

"You'll have to keep quiet while I finish," she said, and hurried through the task of concealing his face with gauze wrap. She covered one of his eyes but left the other one free. That one eye scolded her for not answering his question, and he had been about to pose it again when the door to the inner room opened.

"I'd like to speak to him," said Colonel José Ramon Riaz.

"Gentlemen, this is President Riseman," the President said into the speakerphone on the desk in his study. "Colonel Eastman, are you there?"

"Yes, sir."

Alan Eastman was in the backseat of a car weaving through traffic en route from the Pentagon to Andrews Air Force Base, where a government Learjet was waiting for him. Eastman was the army's chief intelligence specialist in covert operations and terrorist activities. In the many power struggles he had been involved with on behalf of the United States, he had wooed groups devoted to every facet of political thought. As a result, he believed he could predict their reactions to any sort of stimulus or provocation.

"Are you there, Major Brickmeister?"

"You got the Brick, boss," said the head of the Delta Force antiterrorist unit from the cockpit of the C-130 already streaking toward Newport, Rhode Island.

The President looked at Charlie Banks, who could only nod, holding John Brickmeister's file open on his lap. Brickmeister was a career combat soldier who'd learned his trade as staff sergeant in Vietnam and stuck with the army ever since. He was forty-six years old, but his looks had not changed appreciably for the last decade. At six feet and two hundred pounds of rock-hard muscle, curly hair cropped close, he was the embodiment of the phrase "born to be a soldier."

The major's father, a wealthy South Carolina plantation owner, had carried on an affair with one of his black house maids and Brickmeister was the result. He had grown up an outcast, accepted by neither race. He learned the only way to survive was never to back down. Authority had little meaning to him unless it was duly earned, and though he was a soldier, the formalities of respect were lost on him.

Brickmeister had been put in charge of Delta because he was the best damn crisis field commander an exhaustive search could turn up. In the transport plane he was dressed just as his men were, in green fatigues and cap. Amongst them he blended perfectly. There was no assigned training regimen that he did not complete himself along with them. Right now, in fact, Brickmeister would have much preferred being back in the cabin with his seventy men instead of in the cockpit with headset pressed tight, talking to the President.

"Very well," Bill Riseman continued. "For your information. I have National Security Adviser Roger Allen Doane and my chief of staff, Charlie Banks, here with me. The rest of the cabinet will be briefed once we've concluded our business. This group is small for a reason, gentlemen. I want us on subject and with all the facts. Colonel Eastman, have you had time to review the data?"

"I have, sir."

"And your assessment?"

"Logistically, this is a nightmare. Of available land, sea, and air approach routes, a viable counterstrike in any situation makes use of a minimum of two. We don't have that window."

"Negotiation is obviously the first option we will pursue, but we must be prepared on other fronts in the event that fails."

Eastman caught the President's meaning instantly. "Realistically our only viable option is a nighttime helicopter assault. But in a contained hostage situation like this one, we'd be almost certain to encounter friendly casualties."

"Do you agree with that, Major Brickmeister?"

"Only the part about dead friendlies," the Delta Force commander replied in his lazy South Carolina drawl. "See, boss, it's like this. Al's right about dropping troops off a chopper into a landing zone this hot. On this island, they'll see and hear 'em coming from a mile or even two away, especially with eyes in that steeple tower I already been warned about. We got about as much chance of pulling off a safe quickdrop as you would keeping your shoes clean in a cow patch at night. Thing we gotta do in that case is shovel all the shit aside first."

"I don't think I follow you, Major."

"Al's right in saying we need two legs to make a counterstrike, but he's wrong in ruling out one coming in from the sea."

"You're talking about a much longer window of sight zone than the choppers, Major," Eastman argued. "They'd be sitting ducks."

From the speaker, Brickmeister's heavy drawl again filled the study. "Yeah, well, I heard it said you bring protection with you to a whore, you end up doing things you ain't protected for. What we gotta do, we gotta give these shit-eaters what their eyes expect so their minds won't look for more."

"Do you have a plan for that, Major?" asked the President.

"I'm bettin' I do."

"Care to enlighten us?"

"Nope. Need to get a few things nailed down first."

"Such as?"

"These shit-eaters did us a favor by going after St. Michael's. There's a navy SEAL training base spittin' distance away. Give me a dozen SEALS to go with my men and we'll have Castle Island back before they have time to piss on the flowers. My boys'll come in by sea, which means we'll need reinforcements to handle the chopper drop into the LZ."

"There's a detachment of Rangers on alert at Fort Stewart in Georgia," said Roger Allen Doane.

"Well, they ain't doin' us no good down there pickin' cotton. Get 'em airborne for Newport."

"How long until you can be functional?" asked the President.

"Five minutes after the Rangers roll in, boss," Brickmeister assured.

"On that subject," Eastman picked up, "I requested a full recon sweep. Mr. Doane?"

The national security adviser moved closer to the speaker. "The closest Blackbird SR-71X jet was in at Brandenberg for some minor repairs. She's airborne now and will dispatch her photos direct to you. We've set up a command center at the former Quonsett naval air base across the bay from Newport."

"Move it," said Brickmeister.

"Excuse me?"

"Quonsett's too far from the zone by road, and road's the way my boys'll have to get to the water. Besides, the shit-eaters woulda figured on Quonsett. Everything we do to cross them up scores us points. We'll fly these big C-130 suckers into Quonsett and then chopper over to Newport State Airport in Middletown, our new command center."

"Less than two miles from Castle Hill," noted Charlie Banks after consulting his map.

"You got that right. What we're gonna need at this point is the area sealed tight as can be. Once word spreads, we're gonna have more traffic up there than a whorehouse give-away. Call up the local national guard and the coast guard and tell them to give us a firm perimeter. Nobody gets through, including the media. I don't want the shit-eaters tuning in to our plans on television."

"Also send a small squad of guardsmen down to the area of the causeway," added Eastman. "The terrorists will be expecting uniforms, and the sooner we provide them, the better they'll feel."

"See," picked up Brickmeister, "we want them to figure they got us as dick-whacked as a Milquetoast groom. They don't see Delta until Delta's ready to roll."

"Nobody said Delta was going to roll, Major."

"You ordered us functional. Functional means ready. Like a bull in heat, boss. We assume we're going in until the cow tells us otherwise."

"Anything else, Major?"

"Yeah. You ready for my shopping list at the Washington General Store?"

"Mr. Doane has his pen out."

"Fix me up with eight of the fastest speedboats your people can lay their hands on, and the same number of attack rafts. Ravens would be my top choice. Those black bastards ride the waves as good as a five-hundred-dollar whore rides the sheets."

Doane looked up from his memo pad. "What do you need with speedboats *and* rafts, Major?"

"Gotta give the shit-eaters two things, boss. First makes 'em turn the way we want 'em so we can drive the second straight up their backsides."

Colonel Riaz stood in the doorway, as if waiting for Chimera to invite him inside.

"Who is he?" the colonel asked.

"I don't know. He hasn't spoken."

Riaz stepped inside, clothed now in sport jacket and slacks, just as were those of his men mixed among the St. Michael's population to confuse any aerial or land-based reconnaissance. Everything possible had to be done to thwart all types of surveillance. He moved forward and leaned over Jamie's still form on the table.

"Badly injured?"

"A concussion, some serious facial lacerations, and severe internal bleeding. There's not much more I can do here. My suggestion is he be brought to a hospital."

"That will have to wait." He regarded her closely with his one eye. "The headmaster tells me you were merely interviewing for the nurse's job today."

"I suppose this means I've gotten it."

Riaz smiled. "You've kept your sense of humor. That's good."

"I'm not scared. If you had meant to kill us, we'd be dead already."

Riaz was looking at Jamie. "I'd like very much to know who he is and what brought him—a civilian—across the bridge with the police."

"Maybe you've got the scenario wrong. Maybe he's a

teacher here at the school and was trying to escape when the bridge blew."

Riaz turned back to her. "I hadn't thought of that." Then puzzlement crossed his features. "Interesting that you should know the bridge was blown up."

Chimera knew she'd slipped up and been caught at it. "One of your men who brought him in here was quite specific about how he may have received his wounds," she said.

Riaz seemed satisfied. "I will send the headmaster here to see if he can identify him. It is possible he could be offered to the authorities as a sign of good faith once contact is established."

Chimera made herself look relieved. "That's very kind."

"We are not murderers. Please believe that."

"I'd like to."

As if on cue, a younger man with a bandana tied across his forehead over the coldest eyes Chimera had ever seen stormed to Riaz's side. He adressed the colonel rapidly in Spanish.

"I have ordered the men not to check the nets as planned. A pair of coast guard helicopters are flying overhead. They are watching our every move from the mainland. If the men were seen—"

"Your logic is sound," Riaz interrupted. "It was merely a formality in any case."

"The arming systems do check, though."

"I understand." Riaz gazed one last time at Jamie's apparently unconscious form. "You will inform me immediately if he regains consciousness," he ordered Chimera. "I will send the headmaster here as soon as he assists me in making the students more comfortable. If I decide to let him be transported to the mainland, I will let you know."

Riaz departed with the smaller man by his side and the door left open behind him. They were heading down the corridor back for the dining hall when his walkie-talkie squawked.

"Come in, Colonel."

"This is Riaz."

"Sanchez here, Colonel. Javier was injured in the bridge explosion, sir. He tried to bandage the wound himself, but the bleeding has gotten worse."

"Send him to the infirmary," Riaz ordered. "There's a nurse waiting."

Chimera didn't close the door until Colonel Riaz and the smaller man had passed out of sight. She was moving back toward Jamie when he at last succeeded in propping himself up on the table.

"He said something about arming systems," he said. "I didn't catch much, but I caught that."

"Keep your voice down!"

"Tell me what it means." And then Jamie remembered something else. "Nets! One of them mentioned nets, too!"

Chimera was just comprehending the meaning of the words for herself. "The Valhalla Group planned this entire operation to the letter, and that includes a complete grasp of all potential countermeasures. If the forces on the mainland strike, the initial wave will come in the form of scuba divers, Navy SEALs probably. So Valhalla must have managed to have nets erected around the island, undoubtedly mined with explosives. A diver brushes up against one of them and he's blown to bits. It's what they want. It's when they'll trigger the Quick Strike."

"Quick Strike . . . You mentioned that in Nicaragua; it was part of the message I delivered. Quick Strike explosives stolen from Pine Gap. Esteban said something about them to Riaz on the microchip. What exactly can they do?"

"They must have used C-4 *plastique* on the bridge, Jamie, say about twenty pounds of it. Each Quick Strike charge is worth ten times that."

"Jesus," Jamie muttered, recalling his sighting of what had remained of the causeway. "And just how many charges do they have?"

"Eight of Quick Strike . . . and four of something worse."

"Something *worse*?"

It was time to get everything out, Chimera figured. "Valhalla thought they came out of Pine Gap with a dozen charges of Quick Strike. But they got more than they bargained for. Four of the charges are actually containment shells for antimatter."

Jamie's single exposed eye regarded her questioningly.

"It's the most volatile material ever discovered, so volatile that when Castle Island gets blown, nobody knows how far-reaching the effects might be."

"What do you mean *when* the island gets blown?"

"Riaz will threaten to destroy the school if his terms aren't met. But the school is going to be destroyed, the charges detonated, regardless. The present administration and its policies must be disgraced. The groundwork for Valhalla's ascension to power must be laid."

"I know Riaz. He'd never do something like that," Jamie insisted.

"Maybe. It doesn't matter, because he won't be the one to press the button when the time comes. Valhalla's planted their own man in his group."

"And the man running things now is going to go through with it anyway, even though he knows about the antimatter?"

"He seized this as his opportunity to take over." The irony of it all suddenly occurred to her. "I don't know, maybe the risks don't bother him. Maybe there's something else I haven't figured out yet."

Jamie hesitated. "Have you figured out what we can do?"

"For starters, get word off the island to the authorities about the existence of this mined net. Let them know they've got help on the inside."

"Impossible!"

"If that's the case, my only option is to hunt the terrorists down and kill them one by one."

"Alone?"

"It's what I do, Jamie, what I've always done. They don't know I'm here, and their numbers are spread throughout the island. Those are advantages I can make use of."

"I won't let you," Jamie started, "I won't—"

The door crashed open to reveal one of the commandos still dressed in the uniform of a state worker, his small machine gun thrust forward.

"I think the colonel will be most interested in hearing about this," he said in English.

CHAPTER 29

"A GOOD idea, don't you think, Mr. George?" Colonel Riaz asked.

The headmaster of St. Michael's School looked suddenly more relaxed. "Most certainly. The faculty and I have been circulating to reassure them, but the fear's still growing. Back in the dorms, even jammed that tight, we'll have at least the facade of normalcy."

"But they are not to leave them under any circumstances, not to be seen in the corridors. The outside windows have been wired with explosives that will go off if they so much as open the latch. You will make that clear to them. You will separate the faculty equally among the dormitories and the same rules will hold true for them as well."

"I understand."

"My men will be guarding the four dorm buildings in question. Of course, they won't be able to see everything, but the members of your community will have nothing to gain by taking advantage of that."

"Of course."

Riaz looked at his watch. "We will begin the process of moving students from here back to the dorms immediately.

Four major dormitories, one to be filled every fifteen minutes. The entire process must not take more than one hour."

Headmaster George smiled, as if the gesture might have some impact on Riaz. "I can assure you such precautions are not necessary."

"It has nothing to do with precautions, Mr. George. I assure *you* I have my reasons."

As if on cue, the colonel's walkie-talkie let out a squawk.

"This is Beide, sir," came the voice of his spotter on duty in the steeple tower that stretched high above the school's famed chapel.

"I read you, Beide."

"Looks like the man you've been expecting has just arrived on the mainland. Brown sedan, government plates. Stepped out of the backseat like he means to be in charge."

"FBI," Riaz said, mostly to himself. Then, after a glance at his watch, "Right on schedule."

"He's talking into a microphone now. Has his eyes on what's left of the bridge."

"I know the frequency. Perhaps it's time to give him a call."

The commando dressed as a state worker stepped farther into the infirmary. Blood had drenched a makeshift bandage he had tied around his forearm. He seemed to be enjoying himself.

"You will both stay where you are and raise your arms slowly into the air," he ordered, keeping his gun level.

But the commando had positioned himself in a way that made it impossible for him to look at both Chimera and Jamie simultaneously. Chimera waited until his eyes had turned toward the examination table before lunging. Her initial move was to lock the rifle down with one hand and jam the second hard under his chin, with palm heel leading. But the man shifted, and all she managed was a glancing blow to his cheek. She heard him wheeze in both pain and anger, and she was helpless to ward off the elbow he snapped toward her head. She managed to duck, but the strike stunned her nonetheless, enough perhaps for him to regain control of his gun.

Knowing the sound of gunfire would bring reinforcements, Jamie dropped down painfully from the table. He had only one eye to work with, enough because it had to be. He grabbed the glass jar full of cotton balls Chimera had been using and thrust himself at the commando, leading with the jar.

The glass shattered against his face. The man stiffened horribly and would have screamed if Chimera hadn't clamped a hand over his mouth. Enraged, the man bit into her flesh and seemed to be struggling to right his grip on his rifle when Jamie brought a jagged edge of glass he still held forward. It missed Chimera by no more than an inch, passing into the hard flesh of the man's stomach and digging deep through muscle and sinew.

The man's head snapped backward. His eyes bulged. Jamie could see his mouth drop behind Chimera's hand, but the only sound heard was the air escaping his body with the last of his life. His eyes grew glassy as he started to slump down the wall, glazed over by the time he reached the floor with Chimera's hand still covering his mouth. She pulled it back to find the man's blood coating it.

Jamie sank to his knees huffing. His hand was bleeding from several lacerations caused by squeezing the jagged shard as he drove it deep into the man's gut. But his mind had sharpened anew. His heart pounded and he could feel much of his pain receding. Then Chimera was kneeling near him, checking his hand, reaching for yet more bandages to wrap it with.

"I guess this changes things," he said in purposeful understatement.

"He won't be missed for a while," Chimera surmised as she wrapped Jamie's hand. "His clothes indicate he was on the demolitions team that blew the bridge. His assignment from there was probably a patrol area. By himself."

"He'd have reports to issue, regular ones, right?"

"Riaz has more important things to concern himself with. We'll have time. Some. Enough."

"Not enough to follow your original plan. They'll know someone's here. They'll know something's wrong."

"There never was an original plan, just thinking, and now the thinking has to change. I can't do it alone. *We* can't do it alone."

"We *are* alone."

"No, we have hundreds of commandos at our disposal, thousands maybe. The best military minds, the finest soldiers, the best equipment."

Jamie caught her meaning. "Sure. On the mainland a mile away. It might as well be a thousand."

"Don't be too sure. Our primary task is to help them so they can help us. They won't be able to make it without that help. Unless we get word out, their operation will come to a sudden end as soon as the Navy SEALs swim into those mined nets. So might plenty more if that leads to detonation of the Quick Strike . . . and the antimatter."

"You're forgetting something, aren't you?" Jamie asked, with his eyes on the corpse propped against the wall. "Even if what you say is true, we've got to dispose of his body, and we don't exactly have free range of the premises."

Chimera nodded her acknowledgment. "Help me get him on the table. He's going to become you."

Bart Jacoby couldn't believe his eyes. All the on-the-scene reports couldn't do justice to the mess he was looking at. Whoever had blown the bridge had knowledge as well as firepower. This was no ordinary hostage taking and would require anything but normal procedure once the terrorists initiated contact.

If they ever did.

It seemed strange to Jacoby that not a word had been heard from them yet. In most cases the bastards couldn't wait to talk, get their demands out in public and let the world know why they were here. Maybe they hadn't broken their silence yet because they were too busy watching the tube. So far all three major networks had broken in with bulletins, and CNN was already running continuous coverage. Up to now that coverage had focused on the dramatic and violent means of the takeover, with a shot of the remains of the causeway bridge projected over and over again. The scavengers were indeed circling, and the primary task of the coast guard choppers was now to shoo away other helicopters toting newsmen in quest of a closer look.

At the edge of Castle Hill, Jacoby found things calm enough, though he had to skirt between over two dozen parked police cars to reach it. The crowds had begun to gather a half mile away. The newspeople were permitted in a bit closer merely to make them feel they were receiving special treatment.

The Castle Hill Coast Guard Station a few hundred yards behind the shore had become the authorities' makeshift headquarters, and the ancient shoreline lighthouse was being manned by spotters. Even with binoculars, however, they couldn't really see anything worthwhile, and Jacoby didn't bother to join them in the tower. He'd stand here and wait for the terrorists to call. It was just after three-thirty now. By five, all of America would be settled behind their television sets listening to an endless parade of military and terrorist experts speculating on what had already happened and what would happen next. There would be maps and background stories, interviews with anyone they could lay their hands on with knowledge of St. Michael's, including some of the parents of those held hostage on Castle Island.

Jacoby saw it all evolving, and gnashed his teeth. It was only a matter of time, he supposed, before something like this was bound to happen. The United States had gotten off too easy in the terrorist game. He always feared that when the luck ran out, it would do so big time. This was Munich, Entebbe, and the Iranian hostage crisis all rolled into one. He would be running point against terrorist minds that promised to be as ruthless and driven as anyone could imagine.

But what did they want?

As Jacoby allowed himself to speculate on the answer to that question, a Rhode Island state trooper approached and jostled him from his thoughts.

"Excuse me, sir, but I think I've got a call for you. From the island."

"Me?"

"Well, I think so. The voice on the other end asked to speak to the FBI man who had just arrived in the brown sedan."

"This is Colonel José Ramon Riaz," came the accented voice over the microphone, "of the People's Republic of Nicaragua. A country ravaged first by your bullets and now by the flood of your dollars and your high-handed puppet government."

Jacoby nodded to a subordinate who'd been listening in on a different mike. Instantly the man let it dangle and rushed back to the brown sedan to learn what he could from the laptop computer plugged directly into the FBI and CIA data banks in Washington.

Back on the island, Colonel Riaz gazed out the huge bay window that overlooked the mainland from the headmaster's office. Not much was visible so far other than a tangle of cars, but the rest of the picture was clear in his mind.

"You will find a very large file on me, I'm sure," he followed into the microphone. "I would like to know to whom I am speaking."

"Special Agent Bart Jacoby of the FBI."

"And your title?"

"Assistant director of counterterrorism and intelligence."

"Good."

"Is anyone on the island hurt?" Jacoby asked, tapping the top of the car roof impatiently while he waited for his subordinate to return with a report on Colonel Riaz. There were plenty of inconsistencies already, not the least of which was the fact that a report out of Managua had Riaz being gunned down in his home ten days before by marauding Contras.

"The bridge explosion blew out a number of windows, and several students suffered cuts. Not very severe, I'm told, and if any turn out to be, I will allow you to come and get them."

"That's very kind."

"We are not murderers, Mr. Jacoby. This does not have to end unpleasantly for any of us."

"You'll have to excuse my impertinence, Colonel, but reports handed me indicate at least nine policemen are dead or unaccounted for."

"And that is on my head. Whatever happens from here on in will be on yours."

Jacoby swallowed hard. "I'm not the one threatening the lives of children."

"Not just any children, though, are they?"

"I don't know what you mean."

"Yes, you do." Still standing by the window, Riaz recited his next lines from memory. "No less than sixty-five of the students enrolled here are the children of senators, congressmen, or cabinet members. Another forty are in some way related to such government officials. The hundred largest corporations in your country are represented by one hundred and sixty-four students."

"You've made your point."

"On the contrary, Mr. Jacoby," Riaz said into the mike of his portable radio, "I haven't even begun to make my point yet. Here at St. Michael's reside the children of those men, the lawmakers and the business leaders, who have taken over my country with their industry, their dollars, and their despicable puppet rulers. After failing to conquer us with your bullets, you now try to corrupt us. You wish to destroy the life that belongs to us for us and our children."

Keep the issue defined in terms as limited as possible, Jacoby reminded himself. *Don't belittle the opponent, but keep everything in a containable focus.*

"I'm not a politician," he said, "and I'm not a businessman either."

"All Americans are politicians, Mr. Jacoby. Having to deny you are only reaffirms that fact."

"I can't change American policy. I think you know that."

"But I can. And you, I'm afraid, have been placed in the unenviable position of helping me."

Jacoby's out-of-breath subordinate returned with a pile of faxes haphazardly wedged in a manila folder. Jacoby took the folder from him but didn't open it, careful not to do anything that might cause him to lose his train of thought.

"If that's the case, Colonel, it would be useful to know exactly what I was helping you to do."

"Change the world, Mr. Jacoby, and that's just for starters."

"Then everything makes sense now," concluded the President, pacing the room ferociously enough for sweat to show through his warm-up suit. "Our shadow government killed Riaz's family and convinced him to blame us. Now he's up there in Newport with the means to do plenty more than keep us out of the White House for a second term."

The President's hands turned to fists, and he drummed the desk. "Well, at least we're aware the demands Riaz issued to Jacoby are academic. They know we can't act upon them, and so do we. By the same token, they know our only chance is a counterstrike, and that's probably just what they're hoping for so they can detonate. And yet if we don't hit them, they could use the excuse that we've missed their deadline and detonate the explosives anyway. Catch twenty-three, gentlemen."

"Unless we call their bluff," raised Banks. "Just say fuck it and call their bluff by giving in to their demands and ordering our people to evacuate Nicaragua."

"I'm not sure we have the right to do that," countered Doane, "even under these circumstances."

"You're missing my point. We know from Skylar's statement that they killed Riaz's family to coerce the colonel into leading this operation. You read the same file on him as I did. He come across as the mass murderer type to you, Roger?"

"Not before his family was massacred, no. Now, who knows?"

"And I'm not about to base our judgement on psychological profiles," said Bill Riseman. "We know their intention is to detonate no matter what our response is, whether it's Riaz who pushes the button or someone else. The presence of the antimatter changes everything. Now that we know the site, Roger, I want the scenario if the bastards detonate."

The national security adviser cleared his throat. "The location couldn't be a worse one so far as the effects are concerned. The explosion would send ripples up and down most of the East Coast and hurricanes caused by air flooding in through the hole ripped in the atmosphere. Worse than that, coastal cities will be facing tsunamis traveling at upwards of 650 miles per hour." Doane hesitated, to do some calculations in his mind. "Within two hours after the blast, the East Coast down to Washington will be underwater to a hundred miles inland."

"My God . . . the cities, the *people*!"

Doane's grave stare provided his only response.

"We can't let the bastards detonate these explosives," Bill Riseman said, with less assurance than he had tried for. "We've got to put this in Brickmeister and Eastman's hands and let them do what they've been trained to do."

"Mr. President," said Banks formally, "just how much do you intend to tell them?"

"What they need to know to get the job done. They're employees of this country, Charlie, just like we are, and today all of us are going to be earning our paychecks."

The Learjet carrying Colonel Alan Eastman landed at Newport State Airport forty minutes after Brickmeister and Delta Force had come in. Blackhawk UH-60 helicopters had ferried Delta across the bay from Quonsett to the command center Brickmeister had chosen. The first thing Eastman saw upon deplaning was a number of Delta troops downloading equipment, weapons, and ammunition into the airport's single hangar. A number of single-engine planes that had been shoved outward to make room now cluttered the off-ramp areas of the tarmac. Eastman reached the main building to find Brickmeister supervising the rest of his men and some national guardsmen in the transformation of the airport lobby into a command center.

"Over there with that, I said!" Brickmeister was roaring. "Over there!"

The lobby's sixty-by-forty floor was being filled with tables, computer terminals, communications outlets, a Med-Vac center. Those not busy with the hefting and hoisting were unfolding recon maps and arranging them in the proper order. The elaborate typographical maps had been delivered by both the Army Corps of Engineers and Rhode Island's Department of Public Works. One of the reasons Brickmeister was fuming was that neither set included very much at all about Castle Island.

"Delta's used to blueprints and scale mock-ups, Al," Brickmeister explained after they exchanged greetings. "These things are 'bout as useful as plastic wrap for a condom. Come on upstairs and I'll show you the best we got to work from."

The best thing about using the lobby as a command center, other than that the three windowed sides provided plenty of light, was the private office on the second floor, easily accessible by a set of stairs. Brickmeister closed the door to the wood-paneled, carpeted office of Newport Helicopters behind Eastman. This room, too, was messily cluttered with new machines and tables that had been delivered in the past ninety minutes on instructions issued by the major from the air. Standing upright on one of the tables against the wall was a massive painting of what Eastman knew was St. Michael's School. Drawn to scale and still in its frame.

"It ain't much," said Brickmeister. "But it'll have to do for now. Don't matter anyway now, since the first pics from the Blackbird just came through."

He led Eastman to a table set in the center of the office. Across its top a series of eight-by-ten photographs had been laid out.

"Got us a computer that's running what they call heat-enhancement programs to pin down explosives and stray bodies. But what do your eyes make of these?"

Eastman took a magnifying glass from the Delta Force commander and ran it along the series of photos the recon plane had come up with. He stopped occasionally but gave no hint of response or reaction until he had surveyed them all.

"They're moving the students," he concluded.

"From the dining hall to the dorms," Brickmeister elaborated. "Blackbird caught two batches in transit, one in each of her passes."

"Routine terrorist strategy. Splintering the hostages to make our job tougher. We helped write the book, after all."

"Well, this one's got a few different pages. The shit-eaters wait over two hours after taking the island to move the hostages, and when they do move them, it's done in shifts about fifteen minutes apart. Ring any bells?"

"Christ, they planned it for our benefit. They knew about the Blackbird!"

"Ding-dong. Know what else? They wanted us to know they knew," Brickmeister said over the din of machinery still being assembled in the makeshift command center beneath them. "They're showing us they know what hand it is we wipe our ass with."

A phone placed on a desk that had been wiped clean of the usual occupant's paperwork rang.

"Direct line to Washington," Brickmeister said as he moved for it. "Sixteen hundred, if you get my drift . . . You got the Brick," he said when he got there.

"Bill Riseman here, Major. Is Colonel Eastman with you?"

"Hold on and I'll put you on speaker."

"For the record, will that enable anyone else to hear this conversation?"

"Negative, sir," Brickmeister replied, and switched the call onto the speaker.

"Also for the record, Roger Doane and Charlie Banks are with me. Gentlemen, we have established contact with the perpetrators of the seizure. All pertinent intelligence material will be faxed in a matter of minutes, but part of it I wanted you to hear from me. The group is made up of Nicaraguan left-wingers who resent the American presence in their country. The group's leader is one Colonel José Ramon Riaz."

"El Diablo de la Jungla," muttered Eastman.

"I see you've heard of him."

"Only of his exploits. And if half of them are true, then we're facing one hell of a formidable enemy. But wait a minute, last week in Nicaragua . . ."

"He wasn't killed, Colonel, but his family was."

"Oh Christ . . . The report mentioned Contras. He blames us. That's what this is about, isn't it?"

"His terms include the abandonment of all American corporate interests in Nicaragua, so the answer must be yes. Construction sites are to be abandoned and then either bulldozed, razed, or demolished. He gave us forty-eight hours to complete the task, and if we fail to meet his deadline, he will blow up the island."

"The school, you mean, sir," corrected Eastman.

"No, Colonel, I mean the island. Gentlemen, here's where things start to get touchy," the President said. "Colonel Riaz has in his possession a dozen charges of a new kind of explosive called Quick Strike. What it is or how he came to possess it are not relevant at this time. What is relevant is that he has the firepower to follow through on his threat."

"Jesus H. Christ," muttered Brickmeister.

"Gentlemen," Bill Riseman continued with his eyes on Doane and Banks, "it is our feeling that Colonel Riaz has purposely issued a series of demands we cannot possibly fulfill. It is further our feeling that he intends to detonate the explosives as promised when that inability becomes clear. I am therefore authorizing a military option to be undertaken. I want to know what we can pull off and how soon we can do it. Major Brickmeister?"

"It goes like this, boss. Under cover of darkness we can be up their backsides quicker than a hot summer itch. The sun sets up here at 4:59, and one hour later it's completely dark. There's no moon, and the forecast calls for overcast skies."

"*Tonight's* forecast, Major?"

"Sir," picked up Eastman, "if we're going to hit them, it's got to be tonight. Each hour they settle in and control the territory lengthens the odds of our success."

"Colonel, it's already after four o'clock now."

"We got bigger problems than that, boss," said Brickmeister. "The presence of these explosives means we can't do diddley until they're secured. That means no chopper quickdrop for the Rangers and no sea staging for Delta."

"Can they be secured under the circumstances?"

"If the Blackbird can pinpoint their locales and if the SEALs can work their magic, you bet."

"Tonight, Major?"

"We'll hit 'em at nine," assured Brickmeister. "That gives us almost five hours. I need any more time than that, boss, you might as well reassign me to the Boy Scouts."

"You didn't tell them about the antimatter," said Charlie Banks somberly.

"No, I didn't."

"Bill, in my mind those men have a right to know what they're up against, what the real stakes here are."

"Only if it could help them, Charlie. Let them think they're just saving the island. That's plenty enough for them to worry about."

CHAPTER 30

"YOU really think this is going to work?" Jamie asked as Chimera completed the task of covering the commando's fatal stab wound with tight bandages.

In essence, Jamie had exchanged clothes with the dead man, everything except shoes, since the soldier's were hopelessly too small for him. Jamie felt chilled pulling himself into the corpse's pants and blood-soaked shirt. He did his best to focus on Chimera as she carefully wrapped the commando's face and scalp to match Jamie's appearance as Colonel Riaz had seen it.

"It's got to if we're going to save ourselves and get word off the island about the nets. This way the forces on the mainland can snatch the element of surprise from Riaz and use it for themselves. The colonel's depending on the nets to alert him to the strike when it comes. No explosives set off, no strike—and here we are to help the good guys when they storm the island."

"You still haven't told me how we're going to tell them about the nets without getting off the island ourselves."

Chimera finished wrapping the corpse's face and made a few minor adjustments. Satisfied, she turned back to Jamie.

"Just help me find a pen. . . ."

* * *

The last of the students were just leaving the dining hall when Chimera approached Colonel Riaz.

"The man your soldiers found washed up onshore has died," she reported. "There was nothing I could do."

Riaz showed no reaction. "You did your best."

"He was a plainclothes Newport police officer. He regained consciousness briefly and thought he was still in the car crossing the bridge. Apparently your men shot up that car prior to blowing the bridge."

The colonel was still wondering what had brought that car to the island in the first place, with three officers inside, no less. "Regrettably, yes."

"What do you want me to do with the body?"

"Get it ready to be moved. We'll let the dead officer go home."

"Do you read me, Mr. Jacoby?"

"I'm here, Colonel Riaz."

"You've spoken with the President, I assume."

"Yes."

"Can I assume he is considering my ultimatum?"

"You've left us no choice other than to consider it. But, Colonel, providing us with only forty-eight hours for such a task is hardly realistic."

"If I give you more time, you will squander it. The demolitions process will not be difficult once you undertake it."

Jacoby hesitated. "The press has obtained the precise details of our arrangement."

"Have they?"

"They had them in hand minutes after our discussion."

"Quite efficient, aren't they?"

"You arranged for the information to be leaked to them."

"Mr. Jacoby, you overestimate me."

"The President requests that I ask for more time."

"Of course he does. My answer is no. Now, let us dispense with the formalities, Mr. Jacoby. We are both professionals and, I hope, respect each other for that much. The President will have strategy meetings and various agendas to fulfill, but in the end he will see that he has no choice other than to submit."

"Why are you doing this, Colonel? Do you really think Nicaragua is better served by having us out of it? Don't you want your nation to have an economic future?"

"At what price, Mr. Jacoby? Everything has its price, and this one is too vast to pay. We will become another of your satellites, another of your wretched dependents where the wealthy prosper and the poor share nothing, ruled over by corrupt leaders who grow fat on our poverty. And beyond that, many of the most vile of the Contras we forced into exile have now returned. They have not changed, Mr. Jacoby. Nothing has changed."

"You blame us for what happened to your family."

"I blame you for creating the atmosphere that allowed it to happen."

"Killing more children will not bring yours back."

Jacoby had rehearsed that line several times, wondering what Riaz's reaction would be. He thought he had considered all the possibilities, but he must have missed one.

The colonel laughed. "I was waiting for you to say that. I wondered how long you'd wait. You Americans are so predictable. You are so ruled by your emotions that you believe the rest of the world to be equally vulnerable. You are wrong, Mr. Jacoby. If this was about emotions, another man would be leading my mission."

"And that's why you've mentioned nothing about your own future. You don't care. When all this is over, you don't care what happens to you."

"I am yours to take into custody, Mr. Jacoby. I would welcome the trial. I would welcome the chance to tell my side of the story. You will either let me go or kill me, because you cannot let that side be told."

"So you kill more children in the name of justice. Is that it?" Jacoby challenged.

"I have killed no children. Not yet, not ever if you accept my terms. But I did not call you to discuss politics. A policeman who managed to reach shore has died. I would like to make arrangements to return the body."

"Just name them."

"You will send a small boat with two men to the pier on the eastern side of the island facing Castle Hill. Two of my men will be waiting there with the body."

"You'll guarantee my men's safety?"

"I have no need for further hostages."

"How long?"

"Twenty minutes."

"We'll be there."

The van reached the pier ahead of the boat dispatched to pick up the dead policeman. The rickety structure could never have accommodated its weight, so the driver brought it to a halt while still on the road that circled the entire St. Michael's complex. The two men in the rear threw open the van's doors and took the stretcher out after them.

They could see the boat drawing closer as they started to advance down the pier, choosing their steps carefully, their balance threatened by the sway. The corpse rocked on the stretcher, listing from side to side to the rhythm of the men's steps. The van's driver had advanced ahead of them to tie down the small boat when it was close enough.

Motor cut now, it drifted with the currents the last of the way. The other commandos stopped ten feet from the mooring and lowered the stretcher to the pier before the final effort of passing it onto the boat. One of the men lost his grip, and the stretcher rocked hard to the left, sheet-covered corpse teetering on the edge before a quick twist righted it.

In the process, one of the corpse's arms slipped out, its sleeve pulled back, and the skin exposed to the light.

The man at the head of the stretcher had reached down to push it back beneath the sheet when he froze, screaming as he went for the rifle dangling at his shoulder.

"Por Dios!"

Clearly the men who had come in the boat could not be the object of his wrath, and just as clearly the commando had not intended to fire on them.

But the FBI men saw the gun coming around nonetheless and drew their own in response.

"What the *fuck* is—"

The commando who had tied down the boat heard that in the wake of the scream from behind him, saw the men's guns, and responded. Before the nearest one could complete his question, he had shot him in the head four times. The second FBI man had spun unsurely and been cut down by shots coming from the stretcher bearer who had first seen the corpse's forearm exposed.

To reveal the tattoo of a cobra coiled to spring.

The same tattoo all the members of the commando team wore in the identical spot.

Bart Jacoby had watched it all through his binoculars from the lighthouse, watched it unfold the way a massive accident does on the highway. He was too far away to hear the gunshots, so the sight of smoke and muzzle flashes seemed almost surreal.

"My God, my God . . ."

Then he was clutching for the microphone, composure lost and all trace of professionalism gone. Those were his men, damnit, *his men*!

"Riaz! Come in, Riaz! What the fuck's going on? . . . Riaz, do you read me?"

Riaz heard the question through the radio but didn't heed it. He grasped for his walkie-talkie instead.

"What's happening? What's happening?"

"Colonel," came the frenzied voice of one of his men, "the corpse wasn't a policeman. *It was one of us!* Javier, I think . . . yes, Javier."

Riaz went cold as he absorbed the implications. Javier had gone to the infirmary to have a wound bandaged. The infirmary!

"Bring me the nurse! Do you hear me? *Bring me the nurse!*"

Chimera was standing by the window when the door to the infirmary burst open.

"Come on!" Jamie ordered. "You've got to get out of

here!'' She tried to speak, but his words rolled over hers. ''There's no time! They know! Do you hear me? It didn't work! They're coming for you!''

And together they rushed into the corridor.

They darted through an open doorway and pressed their backs against the wall, holding their breaths. After the sounds of charging feet had passed by, they ducked back into the hall and ran for the chapel.

''I was on my way to the chapel when I felt this bouncing around in my pocket,'' Jamie whispered as they moved, and produced a hand-sized black transmitter. ''One of the walkie-talkies they've been communicating with. We never searched the man in the infirmary, so we didn't find it. Anyway, I turned it on, and that's when I heard the order to seize you.''

''What happened?''

''I'm not sure. I didn't catch it all. Anyway, they figured out the body was one of their men, that much is for sure.''

''I heard gunshots.''

''I think they shot the FBI men who came to pick up the body. I'm not sure, but I think so.''

They snaked down the last corridor leading to the chapel.

''What do we do now?'' Jamie asked.

''The only thing we can do,'' said Chimera. ''We hide. We hide until I can figure out another way to get word about the nets off the island.''

Colonel Riaz gazed down disbelievingly at the corpse of Javier. The bandages had been removed from his face to reveal the dried blood where the shattered glass had left its mark. His torso had been bared to show clear evidence of the stab wound that had ended his life.

''How, Colonel, how?'' one of his men asked him.

But Riaz chose not to hear. Instead he returned his attention to the note that had been taped to the flesh beneath the shirt the woman had dressed him in, focusing on the part that most intrigued him.

. . . *A net has been placed around the island. It is mined with transistorized explosives wired to go off when the force of a man's weight comes into contact with it. Your SEALs will be swimming to their death unless precautions are taken. I will be ready to take them from within as soon as your strike begins. . . .*

There was more that came before and after, but those words contained the essence. Riaz actually felt quite relieved. If this note had in fact reached the FBI on the mainland, those words might have become prophetic. After all this, his operation would be threatened with failure. But the ruse had been found out in time. The advantage remained with him. Yes, the woman was still at large, but she was a fugitive now, and those commandos not actively searching for her were wary of her presence.

Riaz had ordered that new transmitters tuned to a different frequency be issued, rendering Javier's device now in the woman's possession worthless. And since her note had never reached the mainland, she was effectively isolated. But this gave Riaz no cause for celebration. It was clear that she was a professional, as cold and cunning as any of his men. He couldn't even be totally sure she was operating on the island alone. After all, since it was Javier the woman had tried to deliver to the mainland, what had happened to the *real* man who had been found at the shoreline?

"There is no sign of her," Captain Maruda reported.

Colonel José Ramon Riaz turned slowly toward him from the window.

"And now you will have the men suspend their search."

Maruda looked stupefied.

"We have more important tasks before us, Captain," the colonel continued. "The explosive charges must be set. We cannot effectively accomplish this if our men are searching the island for this woman. Beyond that, we do not want the American spotter planes to note any anomalies in our movements. We cannot permit our opponents to even suspect a measure of control has been lost."

"The woman still concerns me," Maruda persisted, not able to explain more fully without giving the truth away. It had been a rogue female agent who had killed Maria Cordoba and then sprang Jamie Skylar from jail, proceeding to kill well over a dozen men herself. Could this be the work of Chimera as well?

Maruda tried to dismiss the thought. The ramifications of Chimera being on this island were too dangerous to consider. It could only mean she had linked Nicaragua with the secretive organization behind the operation. And if that was the case, might there be others who knew everything as well?

No, Maruda told himself. She wouldn't have come alone if there were others.

"The Quick Strike explosives are the things now, Captain," Riaz was saying. "Would you like to accompany me while I pull them out of their hiding place?"

"I'd rather continue a private search for the woman."

"Suit yourself. If you want me, I'll be in the kitchen."

Riaz threw back the heavy walk-in freezer door and searched about for the case with the proper label. White, frosty air surged against him, and he could see his breath misting before his face as he stepped farther inside.

The Quick Strike explosives were most stable under cold conditions. They had been brought here under the guise of frozen turkeys not on the menu until the school's traditional pre-Thanksgiving dinner six weeks from now. No need to transport or guard them this way. It was an element of the plan he found most brilliant from the beginning.

Riaz quickly found the crate in question and signaled the two commandos who had entered the freezer with him to help hoist it out. From there, Sanchez would personally supervise its careful unpacking and then plant the charges in previously determined strategic locations about the school grounds.

Shoving the crate across the floor now, the colonel felt a coldness inside him that had nothing to do with the freezer's temperature. Before him was more firepower than one man had a right to possess. Before him was the means to bring about the deaths of over five hundred people who were as innocent as his own children.

I must save my country. I must stop Casa Grande from ever happening again.

That argument made the weight of the Quick Strike explosives no lighter as he helped shoulder them out of the freezer.

After entering the chapel, Jamie and Chimera made for the altar. Atop it was an ornamental rug half covering a steel grating, beneath which lay a hidden chamber Chimera had discovered in her earlier reconnaissance of the school. She rolled the rug off the grate and pried it upward. It resisted at first until Jamie lent his strength as well, and the grating lifted easily to reveal a chamber perhaps eight feet square and four feet in height. They eased themselves down into it and returned the rug into place as best they could before sealing the grate again. Despite their best efforts, part of the grating remained exposed, dooming them if a very careful search was conducted.

"Why can't we just use the walkie-talkie to call the mainland?" Jamie wondered.

"It's a one-channel device. Special chip to make eavesdropping impossible, also communication on any different frequency."

"Then it still might do us some good."

"No," said Chimera. "Riaz would have come with a backup set."

"So where does that leave us?"

"The first wave of underwater response will be destroyed by the mines. The other phalanxes will attack in a battle they cannot possibly win and will have provided the terrorists with a reason to detonate their explosives in the process."

"Jesus . . ."

"That's why I've got to find another way to get word out. Otherwise . . ." Her voice trailed off and she looked up. "Wait a minute."

"What is it?"

"This building. Above the chapel is the—"

She silenced herself as she heard the telltale squeal of the double doors opening into the chapel. Whoever had entered was making no attempt at silence, and the sound of his boots grew louder as he strode up the center aisle. Chimera could detect no immediate purpose in the footsteps, even after they had clip-clopped atop the altar.

The sounds ceased when the figure reached the soft cushion of the rug. Chimera peered up through the grate and noted the figure had come to a halt. His face was clear enough for her to see a red bandanna holding his long hair in place. Chimera remembered him from the infirmary. An especially brutal-looking sort with a devilish smile that could make ice in a fire. She knew the smile well, that of a man who enjoyed killing more with each life he took. Only when the commando had spun in his tracks did she turn back to Jamie.

His mouth had dropped. His eyes bulged. Words pushed their way forward and hammered inside his mouth, but he held them back until a brief cackle from the man's walkie-talkie was followed by the double entry doors squealing closed once more.

"I recognized him," Jamie said.

"What?"

"I recognized him from Nicaragua. From the colonel's farm after the massacre. He's the captain in the militia who put me in jail. His name's Maruda."

Even in the dim light of their cavern, he could see Chimera's face pale.

"Maruda . . ."

"You *know* him," Jamie realized.

"Because Maria Cordoba knew him. He was in charge of the team that murdered your sister."

"It's a mess," Bart Jacoby reported to Major Brickmeister and Colonel Eastman. His radio had been patched through a special land line to Newport State Airport.

"You're sure they're dead?"

"I watched the shootings with my own two eyes. The boat's still moored at the island pier. Riaz isn't talking. I'm not about to send anyone else over, under the circumstances."

"Why did the shit-eaters shoot?" Brickmeister wondered.

"Why does it matter?"

"Tell ya why, boss. Cows lie down 'fore the rain comes, but never in their own piss, and that's what Riaz and his boys just did."

"Major, I don't know what you're talking about."

"You say the king shit-eater contacted you to arrange to return the body, and everything was going just as planned."

"Major, I don't see—"

"Something changed, boss. Something made those shooters lie down in their own piss. I'd like to know what you saw. Mighta been something, anything."

Jacoby hesitated. "I was watching my men in the boat. One of Riaz's men was standing on the pier. Two more were carrying the stretcher. Nothing else." Then, remembering, "Except . . ."

"Except what?"

"They dropped the stretcher. Or they almost dropped it, and the shooting started almost immediately after."

Jamie had felt his breath desert him with Chimera's words.

The man who had killed his sister was here!

And as the hate boiled in him, the anomalies of the situation rose quickly one after another.

"It makes no sense," he muttered. "Why would Riaz be working with the man who killed his family?"

"Because he doesn't know." Chimera's eyes blazed in the half-darkness. "Listen to me. The Valhalla Group wanted Riaz to lead this operation. When he refused, they sent a team disguised as Contras to effect the massacre so he would change his mind. Maruda led that team and then had the members who survived killed. I was the one who was supposed to do the job. But I got sidetracked in New York and they retained someone else. We found the bodies of the rest of the team in the woods." She paused. "Maruda is *Valhalla's* man. They planted him in this group so he could take over when the time is right."

"But—"

"Don't you see? To Riaz, the explosives are just an option to be exercised if his terms are not met. It's Maruda who's going to detonate them as soon as the battle's under way, tonight probably. But we can stop him. We can still stop him."

"Not from here," said Jamie. "Not very likely."

"There's a way," Chimera told him, peering out through the grate. "There's a way."

"You better have a look at these, Major," Eastman said to Brickmeister when the two men were alone in the private office upstairs from the command center.

For the past hour, until the colonel had summoned him back inside, Brickmeister had been out in the field enclosing the airport with his troops. There was equipment to be inventoried, and beyond that, more importantly, an operation plan that had to be thoroughly understood by all parties. By now, Delta had been joined by a dozen navy SEALs along with a detachment of Airborne Rangers who were setting up shop as well.

They probably could have done without his presence, but Brickmeister had reached the stage where he had to get out of the stuffy confines of the command center. Intelligence communiqués were yielding nothing new. On-scene reports were mere repetitions of the previous ones, and there had been nothing yet on the planting points of the deadly explosives.

"More pecks from our Blackbird," said Brickmeister, noting the neat arrangement of eight-by-tens laid out on the table before him.

"Latest batch taken just five minutes ago. A few patches are worthy of special interest," Eastman said, and handed over the magnifying glass.

Brickmeister scanned the photos carefully, holding the magnifying glass over tiny areas that had been darkened under computer enhancement. Such "hot spots" marked the locations of explosives concentrated enough to give off a different thermal signature to the camera passing overhead. The Delta commander compared the shots containing them with the ones taken earlier and arranged them in chronological order on the table.

"Twelve canisters," said Eastman. "Two each planted

around the four dormitories the students and faculty have been contained in, with the remaining four placed—" Eastman maneuvered a pencil adroitly across the retouched photo from memory "—here, here, here, and here."

Brickmeister noted Eastman had drawn what amounted to a perfect rectangle over the area of the island dominated by the complex of school buildings. "Now, ain't that a pretty picture. Think I'd best brief the SEALs."

"I'll contact the President," followed Eastman.

"And you feel they can be safely disabled, Colonel?" Bill Riseman questioned after Eastman had completed his report.

"I can't offer any guarantees, sir. That's why it has to be your call."

"Major Brickmeister believes it can be done, though."

"He's briefing the SEALs now."

"And how do you feel personally, Colonel Eastman?"

"If the SEALs can gain the island without being compromised, the grounds will belong to them. The explosives are on the grounds, Mr. President."

"Then, Colonel, I am advising you to go the fuck for it."

"What do you mean, the tower?" Jamie asked.

"We have to get up there," Chimera replied. "We've got to take it after sunset."

"And that's how we're going to warn the commandos about the nets surrounding the island?"

"That's how we're going to try."

"How? You said there was a commando up there."

"Of course. The tower's got the best view of the surrounding waters as well as the mainland. It's the first place Riaz would have placed a man. Give him a pair of binoculars and the element of surprise is removed from an attack."

"The authorities would know that."

"And plan accordingly. SEALs take the island first, and by the time Delta Force and their airborne backup is ready to move, it won't matter what the spotter sees."

"So Riaz uses the mined nets to eliminate the only approach point he can't watch."

"Except we're going to open it up again. We're going to take the tower and help the SEALs get a free ride in."

"Come in, Mr. Jacoby."

"It's about time, Colonel Riaz," the FBI man barked into his microphone on the mainland. "What the hell happened to my men? You gave assurances. You gave your word!"

"The responsibility for the tragedy rests squarely with me. My men mistook the movements of your men. They overreacted."

"Overreacted? What the fuck is that supposed to mean?"

"Your men were carrying guns. That was not part of our arrangement."

"You didn't say anything about coming unarmed. You never said anything of the sort."

"I accept the responsibility for that. It changes nothing. I have called for a progress report."

"Hold on. It changes plenty. You broke your word, Colonel. What guarantees do we have now that you'll free the hostages once we comply with your instructions?"

"The situations are different."

"Not in my mind, nor the minds of my superiors."

"What do you want?"

"Release half the students."

"You ask for too much."

"Not from our perspective, Colonel. Half the students released as a sign of good faith."

"A quarter released tomorrow morning at dawn, providing work is under way in Nicaragua to follow up on my terms. What do you say to that?"

"The key is that we avoid more killing, Colonel. It does neither of us any good. Let's finish this by the numbers."

"Do nothing rash, Mr. Jacoby, and you will have your wish. Challenge me and the blood will be on your head."

Colonel José Ramon Riaz walked anxiously about the grounds of St. Michael's School as the last of the sun clung to the horizon. He had changed into his dark green battle fatigues, because the time for him to become a soldier was rapidly approaching. Retaliation on the part of the Americans had been inevitable from the start, and his plan had made use of that certainty.

The underwater commandos comprising the first attack wave would swim straight into his nets and be blown to bits. The others, if they came, would face wholesale slaughter. The Americans would then either give in to his demands in the wake of their disgrace or attack in a more direct line and leave him no choice but to detonate his explosives. Either way, the U.S. presence would be gone from Nicaragua. Either way, he won.

But he didn't feel like a winner.

Could he murder children as his own children had been murdered? Could he push the button that would detonate the explosives?

He pulled the black transistorized transmitter from his jacket pocket and fingered it lightly. The Quick Strike explosives had been wired and were ready to go. For a moment, Riaz was tempted to raise the transmitter overhead and hurl it into the ocean beyond. Remove the temptation. Remove the possibility.

But he couldn't. When it came right down to it, destroying the island might yet be the only way he could achieve at least a measure of what he wanted: revenge on the Americans who were responsible for the death of his family. He had hunted their Contra allies through the jungles for years, and when he was ready to retreat, they could not let him. To avenge a massacre, perhaps he would have to become the maker of one. The outcry would be incredible. No American would want anything to do with anything Nicaraguan. The country would be returned to its own people, the capitalist puppets ousted just as Somoza had been.

Yet he wondered how long it would be before the same problems would have to be faced again. Memories were short. The steps taken today might mean nothing tomorrow. His own family could not be brought back.

Feeling himself weaken, Riaz summoned the sights of Marco lying dead on his back, of his daughter staring up in silent accusation from the bottom of the stairs, of the twins' bodies lying on their beds with their throats cut, of the body of Beth Skylar sprawled across the steps. The rage swelled in him. The rage had to be vanquished.

Riaz held fast to the detonator, a part of him he wanted to shed but could not. The last of the sun was sinking from his view, giving way to darkness.

He lifted the walkie-talkie to his lips. "Sanchez, do you read me?"

"Here, Colonel."

"Activate the nets."

CHAPTER 31

THE mist rose from the ocean, casting an eerie translucence on Castle Island. From time to time parts of its shore disappeared from view. At other times the mist gave the illusion of motion to the island itself, making it seem as if it might drift out to sea.

In the lobby of Newport State Airport, powerful floodlights had been set up to facilitate the work of technicians and communications people. No detail could be overlooked. There was plenty to be confirmed and double-checked. The lobby smelled of strong coffee. Cigarette smoke floated in the heavy white beams of light.

In the office upstairs from the command center, Major Brickmeister was holding a meeting at a table dominated by a recently completed scale model of Castle Island, along with surrounding waters and land masses. The model was fashioned of wood and plaster, its most telling feature being the twelve red dots denoting where the explosive charges had been planted amidst the buildings. With Brickmeister around the table were Colonel Eastman, SEAL commander Thomas Balley, and Major Luke Roth of the Rangers.

"Once Lieutenant Balley and his men have secured the explosives, the eight speedboats will come like shit out of a baby's backside from the west,'' Brickmeister explained, touching the edge of Jamestown on the mock-up. ''Enemy might still figure we're staging from Quonsett, so that's the direction he'll be looking.''

''And we're giving them just what they expect,'' from the Ranger commander.

''You graduate at the top of your class, Luke? Anyway, once the speedboats take fire, my boys'll slip through the back door. That's where you come in, Luke.''

''Ten Blackhawk UH-60s,'' Roth picked up instantly, ''loaded eight men each. Our quickdrop LZs will be east and west of the nest of buildings here and here,'' he said, and gestured toward both with his hand.

''Shit,'' noted Brickmeister, ''they must have built them playing fields with us in mind.''

''What about enemy fire?'' Eastman asked Roth.

''Negligible with the SEALs having already secured. We'll be coming in with 7.62 M-60s ready on each side to reduce the heat.''

''Music to my ears, Luke,'' said Brickmeister. '' 'Course, you won't drop until we're at the hill crest. With the SEALs in place, this battle might be over real quick. Colonel Eastman will be running point from the mainland, along with the civie Fed Jacoby. Any questions?''

Before any of the leaders could pose one, a Delta Force sergeant knocked and entered. He looked haggard.

''Sorry to interrupt, sir,'' he said to Brickmeister, ''but you have a visitor.''

''A what?''

''A visitor, sir.''

''Cut this bullshit,'' boomed the voice of Monroe Smalls from the stairway. ''Just take me to the man.''

''Don't I know you?'' Brickmeister asked as he moved in Smalls's direction and met him halfway between the door and the table.

''You watch football?''

''Every Sunday.''

The big man smiled, then winked. ''Yeah, you know me.''

Brickmeister looked up at him. "No, it's something else."

"You outta Bragg, right?"

Brickmeister nodded.

"Well, I'm Eighty-second Airborne, Special Forces reserves. Name's Monroe Smalls."

"You cross-trained with my unit last spring."

Smalls's eyes gleamed. "Only dudes I couldn't twist into pretzels."

"My sarge tells me the ones who tried to stop you at the airport gate ain't exactly standing straight."

"This be different."

"Different how?"

Smalls looked at him closely. "I come to join up, brother."

"I ain't your brother."

"Well, Major, there's someone on that island who is."

The chapel was bathed in darkness. With its interior lighting off, the sole illumination came from the slivers of light that strayed through the stained-glass windows.

After removing the grating above their heads, Chimera and Jamie climbed out of the cramped chamber where they had been hiding. They took a few moments to stretch their limbs before proceeding to the side of the chapel that held a stairway leading up to the tower.

"This door over here," Chimera directed, recalling her reconnaissance of the school that morning.

She moved ahead and eased it soundlessly open. A musty, cold staleness filled their nostrils. Before them, the darkness looked endless. There was nothing to pick out amidst it, including the very shape of the ascending stairway.

"Almost like playing a night game without any lights," Jamie said as they started their ascent.

The ancient stone block construction precluded the placement of railings, further complicating their climb. There was only the wall to follow, and they had to scrape their hands along cold stone for guidance. The stairway swept upward in a continuous, snakelike spiral. Jamie chose his footing carefully, aware that a single misstep could give away their position to the commando in the tower.

His attention was so focused that he had no real sense of Chimera until a light touch of her hand on his chest signaled him to stop.

"There," she whispered.

Jamie gazed forward to see the soft glow of a light flickering beneath the floor crack of a door just ahead. He probed about with his feet and found quite happily that the floor was leveled out, no more steps to negotiate. The door before them would permit access to the tower. Since the tower was open on all four sides, though, another brief climb must lay ahead of them before they could gain entry. The problem was how to manage it without drawing the immediate attention of the man within.

Chimera had the answer. Easing Jamie backward, she moved to the door and pounded it heavily with her fist. The sound made his heart jump. She pounded it again, even harder. A muted voice from within called out something in Spanish, and much to Jamie's surprise, Chimera barked out a reply in a voice low enough to be confused for a man's. She waited before the door like a cat ready to spring.

"I thought you said it was locked," said the commando as he thrust it open.

And that quick, Chimera was upon him. In the thin light the open door revealed, Jamie saw her pounce. God, he had never seen anyone move that fast, on or off the football field. Her charge simply engulfed the man in a quick fury of blows that crumpled him before Jamie had finished his next breath. Not even breathing hard, Chimera turned and beckoned him to enter.

"What now?" Jamie asked.

"That depends."

A circular steel ladder rose from the floor of the inner room the rest of the way into the tower. Chimera climbed a few rungs and then told Jamie to hand the commando's body up to her. With some help from him, she proceeded to hoist him through the opening into the tower ahead of her. Jamie pulled himself in quickly after and found Chimera already moving toward a battery-powered lantern forming the source of the light they had glimpsed from the corridor.

"Perfect," was all she said.

Bart Jacoby was on the phone with Major Brickmeister, who was already deployed on the water beyond the staging area, when a state trooper rushed to his side.

"Sir, you better have a look at something."

Jacoby was about to chastise the officer for interrupting him, but the look in the man's eyes convinced him not to. The SEALs were en route to the island now, with the operation standing at T minus eleven minutes. The Delta commandos and Rangers were waiting for the signal to follow them in.

"Hold please, Major," Jacoby bid Brickmeister, and reached down to the binoculars dangling over his chest. Then, to the trooper, "What is it?"

"A light blinking in the tower."

Jacoby found the dim occasional splotches of flash in his lenses just as the trooper spoke again.

"Sir, I think someone up there is sending us a signal in Morse code."

Jacoby lowered his binoculars. "And just what are they saying?"

"I haven't had time to decipher the whole thing, but a part of it reads something to the effect of 'DON'T RESPOND. MESSAGE FOLLOWS.' "

"Just how well can you read Morse, Officer?" Jacoby asked as he eyed the irregularly spaced flashes.

"I was trained as a signal man in the naval reserves."

"I want to know what it says. I want to know every word."

"Yes, sir."

Still holding the binoculars, Jacoby brought the mike back up to his lips. "Major, we are receiving what may be a Morse code signal from Castle Island."

"Say again, boss."

"A Morse code signal is coming from the tower. A dim flashing light. I'm looking at it now. Can you see it from your position?"

"Through this soup? Shit, I'd have to light a flare to find my dick right now. You're certain it's Morse?"

"A former navy signalman on duty here on the hill is. But so far all we've got is 'Don't reply. Message follows.' "

"Makes sense. If there's a non-shit-eater over there and he managed to take the tower, it's likely no one on the island would notice him sending. But our reply would look like Christmas lights to Riaz and his boys."

Jacoby was about to reply when the state trooper handed over his notepad with completed code translation in capital letters.

"Hold on, Major. I've just been handed the message in question. It says— Oh my God . . ."

"He ain't Delta, Jacoby. I am."

"I'm reading verbatim, Major. *'Nets mined with explosives have been encased around island. SEALs are swimming into a trap. Repeat, SEALs are swimming into a trap.'* . . . That's it. Wait a minute; how did whoever the sender is know about the SEALs?"

"Must be someone on the inside. Riaz figured out we'd be sending them in, so he set up the net, and this someone found out about the net from Riaz. *"Jesus H. Fucking Christ! . . ."*

"Major, what is it?"

Brickmeister fought to recall the whole of the bizarre story told him by Monroe Smalls. The all-pro Giants lineman, who spent ten weeks of every off-season training with the Special Forces, had come here on the trail of a reserve running back named Jamie Skylar. The night before, a microchip Skylar had brought out of Nicaragua was found to contain mention of St. Michael's School. Skylar had come here as a result, and Smalls had come after him. Skylar was on that island now. Skylar might very well be the man in the tower.

Nica-fucking-ragua, thought Brickmeister, with a chill settling at the base of his spine.

"Are you still there, Major?" Jacoby was saying.

"Tell you what you do, boss. You call Washington and tell 'em we're gonna burn some more of Uncle Sam's money. I'm calling back the SEALs."

* * *

The SEAL brigade was five hundred yards from Castle Island when the order came down.

"The fuck you say!" came the response, garbled intermittently by distance and water.

"I say, and you do, Lieutenant. Read me, son?" Brickmeister shouted.

"With all due respect, sir, I'm sweeping my light well ahead and can find no trace of any net."

"Due respect don't mean shit to me, son. I got no choice, which is still more of one than you got."

Maruda had always loved the night. In his early years he loved it for the coolness it brought at the close of the hot Nicaraguan day, and in his later years simply for the dark. No stars, no moon. Just the black everywhere for him to lose himself within.

Killing at night was easier and, Maruda believed, almost spiritual. The idea of the victim's soul being given up to the dark had a symbolism he quite fancied. Night, after all, was always an end of something. Except for Maruda, though, because it belonged to him. Night was his to do with as he pleased.

But this night for the time being he had to share. The Americans would be coming soon. Any minute now the first explosions would sound. Maruda knew what his role would be from that point on, and if he was going to perform it properly, another piece of business remained to be accomplished:

The death of Riaz. The colonel had outlived his usefulness. Maruda had kept close tabs on his whereabouts, knew just where to find him. He would make it quick. After all, Riaz had once been a hero and deserved that much consideration. A knife jammed hard from the rear would do the job well. Ease himself through the wind currents of the night and be done with it before the colonel could so much as scream.

Excited now, Maruda quickened his pace.

A tense and uneasy Colonel Riaz strolled about the rolling green in front of the administration building. He could feel the Americans out there preparing. But the anticipation brought about by that certainty was wholly different from the anticipation he had experienced back during his days in the jungle. Then there had never been any question as to right and wrong. He was avenging specific acts, pursuing specific offenders. Tonight, though, the enemy and the cause he was fighting for had become equally vague.

He hated to kill a man he could not see and who could not see him. Otherwise, whatever honor could have been derived from the act would be lost. And yet tonight his nets and his well-prepared commandos would very likely kill without ever seeing a single victim. Riaz himself might not fire a single shot if all went as to plan. That task would be left for Maruda and the commandos, men who had no concept of honor.

He asked himself again what he was doing here. He had struggled with that question from time to time since agreeing to lead Operation Thunder Clap, but never more than in the last few hours. He felt empty. Since nothing could bring his family back, the vengeance he sought was barren.

And yet perhaps the vengeance was enough by itself. If it soothed him, eased his hurt, and distracted him, it would serve its purpose. He knew the preparation and training for this mission had saved his spirit and soul. Calling a halt now would surely plunge him back into the dark depths of depression that had engulfed him upon his return to Casa Grande for the last time.

Riaz felt for the welcome steel of his rifle. Let the Americans come. But this was the way he wanted it. Not explosives or tricks. Man to man. Eye to eye even in the dark, that final glare felt by his victim if not seen. He was a soldier. There was no shame to die like one, and if it came to that, he would die triggering his detonator so the explosives might serve as his epitaph.

Head pounding from the tension, Riaz turned round and stretched. In the midst of the motion, his eyes caught the flicker of stray light. It came again, and he pinned it to the tower room. Gazing harder, he saw the flickering seemed to come in bursts. Difficult to tell in the dimness, especially with the mist rolling across the island. Perhaps the mist was responsible for the illusion itself.

Riaz might have let it go at that if not for the woman. He felt chilled at the memory of the note she had tried to smuggle to the mainland on Javier's corpse. If sending a message was still her prime concern, what better place to use than the tower?

The flickering light had faded altogether now. Perhaps it had been caused by the whims of the sea mist and the stretched limits of his imagination. Still Riaz had to make sure. Not wanting to summon any of his men from where they lay in wait for the Americans, he determined to check for himself.

Pace quickening to a trot, the colonel made his way toward the tower.

"How can we know they got the message if you told them not to reply?" Jamie badgered when Chimera was finished.

She sat there trying to rub feeling back into her fingers where the continual pressure on the lantern switch had made them first numb and then raw at the tips.

"We have to proceed on the assumption that they did get it, because if it didn't get through, there's nothing more we can do here. Not alone."

Her assessment was difficult to accept but accurate. Jamie could do nothing but shrug.

"And if they did get it?" he asked finally.

"They'll figure out a way to get through the nets. The element of surprise will be back on their side."

"And will they be able to figure out a way to disarm the canisters?"

She looked at him closely in the bluish light cast by the lantern. Its batteries were wearing down. "That's where I come in, whether the cavalry gets here or not."

"You're going way out of my league."

"All of this was out of your league until two weeks ago. You won't have to do anything but watch my back while I disarm the charges."

Something bothered Jamie about her tone. It took him a while, but then he identified it.

"You sound like you're enjoying this."

"Not enjoying, merely accepting. You know my background. In the whole of my life this kind of work is the only thing I've ever been good at. I don't enjoy it, Jamie, but I accept it because it makes me feel I'm worth something."

"Like me playing football."

"I suppose. I guess the key is focus and what happens when you lose it."

Jamie's face turned sad. "I lost it."

"And found another. You've learned to excel in this world, my world."

"But what happens when the time comes for me to go back to *my* world?"

"That depends."

"On what?"

"On plenty." Suddenly some of Crane's final words to her gained meaning. "You succeed at something and you can walk away. What you did matters, so you don't have to look back and keep reliving it. That's the key. If we succeed here, maybe that'll be enough for both of us. And if we don't, it won't matter."

They both felt the sudden rush of a cold, clammy breeze slithering through the portal that led up into the tower.

"Someone's coming," Chimera whispered.

Riaz had approached in silence, not so much as a stir until he reached the door leading into the room directly beneath the tower. He could feel the chilly air that had accompanied him pour through in his wake, and he froze in anticipation of a reaction from above.

There was nothing, not so much as a sound. The dim light shone down the ladder hole to provide the sole illumination. He did not call up to Beide for the same reason he had not tried for contact with the walkie-talkie: He didn't want to reveal his approach to whoever might be listening. If the woman had overcome Beide, then she had another working communicator in her possession.

Riaz reached the ladder and started to climb. Fearing the constant clamor a shoulder-held machine gun would make, he had left his at the foot of the ladder. His pistol was all he allowed himself, and he held it high in his right hand, using only his left to climb the rungs. Silence was nothing new for him. He had learned long ago how to shift body weight to avoid even the slightest sound. His boots touched the rungs with the motions of a graceful dancer.

Near the top of the ladder he heard the stirrings of someone within. He sniffed the air as if it might tell him something, and he came back with a feeling. The woman was up here, all right; he knew that even before a shifting shadow betrayed her. His best hope to overcome her was that her attention would be so rooted in the sending of the message that she would never hear him coming.

Riaz's head was even with the top. He readied himself for the final lunge. When it came, the gun was outstretched, seeming to lead the way. The rest unfolded between breaths and blinks. Upper body raised into the tower, he saw the woman. She twisted from the window that looked out to the east with hair swinging in the dim light. She froze when she saw his gun.

"Don't move," he said.

"Put your hands up," came a voice from behind him.

Major Brickmeister was waiting when Lieutenant Balley and his SEALs came ashore at the staging area in Pirate's Cove. Colonel Eastman had joined him there from his post with Jacoby at Castle Hill, where Eastman was acting as mission liaison with Washington. Castle Hill is part of a jagged peninsula which juts out into the bay from the body of the mainland. Pirate's Cove lies on the southeastern side of that peninsula, out of sight from even the steeple tower on Castle Island.

"We got ourselves confirmation from the local authorities that Coastal Resources crews have been working around Castle Island for over a week, son. Trouble is, Coastal Resources Management doesn't know a damn thing about it."

Balley stripped off his scuba tank. "So that's how they got the nets in place. . . ."

"Yup. Strung 'em the same way the huge fishing trawlers do. Tech boys would call it a monofilament design that would make it invisible to our people under standard underwater light. One or two of them hit is all Riaz needs to tell him we're coming. Explosive charges set but not activated. Nets placed deep enough under not to bother boat traffic. But divers would come in much lower to stay concealed. Your divers, son." Brickmeister paused. "Thing is, under black, ultraviolet light, the shit-eaters' nets will show up clear as a naked broad in a prison yard. Got us a bunch of those en route now. Soon as they get here, Lieutenant, you and your boys get to go swimming again."

For a brief moment Riaz considered shooting the woman and taking his chances. But the voice behind him had stirred a cord of familiarity, and the resulting hesitation dictated his action.

"Now hand the gun to the woman, slowly," Jamie continued after Riaz had raised his arms.

Jamie watched Riaz hesitate briefly and then place his pistol in Chimera's outstretched palm. Jamie's hand was trembling, but it didn't matter, because Riaz's focus had remained on Chimera. She had elected to use herself as bait, and Jamie had played the role she had given him to perfection. Riaz turned slowly toward him, and his single eye bulged disbelievingly.

"Jamie?"

"Hello, Colonel."

Shock had replaced disbelief over Riaz's features, shock and sadness as the sight of Jamie brought all the pain of Casa Grande back to him.

"How can this be? How could you be here?"

"My sister sent me."

Riaz's mouth dropped.

"You knocked me out back at your house, Colonel, I guess to buy yourself some time. They found me and put me in jail. When they marked me for death, she saved my life." He nodded in the direction of Chimera.

Riaz's suddenly enraged eyes flashed between Jamie and the woman. "But I gave explicit instructions that you not be harmed!"

"No one was listening," Chimera told him. "They never listened. You were just a pawn to them. A piece to move across their game board."

"What? Who *are* you?"

"It doesn't matter. To you—everything. Also nothing."

"Don't play me for a fool."

"Someone already beat me to it. Never mind why we're here. The important issue is why you are."

Riaz's eyes went cold. "You flashed a message to the mainland. You told them about the nets."

"And now they'll be able to reach the island with none of your men being any the wiser. Believe me, I did you a favor."

"Believe *what*?"

Chimera looked to Jamie. "Tell him what brought you here."

Jamie didn't hesitate. "You had a meeting with a man named Esteban, Colonel. He described this operation to you and asked you to lead it. You refused. Then Casa Grande changed your mind."

"How do you know all this?"

"Because the meeting was taped," said Jamie, "by my sister."

"She was CIA," Chimera continued. "They planted her with you."

For what seemed like a long time, Riaz said nothing. When he finally spoke, the emotion had vanished from his voice. "But they didn't plant you here, did they?"

"Not by a long shot. My interest in this began when a man named Crane was killed. His own people—my own people—were after him because he had discovered what they were truly about. He had just finished a job in Australia: the acquisition of a dozen explosive devices."

"The Quick Strike charges," Riaz realized. "But why would this man be working for the NNSC?"

"There is no NNSC, Colonel, not so far as Operation Thunder Clap is concerned. What there is, is an American group called Valhalla that has been convinced for decades that it alone knows what's best for the United States. When its leaders were ready to emerge from the shadows, they needed to concoct a scheme to shock the American people and discredit the present administration. That's what Castle Island is a part of—a crucial part, but still only a part."

"Then . . ."

"Then Nicaragua's interests don't enter into this; they never did. After you refused Esteban's request, Valhalla elected to utilize another means to make you cooperate."

And with that, Riaz realized. "No! *No!* I can't believe this! I *won't* believe this!"

"You do believe, Colonel. You probably would have from the start if you had been able to think clearly. But they counted on your emotions to cloud your judgement. *El Diablo de la Jungla* . . . What made you a hero was your incredible focus, your refusal to be swayed once having undertaken a mission, a task, an ideal. They used that, Colonel. Your family was used, you were used, your whole country is being used."

"The bastards . . ."

"There's more. For this operation to achieve its purpose, this island must be destroyed, your hostages murdered. Valhalla knew you would never agree to such a thing, especially without provocation. So they planted someone in your team who would."

"Maruda!" the colonel blared.

"He was part of the team behind the massacre," interjected Jamie. "He was the leader."

Riaz's face betrayed both sadness and rage. His one eye glistened with tears.

"If what you say is true, I will make them pay. I will make them all pay and I will see the two of you safely off this island."

"It doesn't matter, Colonel, because I've saved the best for last. You see, Valhalla was only supposed to receive eight

Quick Strike charges. They ended up with twelve, and the additional four you've planted are something else entirely.''

Riaz just looked at her.

''Antimatter, Colonel, and when the seals on their containment shells are ruptured, a good portion of the northeast United States will perish in the process. And the effects won't stop there.''

Riaz pulled the detonator from his right-hand pocket. ''Then if what you say is true, we have nothing to worry about. This is the only detonator. If I deactivate it, there can be no explosion.''

Chimera shook her head. ''Another illusion, Colonel.''

''How can you be so sure? How can you prove all this?''

In the shadow of an instant, Chimera swept a hand out and stripped the detonator from Riaz's uneasy grasp. Her other still held the pistol trained on his face.

''Maruda's in charge now, Colonel. He will be the one to detonate the explosives,'' Chimera said, and extended the detonator's small antenna. ''And he will do so once the Americans' counterstrike has begun tonight.''

''That's crazy!''

''Let's see.''

And with that, she pressed the detonator's single red button.

CHAPTER 32

THE black motorized rafts slid through the water, at one with the current. Motion was the only thing that might have made them visible, and this the sea mist shielded. Beyond that, there was nothing but black to discern about them, including the covered hands and faces of the occupants.

There were eight rafts in all, each containing seven Delta Force commandos. They had staged from Pirate's Cove, pushing out silently into the night. They continued to paddle their way through the currents at an unchanging speed. Motors would not be activated until the enemy was sufficiently distracted by the appearance of the speedboats. The speedboats were simply decoys, nothing more than drones controlled from the Jamestown shore by radio. Riaz would see them coming, loaded down with dummies, and be forced to respond. While his attention was focused on the west, Delta would storm the island from the south, with the Rangers joining them in a quickdrop along the east and west enemy perimeters. The key was to make the shit-eaters overextend themselves in more directions than they could possibly handle. All Brickmeister needed was word from the SEALs, and chew-ass time was here.

"Black Leader," he said softly in his microphone to Luke Roth of the Rangers, "this here's Red Leader. You copy?"

"Loud and clear, Red Leader." In the background Brickmeister could hear the whirling of chopper blades at Newport State Airport. It was a sound he loved as much as any.

"Black Leader, we are in the bay."

"And we're locked and loaded, Red Leader. Wind report is favorable. ETA to target site three minutes."

The Blackhawks would sweep the long way around the mainland and come in low over the water at speeds approaching 180 knots. They would be flying dark until the last possible instant, the hope being that the enemy's battle with the speedboats in the opposite direction would keep them distracted.

"Affirmative, Black Leader. Hold in pattern until you have my mark."

"Roger, Red Leader."

Now to Lieutenant Balley of the SEALs.

"Blue Leader, this is Red Leader. Report your position."

"Closing on nets now, Major, black lights working wonders. You gotta see these things to believe them. Looks like a goddamn underwater spider's been spinning his web. Too bad he ain't gonna find us stuck in it when he comes back."

"What's your ET to circumvent?"

"We got the gaps clear in sight. Estimate three minutes more to shore, another four after that to secure explosives."

"We'll wait for you before we head down the pipe, Blue Leader."

"Ready to rock and roll, Red Leader."

Riaz had flinched at Chimera's motion, tensing in full expectation of the momentary obliteration of Castle Island. When no explosion followed, his features tightened in an awkward mix of rage and confusion.

"Something must be wrong" was all he could say.

"If I had pressed Maruda's detonator, the results would have been considerably different."

The rage showed through. "He killed my family. . . ."

"Part of the plan from the beginning."

"I moved to Casa Grande and tried to tell myself you could run from what you are. I really had myself fooled. But I had no right to fool my children."

"You can't get them back," Chimera told him, "but there's millions more you can help to save."

Riaz's face turned stonelike. "Give me back my gun. Let me go. I will find Maruda and kill him."

"And what of his detonator, Colonel? What happens when you're holding it in your hand?"

"Those I must punish will not be found on this island, and I will not need explosives to kill them."

"They're already dead, Colonel. Killed by a traitor in their ranks who would not cancel this operation. You see, they had learned about the antimatter. What they saw as a huge mistake, a near cataclysmic accident, the traitor must have seen differently. Don't ask me how or why, but he must have his reasons for wanting this operation to go forward."

Riaz started to ease himself back toward the ladder. "I'm going to leave now. You can shoot me if you wish or you can give me my gun back."

Chimera handed him his pistol, butt first. "The three of us will leave together, Colonel. We've all got our work cut out for us. The problem is how Delta Force is going to figure out we're on their side."

For the first time since the operation began, Captain Maruda was nervous. Colonel Riaz was nowhere to be found, and with him still on the grounds, the rest of the operation could be thrown into jeopardy. By the first sign of shooting or explosives, it was expected Riaz would have been eliminated, leaving Maruda in charge. But with the colonel still alive, Maruda ran the risk of complications he was not prepared for.

Colonel Riaz has been killed by the Americans! You will respond as follows. . . .

The words were well practiced in his head. Now he could not deliver them. He had to find Riaz. Quickly.

Before the Americans came.

* * *

"Red Leader, this is Blue Leader," came the call from Lieutenant Balley to Major Brickmeister.

"Read you, son."

"Beachfront positions taken, sir," Balley's voice was hushed, barely a whisper. "Estimate three minutes time to reach designated positions following strip-down and regear. Another one to secure explosives."

"Roger that, Blue Leader. We're ready to grease up their backsides when you call."

"On our mark, Red Leader."

The SEALs' part in the mission required that they remain out of sight from one another as well as maintain radio silence. The dozen black figures crept in eerie unison across the upward slope of sand, rocks, and sea grass toward the school grounds and their assigned positions within the perimeter.

A SEAL operating in the approximate center of the team approach line tripped over an object rising above ground level directly in his path. Swearing under his breath, he pushed off and felt a boot under one hand. Flicking his flashlight on momentarily, he saw the body of a man dressed in camouflage, one of the terrorists. His throat had been cut.

The SEAL's first thought was that this was the deadly handiwork of another on his team. But closer inspection revealed the man to have been dead for some time. Whoever the killer was had struck before the SEALs had even reached the island. Something was wrong, and in the millisecond the degree of the anomaly registered with him, the SEAL decided to break radio silence.

"Blue Leader, this is Blue Six."

"Read you, Blue Six," returned Balley. "What's the problem?"

"I've got a dead terrorist under me, sir. Someone else's work in advance of our arrival."

"Report your position."

Balley heard a soft flutter as Blue Six shifted suddenly.

"Blue Six, what's wrong?"

"Thought I heard something, sir. Thought I—"

pffffft . . . pffffft . . . pffft . . .

Balley knew the sounds of silenced gunshots even when muffled through a walkie-talkie.

"Blue Six, are you there?"

The thud told Balley he wasn't. The lieutenant dived to the ground, spinning so he came to a halt on his stomach facing Blue Six's position. His M-16 was steadied before him, switch on full auto. Thoughts rushed through his head as he lay there in the sea grass halfway up the hill.

One of Riaz's commandos had been killed, and now Blue Six, too. Balley didn't bother with conclusions; he knew the essence of his mission had changed drastically. He had to alert his men, then contact Brickmeister.

What the fuck was going on?

"Blue Team members, acknowledge."

Silence.

"Blue Team, this is Blue Leader. I say again, acknowledge."

Static.

No use checking the communicator to see if it was tuned to the wrong frequency. He knew it wasn't. And he also knew that the rest of his team had all gone the way of Blue Six.

Impossible!

Eleven SEALs taken out in the space of a two-minute spread was unthinkable, imponderable. Unless . . . Unless . . .

Balley switched to the command frequency.

"Red Leader, this is Blue Leader."

"Read you, son," said Brickmeister. "Are you in position?"

"Negative! My whole team has been—"

Balley broke off his own words when he caught sight of a flash of motion on the hill to the right. He heard the scampering, and figured he had the man if he fired now.

"Fuck you, asshole. . . ."

Balley squeezed his trigger and held it, rotating the M-16 in an arc guaranteed to catch the bastard. Twelve rounds were exhausted when a burst fired from ten feet behind him blew apart the lieutenant's head. His death grip held on for an additional six volleys. The last three burned futilely into the ground a yard in front of him, dirt leaping up to join in the spray of blood and brains.

"Major, what the hell's going on?" blared Colonel Eastman, who had been tuned in to it all.

"You heard it, boss. SEALs been bushwhacked."

"What?"

"Walked right into some kind of trap, by the sound of it."

"But—"

"Got no time for chat now, boss. This changes the game. Black Leader, you copying this?" he asked the commander of the Rangers.

"Roger, Red Leader."

"We don't take 'em now, we never will."

"We're talking a hot LZ, Major."

"Hotter than an Alabama August, Luke, but I don't see we got much of a choice."

"We're in the air," said Roth.

"Send in the speedboats," Brickmeister ordered his men on the Jamestown side of the bay.

Maruda was still awaiting the sound of underwater explosions when he heard the burst of gunshots. A quick sprint down the hill to the southern edge of the jagged shoreline found him gazing down at a figure that could only have been a navy SEAL. Somehow they had gotten through the nets. And someone had stopped them before they could get to the school.

But if not one of his men, then who? . . .

Before he could consider the question further, a squad of speedboats split the silence of the night, roaring with Delta commandos on board for Castle Island toward the western shore from Jamestown. Their running lights and full floods blazed blindingly through the dark. The glare cast a surreal glow over and beyond them, until it seemed there was simply light coming and nothing more. Maruda grabbed for the walkie-talkie that connected him to his men, no longer caring where Colonel Riaz might have been.

"Maruda to all gunnery teams! Maruda to all gunnery teams! Speedboats approaching from the west! Take them out! *Take them out!*"

Riaz, Chimera, and Jamie had just emerged from the chapel when they saw the blistering lights approaching the island from the west.

"Delta Force!" Chimera exclaimed in the instant before the first bursts from the commandos' small artillery fire sped outward in the running lights' direction.

"Something's wrong," said Riaz. "The SEALs would have taken those men out before Delta made their move."

"Could Maruda have killed them?"

"No. He was waiting for the explosions, just as I was. Something else stopped the SEALs from reaching their marks."

Out at sea, one of the commandos' RPG rockets turned a speedboat into a fireball, orange light replacing white. The blast mushroomed briefly and then receded into a shower of death and debris. Chimera barely had time to take a breath before a second speedboat fell to another missile, a Stinger this time, judging from the blast. In spite of this, the other boats kept coming, closing on a shore they could not possibly reach before the commandos' fire found them.

"*Madre de Dios,*" muttered Riaz while next to him Jamie let his shoulders sag against the building.

Chimera had grabbed the colonel's arm before Riaz could speak again. He gazed up at her, his single eye a mixture of fire and confusion.

"It's just us now," she said. "Tell me where the explosives are planted. Tell me!"

The speedboat segment of the plan had worked even better than Brickmeister had hoped. The focus of the commandos was thrown totally to the west, thus allowing the eight black rafts to reach shallow water on the island's southern shore without a single eye noting their presence. The strategic landing point had been chosen because it placed them closest to the dormitories the majority of students had been packed into.

The Delta team members spilled over the rafts' sides, hardly making a splash, and held their weapons overhead to keep them from getting wet. The water chilled the flesh right up to their thighs, but not a single man felt it, certainly not Monroe Smalls. It went totally against procedure to let a civilian accompany Delta in the strike, but there was something in Smalls's eyes Brickmeister recognized from the mirror. The major knew that kind of resolve was not going to be denied. Smalls might have lacked some of the training his men had under their belts, but he carried an M-16 as well as any of them and had a personal interest in taking the island. Besides, if Jamie Skylar really was at St. Michael's, how was the major supposed to recognize him without the all-pro?

The rationale almost made him smile. The biggest problem had turned out to be finding a uniform Smalls could squeeze into.

Brickmeister himself took the point, and with a wave of his hand signaled his men on in assault formation. With Riaz's commandos distracted for the time being, the rules for the encounter had changed only slightly. The element of surprise would still be on their side, but they would be coming into a situation knowing help from the SEALs' secured positions would not be forthcoming and knowing too that the explosives remained to be disabled.

This meant that any moment could see the detonation of the Quick Strike canisters. Brickmeister supposed he should have aborted as soon as the fate of the SEALs was obvious. That would have been playing it safe and by the book. But it was his belief that playing safe led to more people getting killed, not less. Whatever second-guessing he might have been doing vanished when he came upon the twisted corpse of one of the SEALs. Resolve seized him anew. He might have to face a board of inquiry over this, maybe even a court-martial, but at least he'd be able to face himself. No sense reporting to Eastman or even calling in. In a further act of purposeful defiance, he switched his walkie-talkie to the channel only Roth and the Rangers could receive, thereby shutting everyone else out. The ball was his all the way now.

The school sharpened in focus.

The night belonged to Delta.

Brickmeister hit the beach, and with upraised hand he held his troops up one last time as he lifted his walkie-talkie.

"Black Leader, this is Red Leader," he said to the Ranger commander soaring toward Castle Island. "Got ourselves a prime stretch of beachfront property here."

"You should be able to hear us coming up on your backyard any second."

"Gonna need you to handle the shooters concentrated to the west."

"That's a roger, Red Leader. We have the LZ in sight."

As if on cue, Brickmeister heard the heavy *wop-wop-wop* roaring toward him over the water.

"Let's party," he said.

With the victory of his forces apparent, Captain Maruda thought he had figured it all out. He hadn't been able to find Colonel Riaz because Colonel Riaz had been lying in wait for the SEALs. When they had come, he had killed them one by one, had ultimately been wounded himself, and now lay dead or dying. The irony was as strange as it was pleasant. Riaz had more than done his work for him: he had done it and assured the success of the mission at the same time.

From here, Maruda's role was clear. A boat had been left for him on the northern side of the island, camouflaged to avoid detection by aerial surveillance. Intelligence had virtually guaranteed that the north would not be used as an attack route since the backdrop included the lights of Newport. This way, if Maruda needed to make his move in the midst of battle, the path would be clear for him. Upon reaching the boat, he would press his detonator and flee to the rendezvous point, with St. Michael's School smoldering behind him. The explosion would be horrific. The whole of the school would explode in a monstrous, contained fireball that would leave nothing but embers behind. No piece of any structure would survive. Total obliteration. Maruda had to remember to put in his earplugs before pushing the button.

He was heading across the school grounds, slithering through the night, when he heard the fresh gunshots split the night from the south and realized the battle wasn't over yet.

"Delta Force!" Chimera said in the wake of the first exchange.

Riaz looked befuddled. "But the speedboats . . ."

"Looks like they were one up on you all along, Colonel. You thought they were playing into your hands when all the time you were playing into theirs."

"We've still got to disable the explosives," he reminded her. "I can help you."

"No," said Chimera. "You were right before. You've got to find Maruda. He's the only one who can trigger the explosives if they can't be disabled. One of us has to succeed. Otherwise . . ."

"Wait a minute," Jamie interrupted, "there's another one of us here."

She looked at him before heading off. "Leave it, Jamie. Stay here and stay covered. You'll be safe."

"But you won't. You know you can't pull this off, and you're going to try anyway."

"I've been there before."

"Well, so have I. And if you think I'm gonna sit on my ass and wait for this island to blow up, you're crazy."

"All right," she relented. "My back will be exposed." She thrust the rifle that had belonged to Riaz's tower commando at him. "If any of them come up from behind, shoot. Think you can handle it?"

"Damn straight."

"Then let's go to work."

"Goddamnit! What the hell happened?" Brickmeister asked the head of his advance team, which had just plunged back down over the crest of the hill leading to the dormitories.

"Heavy fire encountered, sir. They were waiting for us."

"Fuck me they were. Shit-eaters guarding the dorms got lucky is what happened. Just turned around at the right time." He gazed up as the squadron of Blackhawks soared overhead. "We'll take 'em once the Rangers quickdrop. Stand easy."

Maruda managed to get his two .60-caliber machine gunners in position before Delta Force chanced a rush over the hill again. The rest of his men were still in the process of scurrying back from the western perimeter of the island when the helicopters soared overhead with heavy fire coming out their sides. Four of his men were cut down instantly. The rest managed to find cover while the Blackhawks dropped lower and began to split to the east and west.

All this was going according to plan.

Taking cover himself, Maruda gazed up at the Slater House dormitory roof, where Rodrigo was perched with his .50-caliber machine gun and affixed grenade launcher. The point to Maruda's strategy now was strictly to buy himself enough time to reach his boat on the northern side of the island. He'd trigger the explosives while the battle raged. The mission would end in success. He would finish this as it was meant to be finished.

Maruda grasped the detonator through his jacket and rushed away from the battle zone.

"Black Leader to Red Leader!"

"Read ya, Luke," said Brickmeister. He shouted to be heard over the firefight raging near the southern hill crest.

"LZ too hot for quickdrop. Repeat, LZ too hot for quickdrop!"

"You don't zap 'em, your men ain't worth shit to me."

"They're not worth any more dead, and we've encountered heavy machine-gun and light artillery fire. Two choppers already hit. I got casualties!"

"What about your .60s?"

"Fire is coming from a dorm roof. We got friendlies in there, and these 7.62s will cut them to shreds. I'm gonna have to circle and let you get through first."

"Stay cool, Luke. We're almost there."

* * *

Riaz slid off into the night first, leaving Jamie and Chimera against the building. Chimera knew the chances of her recovering all twelve of the canisters were slim at best. But if she was lucky, those containing the antimatter would be among those she disabled. Riaz succeeding would be a bonus. Maruda would have waited for just this scenario to unfold to perform his final duty. Just grab enough time to get clear and use his detonator.

With gunfire splitting the air, Chimera led Jamie around the main building and indicated the perch he was to take. Then she proceeded on to the first implantation point of the canisters. This close to the battle a hail of automatic fire burned the air nearby, followed by desperate shouts in Spanish.

Ignoring the melee, she focused her attention on where the first charge was planted. She had to snake into a nest of bushes planted almost directly in front of the Headmaster's office.

She felt and saw the hole at the same time, an empty cavern of dirt where the explosive charge was supposed to be. Confused, Chimera probed further and succeeded only in sifting more dirt through her fingers.

The canister was gone. Someone had gotten here ahead of her. . . .

She slithered out from the nest of bushes and signaled Jamie to ease forward. She waved a hand at him to stop when he reached the front edge of the next building, a dormitory three down from the shore and the front line of the battle. That position would provide her cover for a straight run toward the next canister site.

Such thoughts kept her mind sharp as she reached the second spot Riaz had sent her to. There was nothing but another depression in the ground, evidence that a second device had been yanked out. Chimera's thoughts swam wildly. Could some of the SEALs have gotten through after all? And if not, who had removed the explosives?

She would press on. She would check each and every site on the chance whoever was ahead of her had missed one, or had been killed before he had a chance to finish. But the next site necessitated a dash in the open to the side of the Slater House building. Chimera elected not to signal Jamie this time. She would leave him back here under decent cover and hope he could stay alive while she continued on. Taking a deep breath, she bolted forward and reached the other side of the dormitory just as a vicious hail of return fire from Delta Force pinned her down. It clamored incessantly, battering Chimera's eardrums as she slammed against Slater House and sank into a nest of shrubbery for cover. The position was only safe until a shooter from either side found her in his sights. She had to take her chances on the move or, or . . .

A few yards to her right was a window that must have led into the building's cellar. Trying for more of the explosives was sure to get her killed fast, so she might as well wait out the battle or use the basement to move about instead of doing so in the open.

She used the butt of her rifle to break the glass and then knocked the largest shards free to clear her path inward. The basement she was dropping into was pitch-black and she lowered herself in feet first. She slipped when a barrage of fire surged dangerously close, and dug her hands into the remaining jagged shards for purchase out of instinct. The pain jolted her and forced her to let go. Chimera felt herself tumbling and crashed to the cement basement floor, with the small of her back striking first.

She felt numb everywhere as the sounds of the battle dimmed and then disappeared altogether.

CHAPTER 33

COLONEL Riaz searched the night for Captain Maruda. He was keeping to the shadows as best he could, staying on the move. If Chimera was right, Maruda would be on the verge of fleeing the island. He would want to reach a safe point before detonating the explosives and then take off by boat.

Accordingly, Riaz concentrated his search to the north, facing Newport and the easiest escape from the battle raging between Delta and his commandos. No, Riaz corrected himself, not *his* commandos. Never his. Always Maruda's, or at the very least, the force behind Maruda. The feeling of being used and manipulated from the start gnawed at him. Never had he wanted to kill a man more than he wanted to kill Maruda now, the man who had butchered his family. He wondered if Maruda's death would be enough for him. But it would have to serve. Chimera had said Valhalla had been destroyed by one of their own, and Riaz believed her.

His mind locked on that last thought. She had brushed by the member's identity without full explanation. But so long as that person was alive, Valhalla would be as well. Perhaps, then, there was a target beyond Maruda. Perhaps

Riaz would have to find his way off Castle Island in search of it.

Riaz was just swinging around the side of the building to the right of the chapel when he saw a figure darting under the trees, making directly for the island's northern shore. Maruda! It had to be!

The colonel bolted from the shadows. He had nearly three hundred yards to cover but would have a clear shot as soon as he reached the crest overlooking the shore. Riaz was determined to get that shot, and get it before Maruda could press his detonator. Short of this, the colonel could only hope Chimera had managed to disable the explosives. He calculated in his mind the time she had had, and he seriously doubted it had been sufficient to reach all the sites.

Riaz had just passed into the open near the administration building when he was cut down by a deadly hail of bullets, the force of them jetting him sideways. He saw the blood spilling from his body and felt coldness and heat clashing inside. He spun to the ground and crashed into a thicket of bushes, where his life continued to leak out with the taste of Casa Grande on his lips.

Rodrigo had found the colonel in his sights quite by accident. With the helicopters soaring away, he was swinging round to level his .50-caliber machine gun toward the enemy at the hill crest when a flash of movement drew his attention. He recognized Captain Maruda and followed him as the captain hastened toward the northern shore.

The second shape appeared just as Maruda disappeared over the crest. Rodrigo knew it was Riaz, the line of his pursuit making clear his intentions. In that instant Rodrigo somehow grasped that the colonel knew the truth, of both Castle Island and Casa Grande. That made him an even deadlier enemy than the troops that had landed on the island's southern front.

Not hesitating at all, Rodrigo trained his machine gun on Riaz and cut him down with a single burst. The man seemed to be dancing when the bullets struck him. It made Rodrigo's ever-present half smile widen, and he snapped another pack into his machine gun.

In the doorway where Jamie had taken refuge, bricks trembled in their mortar as more rapid fire blitzed his ears.

It's coming from right above me, he realized.

The school building shook from the concussion of gunfire that held the friendly forces at bay beneath the hill. So long as it continued, the soldiers could not retake the island. He wondered if Chimera was realizing the same thing he was, wondered if she was even still alive. It was his task alone to deal with the gunman on the roof. As that realization sank in, he took a deep breath and started to ease himself from the alcove. Jamie's intention was to work his way around the back of the building and ascend the fire escape on the other side.

Instantly, though, brick exploded around him. As Jamie ducked free to avoid the fragments, the motion drew him farther into the open than he had meant to go. A hot, sizzling pain seared the right side of his head and he tumbled to the ground with the world turning upside down.

"That's him, all right," said Monroe Smalls, with the binoculars pressed close to eyes raised just over the hill crest.

"Which one of my men shot him?" Brickmeister wanted to know when Smalls eased himself back down to the cover of the landscape.

"Couldn'ta known he was one of us in all this shit, Major. The little fuck don't die too easy anyway. I'll have him safe and sound in three minutes."

Brickmeister's hand closed as best it could around Smalls's upper arm. "Don't know if I can allow that."

"I owe the man, Major, so I got me no choice. Just close your eyes ten seconds and I'll be gone."

"Plan on coming back?"

"Got a game Sunday and seven more after that, Major. Can't go to the Super Bowl if you're dead."

* * *

Captain Maruda found the boat easily. It was black and sleek, top speed probably fifty to fifty-five miles per hour. A thick, coarse rope secured it to a pylon driven deep into the water, the rope accessible only by probing beneath the surface. He waded twenty feet offshore to reach it and stripped off the camouflaged cover that made the boat seem part of the water.

Feeling almost gleeful, Maruda climbed on board and yanked the detonator from his pocket. He didn't want to risk straying beyond its range. Blow the island here and he would be far enough away from the brunt of the blast to avoid injury. Escape was his. Success was his. He would be a rich man as a result, and there would be plenty more assignments for him down the road. He remembered his earplugs at the last and wedged them in before easing his finger over the red button. Holding the detonator out before him, Maruda pressed it, flinching involuntarily in the process.

Nothing happened. No rumble, no blast, no blinding fireball that shook the island to its core. Maruda pressed again. Starting to panic, he switched hands and repeated the motion deliberately.

Still nothing.

Could he have been out of range, the transmitter weaker than he had been told? No, it had to be the explosives! Something was wrong with the explosives. Maruda shuddered at the only option open to him.

He had to return to St. Michael's School. While Delta overcame the last of his commandos' resistance, he had to reset enough of the outlying explosives to assure at least a measure of success.

Maruda plunged over the speedboat's side and rushed back into the night.

To reach Jamie, Monroe Smalls took the long way around through the fields to the west of the chapel. With the fire concentrated elsewhere, he knew he had a good chance of making it. As long as there was a chance he could get Jamie out, it was worth it. Smalls pressed himself against the field house and steadied himself for the dash to the dorm building where Jamie had gone down. He reached it safely and made his way around the side of Slater House on his belly, grateful for the sheltering bushes scraping his exposed face and palms.

He found a position where he figured Brickmeister could see him if he was looking, and waited. Sure enough, a few seconds later the fire from Delta intensified and was returned by the terrorists in kind, all their attention drawn.

thump, thump, thump . . .

The fire came like chunks of noise smashing his ears. Smalls gazed up. This was the rooftop that was fucking everything up. Lone gunman by the sound of it, but a damn good one.

thump, thump, thump . . .

Under cover of the stepped-up Delta fire, Smalls emerged. He grabbed hold of Jamie with a single arm and pulled him into the cover of the bushes.

"Monroe? Is that *you*?" sighed Jamie when the water from Smalls's canteen had revived him.

"Shit, you done died and gone to all-pro heaven."

Jamie tried to move a little. "My head hurts."

"That's 'cause it got grazed by a bullet that was maybe deflected by those Samson locks of yours."

"What are you doing here, Monroe?"

"Saving your ass, case you didn't notice."

"Not your typical uniform."

"Joined up with a different team. Now, what you're gonna do is work *your*self round the other side of this building, where it's clear, and stay put till you hear otherwise."

Smalls stripped his machine gun off his shoulder and handed it to Jamie.

"You might need this."

"And you won't?"

Monroe's eyes drifted toward the dormitory roof. "Not where I'm going."

Smalls found the fire escape ladder at the back of the building and climbed quickly into the night. The heavy discharge from the machine gunner stung his ears, and he busied himself with trying to pin down the man's exact position.

"Here I come, you fucker," he muttered to himself, and began to climb.

The climb was the thing. He had to make it up fast and silent, and the weight of the rifle he'd given Jamie would have made both difficult. The lack of a weapon bothered him only slightly. Monroe had his quickness, and that would get him where he had to be so his strength could finish the job. Maybe he'd toss the dipshit off the roof for all of Delta to see. Monroe liked the feel of that.

He reached the top with mouth dry from excitement. This was one of St. Michael's older dorms, and the roof came to a v-shaped peak. The angled descent on either side finished in a wide gutter strip. Smalls had already pinpointed the dipshit's position on the strip on the dorm's opposite side.

Monroe started toward him. Slip now and his fall would end four stories down, the side of the roof a mere memory he had no chance of grasping. That thought returned him to the arena where he was most comfortable. The roof was no different than a football field. You kept going until they got you. You didn't stop until somebody stopped you.

Smalls didn't stop. A few breaths later he reached the peak in the roof and gazed downward. His eyes bulged. The dipshit gunman was a monster, huge neck and shoulders and a massive, stubble-haired head, big as any Smalls had faced across the line. Dude was holding a machine gun that looked like it belonged on a tripod, firing it now in regular bursts to keep Delta pinned on the beach. The sound burned Monroe's eardrums, but he welcomed it for the cover it would afford his approach.

He drove himself into a charge down the roof. He came in from an angle, the plan to take the man down sideways to prevent momentum from tipping both of them off.

The dipshit turned at the last possible time and was able to brace himself. The impact was stunning, a Mack truck into a cement wall. Neither man gave in the slightest. But impact spun the gunman around and separated him from his monstrous gun, which clamored to the gutter strip. Smalls went for him again with his shoulder, but the gunman's knee jerked into his face and sent him reeling backward to the roof with a thud. Smalls found his shoulders propped on the slope of the roof, absurdly eye to eye with the dipshit.

The big man came forward in a quick burst, as fast as the best offensive lineman Monroe had ever faced. He managed to twist aside in a motion that took him from Stubble Head's direct path and showed him the huge blade that was now in the dipshit's hand. He plunged the knife downward with all his great force, and it lodged through a shingle when Monroe rolled sideways. Instead of abandoning the knife, Stubble Head tried to pry it free, which gave Smalls his outstretched arm as a target. It was as welcome as a fumbled football rolling his way.

Monroe Smalls threw all his weight into a thrust against that arm. The limb took the entire 300 pounds of his force and cracked inward upon impact. The dipshit's scream bubbled in Monroe's ears, but instead of protecting the shattered arm, the dipshit lashed it upward against the side of Smalls's face. The blow caught Monroe by surprise, and its force pitched him toward the edge of the roof.

Stars were still flashing before Smalls's eyes when Stubble Head lurched awkwardly to his feet, shattered arm hanging limp by his side. Smalls's vision cleared in time to see the man lunge and reach down with his working arm. Monroe tried to roll free, but Stubble Head's good arm clamped onto his throat and lifted him effortlessly up.

Monroe responded by latching both his meat-claw hands onto the dipshit's neck, trying to force his thumbs against the man's Adam's apple, which was lost in a slab of muscle. The result was to place the two giants eye to eye on equal footing a breath's distance from each other. Since Monroe's feet were dangerously near the precipice, he knew Stubble Head held the advantage. All the dipshit had to do was to mount a thrust powerful enough to shove Smalls backward off the gutter strip.

Yup, that was all. Dipshit gave it everything he had with the sudden heave Monroe had been waiting for. Smalls let go with both his arms and ducked low, tearing from Stubble Head's one-handed grasp. Before the dipshit could do anything about it, Smalls hit him with a shoulder just over the knees. The leverage of both their weights joined in that instant. Monroe felt Stubble Head going up and over him, the stuff highlight films are made of. Only, in this film, there was no turf to break his fall, just air.

The sensation of impact this time was negligible. He wasn't sure whether he or Stubble Head screamed at the last. By the time Monroe caught his balance and swung round, the thud had already sounded. Gazing down, he found the dipshit's corpse lying in a big heap four stories below.

"You been retired, motherfucker," Smalls said after him.

But the celebration stopped there. The terrorist fucks were still keeping Delta pinned down from their positions around the buildings.

Well, ain't they in for one big-time surprise, Monroe thought as he lifted Stubble Head's .50-caliber and angled it their way.

"You read me, Luke?"

"Loud and clear, Brick."

"Door's been open wide. Drop on in and unass 'em."

"Roger that."

But Brickmeister wasn't going to wait for the Rangers to show up.

"The dorms!" he screamed as waves of his Delta troops followed him over the crest of the hill. "We gotta own them dorms!"

The last of the machine-gun and rifle fire that had been holding them back had stopped, thanks to a barrage turned on the terrorists from their own rooftop stronghold. *Monroe Smalls,* thought Brickmeister, wondering if Delta might be better off hitting the NFL for its recruits. The major led Delta's charge into the bursts of fire coming from within the Slater House dormitory building, where a bulk of the students had been placed. Damn terrorist fucks must have pulled back inside there. The bastards!

"Go! Go! Go!" Brickmeister heard himself scream, while around him bullets flowed from his men's rifles like water from a hose.

The ceaseless hail of fire punctured a number of windows in Slater House. In the rooms a hefty contingent of the students of St. Michael's cowered low beneath makeshift cover, too terrified to do anything else. The pungent stink of gunsmoke sulfur poured through the corridors, and the students tasted it on their breath.

On the first floor, doors were kicked open one after another by the terrorists who had taken refuge inside.

"Out! Out!" the three commandos ordered. "Get into the corridor!"

One shouted his orders in Spanish, and when a quartet of boys didn't heed the words, he shot them in a burst that swallowed even their screams. The echo of gunfire inside the building was thunderous, and the students already in the corridor starting wailing. Two of the commandos herded them together while the one who had shot the four boys grabbed a girl by the hair and moved for the front door. He reached it ready to show his prize to the approaching Delta troops. He gambled they would hold their fire when they saw her. He and his two fellows held forty hostages on this floor alone, after all. This advantage could provide a stalemate that would help them win their freedom.

The commando thrust open the front door, holding the girl before him. He had thought there was enough light inside to make the situation clear. But his frame shielded the rays cast by the fixture hung behind him on the wall. As a result, the response from outside was a hail of bullets that hit the girl and shoved her back at him. Bullets from the same barrage grazed the commando next, forcing him to drop his shield, which created an open target. Automatic fire ripped into the commando and tore him apart before he could even manage a single shot of his own.

* * *

"Cease fire!" Brickmeister ordered. "Cease fire! Jesus fuckin' Christ . . ."

The frenzy of the moment had caught up Delta in its ra pant bloodthirst. Brickmeister figured he was the only o who had seen the hostage girl fall to the hail of bullets at t entrance to the dorm.

"Cease fire! Cease fire! Cease fire!"

They had fucked up, but there was no sense in crying ov it now. There were over a hundred kids still *alive* in Slat House. Brickmeister didn't know how many would die in all-out assault, but he knew all of them would if the buildi wasn't secured and one of the terrorists still managed to s off the Quick Strike.

Brickmeister moved to the closest of his unit commande "Right side door belongs to you, son," he ordered. "V storm the building in one minute."

Chimera had lain on the basement floor for what seem like a very long time. Awareness of the battle returned gra ually, but still she didn't move. Afraid to try, afraid to anything.

And then she heard the gunshots and screams coming fro the floor directly over her. Chimera's mind cleared. The wa of terrified children brought her to her feet. She realized t sounds of the battle had otherwise ceased. This building h become the point of the terrorists' last stand. They wou hide behind innocents as long as necessary, *kill* as many necessary.

Chimera crouched and felt around the dark floor for h rifle. Her back ached and the lower parts of her legs we still numb from the fall. She found the weapon and relied her bearings to find the staircase. The darkness gave it quickly and she ascended, needing the banister to pull hers up. She reached the door as another series of screams a gunshots came, and she didn't hesitate now.

She crashed through the door and rushed toward the e of the first hallway, around which lay the cluster of hostage She checked her rifle one last time and steadied her breat ing. She spun with a scream echoing ahead of her.

"Get down!"

She fired her first hail of bullets purposely high to reinforce the point. Chimera knew the commandos wouldn't duck, and she was right. Both of them twisted her way and pulled their triggers while she was still squeezing hers.

She felt her chest cave inward as a series of bullets pounded her. She knew she'd been hit many times. But her aim had been true. The last bursts from the commandos' guns sprayed wildly upward as death overcame them. They slammed into walls opposite each other and left a trail of blood behind them as they slid down.

Chimera sank to her knees. She tasted blood in her mouth and coughed up a huge froth that made a pool on the floor. Chimera did her best to hold on to life as she watched the pool widen.

Delta Force was still thirty seconds from storming Slater House when Brickmeister heard the sounds of gunfire from within.

"What the hell . . ."

As Brickmeister sprinted toward the front door, his command echoed behind him.

"Chew ass!"

After Monroe Smalls slid away, Jamie moved in a daze to the northern side of Slater House, safely away from the battle raging to the south. He kept himself pinned motionless against the red brick. He squeezed Monroe's rifle tightly, but he could only hope he had no call to use it. The gunfire had become more sporadic, the battle perhaps drawing to a close with Delta Force at last able to storm the school.

Gazing into the distance, he caught sight of a lone figure approaching from the north. The figure was sticking to cover as best it could, indistinguishable from so far away, except for a shiny red bandanna.

Maruda!

Jamie's heart thudded against his rib cage. Slowly, almost imperceptibly, he eased away from the safe haven of the building. He did not question what great stroke of fortur was delivering the butcher to him. But he was determine that his sister's murderer not leave this island alive. The surg of adrenaline brought on by his hate and resolve swept awa any remaining fuzziness from his head wound. He felt re freshed and ready.

Only dimly aware of helicopters dropping men on bot sides of the complex of buildings, Jamie brought Monroe gun up before him and bolted outward. He crouched lo and followed the line of shrubbery planted neatly befo the red brick. Maruda had darted through the night acros a soccer field to the structure on the end of the row. A Jamie had to do was wait. Maruda was coming rig toward him!

He watched the murderer lean over to check something o the ground and stepped out into the open so Maruda woul see him as soon as he looked up. He sighted down the bo of Monroe's M-16 and just stood there.

Maruda was moving away from the spot he'd just in spected when at last his eyes found Jamie. He started to reac back for his rifle, then stopped.

"Fuck you," Jamie said, hoping the murderer heard i and pulled the trigger.

Nothing happened. The safety, the damn safety must b on!

Maruda had whipped his own gun around when a flash c recognition crossed his eyes. "You!"

His rifle continued up in agonizingly slow motion. Jami probed desperately for the M-16's safety, knowing he coul never both find it and fire before Maruda's bullets burne into him.

"You," Maruda said again, more softly, as his finge tensed on the trigger.

Before the murderer could pull it, a figure lunged o of nowhere and hurled himself upon him. Jamie saw was Riaz an instant before Maruda twisted his head an realized the same thing. He was trying to bring the gu around when Riaz plunged his knife through Maruda back, splitting ribs en route to puncturing his heart. Dea came almost immediately. There was just enough time for the colonel's own fleeting breath to pour a message into Maruda's ear.

"I wanted you to know it was me. I wanted you to die knowing that."

Maruda's eyes locked open and he collapsed out of the colonel's grasp to the ground. Riaz wavered on his feet briefly before sinking to his knees and then keeling over. Jamie reached him and lifted his head gently upward. The colonel's midsection was drenched in blood, while globs of it slid from between his lips. His wounds should have been instantly fatal, but he had kept himself alive long enough to get one chance at Maruda, one chance to set things right.

"I'm sorry," Riaz rasped, "about your sister."

"It wasn't your fault. It's over now."

The colonel grasped his forearm in a sudden burst of strength. "Not over. I saw . . . him."

"Saw who?"

"You must stop him!"

"Stop *who*?"

"He pulled the explosives from the sites and ran . . . toward the sea." Riaz's eye showed the way. "A boat . . . He must have a boat."

"He's dead. You killed him."

"Not Maruda," the colonel rasped with his breath failing. "Someone . . . else. I saw . . . him. I . . . saw . . . the canisters. *Stop him! You must stop—*"

A spasm coursed through the colonel's body, and then it sagged and went limp. If not Maruda, then whom had he glimpsed? Who was the someone else trying to make off with the deadly explosives? Riaz would have stopped him if he'd lived, but now it was up to Jamie. He knelt back down to retrieve Maruda's rifle and then rushed off in the direction Riaz had indicated.

Delta Force crashed into Slater House with the Rangers right behind. Brickmeister took point and halted at the sight of a large group of students cowering on the floor, unhurt but terrified. His trained eyes immediately picked out the dead bodies of the terrorists and swung next to the female figure sitting propped against the wall. She was drenched in blood, and a pool of it spread beneath her. Her eyes met his weakly as he made his way over with his walkie-talkie pressed to his lips and tuned it to the open channel once more.

"This is the Brick. Area is secure. Repeat, area is secure, Colonel."

"What the hell's been going on over there?" demanded Bart Jacoby. "Why'd you break off contact?"

"Just let me talk to Colonel Eastman, boss."

When the pause came, Brickmeister knew something was wrong.

"You mean he's not with you?"

"Not since he left the staging area after the SEALs came back."

"Sorry, Major, I haven't seen him since before then."

Brickmeister was baffled. "But I talked to him."

"Not from the mainland, you didn't."

"What the hell . . ."

"Valhalla," the bleeding woman muttered while the Delta medics administered to her.

"What, ma'am?" Brickmeister asked, leaning over her and figuring now she must have been the one who had alerted them by Morse code about the nets. "Didn't catch that."

Through the blurring of her own consciousness, everything became clear to Chimera. How else could Colonel Riaz know so precisely what Delta Force's response would be? Who else could have known the exact location of the explosive charges? Valhalla had learned of the antimatter and elected to cancel the operation. But Marlowe, their military representative, couldn't allow that, not with so potent a weapon within his reach. So he had killed the other members of the Valhalla Group's executive board and then he had come here to retrieve the explosives for his own use.

"Marlowe" was the only name Valhalla had ever known him as, all of Valhalla except for Simon Winters, who also knew him as Colonel Alan Eastman. The Pentagon's top expert on counterterrorist strategies, a man who knew all along he would be dispatched to Castle Island once the take-over was complete.

"Eastman's one of them," Chimera told the Delta leader crouching near her. "Eastman's one of them, and he's got the explosives."

CHAPTER 34

EASTMAN had been dressed in the black Delta uniform from the start. He'd worn it under his wet suit during his underwater swim to Castle Island. Negotiating the mined nets was no problem since their precise placement and layout had been by his design. Killing a dozen SEALs in a two-minute time frame had proved the most difficult task of all. But Eastman had learned long before that the easiest to surprise were those who felt they had surprise on their side.

He had never intended things to finish quite in this fashion. His original plan had been to make his way to Castle Island in the chaos that would follow the triggering of the mined nets. Once there, he would activate a device that would jam the signal coming from Maruda's transmitter so the captain would not be able to detonate the explosive canisters. This would give him ample time to retrieve them. He'd be dressed in camouflage fatigues with a black patch over his left eye, and the commandos would think he was Colonel Riaz. Then when Maruda appeared, Eastman would kill him. He had spent the past twenty-four hours putting the scenario together.

But then a message from the island had alerted Brickmeister about the nets. The SEALs were called back and equipped with lights to get them through clean. A new strategy was called for, so Eastman had slid off before the new equipment was distributed and reached Castle Island several minutes ahead of the SEALs to lie in wait.

With the dozen in their troop eliminated, he knew just how much time he had to gather the charges from the planting sites he had laid out as well. Locating them became a simple matter of reconstructing the school layout in his mind. The retrieval process went more smoothly and quickly than he had hoped for, and now Eastman was carrying the canisters in two separate padded packs, six in each. He had been in the midst of retrieving them when he had spoken to Brickmeister by walkie-talkie. The grunt never even suspected he wasn't on the mainland.

In his possession now was the greatest weapon man had ever known. With it, no goal would be beyond his reach, nor beyond the reach of the new Valhalla Group for which he would handpick his own people. They would be just military men who could look at issues with a view unspoiled by any but pure and reasonable concerns. There had been too much gray for too long. Black and white were much better shades. The antimatter would allow him to dictate his own terms, or destroy the enemies of the United States without dictating any terms at all.

Eastman could barely contain his exuberance. It was when he had realized that the withered, gun-shy members of Valhalla actually intended to *return* the canisters that he knew a break was required. And the break had to be clean, with no trace left of the past. The other members had had the foresight to choose the best route for the country, but lacked the fortitude to carry it out. It shouldn't have been a surprise. After all, the mythological Valhalla was reserved only for soldiers, and now Valhalla would once again be pure.

Eastman quickened his pace down the hill to the shore and the hidden speedboat Maruda had been on the verge of using. Eastman knew he would return to the school when his detonator failed, and he had waited for that moment for his own flight. Nearing the water, he heard the sound of a boat's motor and found himself caught in the spill of a coast guard speedboat's floodlights as it patrolled the shore area.

"Please raise your hands in the air and identify yourself," a voice over a bullhorn instructed him.

Instead, Eastman waded out into the water and signaled the boat toward him.

"I'm Eastman, damnit!" he shouted when it drew nearer. "Operations commander. I need your boat. Their leader slipped away from us and escaped by sea."

"We haven't seen anyone, sir!"

"Of course you haven't. He's good, very good. But I am, too. Help me aboard. I think I know where he's gone."

The seaman lowered a hand to Eastman, who accepted it gratefully, flinching only when his two packs loaded with the canisters clanged together. All three men were in view when his feet touched the deck. Before the guardsmen knew what was happening, he had drawn his pistol and opened fire. A pair of bullets for each fired in the space of barely four seconds and they were dead. No time to even toss their bodies over the side.

Time only to make his escape from the area in a boat no one would think to question.

"Seal the bay!" Brickmeister ordered.

"Say again, please," responded the coast guard duty officer at the Castle Hill station back on the mainland.

"I said, seal the fuckin' bay, son. Concentrate whatever forces you got out there to the south and east. That's where our man's headed. I don't want you lettin' even a goldfish through."

"Do our best, sir. But it's a damn big ocean."

Jamie had just reached the crest of the hill over Castle Island's northern shore when the shots erupted on the deck of the coast guard boat. He saw the uniformed shapes fall, the figure in black maneuvering between them, and knew instantly it was the figure Riaz had seen with the explosives. He had chosen the perfect means of escape. Once he was in the open water, no one would even think to stop him.

He brought Maruda's gun up fast and fired a burst across the water. But the boat had already torn away, the sound of the gunshots lost in its wake. What now? A boat, he needed a boat!

There was a small pier down the shore about twenty yards, and when Jamie had rushed down the hill toward it, he saw a speedboat bobbing in the water not far from shore. The figure in black must have been making his way toward it when the coast guard boat came along. Of course!

Without thinking further, Jamie rushed into the water and vaulted into the speedboat. He stretched his arm underwater at the stern and released the boat from the pylon it was tied to. Reaching the helm, he found the key waiting for him. He turned it, and the engine roared instantly to life. He jammed the shift lever into gear and shoved the throttle forward. The speedboat shot out into the water, tip rising over the currents.

The red and white coast guard boat had a hefty head start, and Jamie had the feeling its engines could outrun his. He would be able to close the gap for a while, at least until the murderous driver of the lead boat realized he was being pursued and moved to widen the gap.

He had closed to within two hundred yards when he saw the figure behind the wheel swing back and notice him for the first time. Instantly the ground he had gained began slipping away.

"Come on!" Jamie urged his speedboat. "Come on!"

He knew he would never be able to catch the guard boat at this rate and was hoping only to hang close for as long as it took for the authorities to catch on to what was happening. The southern tip of Newport was coming up fast, and with it, the spectral lights of a far-off bridge.

Never in his wildest imagination could Jamie have foreseen the sight that greeted him next: a dozen coast guard crash ships and patrol boats converging from the north and south, a cutter in the center of the two phalanxes bringing up the rear. Their approach placed them in the direct path of the boat Jamie was pursuing. A pair of guard helicopters soared overhead in the next instant with their floodlights searching the bay for the renegade patrol boat. With no other choice, the murderer on board swung left when he reached Newport's southern tip and headed north.

"Gotcha, you bastard," Jamie said, smiling broadly. "Gotcha."

"Major, this is Castle Hill Station."

"Read you, son."

"We are pursuing two boats through the bay. One is a guard patrol we can't raise on the radio, the other a black speedboat with no identifying markings. Please advise."

Again Brickmeister was mystified. The lead boat must have been driven by Eastman, but who was giving chase? The only person he knew to be unaccounted for at this point was Jamie Skylar. The major felt a slight tremor move through him. If half of what Monroe Smalls had said about Skylar was true . . .

"Keep your men in visual contact," Brickmeister finally replied. "But make sure they don't approach."

"Sir, our ships are close enough to overtake."

"Just keep your distance, cowboy," Brickmeister ordered, knowing with cold certainty that the missing explosives were with Eastman on board the lead boat. "I'm dealin' you in, but you ain't got the hand to play."

"Roger that, I think. . . . Sir, word from the bay is the lead boat has been driven up on the rocks and abandoned."

"Shit! Coordinates?"

"He turned north when he saw us and went aground at Cliff Walk beneath Marble House and—"

"I don't know what the fuck you're talking about. Just give me the fucking directionals. We'll go by chopper. Jacoby, you copy that?" Brickmeister demanded.

"Yes, Major."

"Close every road off. Seal this whole fucking area." Brickmeister turned to Roth. "I need to hitch a ride on your birds, Luke."

"Long as I get the seat next to you."

In Eastman's mind, beaching the boat was his only chance. He knew the Newport area well from numerous lectures he had given at the Naval War College, and that would work mightily in his favor. Directly above him now lay Bellevue Avenue and the collection of Newport's famed mansions and estates. The expanse of the area would provide innumerable escape options for him. In Vietnam he had survived and eluded capture for three months in enemy territory by using what the landscape gave him. But first he had to reach that landscape, and that meant conquering Cliff Walk.

Cliff Walk was a man-made breakwater constructed by the wealthy residents over a century before to protect their magnificent homes. Averaging forty feet in steep height, it was composed of rocks, boulders, and shale held in a precarious mold that was actually much more steady than it looked. Still, he had to mount it with the utmost care considering the two sackloads of canisters he wore strung over his back.

He had started to do just that, settling almost immediately into a climbing rhythm, when a gaze downward revealed the second boat arriving at the beach.

Jamie drove his speedboat aground in the patrol boat's wake. Because it carried less weight, it actually skimmed across the rocks that had torn the patrol boat's bottom out and came to rest against the first rocks of Cliff Walk itself. He leaped out with Maruda's rifle in hand and thought of chancing a shot at the figure ahead until consideration of the canisters made him toss the gun aside into the water. He had to stop this man from fleeing, but he also had to make sure the deadly charges on his back were kept intact.

He started to climb after the man in black, who was fifteen feet up the rocks. Without the extra bulk of the canisters to weigh him down, though, Jamie's progress was significantly faster than his quarry's. Beyond that, Jamie was driven by the importance of this pursuit; as much for himself, as the world. The pain and madness had started for him with the murder of his sister, and above him was the man who had orchestrated it. Maruda had been merely a pawn, just as Riaz had. The real killers were Valhalla, and here was the last of them, his to catch.

For the first time, Jamie felt in control. The whole vast

affair had been reduced to a simple one-on-one battle. No more surprises. No more tricks. Just one man against another.

As he climbed with the professional athlete's grace and sureness, Jamie's forward movement never slowed for even an instant. His arms and legs worked in perfect concert, almost like the limbs of a four-legged animal instead of a man. His balance became his greatest ally, and suddenly the feet of the man in black were a mere eight feet up and to his left.

The figure continued to paw over the rocks, holding his own, with knowledge of his pursuer driving him to risk a quicker pace. Jamie decided to keep climbing straight up instead of altering his angle. That way, although his quarry might widen the gap between them sideways, Jamie would reach the top at the same time he did.

He pushed himself over the rocks, never slowing up, vision fixed on the man before him and nowhere else.

Even when his hand touched the grass over the edge of Cliff Walk, Eastman knew he could not escape this pursuer. He had already pondered the man's identity, to no avail. Not a Delta, that was for sure, and not a SEAL. He could have been both, but he was neither. Who, then, and why?

For some reason his mind conjured Jamie Skylar up for him. A thorn in the side of his plan from the beginning, close to being the reason for its abandonment, and now the final obstacle for him to overcome. Skylar! It had to be Skylar!

Eastman turned to see Skylar climb to his feet above Cliff Walk an instant after him. The colonel had already steadied his nine-millimeter pistol when his pursuer broke into a run.

Eastman fired.

The bullets meant nothing to Jamie, though he could feel their heat as they surged by him. A few times he might have dodged or darted. It was difficult to say. Instinct had taken over, as it must in the open field. Think and you're finished. Hesitate and you're done. The great ones keep going. The great ones have a way of attaining a fresh position while still seeming to occupy the previous one.

The figure ahead was starting to backpedal, firing his last rounds as he turned sideways to charge away. Jamie made up the distance in a final burst of speed, which left him with only one available move. The figure's pistol had erupted one last time when Jamie crashed into him, which plunged both of them over the edge.

The choppers' floods poured light over the scene. Brickmeister held the binoculars to his eyes and reckoned there had never been a time when he felt more helpless.

"Jesus Christ," he muttered.

His vision filled with a picture of two figures rolling on the rocks, struggling, one with four canisters of death hanging on his back.

Thinking of the canisters, Jamie had actually twisted in midair to insure impact came with him on the bottom. The blow shook his insides but left him his wind. He'd been hit harder than this on the field, often when sandwiched by two tacklers.

He knew he was stunned, but he could tell the other man was, too, as they began to grapple for position. The figure went for his throat, and instinctively Jamie kicked out. They separated, and both fought successfully for their feet.

As they circled each other, the man gave a fleeting glimpse at the approaching choppers, and Jamie lunged against him into the spill of a powerful floodlight. The figure twisted, lost his balance, and started to slide. Jamie responded in time to reach out and grab the man's shoulder to keep him from a fall that might breach one of the antimatter containment shells. The figure lashed out at Jamie with a free hand, but Jamie was up to that task as well.

He rammed the man's face hard against the rocks, but he was able to gain his feet again and he launched a powerful fist forward. Jamie turned and accepted it on the side of his skull. The impact numbed him. The figure lashed out again, first with a foot and then another fist. Feinting left and right, using the night, feeling it. The man was a pro and he was making his skills count.

Now it was Jamie's head being pounded against the rocks. He could feel warm blood oozing from gashes the blows had opened up. His eyes had misted over. His legs were wobbly. The figure pounded his head forward again, and this time Jamie flirted with the unconsciousness sure to come with the next blow.

And then he remembered his sister, her face recaptured at last. There was her face and nothing else. Something snapped inside him.

As the next blow came down, Jamie spun and crashed his shoulder against his enemy. The hit seemed even harder than the one he'd given Roland Wingrette in the Eagles game.

The colonel felt his breath flee him like air from a punctured balloon. He knew ribs had been cracked, and already the taste of blood was coming to his mouth. He at last grasped the reality of Skylar's strength, and with it the awareness that he had to use it against him. The next time Skylar pushed, Eastman let him, intending to twist away at the last and basically reverse their positions to send Skylar hurtling into the air.

The move should have gone off perfectly, but Jamie instinctively sensed the intention the way he sensed a tackler coming from the side. When the black shape twisted, Jamie spun into the vortex of his movement and hurled him outward with both arms. The result was to project the figure up and away from him toward the darkness and the rocks below.

No! . . . *No!!!!!!!!!!!!!*

He had forgotten the sacks holding the explosives, but he remembered them in the instant before the figure was free of his grasp. His hands had just managed to close around coarse nylon when the scream burned his ears.

"AHHHHHHHHHHHHHHHHH!!!!!!"

Until the very last, Jamie wasn't sure whether he had stripped the bags free or not. But as the figure crashed into the rocks below, Jamie felt the weight of the sacks in his hands. Their momentum almost cost him his balance.

Almost.

Jamie pressed his back against the rock face and stayed there. A glance down toward a numb hot area of his side revealed blood staining his shirt and spreading.

I was shot! he realized.

But he hadn't felt it then and he didn't feel it now. There was the sound of the sea, the fresh smell of salt air suddenly stinging him, and all Jamie could find the strength to do was smile.

EPILOGUE

"So what do ya figure?" Jamie asked Monroe Smalls, who was standing over his hospital bed.

"Fuck, Ivy," Smalls answered. "The docs say next season, not four weeks. Anyway, you done enough for a while."

"But you're planning to play tomorrow."

"You bet your ass." Smalls winked. "Time for me to get back to the real war."

"Front office been understanding?"

"They went fucking bullshit, 'specially since I couldn't tell 'em the whole truth on account of a deal I made with Brickmeister. Anybody finds out the whole truth, my ass is grass along with his."

With that, the door opened and Major John Brickmeister strode in. His eyes fell first on Monroe Smalls.

"Howdy, brother," greeted the major.

"I ain't your brother."

"You're Delta now, man. That makes you my brother, like it or not."

"Not."

"Which wasn't the case last night."

Smalls looked at Jamie. "That was different."

"We're even now, Monroe."

"Shit, Ivy," Smalls scowled, "last night was so much fun, I owe you more than I did before."

"Okay if we talk alone, son?" the major asked Jamie.

Jamie looked at Smalls and nodded.

"You sure, Ivy?"

"I need ya, I'll scream."

Smalls was halfway to the door when Brickmeister produced a memo pad with uncharacteristic hesitance. "Got a twelve-year-old son I know would really love your autograph."

Monroe's grin was tunnel-wide as he took it and the accompanying pen. "Since you and I be brothers, I guess he's my nephew."

"Kid's got plenty of uncles."

Smalls flipped the pad closed, handed it back, and moved on through the door.

"You been keeping tabs on me," Jamie said to Brickmeister.

"How'd you come to know that, son?"

"Monroe said a couple of your boys been in the lobby all night."

"For your own good. I ain't no regular suit. Neither are they."

"And they've been guarding me from people who are?"

"Don't hurt to play things safe." Brickmeister eased a little closer to the bed and folded his arms. "Heard they pulled two bullets out of you."

Jamie folded his arms gingerly behind his head. In addition to the bullet wounds, both his eyes were black, his cheek was swollen, and lines of stitches crisscrossed his face.

"Doctor's saved them for me in a jar," he told Brickmeister. "Said either one could have been fatal if you hadn't used your helicopter to get me to the hospital."

"Least we could do, son."

"You brought the woman somewhere else, though."

"Doc tell you that?"

"He didn't have to."

"I hear she got moved to Washington this morning f
debriefing. They pulled five slugs out of her."

"Her doctor save them, too?"

"No need. She got plenty of others already saved up."

"That's right. She used to be one of you."

Brickmeister stiffened at that. "Not one of me, son. I'
no suit, not even close."

"But you fight the same war they do. Isn't that the point?

"Point is I'm here—they ain't."

"Not yet."

"Explains why I came first."

"Really?"

"You sign up with my boys, everything else gets close
up neat. Nobody worries."

"So I sign up and help you keep the Valhalla Groups
the future in check."

"They end up keeping themselves in check, son. Worl
only lets them get so far before it yanks in the leash and le
them strangle on it."

"But they get further each time, don't they? And each tim
it gets harder to yank them back in. Think about it, Major.
don't get lucky and grab Eastman's sacks and maybe there
a big hole where New England used to be."

Brickmeister came even closer. "It ain't none the wors
for wear, thanks to you."

"Kids died, though, didn't they?"

"Five."

"You don't sound broken up over it."

"I got kids of my own, son," responded Brickmeiste
sounding hurt. "When it comes to the job, I gotta live wi
acceptable casualties."

"Well, let me tell you something none of us can live wit
Two weeks from Tuesday is Election Day, and saving Ca
tle Island didn't remove Valhalla's candidates from the ba
lot."

"With the overall plan fucked, their tools are gonna lose.

"But that won't stop the people behind them from trying again."

" 'Less those people get stopped."

"By you?"

"Just waiting for the call."

"Speaking of which, I was thinking about calling you when Monroe told me you were coming."

The major's eyes grew wary.

"I want to talk to the woman, Major."

"Suits won't like that, son."

"I don't really give a shit. You see, I figure you and I are men who can understand each other. I know the woman poses a pretty big risk to you and I know that might make it tempting to take some unfortunate steps regarding her."

"You said 'you' again, son. And you're wrong again."

"I'm speaking in the collective. You can reach them; I can't. And I want them to remember that I know everything she knows about what almost happened. I know about the antimatter and Valhalla and the people the Group has left out there." Jamie hesitated. "It would be a good idea to resist temptation, Major. It would be in everyone's best interests to keep the woman safe."

A slight smile spread across the major's face. "You'd like my outfit, son. Fit in better than a horny john's dick in a whore's snatch."

"I belong in a game with shoulder pads, not Kevlar."

Brickmeister was nodding. Then his memo pad was coming forward again.

"That son of mine would love to have your autograph, too."

"Think he knows who I am?"

"Well, he reads *The Sporting News* cover to cover. I figure he's seen your name, maybe knows all your stats. And even if he don't, I'll tell him it's one autograph worth having."

"How you gonna convince him of that?"

"I'll tell him I saw you play. I'll tell him you were one of the best I ever saw."

"Not exactly the truth."

"But not a lie either."

"Good point, Major," Jamie said, taking the pad and pe
from Brickmeister. "Where do I sign?"